Echoes
of Savanna

Parent Generation
Book One

Lucinda Moebius

ECHOES OF SAVANNA
The Parent Generation
Book One
By Lucinda Moebius

Haven Novels
2011
Haven Novels
Boise ID 83713
www.lucindamoebius.com

First Hardcover Edition: 2010
First Paperback Edition: 2010
First E-Book Edition: 2010

Echoes of Savanna: a novel/ by Lucinda Moebius. - 1st. Ed. p.cm.

ISBN 0615581501
ISBN 13: 9780615581507 (Paperback)

Cover design by Aaron Leach

Published in the United States of America
Haven Novels

This book is dedicated to all whom I love.
I would like to offer a special thank you
to all my family and friends who have offered me the love
and support I needed to finish this story.
A special thank you goes out to my husband,
whom I love more than anything.

Prologue

A third part of thee shall die with the pestilence, and with famine shall they be consumed in the midst of thee: and a third part shall fall by the sword round about thee; and I will scatter a third part into all the winds, and I will draw out a sword after them.

— Ezekiel 5:12

Chapter One

HEAT PRESSED DOWN ON all sides, making it difficult to breathe. A flash of sunlight reflected off the glass front of the building, blinding Savanna momentarily. Walking into the waiting room of the clinic, she was confronted by a mass of men, women and children crowded in the tiny space. Dark faces with striking brown eyes stared at her from all corners of the room. The few members of the clinic staff Savanna could see all slouched with signs of exhaustion. A nurse sat at the front desk studying a chart, a medical mask covering the lower half of her face. It took a few moments for her dark eyes to settle on Savanna.

"Can I help you?" she asked.

"I'm Dr. Taylor, University Hospital sent me." Savanna recognized the look in the nurse's eyes when she identified herself. She knew she did not look like a doctor. Although she was nearly six feet tall, her fair skin and pale blonde hair made her look much younger than she was. Graduating from high school when she was twelve and medical school at nineteen didn't help convince people either.

"So, University couldn't spare a real doctor, they needed to send an intern?" Savanna heard the scorn in the nurse's voice.

"I assure you, I am a doctor." She showed the nurse her University ID. "The CDC sent me to take samples and see what we are dealing with here. My team's outside waiting with supplies."

It was obvious the nurse was still wary of Savanna's credentials, but she led her into an examination room anyway.

"What do you need?" she asked.

"My team will be offloading supplies from the truck," Savanna said. "I understand we have a large group of people becoming ill and exhibiting similar symptoms." It was a statement of fact as opposed to a question, but the nurse still nodded.

"We need to find a place to treat those most affected." Savanna continued to speak as she pulled out a data pad. "I've brought a team of nurses and med students with me. Once we establish a facility, we'll triage patients and provide appropriate treatment. My staff and I will be taking blood samples and sending them back to University." Savanna placed her medical kit on the counter and opened it. "We need to take samples from anyone who has been exposed, starting with you." Savanna pulled out vinyl gloves, a syringe and a tourniquet. "Have a seat. I'll give you the form to fill out when I'm done. After this I want you to start collecting data from the patients in the waiting room."

Savanna pulled up the appropriate form on her data pad and filled in the date, August 15th, 2036, and handed the pad and stylus to the nurse to fill out her information.

The nurse took the pad with her when she left in the room. Within minutes Savanna was staring the process of taking blood samples from the others at the clinic. The steady flow of patients kept her focused. She didn't even realize she missed lunch until Dr. Omoto came and told her.

Towards the end of the afternoon an elderly Navajo man was led into the room. He was carrying a young child in his arms. Savanna could see the light sheen of moisture and flushed cheeks on the girl. Her bright eyes had a glassy sheen and lacked focus.

The man placed the child on the exam table and stood at her head, brushing his hands through her long, dark hair. Savanna tied a tourniquet around the child's upper arm and felt for the vein. It took a while to locate a good one. The little one barely flinched as Savanna slid the needle into her arm. Savanna watched the vial slowly fill with dark red blood, much too slow. Savanna studied the child's drawn face noting the chapped, cracked lips. A rash, with lesions oozing clear fluid, covered her face, arms and hands. After finishing the blood draw Savanna used a swab to collect some of the fluid.

"I'm going to start an IV. She's dehydrated and needs fluids," Savanna said. "This child should be in the hospital."

10

"We're moving the worst of the sick into an old airplane hangar outside of town," the man said. "There isn't a hospital close enough to handle all those who are sick. The villagers helped get the hangar cleaned and ready. There are many people who want to help."

Savanna studied the sincere face of the man beside the child. "What's her name?"

"Yanaba. She is my granddaughter."

Savanna finished packaging the swabs from the lesions and turned back to the child. She brushed the girl's hair away from her face. "I'm going to start an IV in her other hand and get her started on lactated ringers before sending her to the hangar. The sooner we get fluids into her body the better she'll be."

Savanna turned to the little one lying on the paper covered table. "Yanaba," she said gently, "I'm going to put a needle in your hand, so I can get fluids into your body. This is going to pinch a little. I'm sorry if it hurts."

Yanaba stared at her with a blank expression in her eyes. Savanna wasn't sure how much the girl understood. She took the child's hand and probed with her finger across the back to locate a vein. As gently as she could, she slid the needle into the child's hand. She didn't get the expected flash of blood. Looking up, she made eye contact with the man.

"I'm going to have to start a central line." Savanna tried to put as much compassion in her voice as she could. She called the nurse into the room and asked for her assistance. The man refused to leave the room, but stepped back as Savanna sterilized, numbed and cut into Yanaba's thigh. It didn't take long to place the catheter and get an IV started. She made sure the line was securely stitched and wrapped so it wouldn't be jarred as the child was moved.

After assuring herself everything was perfect, Savanna turned to the nurse. "I need a wheelchair for this child. She needs to be transported to the hangar until we can get an ambulance to send her to University Hospital. She's to be placed in a critical care unit right away."

The nurse's eyes drooped with exhaustion. "We have ten patients in critical condition already. There are over a hundred and fifty people at the hangar, right now. Your intern is there organizing everything. There aren't enough people to help the sick." Her voice was softened by her surgical mask.

"We need to do what we can. I'm going to send a message to University and ask for more assistants. If it's what I suspect it is, it's going to get worse before it gets better." Savanna dropped her chin to her chest as the nurse wheeled Yanaba out of the room. She took a deep breath and turned back to the girl's grandfather. Gathering blood-soaked towels from the exam table and sanitizing the surface only took a moment. She gestured towards the table, addressing the man.

"You're next. Roll up your sleeve, please." Savanna peeled off her gloves, threw them in the trash, and proceeded to the sink to wash. As she dried her hands she noticed how red they were getting.

When she turned back, Yanaba's grandfather was looking at her. She saw his eyes study her face, roll down and take in her posture and rest on her hands. She paused for a moment, not sure what to make of his perusal. Shaking her head, she decided it was nothing and pulled up her chair to sit across from him. Before she could pull on her gloves, the old man reached and cupped her hands in his.

"I am Chief Etu Silva. These are my people and they are my responsibility. I am placing them in your hands. I have watched you Savanna Taylor and I see you are a compassionate person. I know you will do what is right for my children." Chief Etu folded Savanna's hands closed and wrapped his own around them. She could feel the warmth of his hands encasing hers. When he let go, she could still feel his warmth on her hands and her fingers tingled a bit.

Savanna shifted in her seat, unsure of what to say. "I will do the best I can. We have a long battle ahead of us." She pulled on her gloves and reached for Chief Etu's arm.

"Yanaba's name means 'she meets the enemy'. She does have a long battle ahead of her. I know what this enemy is and the first time the People fought it, it nearly destroyed us. Smallpox is a beast." Chief Etu's voice carried all the emotions Savanna felt: fear, suffering, pain, and hope.

"It may not be smallpox, Chief Etu," Savanna said. "There are a number of other viruses it could be."

Savanna wasn't quite ready to accept this outbreak was a strain of smallpox. The disease was thought to be extinct due to mass inoculations in the twentieth century. No new cases of the virus had appeared in almost eighty years.

It didn't take long for Savanna to draw the Chief's blood. She placed the label with Chief Etu's bar-coded medical information on the three vials and placed them in one of the shipping boxes.

"These samples will be sent to my lab in the city to be analyzed. I want to observe the ill patients tonight before I go back to the hospital in the morning." Savanna closed the lid to the box just as the nurse walked back into the room.

"The last ambulance is leaving for the hangar if you wanted to ride along," the nurse said. "Your team is already there. Everyone in the town knows if they start to exhibit symptoms they're to report to the hangar instead of the clinic."

Savanna looked at the man sitting in the chair and made a snap decision. "Chief Etu, will you ride with me in the ambulance?" For some reason, she was not ready to be separated from him.

Savanna sat in the jump seat at Yanaba's head while Etu sat beside the girl, holding her hand. When they got to the hangar, Savanna was surprised to see the immense size of the building. It had to cover at least two acres. One of the hangar doors was flung open and the ambulance pulled up in front of it. Dr. Omoto, Savanna's assistant, stood just outside the hangar door. He joined Savanna as she stepped out of the ambulance.

"We've separated the hangar into three sections," he said. "Triage, observation and critical care. There's a lot of confusion right now. We need to separate families into different areas and they don't want to go." Dr. Omoto was six inches shorter than Savanna and walked with quick, short steps. Savanna had to shorten her own long strides to keep pace with him as she listened to his report. His English was almost perfect, with just a hint of an undertone of his father's native Japanese. When she first hired him as her assistant he had explained his father insisted he learn Japanese as his first language, even though he had been born in the United States.

Chief Etu walked beside them to the building. As soon as he entered people swarmed to him and started wailing and begging for help. Many of them reached for his hands, pleading with him to do something, anything. Chief Etu reached for Savanna and pulled her beside him.

"Please, my children, calm down, calm down." His soothing voice had an immediate effect. Almost at once, the people stopped pushing to crowd around him and a hush fell over the masses. Many of them knelt on the floor as they listened to his words. "Please, the doctors are here to help. Dr. Taylor and her team are doing what is best for us. Listen to them. Do what they say." The crowd rose from the floor and walked back to the waiting area, almost as one.

Inside the hangar dozens of chairs were set up in orderly rows in front of white cloth screens. An exhausted medical intern was sitting at a table, typing at a laptop computer. As the medic wheeled Yanaba to the desk the intern looked up and sighed. "Patient number?"

The medic handed the intern a form with a barcode on it. She scanned the code in the computer and waited a second for Yanaba's information to appear. "Dr. Taylor has listed this one as critical. Third curtain, last cot. Do you know when Dr. Taylor is going to get here? The Director of the CDC put her in charge. We need her here instead of at the clinic."

"I'm here." Savanna stepped forward.

The medic looked up from Yanaba's gurney. "You're Dr. Taylor? How old are you? Sixteen?"

"I'm nineteen, but my age is irrelevant." Savanna turned to the intern. "Why are the supplies going to take so long? They should only take a few hours to get here."

"We had to send to Salt Lake to get more supplies," the intern replied. "Phoenix is having an influx of patients with similar symptoms."

"Similar or same?"

"We don't know yet. We're trying to document as many symptoms as possible for comparison, but internet service is slow here." The intern turned back to her computer.

Savanna pulled her palm-sized data pad from the pocket on her sleeve and handed it to Omoto. "Start taking pictures of patients," she said. "We'll use my data pad to download the information; it's faster than anything we have here. Where's the camera?"

"One of the interns had it," he replied.

"Ask University to send a more cameras or see if people in the village have some. We need to document the stages of this disease." Savanna turned to Etu, putting her hand on his arm. "Let's go see your granddaughter."

The little girl's fever was climbing. Savanna gently placed an oxygen mask over the child's mouth and nose to assist her breathing. Spending a few minutes listening to the girl's breathing through a stethoscope and adjusting the pillows under her head and shoulders soothed Savanna. She just needed a moment to center her thoughts before she started rounds.

Etu took his place by the child's side, holding her hand and singing to her in a soft voice. It took a moment for Savanna to realize she didn't recognize the words. He must have been singing in Navajo. The words were hypnotic and they resonated in Savanna's chest, matching her heartbeat and slowing the rhythm as it echoed in her chest.

When Savanna moved to Arizona six months ago, she never imagined herself as the head of a team trying to analyze an outbreak of a strange illness. The move from Boise to Phoenix was a traumatic one, for both her and her father, but she couldn't pass up the opportunity to study genetics at University Hospital.

Now, here she stood in a vast airplane hangar, facing

dozens, if not hundreds, of severely ill patients. Her genetic alterations allowed her a heightened immune system, providing some measure of protection against whatever they were fighting. She usually didn't think about the genetic alterations her father built into her DNA when she was an embryo, but now she was glad he had manipulated her genomes.

Savanna lost all track of time as she paced the aisles of the hangar. She didn't have time to think about home and her father. He called a few times, but she was only able to talk to him for a few minutes. His concern for her safety was evident as he begged her to return to the safety and security of Haven. Dr. Jackson Taylor was a leading researcher in the field of genetics and his daughter was quickly following on his heels in her own studies. Taking the job in Arizona was her opportunity to experience life outside of her family home and learn new research techniques from leading geneticists. She earned a fairly substantial paycheck working for University, but it all went into savings. Her trust fund supplied her personal needs would be seen to as long as she wanted. Her family's legacy of wealth was passed down from the time of prohibition. Her great, great, grandfather's legacy of being a bootlegger started her family down a road of prosperity few people were able to match.

Savanna often thought of the comfortable bed in her furnished apartment over the next few days as she struggled to find a comfortable position on one of the cots in the office. At times, as she worked with patients cataloging symptoms and charting vitals, she wished she could escape back to her apartment and hide under the blankets. The moment would pass, and she would turn back to her work.

Chapter Two

SLEEP WAS AN ELUSIVE fiend, coming in two or three hour intervals. During rounds Savanna tried to see all of the patients at least once, stopping by Yanaba's bed as often as she could. University Hospital sent as much cidofovir as they could spare, as well as a number of other supplies, but everything was in short supply. Savanna tried to get her contacts in the CDC to send her more medicine, but there just wasn't any to send.

Savanna took the night shift, allowing her team to sleep as much as possible, although few of them did. She moved from bed to bed, checking and documenting changes in patients. Her footsteps echoed in the silent hours of the night.

She started the most critical patients on medication first, hoping eventually to get more. One face blurred into the next, until all she saw were numbers. Temperature, blood pressure, and heart rate were all too high, all too dangerous. Savanna was overwhelmed by the sheer number of patients. Fifty grew to a hundred, a hundred to five hundred. There was no doubt in her mind they were in a full-blown pandemic.

In the early morning hours the hangar developed an eerie quiet. Family members of the sick had brought in sleeping bags and pillows and were now camped on the floor beside cots. Savanna tried to send them all home, telling them they were at risk of contracting the disease and emphasizing the amount of germs found on the floor. Parents, grandparents, aunts and uncles just looked at her and turned back to sick family members.

She expressed her concerns to Chief Etu. He responded by telling her his people had already been exposed and the best treatment they could receive was to be close to their families. Realizing she was fighting a losing battle Savanna allowed the family members to stay but insisted on keeping the area around the cots clear enough for medical staff to treat patients. All around her people slept, or quietly held hands and talked in gentle tones.

Savanna had brought five interns and ten physician's assistants and nurses with her as part of her research team. The clinic had one physician's assistant, two nurses and a receptionist, who also had a certified nurse's aide license. A large group of people from the village volunteered to help as well. From that group, Savanna was able to pull seventeen more people with medical experience to assist in patient care.

Savanna divided the groups into five teams with an intern as the head of each team. She ordered them to set up a sleeping schedule for the team that allowed everyone to get at least six hours of sleep in a twenty-four hour period while keeping at least three interns on the floor at all times. She put Dr. Omoto in charge of the critical care unit and teamed him with the village physician's assistant and as many of the others as she could spare.

Continuing her rounds through the night, Savanna checked on patients and making sure the teams were following her orders. Even with the divided work load and volunteers there were still too many patients to handle. Savanna ordered nurses to train those who wanted to help in basic patient care.

As she passed by one of the cots on her way back to the critical care unit Savanna noticed the triage nurse taking a picture of a patient with a digital camera. She looked at the picture as it appeared on the screen. The girl's face and shoulders were covered in red bumps just starting to ooze clear fluid. Savanna looked from the camera to the girl resting fitfully on the cot. She appeared to be about thirteen or fourteen. A woman sat beside her.

"Are you her mother?" she asked.

"No. I'm her Aunt Emily," the woman responded. "This is Kai. Both of her parents are ill and her younger sister, Yanaba, is in the critical care section."

Savanna nodded and took a deep breath. She didn't know what to say. As much as she wanted to assure Emily everything was going to be okay, she knew the battle was going to be long and hard. Savanna learned to never tell family a patient would be okay. A stressed family member would take a doctor's word as gospel. Emily turned back to her niece and placed a cool cloth on her head. She took the dripping, melted icepacks from the girl's groin and armpits, placing them in a bin at the foot of the cot.

"It's good she has you here to care for her. Have you been exhibiting any symptoms?"

"No." Emily barely glanced up from her care of the child. "If I was going to catch it, you would think I would have by now. I've been with my nieces since they first started to exhibit symptoms. I seem to be immune to whatever it is, even though I was never immunized as a child." As Emily spoke, a nurse brought a stack of ice-filled Ziploc baggies wrapped in towels and handed four to her.

"I want to get a blood sample from you," Savanna said. "If you are immune we may be able to use your stem cells to help combat this disease." She helped Emily wrap the packs in fresh towels and place them on her niece's body. The girl looked up at her, the pain in her dark brown eyes burning through the fever.

Emily nodded. "They've already taken my blood. I think they've drawn blood from anyone who has walked in here. We were told once we're in here we can't leave because even if we don't have the disease we may be carriers. The Elders are not letting anyone else in unless they're exhibiting symptoms. Many people are setting up tents outside because they refuse to leave their families." She turned back to her niece and continued to gently wipe the sweat from her face and arms.

Savanna left Emily to care for her niece and continued her rounds. She walked through the aisles between patients' cots, listening to the whisper of her shoes on the cement flooring. As she moved from bed to bed nurses would bring her charts for her to review. She finally worked her way to the back of the hangar, where the critical cases were being treated.

As soon as she passed the curtain barrier she knew something had changed. The gentle hum of oxygen machines had increased in noise level. Every patient wore an oxygen mask. Savanna looked over to Yanaba's bed. Chief Etu was not in his customary place beside her bed. Instead an elderly woman, whom Savanna recognized as the Chief's wife, sat beside her. She was helping the nurse change the cool, wet towels on the child's chest arms and legs. Yanaba was propped up in the bed with three pillows, but her breathing was still labored. The child's face was tinged grayish-blue. Savanna walked to the machine measuring Yanaba's oxygen level, blood pressure and temperature. She didn't like what she was seeing.

"We need to intubate. The cidofovir isn't helping block the spread of the virus as it should. Do you know where Dr. Omoto is?" Savanna directed her question to the nurse, but it was Yanaba's grandmother that answered.

"He said he was going to intubate. He went to get the equipment." Savanna noticed the woman's face was slightly flushed.

"I don't think I have officially met you. I'm Dr. Taylor." Savanna held out her hand.

"I'm Rachel. I know who you are, Dr. Taylor." When Rachel took her hand, Savanna could feel the warmth in her fingers.

"Rachel, have you been checked out?" Savanna asked before she released the woman's hand. "Do you have a sore throat?"

Rachel looked at Savanna. "I know I have it. I don't understand. I was immunized when I entered the military." Rachel pulled up her sleeve to show Savanna the smallpox inoculation scar on her arm. "I think there's something really wrong with this virus. It's acting strange. I don't think it's what everyone thinks it is."

"You need to be in bed." It was all Savanna could think to say. She knew the disease wasn't acting like a normal virus. Savanna was torn, feeling the need to be back at her lab studying the virus, but the thought of leaving these people made her chest ache. As an intern she had witnessed death, but she had never seen anything on this grand a scale before and she was afraid if she left many more of her patients would die.

Yanaba's grandmother brushed the girl's hair out of her

face. "I need to be with my granddaughter more." Omoto walked in as Rachel turned back to the young girl.

"Dr. Taylor." He nodded at her and then walked over to Yanaba's bed with the intubation tray.

Savanna took the tray from his hands. "I'll do this."

The nurse removed the pillows from under the girl's head. Sitting at the head of the bed, Savanna placed her hands around the child's head. She could feel the heat radiating through her vinyl gloves. Yanaba didn't regain consciousness as Savanna prepared for the procedure. Tilting the child's head back, she gently pushed Yanaba's jaws open with her fingers. It didn't take long to put the laryngoscope in place and find the swollen, reddened vocal chords. The tube was in place in a matter of seconds. Savanna inflated the bladder and hooked the machine to it. The nurse checked Yanaba's chest with a stethoscope.

"Good bilateral breath sounds. Her O_2 levels are coming up," he said.

Savanna watched as color started to fill back in Yanaba's face. "This should ease her breathing. Let's see if we can get her fever down some more. Keep the ice packs fresh."

Savanna turned to Rachel. "I want you in bed. Where's Chief Etu? I'll have him sit beside Yanaba."

"He's outside. He wants to perform a ceremony at sunrise to cleanse the evil spirits. I don't think it'll do much good. Ceremonies can't defeat this demon."

Yanaba's O_2 level was rising but her blood pressure and fever were still elevated. Savanna monitored her condition for about twenty minutes. The child seemed to be resting a little easier, so Savanna continued her rounds. She made it back to her office to find Omoto waiting for her. Savanna could see he had several charts pulled up on his data pad.

"Dr. Taylor," he said as he handed her the pad. "We've lost patient seven today. CPR isn't effective; the disease destroys too many major organs. The cidofovir isn't working. It's not combating the virus. Something needs to change."

Savanna scrolled down the lists on the data pad. The

ratio of medical supplies to patient numbers wasn't even close to matching up. Omoto just stood watching her as she took in the information.

"Tell the team to stop attempting CPR. We need to focus on those we can save. Send this information to University. Let's see if they can send us another type of antiviral. We're going to have to start experimenting here." She handed the data pad back to him.

Savanna stretched out on a cot in the office trying to sleep for a while, but she just couldn't keep her eyes closed. Finally giving up, she stood, stretched out the kinks in her back, and moved back into rounds. There was an echoing tension in the air as she moved from patient to patient. Savanna could feel it tightening the muscles in her chest. She would give anything to be back in the seclusion of Haven right now, away from all this pain and sorrow. The quiet halls of Haven sheltered the residents from this kind of pain. Eventually, her pacing brought her back to Yanaba.

Rachel was still holding vigil at her granddaughter's bedside. Omoto was standing at the foot of the bed, scrolling through Yanaba's chart on his data pad. Savanna looked at the tiny, flushed body on the bed. Suddenly Yanaba's body arched and her teeth bit down around the tube.

"Febrile seizures." Savanna quickly sat at the head of the bed and placed her hands on either side of the child, creating a barrier, to keep her from rolling off the bed. "Lorazepan, stat." Omoto ran to the med cart.

Savanna looked at Rachel and saw the concern in her eyes. "Febrile seizures only last about fifteen minutes," she said. "This should break her fever."

Savanna watch as the child arched into the tonic phase and relaxed into the clonic phase for about ten minutes. Rachel couldn't be convinced to leave her grandchild's side and go to the cot set up for her in the non-critical ward. When the seizure finally ended, Savanna checked bilateral breath sounds and assured herself the ET tube was still in place. The monitor showed Yanaba's fever was lowered, but it was still above normal. Even though the machine was easing her breathing Yanaba's breaths were coming in short, quick gasps. There was nothing more Savanna could do. She watched as the monitor slowly started decreasing in readings.

"Rachel, I'm going to send the nurse for Chief Etu." Savanna knew the child's situation was becoming desperate. Without effective medicine, adrenaline, IV fluids, all the tools of her trade, everything she didn't have, there was nothing more she could do. "Who else should come?"

Rachel's face settled into a slightly shocked expression, but it was clear she understood what Savanna was saying. Her voice was choked with tears as she spoke.

"Etu knows." Tears flowed freely down her face. "He said he was going to do the ceremony and he would come back when it was done. Her mother, father and sisters are in the other ward. They're too sick to come. It's just you and me. Please, just make sure she doesn't suffer."

Savanna lowered her head and watched as Yanaba struggled for breath. She assisted on removing and replacing icepacks and cool towels. Half an hour into the vigil the child's stats dropped. Savanna could hear the rattling in Yanaba's lungs. The monitor showed two beats, then a flat line, a sudden echoing thumping of five beats and then, nothing. Savanna listened to the steady beep of the flat line for thirty seconds. She used her stethoscope to listen to the child's lungs and heart, brushed her hand across Yanaba's cheek and looked at the clock.

"Time of death: 5:47 A.M." She could feel her throat tighten and tears welling in her eyes and was overwhelmed with a desperate need to escape. It wouldn't do anyone any good to see the doctor they were counting on to break down. "I'm going to find Chief Etu." She tried to take a surreptitious breath before she turned to Dr. Omoto, but she could feel the shakiness in her voice as she spoke. "Put her with the others." He nodded in understanding.

Savanna walked away from the bed, past the white curtain separating the makeshift morgue from the rest of the hangar. She knew she had to leave before she broke down. Out of the corner of her eye, she saw Emily remove a cool cloth from Kai's forehead and brush the girl's hair out of her face before replacing it with another. Savanna walked out of the hangar and into the brightness of the rising sun.

Chapter Three

THE BRIGHT RED SUNRISE colored Savanna's vision for a few seconds. Blinking rapidly, she tried to force the tears away. Still, she could feel them quivering in her eyes, ready to fall. Hopelessness tightened her chest. Everything was so inadequate here. She knew part of the tears came from frustration and exhaustion, but she couldn't shake the feeling she should be doing more. So many people shouldn't have to die. A shadow came between her and the sun. She blinked again and Chief Etu's face came into her field of vision. The tears wouldn't stay in her eyes and she felt them start to fall.

"Chief," she choked out. "Yanaba—" She couldn't get words past the lump in her throat and the tears spilled out in earnest.

"I know, I know." Etu pulled her into his arms. Savanna didn't resist. She needed to draw on his strength. She was beyond thinking.

"You're doing everything you can in this battle. Come with me. I think I can do something to help."

Etu pulled Savanna to an open area, away from the crowds. He stood behind her. Savanna could feel his hands in her hair as he pulled out the pins holding it in place. His gentle caress soothed her as her hair fell and was caught in the wind. Placing his hands on her shoulders, he leaned forward and whispered in her ear.

"Close your eyes. Keep them closed. Listen. Allow the wind to speak to you."

Savanna allowed the warmth of Etu's hands to penetrate her shoulders as she closed her eyes, relaxing into his embrace. She could hear wailing and crying from those gathered around. Slowly, another sound threaded its way into her consciousness. An echo of a chant carried on the wind began to penetrate the sounds of the hospital. The gentle strumming seemed to flow into her chest. Her heart started to beat in the same soothing rhythm.

"Listen to the wind." Etu's voice should have startled her, but it didn't. His words seemed to echo in the wind in her heart. "Draw the wind into your lungs and blow it out." She felt Etu as he moved in front of her, his hand trailed down her right arm and he took her hand in his. Sand trickled into her palm and he closed her fist around the grainy substance.

"Hold your hand in the air and let the wind flow through." Savanna felt him turn her body and she followed his lead as if they were dancers on a stage. The scent of burning sage filled her nostrils. "Fill your body with the wind from the East. Allow your mind to open and think about what's ahead. Turn your thoughts from the past." Her hand was raised into the air and she felt the wind flow over her body. Etu's arms encircled her and she could feel her body start to sway to the rhythm of the chanting.

She felt him turn her again, her body followed naturally. "Feel the wind from the South. This wind will help you plan. Know what you are going to do next, Anaba. You are the warrior maiden. Plan how you will fight this battle." Savanna drew in a deep breath of cool morning air. She could feel the sand trickling from between her fingers. Her body relaxed as the air filled her lungs.

Again, with the grace of a dancer, Etu turned her. "Feel the wind from the West. Allow this wind to carry you through. This is where you will live out your plans. The west wind will support you as you work and fight. Feel the strength of the west wind."

Savanna felt Etu's hand leave her shoulder and travel up her arm. His fingers curled around hers and caressed them as they cupped the sand. Gently, he turned her one more time. She felt him whisper, "Open your hand, Anaba." She slowly uncurled her fingers.

"Allow the North wind to carry away the pain. Focus on how to use your knowledge to help these people. Evaluate. Make things better. Think, Anaba. You know how to defeat this. Fight for our people. You have taken the spirit of our people in your heart. You can help us." Etu released Savanna's shoulders and she opened her eyes. He pulled away and she had to turn to search for him. She didn't know at what point her tears had stopped, but when she turned to him, his face was clear in her vision.

Savanna looked past the deeply etched lines in his face and into his dark eyes. The clear, liquid, brown eyes carried a hope Savanna couldn't help but feel. Warmth spread from her chest through her body and enveloped her. The red of the dawn was fading from the sky and the yellow sun glowed behind Etu. Despite the brightness, Savanna could not draw her eyes from his. Finally, Chief Etu looked away. Savanna realized they were surrounded by people. Most were sitting on the ground clutching blankets and rocking back and forth. Chief Etu walked among them, reaching for one person's hands or brushing his hand through another's hair. He spoke a few words of comfort to his people as he passed among them.

The roar of a large, diesel engine interrupted the peace of the early morning and Savanna looked towards the hangar. A huge U-haul was pulling up in front of the doors. Chief Etu moved to stand beside her and she turned to talk to him.

"This will be supplies. We need to organize them. Can you help?" The words she spoke brought Savanna back to the moment. With her mind on the patients in the hangar, she turned towards the U-haul. Etu followed.

"Chief, I have a question for you." Etu slowed. "Why did you call me Anaba? My name is Savanna. My mother used to call me Anna when I was little, but no one has ever called me Anaba."

Etu's mouth curled into a small smile. "Anaba is a Navajo name. It means 'she returns from war'. You are a Navajo warrior woman now, Anaba. You are my daughter and I have given you a Navajo name befitting your status. You are a warrior who will fight this enemy."

Savanna stopped walking and looked into Etu's eyes. For a moment she thought she should be offended, but she realized he was trying to honor her. Her concern must have reflected in her eyes because Etu smiled and brought his hand up to catch a strand of Savanna's long blond hair.

"Do not be concerned. I know you are a grown woman and a full-fledged doctor, but you are still a young woman, far from home and you need love and support through this battle." Etu's gentle eyes seemed to pierce Savanna's heart. "I cannot help but feel for you and since I do not have the medical knowledge to fight this disease I will give you what strength I can." Etu placed his arm around her shoulders, drawing her into his warmth.

After a moment she stepped back and walked towards the U-haul. Dr. Omoto approached from the hangar entrance, followed by Sam. The robotic S290 was designed to be a workhorse. Compact and strong, the machine was made from layers of tempered steel. He was only about five feet tall with a broad wheel base and a wide range of motion in his mechanical arms. He rolled towards her across the uneven ground, lurching as he adjusted to the variety of turf. Dr. Omoto and the S290 reached the truck just as Savanna and Etu did. The driver hopped down from the cab and handed Omoto a data pad. Omoto handed Savanna the pad and they all walked to the back of the truck.

"Sam, start unloading the truck and assist the staff in organizing and cataloguing supplies." She turned to face Dr. Omoto and the truck driver. "I can tell from the size of the truck we don't have all the supplies we asked for. Dr. Omoto, you need to direct the organization of the supplies. Nothing is to be distributed without my okay." The driver unlocked the back of the truck and rolled up the door.

A crowd gathered around, some begging for medicine, others offering to help. Etu walked among them soothing and calming as he passed. Savanna turned the driver as she looked through the truck manifest. "Is this all there is, or are there other trucks coming? I was expecting ten times this amount."

The driver shook his head. "Hospitals in Arizona, Nevada, and Utah are being inundated with Smallpox patients. There's not enough medicine to go around. We have to transport supplies in unmarked vehicles because medical transports are being attacked and supplies are being stolen." As he lifted his arms to unload a box, Savanna noticed a gun strapped to his waist.

Savanna scrolled through the list of supplies on the data pad. Shaking her head, she looked from the supplies to the hangar. "There's not enough. We're going to lose so many." She was talking to herself, but she noticed Chief Etu heard.

She felt the overwhelming pain as she turned to face Etu. His warm eyes looked into hers and she drew strength from him. "Chief Etu, I have to get back to my lab. I can't fight this battle here, not with these inadequate weapons."

Etu nodded. "We will fight this battle here, my daughter. You fight the war." He placed his hands on her shoulders and then pulled her into himself. Warmth flowed into Savanna as he enfolded her in an embrace.

Pulling away from Etu's embrace, Savanna turned to the truck driver. "Wait for me. I'll ride back with you."

As Savanna walked into the hangar she noticed a crowd of people surrounding Dr. Omoto and the supplies. Members of the medical staff were reaching for boxes to open. Family members begged for medicine for ill loved ones. Dr. Omoto tried to stand between the crowd and the supplies and move people away, but many pushed past him; he was losing ground. Savanna looked at Chief Etu and he nodded, understanding.

"Children, children!" Everyone turned as he spoke, even the medical staff. "Please, let the doctors do their jobs. Move away from the supplies."

The crowd reluctantly filtered away from the pile of boxes. Savanna walked to Dr. Omoto.

"Order the team leaders to the office, now." She turned to the chief. "Chief Etu, will you bring some of your most trusted men over to guard the supplies?" Etu nodded and moved towards the crowd, pointing out men.

Ten minutes later Etu had five men guarding the medical supplies. Savanna stood in the makeshift office, surveying the ten-team leaders. Many of them slouched with exhaustion. She knew they weren't following her orders to sleep.

Making eye contact with each one, she made sure she had everyone's attention. The next orders she issued were going to be hard to follow.

"We don't have enough supplies to treat everyone." She heard a hiss and whispering as the team reacted to the news. Holding up her hand for silence, she continued. "The anti-virals aren't working on the critical patients. Save it for those who are just starting to exhibit symptoms. No one exhibiting symptoms for more than four days will receive anti-virals. No one. We have five hundred inoculations from the military back supply. Administer them in this order: children age two to twelve first, anyone with a compromised immune system next, twelve to twenty after that, and then sixty and over. Those between twenty and sixty will be last. I doubt we have enough for even that many. Keep this protocol even if we get more supplies."

Savanna paused and looked around the room. The tired expressions were slowly being replaced with different levels of understanding. She looked at the village physician's assistant as his eyes hardened.

"I'm not going to sit here and listen to some chit of a girl tell me how to treat my patients. I was treating these people before you had the know-how to wipe the snot off your chin." He stood up to leave, but before he could get to the door Savanna spoke.

"Sit down!" she ordered. "We will do it this way. It gives us the best options to save lives."

For a moment the man glared at her then, like a deflated balloon, he lowered himself back to his chair. He slouched in defeat, seemingly more exhausted than before.

"We're going to give these people the best treatment we can," she said. "Everyone is going to receive comfort measures and the best medicine we can give. I'm going back to my lab at the hospital. I'm going to find out why this disease is not acting the way it's supposed to. Fifty percent of these patients are going to die if we treat them the way we have been. I need to find out what is going to work if we're going to defeat this beast."

Heads nodded in agreement. "Gather every single blanket, sheet, towel, any piece of cloth, and sterilize them. Ask the village members to help you. Gloves are mandatory for everyone. Train everyone in the village to wash their hands and use hand sanitizer. Family members can no longer sit with patients, but they can't leave the area. We can't risk spreading the infection. This entire town is officially quarantined."

"What about you, Dr. Taylor? If we're quarantined, so are you. You can't go back to your lab." The question was asked by the same nurse who had greeted Savanna at the clinic.

"I'm following protocol for my return." Savanna shook her head. "I'm going to do everything I can to stop this. One last thing cremate the bodies. We can't send them out. Find a way to cremate them here."

Savanna again made eye contact with each of the team leaders, looking for the hardened resolve she knew she wasn't feeling. Many of these people sitting in front of her had much more experience than she did. She had to trust that they would obey her orders when she left. At last she looked at the physician's assistant. His eyes narrowed and then he nodded, as if resolving something within himself.

"You're right, Dr. Taylor," he said. "We just don't like to hear these kinds of orders. All of us are in the business of saving lives and it's difficult to think of giving up so easily."

Savanna approached the man and put her hand on his shoulder. "We're not giving up the battle." She spoke in a low tone, but knew everyone in the room was listening. "We just need to move the front line. I'm going to do more good fighting this disease in my lab than here at this camp. You all fight for me here and I'll fight for you there." It sounded corny, even to her ears, but the words seemed to give a modicum of hope to those in the room.

Chapter Four

THE DOOR SWUNG OPEN and Chief Etu entered the already crowded office. "Anaba, a group from the National Guard just pulled up. There's a Captain Grey out here who says he needs to talk to you."

Savanna looked around at her team, all crammed in the tiny room. Each face registered shock, anger, exhaustion, and fear, but Savanna could also see the emotions were for the situation not focused on her. "Dr. Omoto, I'm leaving you in charge here. When I get back to my lab, I'm going to set up a direct video conference link between here and my office. I want continual communication, twenty-four seven." Savanna looked at each member of the team, making eye contact with those who would look at her.

Knowing she had done everything she could, Savanna left the office to meet Captain Grey.

Walking outside, all Savanna could see was chaos. Armed soldiers were herding people away from the entrance of the hangar and separating them into groups. Voices were raised in protest and soldiers were shouting orders. Savanna saw a group of five or six military vehicles only a few yards from the hangar entrance. A helicopter was perched a hundred yards away, its blades slowly rotating as it was powered down. Savanna had no difficulty identifying Grey. He was the man shouting the loudest.

Savanna lengthened her stride as she crossed the hard-packed dirt. All signs of exhaustion dropped away as she approached the man disturbing the calm she had worked so hard to build. She had everything under control and now these soldiers came in and bullied their way around. Striding across the compound, she pushed her way through the crowd to confront the leader. Before she could reach him a woman in full battle gear, including bullet-proof vest, helmet and gun, stepped in front of her, forcing her to stop.

"I'm Dr. Taylor." Savanna said. "I need to speak to the

Captain."

The soldier nodded. "Follow me, Doctor." She turned, and Savanna followed her to where the Captain was yelling orders.

Captain Grey turned around as Savanna approached. The soldier leading Savanna motioned her forward. Grey looked her up and down and curled his lip into a snarl.

"Who are you, little girl?" he asked. "I need Dr. Taylor out here, not a nurse."

Savanna straightened her shoulders and stiffened her spine. Drawing herself to her full height she stared the man down. Moving in so she was only six inches from his face she planted her finger in the middle of his chest.

"Listen, I am Dr. Taylor. I'm in charge here. Pull your men back and let my team do its job."

Savanna knew her voice was about two octaves lower than normal. When she became angry her voice dropped, a technique she picked up in graduate school. No one listened to a screeching teenage girl, so she practiced lowering her voice and speaking with intensity. The technique helped her get through medical school, where she had to deal with doctors who didn't believe she was capable of doing her job. Captain Grey didn't back down as well as the doctors.

"Hey, little girl," he said, "take the bass out of your voice. I'm here to help get this thing under control. I'm taking over here."

Savanna pulled herself up to her full height. Captain Grey was still a few inches taller than her, but this didn't intimidate her. "I have things under control here. You don't need to bully people around and I'm not going to let you add any more stress to my patients."

"You don't even know what you are dealing with here." Grey talked over the top of her as he gestured to one of his men. "This situation is a lot worse than you think. I'm here to debrief you and bring you back to the city."

"No!" Savanna realized the helicopter was powering up and they were expecting her to ride into the city in the thing.

Her heart started racing as her old fear of flying swept through her.

"We need to go now," Grey said. "I don't have time to argue with you." He grabbed her arm and pulled her towards the helicopter. Savanna tried pulling away and digging in her heels, but he had a tight grip on her arm. The chopper's side door was open. He grabbed Savanna by the waist and, lifting her off the ground with ease, sat her in the seat. Before Savanna could react, he followed her in and shut the door. The engine fired up and the blades started twirling before Savanna realized what was happening. The chopper lifted off the ground. Savanna forgot about lowering her voice and screeched at the Captain. Her panic overwhelming all her other thoughts.

"What are you doing?" She could feel the panic constricting her throat. "You can't drag me away like this. I have things I need to do before I leave."

Savanna started to stand up, but the Captain pushed her into the seat. A soldier grabbed her and efficiently strapped her into a restraint harness. He placed a set of headphones over her ears. "Buckle up, doctor," she heard his voice filter through the headset. "We're going to be traveling pretty fast to get you back to the city."

The chopper lifted off the ground as Grey filled her in on the situation. Savanna felt as though her stomach and heart were left on the ground, then swooped up in the air, racing to catch up. Grey's voice cut into her panic, bringing her thoughts back into focus.

"There are riots and mobs everywhere. Our job is to protect your pretty little backside until we get to Phoenix." Grey's voice blended with the echo of the chopper blades. "My men'll set up the mobile hospital and the incinerator to cremate the bodies here. Your job is to find out how to defeat this disease. The Corporal is patching you in to the director of the CDC. He'll debrief you on the situation."

If Savanna could have reached the man she would have smacked him across the head. As it was, she was strapped in too tightly and there were too many buckles to try to figure out.

She sat back as the soldier next to her pulled out a computer and flipped it open. He plugged a wire from the headset into a port in the computer.

"I'm getting the director of the CDC on the line now. He's going to debrief you on the situation. Smallpox isn't the only outbreak we're dealing with," the corporal said.

The screen flickered and an exhausted, middle-aged, man appeared. "Doctor Taylor," he began. "Today the terrorist groups Egyptian Islamic Jihad in collusion with al Qaeda took credit for a series of attacks across Egypt, the United Kingdom and the United States of America. There have been outbreaks of diseases and unexplained illnesses in many urban centers in all three nations. An hour ago, a leader in Pakistan announced the terrorist groups were responsible for sending over a hundred infected individuals to key urban cities in each country."

The significance of this information slowly started to sink in as Savanna listened to the director. She realized he hadn't even introduced himself to her before he started speaking. Savanna had been working with the Director of the CDC Phoenix branch office over the last few days, now she realized she was talking to the Director from Washington DC.

"Do we have a list of the viruses they have released, sir?" She wasn't quite sure how to address him.

"They haven't released the names of all the diseases, yet." His frustration forced its way into his tone. "Al Qaeda has claimed responsibility for releasing chemically engineered strains of smallpox, bubonic plague, and tuberculosis in each nation, but we suspect there are others. So far the only confirmed reports of outbreaks are pockets of smallpox."

"We've advised the general public not to panic," he continued. "We've also advised them not to go to the hospital unless they are exhibiting specific symptoms. We've posted a list of symptoms on the CDC website. Most people are ignoring our advice."

Savanna realized she was going to be flying into a firestorm when she got back to University Hospital. The medical community had thought these diseases had been eradicated, in some cases over seventy years before. Most of them didn't even have vaccines or treatment protocols in place. Things were going from desperate to disastrous.

"Dr. Taylor," the director brought her attention back to the video link. "We're starting to see riots in the streets and overwhelming numbers of patients in emergency rooms. We need to find a way to get this under control. Your lab is the most advanced in the area. We need you to start analyzing the viruses released in your area and find out how they have been genetically altered. We have labs set up in all the affected zones. There's a team waiting for you at your lab."

The soldier flicked the screen off and flipped it closed. The captain's voice came through the headphones again.

"I've been informed University Hospital has been inundated with smallpox patients. Hospitals all over the world are analyzing patient records to see if they have a history of these diseases in the past two months. They haven't been able to identify patient zero in any of the cases. There's no way of identifying the target cities. President Stewart has declared a state of emergency and every medical facility is on high alert. There have been riots in nearly every major city in the United States. The President just held a press conference. She said if the riots don't end she's going to lock down the cities under Martial Law."

Savanna slumped back in her seat, feeling the exhaustion of her sleepless nights. She forgot her fear of flying as other fears replaced it. The helicopter flew over the empty desert and approached the landing pad on top of University Hospital.

As they landed Savanna saw a group of people standing in the sheltered alcove usually reserved for trauma teams as they waited for victims flown in by Air Ambulance. The chopper powered down and the soldier next to Savanna unhooked the harness strapping her to the seat. Her heart raced and she could feel the bile in her throat as the overwhelming knowledge of the pandemic she would be facing overtook her thoughts. The chopper door slid open and Savanna ducked and ran for the alcove. The hospital director and two lab assistants were waiting for her.

"Dr. Taylor, welcome back." Doctor Richard Fallon, the Director of University Hospital, waited for her to pass by and into the door leading from the roof to the main building. "The samples you sent are waiting for you in the lab."

"Dr. Fallon, what's going on here? How bad is it?" Savanna locked eyes with the Director.

Fallon shook his head, explaining as they hurried through the corridors. "So far we've only been dealing with a smallpox outbreak in this region. There have been reports of other types of outbreaks in other cities, including two other smallpox outbreaks in New York State and a smaller one in Pennsylvania. We don't know if they're the same strain of virus."

"Can we get samples of the other viruses here?" They had entered Savanna's lab as they talked and she walked over to her desk. Opening the top drawer, she pulled out two pony tail holders. In a few seconds, her hair was pulled up into a loose bun on top of her head.

"We've requested samples from New York and Pennsylvania, but they're having problems arranging transportation." Dr. Fallon pulled up some files on the computer screen on Savanna's desk. "The CDC is trying to get the samples to us, but transportation is a huge problem right now. Hardly anyone is willing to drive affected samples into infested cities. We have asked for help from the National Guard, but they're busy with riot control. Once the riots are under control the Guard will start transporting the samples."

Savanna pulled her data pad from her pocket. Thankfully, in the rush to leave the reservation, she had placed the device in the pocket of her lab coat. "I want samples of all the suspected viruses and bacteria. If they were created by the same lab they'll have similar mutations. I want to compare the DNA, RNA and cellular makeup of all contaminates."

"Savanna." Dr. Fallon's voice had the same tone a

frustrated parent would have with a stubborn child. "You're the best medical researcher we have in this hospital, but even you're not going to be able to analyze every disease the terrorist released. You should just focus on the smallpox virus. Let researchers in the affected cities figure out how to combat their disease."

"Listen, Fallon." Savanna paused and took a deep breath. "I need to have every weapon at my disposal to combat this outbreak. I need to know what has been done to the genetic makeup of these diseases. Get me those samples."

Dr. Fallon looked closely at her face. Savanna knew he was looking at the dark circles under her eyes, her disheveled hair and paleness in her cheeks and lips. Lack of sleep always made her look washed out and sick.

"When was the last time you slept, Savanna? You look like something the cat dragged in after it was run over by a transport truck."

Savanna gave a small, wry smile. "I slept some at the reservation, but it doesn't change anything. I still want those samples."

"I understand, but I want you to get some sleep. It's going to be a while before the samples are sorted and prepared for analysis. Let's start with the ones we have. The other samples will get here when they get here." Fallon placed his hand on her shoulder. "We have pulled in the entire lab staff to help with the prep work."

Savanna nodded. She lowered herself into her office chair. "I don't want to leave the hospital. Can you set a cot up in here? I'll sleep for a couple of hours."

"I'll get an orderly to bring up a cot." Dr. Fallon turned and left the lab, leaving Savanna to her work. She placed her data pad on its charger and started downloading the data she had gathered at the reservation. She dialed the reservation. It only took a few minutes to call up the address. The view of the hangar office filled her computer screen.

The tired nurse from the clinic was sitting at the computer, staring blankly at the screen. A new mask was covering the lower half of her face, but Savanna could see the bright sheen of fever in her eyes. "Hello?" Savanna's voice caused the woman to start.

"Dr. Taylor? Oh, thank God!" The nurse brushed her hand across her forehead.

Savanna experienced a moment of panic. Things couldn't have gone so desperately wrong in the hour since she had been whisked away against her will.

"What's been happening there?"

The nurse shook her head. "Medically, nothing has changed. We've been following your orders. The National Guard was very heavy handed at first, but Chief Etu was able to talk to their commanding officer. I think they were expecting more resistance here because of the problems they have been experiencing in the city. The National Guard's medic team was able to take over triage and they were a little more forceful when they insisted family members couldn't stay with their sick relatives." The nurse lowered her eyes, when she looked up there were tears in her eyes. "They have also started cremating the bodies. Five more have died since you left."

The doors to the lab slid open and an orderly rolled a cot into the office. Savanna looked away from the computer for a moment. When she looked back, the nurse was removing the surgical mask from her face. Savanna could see the beginnings of a rash creeping up the sides of her face.

"I've been feeling a little sick for a couple of hours. I tried to convince myself I was just tired, but I can't deny it any more. I'm going to let Dr. Omoto know the video connection is up then I'm going to find an empty cot." The nurse wiped her forehead with the back of her hand. "Good luck, Dr. Taylor."

As the nurse walked away, Savanna realized she had never even asked her name. She transferred the video signal to a computer in the main lab and told her staff to wake her if there were any major changes. Closing the door to the office, she curled up under the blanket on the cot, buried her face in the pillow and cried herself to sleep.

Chapter Five

SAVANNA'S FATHER CALLED six times while she was sleeping. The research assistant who brought her the messages also brought her a progress report on sample preparation. Checking the time on the pad, she noticed she had been asleep for seven hours. She stretched to work the kinks out of her back and headed down the hall to the bathroom. Combing her hair and washing her face helped shake the last vestiges of sleep from her eyes. Making sure her hair was tightly braided and that the dark circles had disappeared from under her eyes only took a few minutes and before long she was back in the lab, sitting at her research station.

She was looking at the reports the technician had handed her when her pad beeped, signaling an incoming call. Realizing it was her father, she decided she couldn't ignore it. Transferring the call to her computer screen so she could still study the records of viral loads on her pad, she answered.

"Hi, Dad." Savanna didn't need to look at the screen to see the worry in her father's face. When she did glance at the screen, she noticed he was in his office at Haven, not the one in Boise.

"Savanna," he said. "Where have you been? I haven't been able to get a hold of you for two days."

"I've been working, Dad." Savanna couldn't help keeping a slight bit of sarcasm in her voice. Her father knew a doctor's life was full of emergencies and late nights. "Why are you at Haven? Aren't you scheduled to be at the office?"

"I was working here when news of the attacks was reported," he said. "We decided to close the facility, no one in or out until the outbreaks are under control."

Savanna didn't look up from her work to acknowledge his response, but she did nod. Pulling up the list of results from asymptomatic patient blood draws she started to separate them into vaccinated verses unvaccinated. She wasn't surprised her father had sealed the doors to Haven. He always liked to call the facility a shelter from the storm. Haven had its own two-year supply of food and medical supplies, in addition to resources normally shipped from other locations.

"How are you holding up, Savanna?" His voice softened in concern.

"I feel like I'm back in my residency." Savanna didn't enjoy her medical residency. She always felt the need to prove she was better than the other residents, many of whom where at least five years older than her. Being known as one of the most brilliant minds of her generation caused resentment and anger among her colleagues. One of her most vivid memories from that time was walking into the doctor's lounge and hearing the tail end of a conversation. One of the other residents had blurted out 'genetically altered freak' just as she opened the door. The silence echoed in the room as she walked to the fridge, grabbed a bottle of water and walked out.

Savanna reassured her father for a few more minutes and made a solid promise to call him the next evening. She managed to convince him it was time for her to go. Ending the call, she returned to her work. She needed to get her lab assistants help her sort the samples. Each sample needed categorized based on symptomatic verses asymptomatic patients and then subcategorized based on vaccination status of the individual.

Although the people working in the lab were all competent and followed her directions, she still missed the members of her team. She wasn't quite sure if she could trust the new team members to run the experiments to her specifications, and she ended up looking over their shoulders and double checking their work. The confidence level just wasn't there.

There was a tension in the lab Savanna wasn't used to experiencing. She felt grungy and tired and she realized she hadn't had a good shower or slept in a real bed for five days. The image in the microscope kept blurring under her gaze and no amount of eye rubbing or image adjustment helped. She finally made the decision to go back to her apartment and get some real rest. A five-minute tram ride soon had her at the front door of her glass fronted apartment complex.

Stepping from the oppressive heat to the deeply air-conditioned apartment building was almost a shock to Savanna's system. The security guard at the desk stood as she entered. Mike was a silver haired, gentle-faced man and Savanna had severe doubts he would ever be able to stop anyone from entering the complex. She was grateful for the double security measure of micro-chip coding on the elevator and door locks. She smiled at the kind-looking gentleman as she passed the desk and headed for the elevators.

Her apartment was too high up to hear the sounds of the street and the quiet made it seem empty. She considered turning on the ninety-inch screen television embedded as part of the wall structure for background noise, but just didn't feel like becoming invested in anything at the moment.

Dinner was a quiet, lonely experience. It made Savanna yearn for the chaotic mealtimes at Haven. The shelter, in its present form, was built five years before Savanna was born. The battered woman's shelter sponsored by her mother had become a multi-functional hospital, including an onsite psychiatric treatment center and rehab facility. Much of Savanna's childhood was spent volunteering for the programs sponsored at the facility. Haven was a safe place amidst all the chaos of the world. Her father managed the facility and kept the dream of it alive, in memory of her mother.

The quietness of the apartment was getting to Savanna. Although it was still early, she decided to shower and prepare for bed. She wanted to give her hair time to dry before she had to braid and pin it up in the morning. It was always irritating to pull down the waist-length, blond hair and still have it wet at the roots at the end of the day.

Savanna returned to the lab the next morning refreshed and ready to focus on her work. She helped her lab assistants prepare slides and cultures and organize samples. The sheer number of patients was overwhelming for many members of the team, but Savanna tried to keep them focused on the outcome. She knew they had to find a way to combat the virus before it spread. Savanna was frustrated by the slow process of preparing samples and identifying the genetic markers of the cellular DNA, but she knew there was no way to speed up the process.

Her team returned from the Reservation as stressed and exhausted as she had been. She ordered them to go home and rest for twenty-four hours before returning to the lab. During the early morning hours she was called to the emergency room, a nurse shaking her awake from the cot in her office. Two of her assistants had been brought in exhibiting high fevers and a rash. More casualties in the growing pandemic.

As the weeks progressed the CDC finally identified all the diseases brought in by the terrorist cell. In addition to smallpox, the CDC was able to identify strands of E. coli, tuberculosis, and bubonic plague, all diseases thought to be eradicated, some nearly eighty years before. By tracing immigration visas, the FBI was able to identify a number of terrorists, each of whom had entered the target countries on work visas or under the guise of seeking political asylum. These individuals obtained jobs in the service industry, allowing as much exposure to the general public as possible. The diseases were designed to lay dormant in the host for up to three weeks as they spread them to new hosts. Even during the dormant phase, the viruses and bacteria were still transmittable and the new host would spread the disease, unknowingly.

Many of the disease infested terrorists succumbed to the deadly affects of the various viruses and bacteria by the time they were identified. A few had been found by concerned good Samaritans and brought to area hospitals before dying, others found a nice quiet place to hide away and await death. Savanna was able to obtain some samples from what was now being classified as Patient Zeros on each of the diseases, although most of them were not easily tracked. Many of the original terrorists were still considered missing and at large.

The smallpox virus in the Southwest region was brought in by a woman who worked as a maid in a high-end hotel in Phoenix. She had entered the United States as a political refugee and had been sent to a local refugee center. The center volunteers helped her get a job at the hotel. While in public she wore a burqa covering her face and shoulders so, when the rash started to appear, she was able to hide it. Working in the hotel allowed her to handle many of the items in each room, from bed linens to water glasses and coffee cups. She made sure everything was germ infested before she left the room.

Savanna learned the woman disappeared at about the time the illness would have made her too sick to work. The CDC speculated that once she exposed as many people as she could she used the refugee center car to drive into the desert, park and hike as far as she could into the barren heat. The Tribal police had found her body three days later. Although her body was severely decayed, the virus was still active when she was brought to the coroner's office, another mutation of the virulent strain of the disease.

Savanna had been sent samples of strains of the diseases released by the terrorists. The CDC was able to trace them back to a defunct lab in Russia. When the Soviet Union dissolved over sixty years before some of the biological warfare labs had been raided in the confusion. No one reported the theft of the biological weapons, hoping they wouldn't be noticed. Unfortunately, the viruses had ended up on the black market, where they found their way into the hands of the terrorists.

Savanna contacted the reservation as often as she could, most of the time talking to Etu. At the end of two months two-thirds of the reservation population had contracted the disease. Over half of those afflicted died. Savanna made many trips to the reservation to gather samples and bring supplies. Although there were members of her team willing to do the grunt work for her, she wanted to be with the people she had come to care for so deeply. Etu always welcomed her into his home to stay while she was there. His wife was bed-ridden, weakened from her bout with the virus.

When news of Rachel's death crossed her desk, she dialed Etu's address as quickly as she could. His face appeared on her screen weathered and worn, showing the ravages of his pain.

For a few moments Savanna couldn't even speak. The normally strong man looked broken and defeated.

"Anaba, my daughter," his voice cracked.

"My father," Savanna had started using this address, like many other residents of the reservation. By now it was rolling naturally off her tongue. "I'm so sorry for your loss."

"There is much sorrow here, my child." Etu rubbed his hand across his face, exhaustion dragging at his features. "Savanna, Emily wants to help. She has been cleared for travel and is coming in on the next transport."

"Are you sure this is wise?" Savanna was concerned for more than Emily's health. Safety was becoming a major concern in the city. A nine o'clock curfew had been imposed and National Guard soldiers patrolled the streets, maintaining crowd control. Reports of hording and theft were rife in the city.

"She wants to be where she can do the most good. The hospital has offered her a job as a lab assistant." Etu gave a weary smile. "My main concern is her living accommodations. There is not a lot of affordable housing close to the hospital."

"She can stay at my apartment." The offer came from her heart. She had more than enough room. Her father had purchased the two-bedroom apartment for her when she first moved to Arizona. She rarely spent two consecutive nights in it anyway.

Within a few days Emily was established in the apartment's second bedroom and she fell right in place with the rest of the lab staff. She brought gentleness and a quiet sense of command to the lab and her presence helped polarize the staff. Emily also reminded Savanna when to eat and sleep and she wasn't afraid to let Savanna know when she needed to take a shower every once in a while.

Savanna had been able to obtain the one known sample

of smallpox, stored in a lab in Norway, and replicate it in her lab. She had a terrorist sample pulled up on a split screen with the Norway sample and was comparing the two. The current strand of the virus was extremely long lived compared to its historical counterpart. Savanna had a feeling there was more to the story than genetic manipulation. She was looking at the protein coating surrounding the virus.

"That's how they did it!" Her outburst drew the attention of her lab assistants. "It's the capsid shell, it's thicker."

"What are you talking about, Savanna?" Emily had looked up from where she was preparing gram stain slides.

"They used a thicker protein coating to protect the viral DNA." The four assistants in the lab all gathered around Savanna's computer. "It's barely noticeable, but it's there. If we can figure out a way to break that protein bond the anti-virals will be more effective."

Savanna called the head of the CDC to report her discovery. It was the first good news she had been able to report in six weeks. The thicker protein coating on the viruses and bacteria allowed for a more stable and transmittable strain, but her discovery allowed for a broader range of treatment options for those afflicted with the illnesses. The news of the find spread across the nation and was the first cause for celebration in months. President Stewart extended the curfew and for a time the riots and mobs ceased their destructive behavior.

The CDC was able to act quickly in the case of most of the terrorists' infestations. Quarantining afflicted areas and creating stringent disinfecting policies in public access areas helped slow the spread of the diseases. The only virus they were unable to contain was the smallpox outbreak. The virulent nature of the disease defied containment.

A mutation on the PB2 gene of the smallpox virus was responsible for the disease's resistance to the original vaccine. Savanna was able to create a vaccine containing the live virus using the samples she had in her possession but replicating the virus and insuring the vaccine was safe for human consumption was taking too much time. The virus spread from city to city and town to town.

Daily reports crossed her desk. Two-thirds of the population coming in contact with the disease became ill with forty percent of those dying. Those who survived were often left with disfiguring scars and, in some cases, blindness. Savanna felt an overwhelming sense of urgency as she rushed to produce a vaccine to quell the spread of the virus. The riots started up again and Stewart reinstated the nine-o'clock curfew.

Death tolls numbered in the millions. Savanna tried to steal herself against the numbers of casualties, but every report seemed to be a personal affront, exposing her failure as a researcher and a doctor.

Chapter Six

MONTHS AFTER THE INITIAL outbreaks the disease had slowed its course in the Northern Region of the U.S., but there were still pockets of outbreaks throughout the United States and Eastern Europe. Savanna was spending days in the lab, extracting stem cells from blood and bone marrow samples from those whose immune system had been able to fight off the disease. If she could identify exactly what it was that gave these individuals the ability to fight off the devastating effects of the disease, she knew she would be able to create a more effective vaccine.

Savanna set up the last samples of stem cells and set them in the culture trays. It was going to take three days for the cultures to grow and there was little more she could do in the lab until that happened, so she decided to go home. Emily had already left and had promised to have dinner ready if she made it home by seven, it was close to eight-thirty and almost curfew. If she left now she wouldn't need to get an escort home. She went into her office, closed the blinds and changed into her street clothes. Any clothes worn in the lab had to be sent to the laundry every day to avoid the spread of contaminants.

The tram was crowded with passengers trying to make it home before curfew and there was no place to sit. Savanna took a handkerchief from her pocket and used it as a barrier between her hand and the rail as she steadied herself from the lurching of the car. As soon as she exited the tram she threw the square of cloth in the trash, squirted a glob of hand sanitizer in her palm and rubbed her hands together briskly as she walked up the sidewalk.

She was near the front door to her apartment complex when she noticed a huddled form on the ground, half hidden in the alley. From the angle of the body she knew there was something wrong. Savanna made eye contact with a soldier standing on the corner and waved him over. He grinned as he approached. Savanna recognized him as a young private assigned with a unit patrolling the University Hospital district.

"Dr. Taylor," he acknowledged her. Savanna was easily recognizable. Her name and face had been splashed across news broadcasts over the last six months. "How can I help you?"

Savanna pointed out the figure huddled in the ally. "I think there's someone over there. Could you go check it out?"

The soldier slipped on a pair of vinyl gloves, now standard issue, and pulled out his taser. Savanna watched as he slowly approached the huddled form on the ground. She knew it was common place to find bodies of plague victims in alleys and abandoned buildings. There hadn't been any found in her neighborhood, though, and Savanna didn't want this to be the first. The soldier gently turned the body over, exclaimed loudly and jumped back.

"Dr. Taylor!" His voice echoed down the street. "It's a girl and it looks like she's been beat up, bad."

Savanna ran to where he was standing. She knelt and pulled the long, black hair away from the girl's face. It took her a second to realize she was looking at Kai.

The last time Savanna had seen the girl was just after the death of her grandmother. Savanna had never spent much time with the fourteen-year old girl, instead focusing on those who were still exhibiting symptoms of the diseases. She remembered Kai had a few scars on her face, neck and shoulders from the smallpox, but the scars were hard to see beneath the bruising and swelling currently dominating her features. She also had finger marks around her neck.

The soldier called 911 while Savanna assessed the girl. Kai's chest was rising and falling with even breaths and her eyes opened when Savanna leaned over her. She whispered something, and Savanna leaned down, so she could hear. The only words she could make out were 'Aunt Emily'. Savanna reached for her data pad and called up to the apartment. Emily made it down the elevator just as the ambulance pulled up. There was only room for one other person in the ambulance. Emily joined her niece while Savanna took the tram back to the hospital.

She arrived just as Kai was being wheeled into an exam room. Emily gestured for her to come into the room. Kai was slipping in and out of consciousness as the emergency room physician did his initial assessment. When he tried to give her a pelvic exam she started screaming. The doctor looked up at Savanna and Emily.

"It appears she's been raped," he said. "But, unless she allows me to do a pelvic exam, I'm not going to be able to confirm it."

Emily leaned down and gently spoke to the girl. "Kai, the doctor is trying to help you. Can you let him do a pelvic exam please?"

Kai shook her head. "No, no Aunt Emily." Tears streamed from her eyes. "It hurts so bad. Please, don't let anyone touch me."

Savanna placed her hand on Kai's arm. The girl looked up at her. "Kai, I can do it." Savanna softened her voice as she spoke to the child. She knew the girl had been victimized, recognizing the mannerisms as those she had seen over her years of working at Haven. It took a few minutes of coaxing, but eventually Savanna and Emily convinced her to allow the exam. Savanna worked quickly and gently, taking swabs and samples.

The police arrived to take a statement and, in fits and starts, Kai explained what happened. She had a tight grip on Savanna's hand the entire time. Savanna was surprised at this. The girl should have been holding her aunt's hand but, for some reason, Kai was developing a sense of trust in Savanna and clung to her.

Kai explained to the officers how she had come into the city with some friends to a party. She had been drinking for a couple hours when she all of a sudden she started to feel sick. After going into an empty room she passed out on the floor. When she woke up a boy was raping her. She screamed and the boy hit and choked her until she nearly lost consciousness. She heard someone say, 'move it's my turn'. She had no idea how many times she was raped, the next thing she remembered was waking up in a park. She was bruised and bleeding, her clothes were ripped and she was missing her underwear.

Her purse was beneath her body and her cell phone was inside. Using an app to locate Savanna's address, Kai walked slowly, painfully to the apartment. Although she had the address she didn't have Savanna's number. She hid in the alley, hoping she would see her aunt coming home from the hospital. The National Guard soldiers frightened her and she was trying to stay as hidden as possible. Knowing it was getting close to curfew, she decided she would try to see if the doorman had seen her aunt and was trying to work her way out of the alley when she lost consciousness.

Emily stepped out of the room to call Kai's parents and let them know what happened. Savanna tried to disengage her hand from Kai's, but every time she tried to move the girl would grip tighter and pull her hand closer. She finally sat by the edge of the bed, allowing Kai to sleep while her hand slowly went numb.

Emily quietly made her way into the room. She raised her eyebrows when she took in Savanna sitting at the edge of the bed, Kai's hand wrapped tightly around hers. Savanna shrugged, silently saying 'whatever works'.

"Her mom's at work," Emily whispered. "They're not going to make it until morning. No one's available to escort them into the city and they can't leave outside of curfew."

The nurse woke Kai to give her a plan B pill, but she complained her throat hurt too bad to swallow.

Taking the pill away the nurse said, "I'll let the doctor know she can't swallow. He'll write a prescription to take home. She'll need to take it in the next forty-eight hours for it to be effective against preventing pregnancy."

When Kai was released from the hospital she refused to go with her parents to the reservation. Emily asked Savanna if she could stay at the apartment while she cared for the child. Since Savanna didn't spend a lot of time at home she allowed the girl to move in with her aunt.

Once she was brought to the apartment Kai hardly moved off the couch. The few times Savanna did come home she found the girl laying on the couch staring at the television. Sometimes it was on; sometimes she would be staring at the blank screen.

Savanna's conversations with Emily were limited but, when they did talk, Emily would describe the ineffective counseling sessions she encouraged Kai to attend. The girl would sit, not saying anything for the entire fifty minutes. When Savanna was home she would attempt to help Emily as she coaxed the girl to eat or clean herself or to motivate her to move off the couch.

It had been nearly three weeks after Kai had showed up at the apartment and Savanna and Emily were both working in the lab, a rare occurrence since the incident. It was quiet as Savanna prepared gram stain slides. Emily stood at the work station, her back to Savanna as she sorted through the samples, labeling them before entering data into computer. The two women worked in companionable silence for a while and managed to get quite a bit of work done.

An easy friendship had developed between the two over the past few months, despite their age difference. Savanna was only a few months away from being twenty and Emily was approaching forty. Emily was the first person Savanna ever counted as a friend.

Emily put down the slide she was working with and turned to face Savanna. "Savanna, has your father lifted the lockdown on the treatment center he runs in Idaho?"

Looking up from the microscope, Savanna gazed into her friend's eyes. Emily was only five-three and, despite being seated, Savanna didn't have to look up to meet her eyes.

"I talked to Dad about Kai last night," she said. "Since she's a minor we would need to have her parents sign her up for the program, but he has a bed for her if their interested."

A relieved smile spread across Emily's face. "I don't know if they'll be willing to send her so far away, especially with everything that has happened since the viral attacks. I'll talk to my sister. We're going to have to get a travel visa added to her papers so she can cross state lines."

Savanna nodded. "After you get her parents' okay, I'll bring her in and get a blood sample. It might take a while, but we'll do what we can. Why don't you see what you can arrange since you have the day off tomorrow?"

Savanna stayed on her cot in the lab overnight. She had several stem cell cultures ready to process and didn't want to leave. She was exhausted when she headed home late the next evening. The apartment was empty when she stepped inside. Assuming Emily and Kai were at another unproductive therapy session, she pulled out one of the dinners Emily kept in the fridge, reheated it according to the note on the foil, and had just sat down at the table when Emily burst into the apartment.

"Have you seen Kai?" Her voice seemed shaky and there was a tension in her eyes Savanna usually didn't see.

"No, I just got here."

"One of her friends called last night about eleven and she took off, completely disregarding curfew." Emily was shaking as she spoke. "She didn't come home last night. I don't know where she is."

Savanna had Emily sit at the kitchen table while she called the police. While they were waiting for the police to arrive, she handed the phone to her friend and had her call the reservation. Emily explained to her sister what happened and told her Kai was missing. Savanna could hear the woman screaming on the other end of the line so she took the phone and tried to reassure Kai's mother. It didn't take long for the police to show up at the apartment complex and so Savanna cut the conversation short. She sent a message to the elevator to allow the officers to unlock the doors and come up to the apartment.

Emily explained what happened as the officers took notes on their data pads. Although the police were kind, they did not leave Emily much hope to find Kai. After the details were gathered, the officers sent their reports to the main computer at the station. They turned to leave. As the older officer reached for the panel to activate the door, the younger one turned back to face the women, he took off his cap and addressed both of them.

"Ladies, I don't want to build up any false hope here," he started. "When a teenager runs away they're always difficult to find. And when they run away once, they're more likely to run away again."

He replaced the hat on his head and addressed Emily. "Ma'am, I doubt your niece is going to be easy to find. If you do find her, I suggest you send her to an in-treatment psychiatric facility. It'll be the best thing for her, and for your family." The officer turned with his partner and left the apartment.

Emily sat across from Savanna at the kitchen table. Not quite knowing what to say to the woman who had become her friend and assistant over the past few months, Savanna sat in silence. Finally, not knowing what else to do, she moved to the stove to make some tea.

As Savanna moved across the kitchen, Emily stood up and intercepted her. "Let me do that." She took the tea pot and filled it with water. "I'm glad I don't have kids. I love my niece, but if I were her mother I would lock her in her bedroom and not let her out until she was twenty-five."

Savanna took the tea Emily offered and sipped it, trying to avoid being burned. "My Dad used to threaten to do that to me." She smiled at the memory. "He said he would slip peanut butter sandwiches under the door to feed me. Of course, I was only eleven when I went through my rebellious phase and it only lasted about ten weeks."

It was easy to see the smile on Emily's face was forced and Savanna didn't know if she felt any better. "Hey." She reached across the table and took her friend's hand. "We'll get her to Haven as soon as we find her. The program has the highest success rate for psychiatric treatment in the United States. We'll get her the help she needs."

Chapter Seven

THE POLICE BROUGHT KAI into the emergency room three days later. When the ER physician asked Kai who her family doctor was she told them it was Savanna. It only took a few minutes for Savanna to get from her lab to the emergency room. She was there when the results for most of the tests came back.

The physician handed Savanna the test results and said, "Should I tell her or do you want to?"

Savanna looked at the results and shook her head. "I'll tell her, she's my patient."

"Her parents are on their way. Other than the high blood alcohol content she's medically clear." He left Savanna in the hallway and walked into another patient room.

As she watched him walk away Savanna could see the exhaustion in the tension of his shoulders. Searching her mind, she tried to remember his name. Stephen Murray, he was finishing his third year of residency. She was thankful her days of residency were behind her, although the hard work and sleepless nights helped prepare her for the continuing work of the pandemics.

Savanna approached the triage center of the emergency room. She gently pulled back the curtain hiding Kai's bed from the probing eyes of other patients. The girl was studying the IV in her arm, watching the steady drip of fluids slowly work its way from the bag, through the narrow tube, and into the machine pumping it into her vein. Savanna pulled the chair close to the bed and placed her hand on Kai's arm.

Kai turned to face her, but when she looked into her eyes, it seemed to Savanna as if she was looking through, not at, her. Savanna had seen this look before, usually on family members of those who had died from smallpox.

Kai was an extraordinarily beautiful girl, despite the smallpox scars. Now, though, her hair was unkempt, her dark skin was smudged with dirt and there was a scratch from the slightly down-turned corner of her right eye ending just above the corner of her full lips. The blood from the scratch was smeared across her face, and some of it was matted in her hair. A nurse tried to clean her up, but Kai kept pushing her away. Giving up, the nurse put down the moist gauze pads on the bedside table and, shaking her head at Savanna, walked out of the treatment room.

"Kai." Savanna paused to make sure the girl was listening to her. "Kai, we have some of the test results back. There is no easy way to tell you this, so I'm just going to say it. Kai, you're pregnant. From the hormone levels, it looks like a little over three weeks. It probably happened the night you were raped."

Savanna knew the moment Kai realized what she was being told. The dead, unseeing look left her eyes and was replaced with rage.

"What? No! Get rid of it! I don't want it! Please." The girl grabbed Savanna's arm so hard her hand actually became pale and started to tingle. "I can't have this baby."

Savanna closed her hand into a fist and Kai released her. "Kai, I don't perform abortions." Savanna tucked the blanket around the girl's shoulders. "We can bring you to an abortion clinic or a doctor here might be able to perform--"

"No," Kai interrupted. "You, only you. I can't trust anyone else. Please, don't tell Aunt Emily."

"I can't." There was real anguish in Savanna's voice as she explained to the girl. "I promised my Dad. The only thing I can do is harvest the fetus for transplant. I've seen too much death and pain already."

Savanna was thinking about the promise she had made to her father when she first became a doctor. Dr. Jackson Taylor was a geneticist. During the course of his career, he had seen a rapid decrease in fertility rates, including the infertility of his own wife. He became increasingly frustrated with the increasing number of abortions performed while many of his patients struggled to become pregnant. Through the course of his research, he developed a method of fetal transplant and vowed he would never perform an abortion, but would instead perform fetal adoption. It took five years for legislation to formalize fetal adoption procedures, but once legislation was in place fetal adoption became a popular alternative to abortion.

Savanna knew how important this work was to her Dad and promised she would never perform abortions. If ever asked, she would offer fetal adoption transplants instead. Looking at the tiny fourteen year old before her she started questioning this vow. She didn't see how a fourteen year old child could make such a devastating decision under these circumstances.

"Fine, then do the transplant. Find someone to take care of it." Kai started to turn away, and then she abruptly turned back. "You can have it! You take the baby. You'd take care of it better than me."

"Let's not talk about it right now." Savanna breathed a sigh of relief. Pulling up a form on her pad, she started to list the supplies she would need. "We need to get the approval of your parents, but I'll send for my equipment and harvest the fetus. We can find suitable adoptive parents once we take care of this." Savanna was thinking of the emotional and physical needs of the patient in front of her, not the fetus she was preparing to harvest.

"No, I will only give it to you." Kai voice had a note of finality to it.

Savanna had her equipment brought to the emergency room within fifteen minutes, but she had to wait before she could perform the procedure. Kai was underage and her parents had to sign off on any medical procedures. The hospital social worker was called in to prepare the necessary paperwork. Kai insisted the contract stipulate Savanna was to be the adoptive parent of the fetus.

Legislation stated the fetal donor mother had to be shown as mentally competent to make the decision before she could sign the adoptive paper work. However, it allowed mothers to make the decision early in the pregnancy since fetal transplants were most successful if the fetus was harvested in the first two months. As long as the procedure was performed in the first trimester the only signature needed for adoption was the donor mother's, though Kai's parents had to sign off on the actual procedure.

The squeal of the curtain being flung open interrupted the social worker's explanation of the procedure. Savanna easily recognized Kai's parents. Her step-father was carrying a white cane with a red tip, his eyes covered by milky-white sheen. His hand was on his wife's shoulder as she guided him into the room. Both had scars disfiguring their faces, making their twin scowls look even more fearful. Kai pulled her body to the far side of the bed, as far from her parents as possible. Her mother turned and addressed Savanna, ignoring the small huddled form on the bed.

"Dr. Taylor," she said, "how bad is it this time? Are we going to be able to take her home?"

Savanna stood and approached the couple. "Let's step into an empty room. We have a few things to discuss in private."

Kai's mother shook her head. "We can talk it over here. I'm not letting her out of my sight."

Savanna explained, in hushed tones, about the pregnancy and what Kai wanted. Before she finished, Kai's mother was reaching for the pad to sign. The social worker tried to explain about Kai's desire for Savanna to adopt the embryo, but the woman held up her hand to stop her.

"I don't care what happens to the baby," she said. "It's bad enough we have to deal with all of this at the Rez. Kai keeps changing her story and, other than DNA evidence, they can't prove who did what when. The boys are claiming it was consensual and someone else beat her up. We have been friends with most of these boys' parents since we were in school and now even they won't talk to us. Everyone is taking sides, the last thing we need to do is throw a baby into the mix." She signed the pad with a flourish.

The social worker cleared her for the procedure, but Kai refused to sign the fetal adoption release until it was modified to give custody of the fetus to Savanna. Feeling this was the best option for treatment of the young girl, Savanna agreed to Kai's terms. There was an intense look in Kai's eyes as she watched Savanna sign the agreement to adopt. When all the paperwork was complete Kai relaxed back on the bed. Savanna convinced Kai's parents to wait with Emily in the waiting room. Kai was transferred to the procedure room where Sam was waiting with the equipment.

Savanna coached Kai to place her feet in the stirrups and scoot down to the edge of the bed. The entire procedure was very simple, one that had been perfected over the past forty years. Savanna kept her voice low and soothing as she spoke to the girl. "Kai this is going to pinch, but I promise it'll only take a few minutes."

Savanna quickly sliding the slim, flexible harvester into place. She used the scope to locate the microscopic, multi-celled organism nestled against the uterine wall. Using the laser, she separated the embryo and drew it into the fluid filled tubing, where it traveled into the test tube. Sealing the tube, she placed it in the small metal container sitting next to her on the procedure table. Pushing the red button on the top of the container caused it to close, sealing the embryo in its protected container.

Savanna looked through the microscope a final time to assure herself there wasn't anything else she needed to be concerned about. Finding nothing, she finished the procedure, withdrawing the scope. She heard Kai release a gasp of air, as if she had been holding her breath. Savanna helped the girl sit up and adjusted her pillows. Removing her gloves, she washed her hands at the sink before turning back to Kai.

"You may have some residual bleeding and cramping, but it should be gone in a couple of days." Reaching up, she brushed Kai's long black hair away from her face. "Kai, your family loves you and wants to help you. It's breaking their heart to see you in so much pain." Savanna felt the moisture from the girl's tears in her hand as she touched her face.

"It hurt so bad. No one understands." Tears now

flowed easily from her eyes. "They all say they do and they want to help, but how can they know. The scars make me so ugly. I just wanted Jimmy to love me for who I am, but I'm so ugly and now this. No one will ever love me." Kai broke down and started sobbing. She curled into the fetal position and refused to talk any more.

Savanna helped the nurse bring Kai back to her bed in the emergency room. The physician walked into the room as Savanna was covering the girl with a blanket. "Are you finished with the procedure?"

Savanna didn't trust her voice to speak, so she nodded. The physician looked down on the young girl curled into a ball in the white sheet draped bed. "Kai, your parents want to see you. Can they come in?" He must have taken her silence as acceptance because he pushed the curtain back.

Kai's mother walked to the side of the bed and put her hand on the girl's shoulder. She sat in the chair by the side of the bed, seeming to collapse into herself.

Savanna approached, sitting on a stool next to her. "Has Emily talked to you about sending Kai to Haven? My Dad has a place for her at the psychiatric hospital. He can get her the help she needs."

Kai's mother shook her head. "We considered it, but we don't want to send her so far away, even temporarily." Tears escaped the corner of the woman's eyes. "Kai is all we have left. Our other two children died from the virus. We do love her, it's just we had so much to deal with over the past year. We found a place closer to home that will take her."

Savanna nodded. Picking up the metal storage container, she slipped out of the exam room. Emily was standing in the waiting room when Savanna walked out.

"Is there anything more you can do for her, Savanna?" She asked.

"She needs more help than I can provide." Looking down at the container in her hands, Savanna thought about the decision she needed to make. "I have work to do in my lab, would you like to help?"

Emily nodded and followed her out of the room. As the curtain closed behind them, Savanna knew Kai's parents were signing the papers to commit Kai into an in-patient psychiatric clinic. She sincerely hoped the doctors and nurses there could help the girl struggling with her insecurities and fears.

The elevator lit up at each floor as it journeyed to the lab. Every few floors it would stop and the doors slid open, allowing passengers to enter or egress. Savanna noticed Emily kept glancing at the metal container in her hands. Neither of the women spoke as the elevator approached the seventeenth floor and the doors slid open.

Savanna walked into her lab, Emily half a pace behind. She walked to the counter at the back of the lab, her own personal workspace.

During the height of the pandemic, Savanna had kept this workspace clear. Even though lab space was at a premium, she just couldn't bring herself to use the same area for analyzing the DNA sequence in killer viruses as she had been using to study stem cells in combating birth defects. This was the first time she used her personal work space in over six months. The experiments she had been working on were all cryogenically frozen. Some of the more sensitive experiments had been sent to her father's lab in Boise since she didn't know when she would be able to continue her own personal research.

Pulling out the electronic microscope, Savanna attached the electrode into the receiving port on the storage container. Within seconds the embryo appeared on the computer screen, magnified one thousand times. Savanna pulled out her data pad and scrolled to the record icon. As she tapped it with the stylus, the screen flashed red and pulled up a word document. She placed the data pad on the counter and started to record her observations. As she spoke, the words typed on the screen.

"The embryo is three weeks, showing normal development. The mother is full Navajo. Father is unknown but is also suspected to be Navajo. Possibility the father could be of Anglo-Saxon descent. Exposure to alcohol and drugs in uteri, unknown quantities, unknown duration. Will use stem cells to try to repair any possible damage from FAS and cellular damage pre-transplant. Will also use stem cells to enhance immune response and prevention of birth defects."

Savanna tapped the screen twice and the recording stopped. Using a microscopic probe, she inserted a needle into the cluster of cells and extracted a minuscule amount of DNA. Emily handed her a Petri dish.

"Is this the right one?"

Savanna nodded and placed the DNA sample in the Petri dish. A final touch of a button on the side of the metal container released the nitrogen, freezing the embryo in stasis until she was ready to transplant.

Savanna placed the container in Emily's hands. "Put this in storage. I need to do some prep work to make sure the fetus is suitable for transplant." Emily took the container and moved to the door near the back of the lab. As she stepped towards the door, she paused and turned towards Savanna.

"What are your plans for this fetus?" Emily asked.

Savanna studied Emily for a minute before she responded. Although the two women lived and worked together for the last six months, Savanna was unsure how Emily would react to any decision she made. After all, the fetus was technically the woman's niece.

Savanna watched Emily closely as she spoke. "The fetus was given up for adoption. I suspect there may be a few problems with the fetal development and I want to use some of the stem cell research I've been working on to try to repair it. Without gene therapy the fetus may not even be viable." Emily's expression was blank as Savanna spoke.

"Emily, Kai wouldn't sign the release unless I agreed to adopt the fetus." Savanna said. "I'm, uh, I'm really considering it. I've just seen so much pain and suffering over the past few months, I think something good needs to come out of this tragedy. I really think I can provide a safe, happy life for the child."

Emily nodded. "I was just curious about any of the

experiments you may be running so I could prep the equipment. I think it will be better this way." She paused, briefly, before speaking again. "You know, I think you should adopt this fetus." Savanna was surprised her friend was so calm. "You don't have to transplant right away, you could wait a few years. I don't have any desire to have children, but you may someday." Emily looked at the container in her hand. "So much tragedy has happened, especially to Kai. Something good does need to come from this."

Chapter Eight

SAVANNA MADE A NOTE to research the treatments she would need to take to prepare herself for fetal transplant. She hadn't made a final decision yet, but she wanted to explore the options before her. Emily came out of the storage facility and sealed the door. Savanna entered the lock code on her pad and pressed send. The click of the door mechanism reassured her that the storeroom was securely locked.

Back at the apartment Emily prepared dinner, a careful blend of textured soy protein enhanced by fresh vegetables. Savanna had become frustrated with trying to find protein untreated with hormones and antibiotics. Over processed foods didn't always agree with her stomach and since shopping for meat products without additives took time and energy Savanna didn't have, she just found it easier to use alternative protein products. While living in the apartment Emily had adopted Savanna's eating habits. The women sat down to eat at the kitchen table.

They ate in silence for a while, but Savanna's curiosity got the best of her. "Emily, why don't you want to have kids?" she asked. "You're young enough. You could still have a child."

Emily seemed to take a long time to respond. At first Savanna thought she had offended her friend, but Emily didn't look angry, just thoughtful.

"I don't know. I never wanted to have children. Did you know I was married once?" Savanna must have shown the surprise she felt because Emily paused for a moment before she continued her story. When she did start talking again Savanna could hear the tension of suppressed emotions in her voice.

"I married my husband when we were both nineteen. He promised we would go to college and get off the Rez. We were both working dead end jobs on the Reservation and I wanted to get out. He talked about wanting kids, but I wanted to wait. I just didn't feel right about bringing a child into the world to live the same life I had. A few years into our marriage he got a job as a dealer in one of the casinos and it's like the casino took over his life. He was making good money, but he would turn around and gamble it away. I waited for him to work it out of his system, but he never did."

Emily paused and took a few bites of her dinner. Savanna wanted to hear more of her friend's story, but didn't want to push her. She ate the last few bits of carrot off her plate and brought it to the sink. Moving back to her seat, she waited for Emily to continue. Emily finished her last few bites of food. Putting her fork across the plate, she intertwined her fingers under her chin and rested for a moment.

"This is the first time I talked about this since the divorce. It's been more than fifteen years. You would think I would be over it." Emily paused and took a deep breath. "I kept pushing him about going to college, I wanted to get of the Rez and make a better life for myself. He told me our life was good enough and stop pushing it. We had been married for five, almost six years. I barely remember the first time he hit me, he didn't leave any bruises and I didn't think it was a big deal. I remember the last time he hit me, though."

Again, Emily paused. This time she just took a drink of water before she continued. "I was just getting ready for my shift. I was working as a waitress at the same casino where my husband was dealing. Rent was due and we were two hundred dollars short. I woke my husband to remind him about the rent and ask him if he had the money. He flew out of bed and tackled me. Within a few minutes of him hitting me I was unconscious. He left me on the floor, took a shower and went to the casino." Emily paused for a moment. Savanna could see the repressed pain in her friend's eyes.

"I gained consciousness after a few minutes and managed to crawl to the phone and call my father. They arrested my husband from where he was sitting at the blackjack table. I spent two days in the hospital and he spent thirty days in jail. My family helped me move out of the apartment and file for divorce before he was even out. I still see him around the Rez every once in a while. He remarried a few years later. From what I've heard he hasn't changed much."

Emily finished her story and moved her plate over to the sink. She efficiently cleaned the dishes. After washing them, she put them in the sanitizer. Savanna watched her for a few minutes, imagining what her friend endured in her marriage. Victims of domestic violence were frequent fliers in the emergency rooms of the hospitals where she had worked. Savanna had treated more than one woman battered by her partner. She had even treated a couple of men who had been assaulted as well. Most of the victims returned to their abusers, despite attempts to steer them towards domestic violence counseling and help-lines.

"My mother's pet projects involved working against domestic violence." As Savanna spoke, Emily returned to the table and sat across from her. "My Dad is a very wealthy man. We have family money and his work in genetics has helped 'pad the family checkbook'. His words, not mine. He won't tell me how much he's worth. Not that it matters much. My mother decided she wanted to open a domestic violence shelter with some of the money. She's the one who actually started Haven."

"I really wish my sister would consider sending Kai there," Emily said. "I've read about the program and its success rate. It would have been nice to know about it when I was younger."

"Some days I wish I was still there," Savanna said. "The whole thing started as a program for women trying to escape abuse, but it has grown into something much bigger. The center is almost a hundred percent self-reliant. My Dad makes sure the Haven Project has everything it needs, in memory of my mother."

Emily started wiping the table and counters with sanitizing wipes. "I've talked to your father a few times." She smiled. "He's very kind. How does he manage to work in research and run a women's shelter? I mean, you come home exhausted, when you do come home."

"My mother ran it while she was alive." Savanna reached up and touched the purple butterfly necklace around her throat. It was a gift from her mother. Kylie Taylor had given the necklace to her daughter when she had her first battle with cancer. She told her she needed to break out of her cocoon and find her wings. Savanna was painfully shy as a child and she knew this was her mother's way of telling her she needed to find her voice.

"Haven isn't really much of a shelter any more. It's become a more like a specialized treatment center. My Dad is more of a figure head than a manager."

Emily put a steaming cup of tea in front of Savanna and sat down with her own cup. Savanna traced the edge of the brown ceramic mug as she waited for the liquid to cool. Emily sipped from her own mug in silence.

"I'm going to do the transplant." Savanna kept her eyes on the steam rising from the mug. "I'm going to start the hormone treatments right away and work on genetic restoration of the embryo." She looked up to gauge Emily's reaction.

Emily's lips thinned as she shook her head. "Are you sure this can't wait?" She drank more tea before she continued. "You have your whole life ahead of you, Savanna. You're not even twenty."

"There's so much pain and tragedy in the world right now," Savanna explained. "Every time I go to sleep I see Yanaba's eyes looking up at me. I can't sleep, I can't think half the time." Savanna reached out and took her friend's hand. "Something good has to come from this madness. I know I can give this fetus a chance at life. A chance others never had. I feel if I give this life a chance, I'll be doing something to make up for the pain and suffering happening around us."

Savanna tested the temperature of her tea, sipping a bit of the sweet herbal mixture, tasting mint. She wrapped her hands around the warmth of the cup. The air conditioner was running full bore, chilling her fingers. The tea warmed her up enough she was starting to get sleepy.

"Why now, Savanna?" Emily sipped her own tea.

"We're still trying to find a better vaccine for the smallpox. Why can't you wait until things calm down a little bit?"

Savanna stood up and brought her cup to the sink. "Are things ever going to calm down?" She rinsed the cup and put it in the dish sanitizer. "President Stewart just announced she's committing another hundred thousand troupes to the Middle East to try to find the terrorists cells responsible for releasing the viruses. There are still strains of all the diseases out there and some of them are still mutating. We can't fight it all." Savanna took a deep breath, trying to calm her nerves. Sitting back down, she pulled out her data pad and checked her schedule for the next day.

"I still don't know why you can't wait." Exasperation was clearly apparent in Emily's voice.

Savanna stood and pushed in her chair. "I need something solid to cling to in all of this. I can do something good, make something right with this. Something like my Dad is doing with Haven." She stretched to work the kinks out of her back. "I have a lot of work to do tomorrow. I'm going to bed. I'll see you in the morning."

Over the next few months Savanna worked with Dr. Omoto to prepare for her transplant. He put her in a daily hormone regiment to prepare her body for the fetal transplant. Together, they developed genetic alteration from stem cells drawn from cord blood and adult donors. Omoto's excitement in the work was apparent. He explained this type of work was why he wanted to join her team in the first place. Both of them reveled in the fact they were finally working on building life as opposed to fighting death.

One of the side effects of Savanna's chosen method of hormone therapy was an increase in ovulation. Dr. Omoto harvested twelve ova in the months she was under treatment. Savanna wanted to fuse some of her own DNA with the fetus, to give the cells the same immune defenses she had been given. She drew her own stem cells from one of the harvested ova. Using some of the genetic contributions from her own research, Savanna fertilized the rest of her ova, creating embryos before cryogenically freezing them.

Savanna prepared several stem cells to fuse with the embryo in hopes to enhance the immune response and fetal development. She used the sample she had harvested from the embryo to assess what else needed to be repaired. Emily helped draw blood and analyze Savanna's hormone levels during her treatment. She also helped Savanna develop the stem cell cocktail used to enhance the fetus. However, Emily wasn't in the lab when Savanna added the feline stem cells to enhance the strength of the weakened sensory cell walls in the fetus.

Combining animal DNA with human was still a new science, carefully regulated by the FDA. The first experiments with the process were greeted with disgust and protests. Originally legally approved in the United Kingdom in 2004, the first embryos created in this process were destroyed after fourteen days of development. Almost immediately letters, threats and protests flooded into scientists and doctors' offices, all littered with biblical references and obscure quotes from *The Island of Dr. Moreau*. It took seven years of research and fighting Congress to develop legislation allowing the combination of animal stem cells with human DNA to strengthen genomes. It took another six years before the first child repaired by animal stem cells was born.

Many of the originally altered children were ostracized and harassed, despite efforts to protect their identities. Savanna wanted to ensure this child had as much anonymity as possible. Noting the modification in the fetus's medical record, Savanna sealed it, allowing access only for medical purposes.

Savanna worked on the embryo every spare moment she could find. After three months of treatment, she finally decided it was time for transplant. She didn't have high hopes for the success of the procedure. Even with strong, viable fetuses the success rate of in vitro was only forty percent and this was a fetus carrying a high number of possible injuries from its treatment in uteri. Dr. Omoto and Emily met her in the lab at five in the morning. No one else was around as Savanna stripped out of her scrubs and put on the paper robe.

She sat on the edge of the bed with a sheet draped over her lap.

Smoothing out a seam on the sheet, Savanna took some deep breaths to focus her thoughts. It seemed silly to sit on the edge of the table with her legs modestly covered. For some reason she felt vulnerable and wanted the extra layer of protection the sheet offered.

Dr. Omoto walked in with the sterile packaging containing the transplant equipment. Emily was carrying the embryo in the transplant vial. They had worked together to prepare the fetus in the days before the procedure. Savanna hoped the stem cell modifications would prove to be effective. There was no way to tell what modifications took and which didn't until the embryo was further along in its development.

Savanna felt her legs quivering as she placed her feet in the stirrups. She scooted to the edge of the exam table and made sure the drape was covering her knees. Dr. Omoto placed his hand on her inner thigh. She could feel the coolness of the vinyl glove against her skin.

"Just relax, Savanna. This will only take a minute."

Savanna took a few deep breaths and closed her eyes. She interlaced her fingers and rested them against her rib cage. Focusing on her breathing, she centered herself. She felt a sharp pain and tensed. Taking a deep breath, she relaxed back onto the bed. After a few moments, she was able to focus on what Omoto was saying.

"Okay, just relax a little more."

Savanna drew her breath and stared at a tiny spot at the ceiling, willing her mind to escape into the darkness.

"We're almost there. Emily, make sure the embryo is prepared." Dr. Omoto paused for a moment. "Here we go, I'm in place. Give me the embryo."

Savanna kept her eyes closed, completely focusing on her breathing. "That's it Savanna." He helped her remove her feet from the stirrups, roll over on her side and curl her legs up to her chest. Emily covered her with a blanket "Relax, don't move for about twenty minutes." He removed his gloves and moved over to the sink to wash his hands. "If the transplant is successful you will have a baby in about eight months."

Emily handed Savanna her data pad and went to work cleaning the room. Savanna spent the next twenty minutes studying the outbreak patterns in different regions. Mass vaccinations helped slow the spread of the diseases, but it didn't stop them completely. The samples from affected regions entering Savanna's lab all had the same genetic markers. Savanna was using stem cells of individuals with natural immunity to develop a therapy treatment she hoped would help strengthen the immune systems of those without immunity.

Emily left her so she could get dressed. Within a few minutes Savanna was at her work station searching databases. Emily was prepping slides, the silence in the room was deafening. Savanna put her data pad aside and turned to her friend.

"Emily, you haven't said a word for two days. What's going on?"

Emily sighed and put aside her work. "I just think you're going a little fast. Waiting a few more years wouldn't hurt. You're really young to be a mother. I mean, you still have another twenty to twenty-five years of fertility."

"Is that why you're so angry with me? You think I'm too young to be a mom?"

Shaking her head, Emily put down the slides. "I'm not angry. I just don't think you know what you're getting into." Emily rolled her chair closer to Savanna. "Also, I have a decision to make."

"What? Are you thinking about moving back the Reservation?" Savanna felt a moment of panic at the thought of losing her friend.

"No," Emily said. "I don't have any intention of moving back the Rez. Your father has offered to pay my way through school. I applied to the Nurse Practitioner program at the University. It's going to take four more years, but I think it'll be worth it. It seems strange to accept full tuition from a man I hardly know. Why would he do this?"

Savanna smiled. "It's for my mother. One of the

promises he made to her before she died was to support anyone he could, if he had the chance. He's just trying to help you, just like you're helping me."

Emily was smiling as she turned back to the slide preps. "I guess I start school next month. You'll help me study, won't you?" She laughed slightly. "I can't believe I just asked a nineteen year old kid for help."

"Don't worry Emily, you won't have any problems. I'll make sure you get through the program." Savanna reached over and grasped Emily's hand. "Besides, in two weeks I'll turn twenty."

Savanna smiled at her friend and reached to give her a hug. After a moment of resistance Emily hugged her back.

Chapter Nine

THREE WEEKS LATER THE home pregnancy test came back positive. Savanna wasn't quite sure if she trusted the results so when she went into work she had a lab assistant draw her blood and run an analysis. The blood test showed an increase of human chorionic gonadotropin, confirming her pregnancy. Since it was Emily's first day in her new classes and she was tied to her computer trying to figure out all the ins and outs of the new online program, Savanna didn't call her. She waited until Emily got back to the apartment to tell her the results.

Savanna had very few problems with her pregnancy. She had heard horror stories about morning sickness lasting the entire nine months, seventy-two hour labors and any number of discomforts and disasters. The stories became even more varied as her due date grew closer.

When she was about six months pregnant she decided it was time to tell her Dad. She waited until Emily was out of the apartment to make the call. Unsure of how her father would react, she typed in his address and waited for him to answer. It took a few minutes because the call had to be routed from his home office to the office at Haven. When he answered he looked so genuinely pleased to see her Savanna couldn't help smiling.

"Hi, Dad. You're looking great."

Nearly seventy, Dr. Jackson Taylor was aging well. A fluff of white hair ringed his head and crow's feet surrounded his light brown eyes. "Savanna. It's about time you called."

"I just talked to you last week." If her father didn't hear from her every week he would call and e-mail five or six times a day until she called him back. "I have some news." Savanna smoothed the front of her scrubs over her burgeoning belly. She knew her father couldn't see the gesture since the video was focused on her face. "Dad, you're going to be a Grandpa."

Her father's face went blank, and then a slow grin

spread across his face. "Well, this is a surprise. I wasn't expecting to be a grandfather for at least another five years. I didn't even know you were dating anyone."

Savanna's face heated and she knew she was bright pink. "I'm not, Dad. I adopted a fetus. The baby is going to be born in about three months."

A smile blossomed on her father's face. "Well, why don't you consider returning home? Haven is a wonderful place to raise a child." This was an old argument. Savanna's father had included a full-scale research lab in the plans when Haven was first built. He wanted Savanna to come home and run it, she wanted to get more experience before moving home.

"I still have work to do here." She smiled indulgently.

"I'll have your lab ready for you whenever you're ready to move home. You can do your work here just as well as you can there. Better, in fact. Haven is very well protected. We've added more security personnel. Haven would be the perfect place for you and your child."

Savanna sighed. "I know, Dad. We're doing well here, though. The National Guard keeps the streets safe, for now. I have to see my research through here."

Her father asked her to send her a copy of her medical records and ultrasounds. Savanna had them ready and sent them right away. She was able to point out the fetus' developing features and gender.

"What do you think, Dad?" Savanna asked. "Isn't your granddaughter adorable?" All of Savanna's nervousness was gone. It was obvious her father had taken her announcement in stride and accepted his new status as a Grandfather.

"I'm sure she's going to be beautiful."

They talked for a few minutes, then Savanna told him she had to go to work. She entered the nearly full tram and worked her way to her usual seat near the door. An elderly woman sitting across from her smiled as she sat down and attempted to position herself in a comfortable position.

"When are you due?" The woman's voice had a gravely quality, as if her throat had been damaged. The woman reached across to touch her belly. Savanna tried to pull away, but she wasn't quick enough. The woman's warm hand brushed lightly against her stomach. Suddenly a hand reached out and grabbed the old woman's arm.

"You should know better than to touch a stranger in these times." Savanna looked up to see a young National Guard soldier tightly gripping the woman's arm. "Do you have your health papers?"

The woman jerked her arm away. "Last I heard health papers were suggested, not mandatory." Bright red spots appeared on the woman's cheeks. "You have no right to grab me. In my day we respected our elders."

Savanna pulled as far away from the confrontation as she could. There wasn't much room on the tram to move without bumping into someone else. Confrontations like these were becoming increasingly more frequent on the streets of the city. Despite the push for uniform health care an entire subculture of citizens was developing in the city's underground. Some residents couldn't afford health care or refused to be vaccinated for any number of reasons.

Savanna was shaking as she exited the tram and headed for her lab. She didn't like being that close to the confrontation between undocumented residents and security forces. The lab, tucked away in the far corner of the hospital, was a safe place away from the turmoil on the streets. Emily was at her station, sorting new samples. Savanna didn't acknowledge her friend as she walked back to her office. She walked across the room to the closet where her extra uniforms were stored. It only took a minute to change her scrub top and throw the old one down the laundry chute.

She left the office to find Emily staring at her. Recognizing the questioning look in her friend's eyes, Savanna shook her head, trying to reassure her friend without making a scene. Emily worked in the lab part time as she was taking classes; telling Savanna school wasn't keeping her busy enough and she needed to keep her lab skills up to date.

Walking to her station, Savanna pulled up the outbreak

pattern map on her computer. She was working with the CDC to try to analyze outbreak patterns to predict where the diseases may spread next.

Emily left her station and walked to where Savanna was working. Savanna recognized the questioning look in her friend's eyes. She shook her head, knowing if she talked about what just happened she would start crying.

Ever since she started her hormone therapy and into her pregnancy it seemed Savanna was always in emotional turmoil. Lately she had been having nightmares about trying to find something, but she had no idea what she was looking for. She had a feeling if she didn't find it soon she would lose everything important to her.

Lately the most frequent dream was one where she was trapped in the airplane hangar that had housed the victims of the plague. The floor was covered waist high with bedding and towels, melting ice packs, IV stands and hundreds of other supplies. She spent hours digging through everything, looking and not finding anything. Finally, not knowing what she was looking for, she sat in the middle of the room and cried. She would wake up with her heart racing and tears soaking her pillow.

Emily placed a Petri dish beside Savanna and pulled up a stool to sit beside her. "Savanna," she said, "what's going on? You're pale and shaky. What happened?"

"Just an incident on the tram." Savanna didn't want Emily to know about the nightmares. It seemed everyone worried about her constantly. She was tired of feeling like she was being hovered over as if she was a fragile piece of art. She had come to Phoenix to gain experience and express a sense of independence.

"I just need to focus on my work." She tried to keep her voice steady. Emily nodded and walked back to her work station. Savanna could feel her eyes on the back of her head as she worked.

Her daughter was born in late winter by scheduled cesarean section. The first thing Savanna noticed about the baby was a shock of black hair standing up on the little head, like a wing of a bird getting ready for flight. When the nurse brought her close, Savanna reached over and brushed the sticky, goo covered hair. "She looks like a little raven caught in a wind storm." The nurse took the baby away to clean her up before she brought her back.

The nurse placed the little girl in Savanna's arms. "She had a little difficulty with her breathing and reflex irritability during the one minute Apgar. The test had her at a seven but now she's at a nine."

Savanna pulled the blanket away from the newborn's face. She was covered in a white, powdery film and wrinkled beyond anything that could ever be considered cute. The blanket was suspiciously wet around the bottom area. Savanna unwrapped the baby and assessed her from head to toe. Everything was there, including eyelashes and toenails. She was holding a perfectly formed little human in her arms and she was all hers.

News of an apparently full-blooded Navajo child born to the white doctor traveled to the Reservation quickly. There were a few rumbles from residents attempting to challenge her parental rights. Some of them approached Chief Etu with the idea. The law was on Savanna's side, though. She had legally adopted the embryo.

When embryonic transplants first became popular the courts made a few preemptive strikes to handle parental rights challenges. They handed down a decision stating an embryo belonged to the woman carrying it unless a binding surrogate contract was in place. This protected the rights of adoptive parents and prevented exploitation of surrogates.

Savanna named her daughter Bly, but the word she first said when the baby was born stuck and everyone was calling her Raven before she even left the hospital.

Savanna was pleased to discover most of the genetic alterations she had performed on the embryo manifested as Raven developed. Her growth and development fell well within the normal range. When Raven was a few weeks old Etu asked

Savanna to bring the baby to the reservation so he could meet her. Savanna spent the last week of her maternity leave at the reservation, recovering and reveling in the obvious joy Etu was taking in the young child. Kai was living with her grandfather at the time, but she rarely left her room and only after making sure the baby was down for a nap or otherwise occupied. Savanna attempted, once or twice, to get Kai to interact with her and the baby, but Kai just looked up with scorn in her eyes and turned away without saying a word.

Savanna had been back to work for a little over a week and was pleased with how well her daughter was adjusting to the new schedule. She carried the infant to work with her in a sling. The twenty-four hour childcare, two floors down from her lab, allowed her to have her daughter close and still work on her experiments. Raven rarely cried and slept well at naptime and during the night, only waking for a three o'clock feeding. Savanna was thrilled with her perfect child.

She was on her way to work on the tram in the early morning hours, Raven sleeping against her chest, when a loud explosion nearly shook her out of her seat. Savanna wrapped her arms around the infant and rolled onto the floor, curling her body around the tiny form.

The tram squealed to a stop but Savanna stayed on the floor, shaking with fear. Looking down, she saw her daughter's bright brown eyes staring up at her. She was awake but didn't look frightened or startled. All around her people were screaming and crying, yet her daughter looked up at her as calmly as if she was lying in her crib. Something had to be wrong. Savanna's heart was pounding with combined fear for what was happening outside and what was going on with her daughter.

It seemed to take forever for the tram doors to crash open. An armed security guard came through. The lower half of his face was covered by a filter mask, muffling his voice as he spoke.

"Is everyone okay?" The voice seemed harsh and Savanna flinched. "Raise your right hand if you think you can walk out of here."

Savanna slowly put her hand up in the air. All around her she saw hands going up.

"If you can walk, stand up and move towards the front of the car." Following his orders, Savanna walked toward the sound of his voice.

Raven's thumb was in her mouth, obviously soothed by the suckling. Savanna exited the tram to smoke and falling debris. She used her hand to shield the infant's face as she followed the soldier. Still, her daughter didn't cry. Something was wrong. Savanna couldn't shake a feeling of fear for her little child. So much noise and craziness, Raven should be crying and screaming.

Savanna clutched the baby closer to her chest as she tried to make her way through the confusion. She heard someone call out for anyone who could walk to move towards the sound of my voice, she turned and headed that direction.

She was directed to a soldier standing by the door of a bus. He held a micro chip scanner in his hand. As people passed he would run the scanner over either their hand or eyelid to read the chip under the skin. Those without a chip were sent to another line and were loaded on a separate bus. Dazed, Savanna held out her hand and then her daughter's. The soldier stopped her from boarding the bus and called another man over.

"Dr. Taylor," he took her arm as he explained, "you're needed at the hospital. We have a mass casualty situation and we need as many trained professionals as possible."

Savanna followed the soldier to a nearby ambulance. They had her sit in the front seat as the ambulance raced to the hospital. The medic called ahead and informed the emergency room that in addition to two critical patients he was bringing in Dr. Taylor and they needed someone from the child care to be prepared to take her infant. A paramedic checked Savanna and made sure she hadn't sustained any injuries while they were on their way. By the time they arrived at the hospital, she had been cleared for duty.

A nurse's aide Savanna barely recognized was waiting for her as she stepped out of the ambulance. The girl reached out to take Raven as soon as Savanna's feet hit the ground.

"Don't take her to the nursery," Savanna ordered. "There's something wrong. She needs to be checked out."

The girl nodded. "I'll get her checked in and watch her." The aide took the infant and walked through the emergency room doors. Savanna experienced a moment of panic as she watched her daughter disappear into the hospital.

The scream of sirens interrupted her thoughts and she turned to see another emergency vehicle pulling into the bay. A nurse stood by the entrance, apparently waiting for the ambulance to come to a stop. Savanna approached the man and caught his attention.

"What's happening here?" She had to yell to be heard over the sirens.

"Explosion at a citizen registration station," he yelled back. "Dozens of casualties. We're going to need all the help we can get."

"What caused the explosion?" Savanna had never heard of an explosion at a citizen registration center before. As far as she knew, the only thing at the centers were microchip programmers and implant devices.

"There are all sorts of rumors," he said, pulling open the doors of the ambulance. "They can't prove anything, but they're pretty sure it was a bomb."

Savanna didn't have time to think about what caused the explosion for the next few hours. She was so entrenched in caring for the injured she didn't have time to think about anything else.

Chapter Ten

THE FRANTIC PACE OF the emergency room had a soothing effect on Savanna. She was able to focus on using the skills she had dedicated her life to perfecting. This was her element. She stitched gaping wounds, tended bruises and breaks and assessed injuries. Savanna made sure Raven was placed in a bassinet by the nurses' station where the aide could keep an eye on her while entering patient data into the computer.

Triaging and treating patients wasn't nearly as frustrating as dealing with frantic family members. The explosion occurred in the early morning hours, before the center was opened. Most of the casualties were a result of flying debris and shock concussions. Savanna was relegated to the minor wound unit, where she worked cleaning and stitching wounds. Since it was the morning commute there was an overwhelming number of patients to be seen. The medics and the nurses worked diligently to triage the injured from the just plain scared.

Savanna was probing the edges of a gash on the inner thigh of an elderly woman, trying to assess the depth of the wound, when Dr. Fallen found her. He handed her the digital scanner and she used it to scan the leg for shrapnel fragments. Seeing nothing, Savanna brought out the suture kit, cleaned the wound and sutured it closed. She had to use soluble stitches to pull the underlying muscle together before she started on the layers of skin. Fallon watched her for a few minutes, she was grateful her hands had stopped shaking before she had been brought to the hospital.

"I understand you were in the hot zone, Savanna." Fallon never took his eyes off her quickly moving hands.

"Raven and I were on the tram." Savanna's voice was steady, surprisingly. "Do we know what happened?" Savanna had been hearing rumors of everything from a terrorist bomb to a natural gas leak. She wanted answers. She needed to know her daughter was safe.

"A group calling themselves America's Soldiers took responsibility for the attack about ten minutes ago." Fallon was angry. Savanna could hear it in his voice. "They claim the centers are substations for anarchy and the microchips are the mark of the beast."

"How bad is it?" Savanna put the finishing touch on the stitches and started to wrap the wound with sterile gauze.

"No one was at the center." He helped bandage the thigh as he talked. "Two people were killed by shrapnel and a third is in critical condition. I know I kept you out of the major traumas, but you keep your head in these situations so well, I wanted you here handling the heavy load of non-criticals."

"I'm glad it wasn't any worse." Savanna smiled at her boss. "I need to go to my daughter now." She peeled off her gloves and scrubbed her hands before searching out her daughter. She found the infant in a bassinet pushed up against the nurse's station. As Savanna approached the aide looked up from the computer.

"Your baby is doing so well. I gave her a bottle about an hour ago." She looked down at the sleeping baby. "I think your right. In all this crazy loudness, she should be startled and crying. She barely fussed when she was hungry. Do you think the blast affected her hearing?"

Realization hit Savanna as she picked up her daughter. Raven had no startle response. She didn't turn to the sound of voices or verbalize sounds like other babies in the child care center. She would need tests to prove it, but Savanna had a feeling her baby was deaf.

It didn't take long to discover her daughter was not just deaf, she was profoundly deaf. Everyone in the infant's life immediately registered for sign language courses and developed the habit of signing as they spoke. Raven was sixteen months old when surgery was performed to give her a cochlear implant.

Despite the hearing loss her daughter's development and progress fell well within every norm Savanna ever read about and nothing brought her more joy than watching her grow.

Emily progressed through her Physician's Assistant program and graduated with honors. She went to work at University Hospital in the twenty-four hour Quick Care Clinic. Savanna missed working with her in the lab and, since their schedules didn't coordinate, they rarely saw each other.

The attack on the citizen registration center was the first in a series. Security forces tightened patrols and were given the authority to make arrests based on suspicious behaviors. Savanna rarely felt safe unless she was in close proximity to a guard or in her apartment and lab.

Phoenix wasn't the only area suffering from attacks and uprisings. It seemed there was enough blame to go around for any number of sins. Savanna heard reports of small town militia's and home-grown terrorist groups organizing attacks against government facilities. Every time Savanna left the apartment, she wondered if she would be caught in the middle of another attack.

Raven was nearly four when Savanna's weekly calls to her father finally convinced her to return to Haven. His health was failing and she felt the need to be with him. Haven would also be a safe place to raise her daughter.

The secluded nature of the facility would protect them from the burgeoning violence and the high-tech lab would allow her to continue her research. The development of a stem cell treatment for strengthening immune system was still years away from fulfillment and everyday more people were exposed to the devastating plagues. She gave notice to University Hospital, explained the situation to Emily and began packing her apartment.

On the day of her scheduled move she had Sam help her pack the crate she was taking with her to Idaho. The robot rolled across the floor, carefully balancing the weight of a metal storage container between its mechanical arms, adjusting its rollers as it shifted over a slight deformity in the carpet. With a hiss, the apartment door slid open, exposing the packing crate standing open in the hall. The container fit perfectly in a niche left in the crate. He slid it in beside the metal hyperbolic storage container holding a hundred embryos frozen in stasis, eleven of those belonging to Savanna. She walked into the room behind the robot, barely glancing up from her data pad as the S290 finished packing the crate.

"Great job, Sam. I'm pretty sure that's the last of it." Savannah looked at the robot that had been a constant companion for the past ten years. "Pack yourself in the crate and power down. We're going to be on the road for a while."

"The Good Will van will be here to pick up the remaining items tomorrow." The voice that came from Sam's digital processor still had a slight mechanical sound despite the efforts Savanna put into its programming to make it sound more human. "All of the items are separated into donation and recycle. The recyclers said they will be here by the end of the week," he said, rolling inside and folding into the only empty niche in the crate. Savanna had always thought of her robot as male though the original designers of the interactive robot claimed the design was genderless.

As soon as the indicator lights in the S290's orbital sockets faded Savanna entered the code to close the crate on her data pad and pressed send. The hydraulic door slowly closed and sealed shut. The six foot by four foot crate held all the personal belongings she and Raven were bringing with them, along with a number of sensitive experiments going with her from Phoenix to Boise.

Most of the furniture in her two-bedroom apartment was being sent to second hand stores or the recyclers, as well as some barely used kitchenware. Pots and pans, as well as several kitchen appliances her father had given her when she first started her studies in Arizona, were neglected as her studies and her daughter took most of her time and energy.

Savanna's father had just earned the Noble Peace Prize in genetics. His partner, Doctor Devon Smith, was snubbed by the committee due to concerns about ethical questions in his own research. Dr. Smith had separated his work from her father's four years previously, under a heated debate over proprietary rights to research data. Although her father never explicitly said anything, Savanna knew the threats Dr. Smith made involved more than just a few mentions of bringing Dr. Taylor before a medical review board. The Idaho Statesman on-line had reported a physical altercation between Dr. Smith and one of his interns when the ethical questions were first raised. Savanna was worried about her father living alone when it was obvious his former partner was quite capable of physical violence.

She wondered what it would be like for her at home since so much had changed in her life in the past seven years. There was a certain amount of acclaim to her name and her image had been splashed on news broadcasts multiple times over the past seven years. In addition to the work she had done with the initial smallpox outbreaks and all the subsequent outbreaks four years ago, an anonymous source leaked the birth of an apparently full-blooded Navajo child to the obviously white daughter of Professor Taylor.

She had her suspicions about the anonymous source, Dr. Smith was an extremely bitter man, but she knew the less fuss she made about it the sooner the media would move onto the next great thing. The news media had speculated about the birth of the girl, but no one had confirmed any rumors and since Savanna had made a name for herself as a compassionate, intelligent doctor, the media didn't pursue the topic.

The data pad in Savanna's hand beeped, drawing her attention away from thoughts of her father. Glancing down she noticed the incoming call was from Chief Etu. Savanna was tempted to ignore the call, but she knew she couldn't leave things the way they were with The People. She respected them too much to do so. After a quick glance in the wall mirror to assure herself that her honey blonde hair was still neatly contained in a French roll, she pressed the answer icon. Chief Etu's face filled the small screen in her hand. "Father, you honor me."

"We appreciate the pleasantries Dr. Taylor, but we want to talk to you about a serious matter." Chief Etu's face was deeply lined and his black hair was liberally streaked with gray.

"I think I know what this is about Chief Etu, but you know I'm not going to change my mind about this." Savanna tried to keep her face stern, but she knew the love she felt for the man was shining in her eyes. "I love my daughter, and I think I know what's best for her. I've also asked you to call me Savanna. My father is Doctor Taylor."

Etu gave a small smile. "Savanna, you are a great doctor. We know you care deeply for your patients. No one here will ever forget what you have done for us, nor will we forget your tireless efforts when smallpox broke out. However, today you are taking away one of the children of our Nation, and it is breaking our heart. Raven belongs with her own people."

"I don't want to leave with bad feelings on either side, Chief Etu." When Savanna announced she was taking her adopted daughter with her to Idaho, a strain developed in the relationship between her and Etu. He had wanted Raven to stay in Arizona. Savanna knew Etu loved Raven. When Raven was born he had asked for grandparents' rights, but the courts had been unwilling to grant them. The fear was any ruling in favor of granting him rights would open the floodgates to challenges of fetal adoption laws. Savanna hadn't objected to Etu spending time with her child, but the courts wanted to clearly define the role of fetal adoptive parents. The legislation was too new to be tested.

"How's Kai doing? I didn't see her the last time I went to the Rez." Savanna tried to steer the conversation away from her daughter, trying to ease the tension between them.

"Kai has left the tribe and no one knows where she is." The pain in the eyes of the chief was unmistakable. Kai was his true granddaughter, not an adopted daughter as Savanna had become as she worked so tirelessly to save the lives of those afflicted with the virus.

Etu's dark brown eyes seemed to penetrate Savanna's own, despite the fact he was looking at her through a video conference connection. "Savanna, my daughter." The endearment brought moisture to her eyes. "Raven is not the only child of the tribe leaving us today. The People love you and we do not want you to leave." He paused for a moment. "I love you, my daughter. I wish you would stay."

"Father." As Savanna spoke her voice softened and she strained to get the words passed her tightening throat. "You know how much I love working here. I don't want to leave, but my father needs me. I'll never deny you from contacting Raven. I've made arrangements for you to come visit us any time you want."

"I know Savanna," Etu responded. "I just thought I would try one more time before you left. I am getting too old to travel and I am afraid I am never going to see my great-grandchild again. May I speak to her?"

"Of course." Savanna carried the data pad to her daughter's room. She knew Etu wasn't as old as he claimed; only being in his late fifties.

Approaching the open door of her daughter's room she passed her hand in front of the motion sensor, causing the light on the desk to flash twice. Raven looked up from where she was playing with her dolls and smiled. As the girl turned, her eyes caught the light and a silver sheen seemed to reflect off them. She blinked and her eyes returned to their natural dark brown. No matter how many times Savanna saw the effect it still shocked her to see the cat's eye reflection.

"Raven," Savanna signed, "your grandfather wants to speak to you. Turn on your implant."

Raven reached up and turned on the implant that gave her nearly perfect hearing. The child reached for the data pad. As soon as Savanna handed over the device, the little girl placed it on the floor in front of her and started jabbering at her grandfather using a combination of English, Navajo and Sign Language, a language unique to the four year old. Savanna heard Etu laugh and admonish the child to slow down. She left the two to say their goodbyes and began her final sweep of the apartment, making sure she wasn't leaving anything important behind.

Memories of her years in Arizona flooded over her as she worked her way through the apartment. Her work with the viruses being the most prominent. Despite the best efforts of researchers and doctors, the viruses and bacteria took a devastating toll on the population. Pockets of disease were still breaking out in rural areas around the world, including towns and cities in the United States.

The vaccine Savanna had developed to combat Smallpox was effective in preventing new outbreaks, but it was impossible to manufacture enough of a supply to keep up with the demand. Smallpox, in addition to the other diseases released by terrorists, had changed the entire global structure. Constant civil wars were breaking out in nations where governments already had a tenuous stand. Health codes were being rewritten. Old prejudices, long thought dead and buried, were resurrected and new legislation about hate crimes needed to be developed.

Walking from the bathroom to her bedroom and back into the open floor plan of the kitchen, Savanna surveyed the home she was planning on leaving behind.

Despite the left-over furniture, piles of clothing and other belongings, the apartment seemed empty. She knew the pain she was feeling was from leaving the people she had come to care for more than the thought of leaving a tiny two-bedroom apartment. So much had happened since she moved to Arizona; it was hard to believe this was the same apartment she had stood in seven years ago, staring at the blank walls, wondering if it would ever feel like home.

Chapter Eleven

LEAVING SHOULDN'T BE SO hard. Savanna rarely allowed herself to get overly emotional. It wasn't healthy for a doctor to get emotionally involved with patients. Her father didn't seem to have this much of an issue with keeping an emotional distance from his subjects. He was known to be compassionate when he dealt with patients, but Savanna never saw him become overly emotional when he was dealing with life and death. The only time Savanna ever saw him cry was right before the death of her mother.

Kylie Taylor had been diagnosed with ovarian cancer, her second bout with the disease, when Savanna was eleven. Her parents had hidden the diagnosis from her since her graduation from high school was looming and she had been accepted to Harvard. They were afraid Kylie's health problems would delay her education.

By the time Savanna was prepared to enter college her mother's condition had degraded to the point she couldn't move to be with her, a requirement of her early acceptance to Harvard. The school was willing to work with her, since she was bringing it notoriety as a rising child prodigy. Rather than move Savanna across the country, Dr. Taylor helped his daughter complete her undergraduate work on-line. He had managed to work out a deal with the school, allowing Savanna to do her course work on-line or on the local Boise State campus. Midway through Savanna's freshman year her mother couldn't fight the cancer any longer.

Savanna had just finished an English final and submitted it when she heard her father walk out of the room he shared with her mother. Wondering why he was leaving her mother's side, Savanna went in search of him. She found him sitting in his study with a glass of whiskey in his hand and tears streaming down his face. Not knowing what else to do, Savanna backed out of the room and left her father to his pain. Three days later her mother died.

Savanna's father wouldn't let her relax her studies, even on the day of the funeral. It seemed all the energy he had put into caring for his wife went into ensuring Savanna finished her education.

Savanna knew her father loved her and there was no way she could deny the love she felt for him, but she couldn't help but wonder if Haven would feel like home after all these years of being away. Returning to Arizona for visits was going to be nearly impossible. Traveling was becoming more difficult as restrictions tightened. Once they were at Haven she knew her work would keep her there for a long time. Savanna's experiments were too fragile to travel in the cargo hold of a plane. Her father was sending one of his employees to bring her and Raven home.

The doorbell chimed, pulling Savanna away from reflections of home. Glancing at the screen beside the entry way she was surprised to see Emily's face. The door slid open, startling Savanna. She didn't do anything to open it. The patter of footsteps registered right before the streak of black hair as her daughter ran by her.

"Aunty Emmy!" Raven flew into Emily's arms and the woman picked her up and carried her into the room. She sat the girl down beside Savanna and stood in front of her. A large suitcase, sitting on top of the packing crate, drew Savanna's eye.

"Emily," Savanna said. "What's happening? Why are you here?"

Emily didn't answer right away. She looked from Savanna to the suitcase by the door. Glancing down at the child, she put her hand on top of Raven's hair. "Savanna, I'm coming with you."

It seemed such a simple statement, but Savanna knew it was more complicated than Emily was letting on. Emily's family was very close, for her to just pack a bag and announce she was moving over nine hundred miles away wasn't a spur of the moment decision.

"Aunty Emmy, you're coming with? Do you know we're moving to Boise to be with my other Grandpa?" Raven's voice had an almost glottal timber, as if she was swallowing part of her words as she spoke. Her sign language was completely subconscious as she emphasized her words.

"Emily, it's going to take some time to get you a state line pass." Savanna followed her friend and her daughter into the room as the door slid shut behind her. "You can't just pick up and move to another state. You need to get a work permit and have a physical to make sure you have a clean bill of health."

"It's all taken care of." Emily put Raven down beside the kitchen table and walked to the sink. She poured a glass of water and handed it to the girl. "Your father offered me a job at Haven. I've passed every physical I had over the past four years. I have a state line pass all ready to go."

"Oh." Savanna followed Emily into the kitchen. "What does your family say? Are you sure you want to do this?"

"Savanna, I've been thinking about this for a long time. I don't belong here anymore. This is the best option I have." Emily opened the refrigerator. "It looks like you emptied out the fridge. Do I have time to order a few things from the market?"

Savanna crossed the room to a small bag on the table. "I have some dried apples if you need a snack. Dad is sending any food we need for the trip. I'm sure if he knows you're planning on coming with us, he'll send plenty for you."

Emily smiled as she closed the fridge. "So, I guess I'm moving to Idaho."

"Yeah, Aunt Emmy's coming with." Raven threw herself into her aunt's open arms.

Savanna smiled at the antics of her young daughter. She plucked the girl from Emily's arms. "Go get your bag, Little One. I need my data pad, too." She gently tapped the girl on the bottom and aimed her towards the bedroom. "Love ya, Baby."

Raven ran back to her bedroom. Within a few minutes, Raven tripped back into the room carrying her pink suitcase and her two favorite dolls. She slipped the data pad into her mother's hands. "Here, Mommy." She ran to the front door and tapped her hand against the signal pad. The door slid open and the girl placed her bag next to the crate.

"All ready? Let's go."

Savanna laughed. "We need to wait for our ride, Raven. We'll leave when he gets here. Let me find your favorite book for you. Maybe you can read it to your Aunt."

Savanna pulled up *If You Give a Mouse a Cookie* on the pad and handed it back to her daughter. Raven pulled up a chair next to Emily.

"Do you want to hear a story, Aunt Emmy?" Emily nodded and pulled Raven's chair closer to her side. Savanna stepped out in the hall to check the controls on the outside of the storage pod. Everything seemed to be in order. She double checked the locking mechanism and pulled out the retractable bar used to maneuver the container from the back. Kneeling, she checked the wheels. She was just getting to her feet when Emily approached her with the data pad.

"I think our ride is here. You have a call from the front lobby."

Savanna took the pad and pushed the answer icon. "This is Dr. Taylor. Can I help you?"

She didn't recognize the deep voice coming from the speaker, but this didn't surprise her. Savanna hadn't been home in over seven years, she didn't know all the people working for her father.

"Hi, Dr. Taylor. My name is Travis Baker. I'm here to pick up your family and bring you home."

The words struck Savanna to the core. She was going home. Her father would be waiting for her at Haven. Together they would continue their research. It would be nice to be able to work side-by-side with her father, instead of communicating back and forth over conference calls and e-mail. The campus at Haven was gaining recognition in its own right and Savanna was looking forward to helping her father.

"Confirm your identity please. There's a micro chip scanner at the front desk." Savanna waited for confirmation before she unlocked the elevator bay. It only took a few seconds. She sent the elevator to the lobby and turned back to the apartment.

"Well ladies, here we go." Raven and Emily grinned at her. "Let's get ready to move."

Raven ran out of the apartment and skidded to a stop in front of the elevators. Emily walked out at a much slower pace.

"I don't think that child has an off switch."

Raven turned back to her aunt. "Yes, I do. It's right here." She reached up and turned off her implant.

Savanna laughed at Emily's shocked expression. "Do you forget how clever my daughter is? You've only been at your own place for two months."

The elevator door slid open. She turned to the opening door and froze. Travis Baker was the most strikingly handsome man she had ever seen. He stepped off the elevator with a grace known only to those who spent their life as an athlete. The man had to be at least six and a half feet tall and his tight black shirt and jeans revealed hard packed muscles and broad shoulders tapering down to a narrow waist. His skin was the color of coffee tinted with a hint of fresh cream. Black hair was shaved close, almost nonexistent, highlighting the sharp angles of his high cheekbones, strong nose and full lips. He flashed a smile, revealing perfectly straight, white teeth.

Savanna felt her heart race as her blood pressure shot up. She grabbed the corner of the crate to support her weakening knees. Quickly turning away from the man standing by the elevator so he wouldn't see the rising blush on her cheeks, Savanna looked into the apartment. Emily was staring at Travis.

Savanna took a deep breath. Clearing her throat, she spoke to her friend and daughter. "Ladies, I think our ride is here. Are we ready to go?"

Emily tore her eyes away from Travis. Raven continued to stare at the tall, muscular man standing by the elevator door. Emily grinned as she looked at Savanna's face. Savanna tucked her chin into her chest as she felt the heat increase.

She had to get her physical response under control. It wouldn't due to embarrass herself in front of this man. They had a long trip ahead of them and it wouldn't do her any good to reveal her attraction to him. Just because she had a strong physical response to him didn't mean he returned the attraction. In fact, from the heightened color in Emily's cheeks, Savanna realized she wasn't the only one attracted to Travis. Waving her hand in front of her daughter's face to gain her attention, Savanna signed for her to turn on her implant. The little girl flipped the switch.

"Dr. Taylor?" The man stepped from the elevator and looked towards Savanna. "I'm Travis Baker. Your father sent me to fetch you."

Savanna turned to face Travis. His dark brown eyes surveyed her from head to toe, taking in her narrow frame. She blushed again when his eyes connected with hers.

"It's a good thing your father showed me your picture. You don't look very much like a doctor to me." He grinned and winked at her. "I thought doctors were all old men with gray hair and glasses."

"I'm in disguise." Savanna couldn't believe she was joking with him. Usually she became defensive when people commented on her age and gender. "How do you know my father? He was pretty tight lipped about who he was sending."

"I was part of a research study involving regrowth of tendons and vascular tissue after I blew out my ACL during a football game." He smiled again and Savanna's heart raced. "With his research, he was able to extend my football career by two years. After I graduated he offered me a job at Haven." Travis moved to the packing pod. "Is this ready to go?"

Savanna stepped away from the pod. "Yes, it's the only crate we have. The three bags need to be placed where they can be easily accessed."

"This is all you're bringing with you?" Travis looked at the crate and the three small bags.

"Everything we need is going to be provided at

Haven." The crate looked pitifully small sitting in the hall.

Travis shrugged his shoulders. The ripple of packed muscle under his shirt almost floored Savanna. Travis turned toward the women once he had the pod in the elevator. Savanna picked up her bag and signed for Raven to do the same.

"Well ladies, it looks like this elevator is full." Travis stepped onto the elevator and pushed the button. "I'll take this down and send the elevator back up. By the time you get down I'll have this stored on the truck and be ready for you." The elevator doors closed, hiding Travis from sight. Savanna couldn't stop staring.

"Oh, my God." Emily's voice broke through her stupor and Savanna turned to face her friend.

"What, what's wrong?" Savanna still shook from her encounter with Travis. Emily grinned.

"Oh, there's nothing wrong. Nothing wrong at all. Wow, I wish I was twenty years younger. I would be all over that."

"Emily!" Savanna was truly shocked to hear her friend talk like this. Usually she was fairly tight lipped about her reaction to men. "I can't believe you're objectifying him like that."

"Oh please, Savanna." Emily looked at Savanna through the corner of her eyes. "I saw the way you looked at him. He's hot and you know it."

Heat flushed Savanna's body. She turned to face the elevator to hide the pink in her cheeks.

"Savanna?" She turned at Emily's questioning tone. "Why don't you go for it? I've never seen you react to anyone like this before."

Savanna stared at Emily in silence for almost a full minute. She could see the woman's shoulders shaking with suppressed laughter. Shaking her head, Savanna couldn't hide the small smile creeping up her face.

"I've never reacted like this to anyone before. He's very good-looking, but I wouldn't know what to say to him." She blushed as she confessed her feelings. Most of the men Savanna worked with were significantly older than her and resented her for her success. Even if she was interested in dating, none of the men she knew had shown any interest in her.

Chapter Twelve

SAVANNA COULD FEEL EMILY studying her as they rode the elevator down to the ground floor. It was an almost complete echo of events nearly six years previous, in reverse. Savanna couldn't help but smile at the child now accompanying her and Emily in the trip down the elevator. Six years ago, the child was a microscopic bundle of cells in a metal container. Now she was a bubbly, extremely active, four-year old.

The elevator came to a soft stop on the ground floor and the doors slid open. Travis was waiting as they stepped off and into the lobby.

"Here we go, ladies. Let me take those." He reached for Savanna's and Emily's bags. He swung Savanna's over his shoulder and reached for Raven's suitcase. "Can I take the bag, Little One? I promise I'll take care of it."

Raven's eyes widened and she pressed her body against her mother's leg. She handed the suitcase over and immediately hid behind Savanna. Travis smiled at her and walked out of the building. Emily followed close behind. Savanna waited until the two were near the door, her daughter wasn't budging from her hiding place behind her leg. She bent down and lifted her daughter into her arms.

"Child, you're getting way too heavy to carry around like this." Raven rested her head against Savanna's shoulder and wrapped her arms around her neck. The little girl played with her mother's butterfly necklace, twisting the chain through her tiny fingers.

"You can carry me, Mommy. You're strong enough."

Savanna hugged her daughter close to her chest and walked outside into the early afternoon sunlight. Emily and Travis stood beside a plain white truck. There was a row of black solar panels across the top of the cab, drawing power from the hot, yellow sun. Emily reached out and took the child from Savanna's arms.

"She's getting too big to carry around all the time."

Emily said. "One of the back seats has a built-in car seat, your father thinks of everything. I'll ride in the back, for now. You take the passenger seat in front." Emily turned and climbed into the truck before Savanna could object. Travis held the passenger door open.

"Dr. Taylor?" He gestured her to get in the seat. "We're on a pretty tight schedule. The solar operated vehicles aren't as fast as others and it's going to take us a couple of days to get home."

Savanna didn't trust herself to speak. She tucked her head down and moved to the passenger side. As she ducked under Travis' arm she could feel heat radiating off his body. He closed the door and moved around to the other side.

Savanna flipped the visor down and opened the flap to reveal the mirror. Her face looked normal, her cheeks only slightly more pink than usual. Well, at least she wouldn't have to spend the entire trip with her cheeks on fire. She closed the mirror and flipped the visor back in place. Turning in her seat, she double checked Raven's seatbelt and glanced at Emily. The woman had a grin on her face and she couldn't suppress a chuckle as Travis buckled his seatbelt and put the truck in gear.

"Well ladies, welcome to the road trip." Travis flipped the on switch to start the truck.

As the truck pulled out of the apartment parking lot Savanna rolled down the window and looked behind them. She blinked quickly to dry her tears. So many emotions were rolling through her as Travis pulled onto the main road. Savanna knew she left herself open to pain and sorrow when she decided to leave Arizona. She just needed the resolve to steel herself against the emotional turmoil she was feeling. Savanna rolled up the window and leaned back into her seat.

Emily reached forward and rested her hand on Savanna's shoulder. "Are you okay, sister?"

Savanna took her friend's hand. "I will be. I just feel like I'm forgetting something. Like, I left the oven on or something."

Emily laughed. "Left the oven on, that's classic

Savanna. I don't think you even know where the on switch is on the oven."

Travis glanced at her out of the corner of his eyes. "You don't cook, Dr. Taylor?"

Savanna never considered her lack of cooking skills a detriment before. "I spend most of my time studying or treating patients. I never really picked up many domestic skills."

Travis grinned. "Well, I guess it's a good thing you're moving to Haven. The food there is great and the nutritionists ensuring everyone is taken care of. Since you're the boss's daughter you won't have to follow the rules like everyone else. I'm sure you won't be required to do any cooking or cleaning."

"Yes, I will." Travis glanced at her. "I signed the same contract as everyone else."

"Why would your father make you sign a contract?" Emily asked. "Doesn't he realize you have a higher calling than to scrub around in the dirt, struggling to raise crops?" Emily removed her hand from Savanna's shoulder.

Savanna tilted her mirror down and watched Raven scroll through books on her data pad. The girl's eyes locked with hers in the mirror.

"Mommy, my head's hurting. Can I turn off my hearing?"

Savanna turned so her daughter could see her face as she spoke. She knew much of Raven's communication was nonverbal. "Go ahead, but make sure your messaging is opened and your pad is set to vibrate. We need to be able to connect with you in an emergency."

Raven nodded. Savanna watched as her daughter set her data pad to the correct parameters and then turn off her implant. She held her hand up to her daughter with her two middle fingers folded down. Raven signed, 'I love you too, Mommy.'

'Do your math,' Savanna signed. Raven pulled up her text book and started on her multiplication tables. Savanna pulled out her pad and plugged it into the charge console. Raven's work was flashing by in real time on the bottom left corner of the screen. Travis glanced over at the math factors flashing on the screen.

"Would you ladies mind if we stopped at a truck stop? Your father provided plenty of food for the trip, but there are a few things I miss working at Haven. I want to get a Dr. Pepper and some snacks." Travis didn't take his eyes off the road as he talked. He turned onto the main drag in Phoenix. The freeway was only ten minutes away. The bright light of the late morning sun shone through the windshield. Travelling during the brightest hours of the day helped the van run at peak efficiency.

"If you really want to load yourself up with that much junk be my guest." Savanna tapped her father's messaging address into her pad. She typed the message, 'Just leaving' and pressed send. Her father's return 'Can't wait to see you.' contained a smile icon. Savanna chuckled at the antiquated symbol.

"You sound just like your father. He's been lecturing anyone who will listen on the dangers of processed foods. It's the one thing I miss while I'm living at Haven." Travis smiled as he turned into a Chevron parking lot. "Do you ladies want to come in? It's your last chance to revel in the sins of processed food products." He parked the truck in a spot on the side of the building.

"I'll wait here." Savanna pulled up the road map on the pad. "I want to double check our route. We need to take the quickest route home. I have sensitive experiments in cryostasis we need to get to my lab."

Emily unbuckled her seatbelt and opened her door. Raven watched her aunt get out of the truck. She looked back at her mother and then at her aunt. Reaching up, she turned on her implant.

"Wait. Wait. I want to go too. Aunt Emmy, wait for me." Raven reached around to unbuckle her seatbelt. Savanna decided she might as well go in too. She followed the others into the store.

Travis was at the fountain, filling a hundred and four ounce jug with soda. Savanna shook her head, so much caffeine and sugar. She headed to the cooler to find a bottle of water. Raven followed her to the back of the store. Choosing a brand she knew was well-filtered and tested regularly, Savanna grabbed two bottles. She headed to the register, followed closely by her daughter.

"Give us a minute, please. I'm paying for all four of us." Savanna waited for Emily and Travis to bring their selection to the counter. The two piled packages of beef jerky, Twinkies, candy bars and soda on the counter.

The cashier rang up the purchases. "Forty-seven, sixty-three." The cashier didn't make eye contact as Savanna waived her hand in front of the pay pass. The machine scanned the tiny microchip imbedded in the pad of her palm, beeping to let her know her payment was accepted.

Back in the truck, Savanna handed one of the water bottles to her daughter and slid the other one into place in the drink holder beside her. She flipped the switch beside the holder to cool. Travis slid a built-in tray from under his seat and set up his drink and snacks. Savanna watched as he opened packages and positioned his drink in the optimum position. As he finished settling everything, he looked up at her.

"Once we're on the freeway we're going to be on autopilot. I want to be all set up and ready to go."

Savanna kept eyeing the huge jug of soda. She couldn't even imagine drinking that much sugary, sweet syrup. Let alone all in one sitting.

"Mommy, what's that?" Savanna turned to see where her daughter was pointing. The huge jug sat so glaringly beside Travis.

"It's soda pop, honey. It's a lot of soda."

"Oh." Raven paused for a moment. "Can I have a drink?"

Savanna didn't know how to respond. Usually she didn't deny her daughter anything, but the thought of all the unhealthy sugar and caffeine gave her pause. "I suppose it won't hurt just this once. I'll go get you a soda." As Savanna reached for her seatbelt, Travis reached over and placed his hand over hers.

"Don't worry about it. She can have some of mine." He popped a straw through the opening in the lid of the jug and handed it back to Emily. She held it so Raven could sip. Savanna watched the straw darken as the carbonated syrup flowed into her daughter's mouth. Raven released the straw and grinned.

"This is so good." Raven put the straw up to her lips and took a long draft. She sighed and grinned as she released the straw.

"Are you done?" Emily moved the jug away.

"I think she's had enough." Savanna reached around and took the jug. Placing it back on the tray, she withdrew the used straw and unwrapped a new one, placing it in the opening of the lid.

"Do you want a drink?" Travis nodded to the jug and looked at Savanna.

Savanna shook her head. "I think I'll stick to water. Caffeine makes me jittery."

"Hmm, well do you want to double check our route before we get on the road?" Travis was obviously deferring to her.

"I've downloaded driving directions on my data pad," she said. "I'll upload them to the truck's navigation computer. We want to take the most direct route, even though it may mean delays at the Hoover Dam. It's easier to cross the state line into Nevada than into Utah." Savanna downloaded the directions into the navigation computer. Within seconds, a map showing Savanna's planned path flashed on the screen.

Travis studied the map. "It looks like we're like-minded individuals, Dr. Taylor. Your path matches mine exactly." He flashed a smile at her.

Travis flipped the on switch to start the truck. His thumb on the print reader unlocked the gear shift. He guided the truck onto the road and aimed it towards the freeway. Once they merged off the I-10 onto I-17, Travis activated the auto-pilot. The truck followed the imbedded computer chips designed to guide traffic on the freeway. Proximity sensors around the truck monitored the vehicles on all sides, adjusting speed and distance based on the surrounding traffic.

The solar powered vehicle couldn't travel faster than sixty-five miles per hour, so it was legally required to travel in the left-side slow lane. The truck's programming allowed it to maintain a safe distance from the scooters, alternative fuel vehicles, and other trucks around it.

Savanna flinched slightly as other vehicles seemed to speed by. Just because the speed limit was ninety-five, didn't mean everyone needed to travel that fast. She never did feel comfortable traveling on the freeway. In fact, if she didn't have to, she didn't drive anywhere. Her apartment and the hospital were connected by the monorail. Any groceries she needed were delivered. Savanna's heart started to palpitate and her respirations increased. All thoughts of the handsome man beside her fled as she tried to focus on staying calm.

She flipped her mirror open and caught Emily's eyes. "Em, did you pack any of the tea your father used to make for me? I think one of them might be nice right now."

Emily reached for her bag. "He had a feeling you'd need some. He also gave me a number of recipes to make teas when we get to Haven. Which one do you want?"

"Give me the chamomile blend, please."

"It might make you sleepy. I have a mint one in here. It only has a mildly sedative effect." Emily held up two small cheesecloth bundles.

Savanna shook her head. "No, I might want to go to sleep. We have a long way to go today."

Emily drew hot water from the tank stowed behind her seat. She set the tea to steep, added a squirt of honey and placed the cup in the drink holder behind Savanna's water bottle. She flipped the switch to hot. "Give it about ten minutes. Be careful; it's going to be hot."

Savanna closed her eyes and tried to relax. She could feel the tension in her jaw as her teeth clinched and unclenched. Pressing her hand against the side of her face, she tried to massage the tension from her cheek and temple. Her right hand balled the beige linen of her slacks, embedding the sweat and oil from her hand into the wrinkles and creases in the simply woven cotton cloth.

Emily pulled the herb bundle out of the hot water, stirred it and snapped on a lid. Savanna carefully sipped the hot liquid, allowing the soothing effects to flow through her veins. It took about twenty minutes to feel the relaxing effects of the herbal mixture. Trying to get her mind off traffic, she focused her attention on her daughter's work.

Chapter Thirteen

EVEN THOUGH SHE KNEW her daughter had turned off her implant, Savanna couldn't help talking while she typed responses to her daughter. "You're doing great, Little One. Work on your nines. You're still struggling with those." Savanna watched the numbers flashing on the screen. "Think about the problems. Subtract one from the number you're factoring with nine. What number added to that one equals nine?" Savanna watched as her daughter worked through the problems. "Great job. Why don't you relax for a little while? Mommy wants to take a nap." She watched as the girl pulled up a video and put on the closed caption.

"She has some pretty impressive skills for a four-year-old. I don't think I could do my times tables until I was twelve." Travis looked at the data pad Savanna held in her lap.

"All children have the ability to learn at an accelerated level. It's the mass-produced school system using antiquated teaching methods that hold them back." Travis' eyes widened as he studied Savanna's face.

"Your father told me you were home-schooled. Are you going to home-school your daughter? Or are you going to send her to the school at Haven?"

"Haven's school is different." Savanna began to feel the relaxing effect of the tea. "Students learn at their own pace. Instructors are just there to guide learning. I'll be focusing on my own research, so I won't have the time to home-school her like I was. But, I'm definitely going to want to be an active participant in my daughter's education." Savanna finished her tea. She rolled her sweatshirt into a ball and tucked it behind her head.

Emily reached up to the front seat and opened her fist. Two little earplugs were nestled in her palm. "These might help you relax."

Savanna rolled the yellow foam disks between her thumb and forefinger until she could insert them in her ears.

The plugs didn't filter out all the noise, but it was enough. She was able to relax enough to fall asleep.

Savanna woke with a start. She felt her body roll as if she were falling. Throwing her arms in front of her, she tried to brace for impact. Her hands didn't make contact with anything and she started flailing her arms, trying to find something to grasp. Something clamped onto her arm and she jerked away. A voice penetrated, muffled, calling her name.

"Savanna, Savanna." The echo of her name broke through her panic. Travis had his hand on her arm and Emily was calling her name. Savanna reached up and pulled the plugs out of her ears.

"Are you okay?" There was concern in Travis' eyes as he leaned over her.

Savanna opened her mouth to speak, but her throat was too dry. Emily answered for her. "She's fine. She just gets nightmares sometimes. It's a side effect of her genius mind and all the tragedy she's seen. Savanna, drink some water. We're just pulling over to eat lunch."

Shaking her head, Savanna tried to clear the cobwebs. She could feel her hair falling around her shoulders. The pins must have fallen out while she slept. She ran her fingers through her hair, pulling out the left-over pins. Bringing all of her hair over her right shoulder, she let it fall until it cascaded with the ends on her lap.

"Wow."

Savanna ignored Travis' comment, not quite sure how to react.

Travis had his hands on the steering wheel. Obviously, he had taken the car off auto pilot. Savanna could see him glancing at her out of the corner of his eyes. She quickly braided her tresses into a single braid.

"You have beautiful hair. I don't think I've seen hair that long before." Travis said.

Savanna pulled a band from her pocket and slid it around the end of her braid. The tip curled against her hip. "My father says hair is a woman's crowning glory. My mother loved my hair. She used to brush it and play with it for hours. At least it seemed like hours. When she lost all her hair from chemo she made me promise I would never cut mine."

There was very little traffic as Travis pulled into the rest area. Emily helped Raven out of the truck and grabbed the sanitizing wipes. Savanna stepped out and took a deep breath of hot, desert air. Keeping one hand on the door, she stretched her arms and bent over to get the blood flowing back in her lower extremities. She arched her back to align her spine and noticed Travis was watching her. Savanna straightened and stepped away from the truck.

"Um, I'm going to the bathroom." Ducking her head so he wouldn't see her blush, she headed towards the red sandstone building. Halfway there she realized what she had just said. She couldn't believe she had just told Travis she was going to the bathroom. She quickened her pace and entered the bathroom just as Emily was helping Raven wash her hands. Savanna grabbed the sanitizing wipes off the counter and headed into the stall.

"Savanna, are you okay?" Savanna could see the tips of Emily's shoes as the woman stood just on the other side the stall door.

"I'm fine. I'll be ready to go in a few minutes. Why don't you and Raven get lunch ready?" Savanna could hear Emily ushering Raven out of the bathroom.

Savanna pulled on vinyl gloves and used the wipes to clean the toilet's seat and handle. She extracted a paper cover out of the holder and placed it on the toilet. When she finished, she made sure to scrub her hands thoroughly, using the paper towel to turn off the sink and open the bathroom door.

As Savanna approached the picnic table she saw Emily had pulled out the bread, meat and cheese to make sandwiches. Raven was carrying a bowl containing a mixture of fruit pieces. She handed the container to her aunt and sat down at the table. Travis approached, carrying his jug and two bottles of water.

"What can I do to help?" Savanna asked.

"We're fine here. Why don't you take Raven and

explore the sights? It's so beautiful here. Watch out for rattlers."

Savanna held out her hand to Raven and the two walked away from the picnic table. Emily was right about the beauty of the area. Outcrops of sandstone, all golden, orange and red, rose out of the rolling hills. Savanna watched her daughter closely as the girl searched for pretty stones buried in the sand. They were never further than two steps apart while the little girl searched for her treasures. After a few minutes Emily called them in for lunch. Savanna gathered her daughter into her arms and carried her back to the picnic table.

"Look at all the pretty rocks, Aunt Emmy." Raven dumped a pile of rocks on the table. The sunlight picked up the quartz crystals embedded in the stones facets and caused them to sparkle.

"Pretty, pretty, Little One. Let's wash your hands and get you something to eat." Raven held out her hands and allowed Emily to wipe them off with the sanitizing wipes.

Savanna used a wipe on her own hands before she picked up her sandwich. The dense, dark, homemade bread was so flavorful after the years of mass produced, over-processed foods. She savored the flavor.

After lunch they took up the journey again. The road opened up before them. Wide vistas of red and orange painted hills dotted with scrub brush and cactus, interrupted by up-thrusts of angular sandstone spread out before them. Blue sky with puffs of white clouds spanned the horizon, lending an unearthly beauty to the whole scene. The clear air of the desert contrasted with the hazy overcast of pollution of the city. Savanna turned to her daughter, who was enthralled with a video game. Savanna typed a message into her data pad and sent it to her daughter.

"Raven, look at the clouds. Let's see if we can find shapes in them." Raven turned off her game and turned on her implant. Time passed quickly as the van occupants pointed out changing shapes in the clouds, trying to outdo each other in the patterns they could find. Raven tried to convince Emily she could see Santa Clause with all his reindeer; Emily argued it was a triple-decker ice cream cone.

Travis pointed to a huge cumulus cloud. "Look ladies, it's Puff the Magic Dragon."

Savanna turned to him. He looked at her face and laughed. "Haven't you ever heard of Puff the Magic Dragon?"

Savanna shook her head.

Travis reached over to the truck's computer and started to scroll through music downloads. "I took a History of Pop Music class at Boise State. I usually don't listen to this brand of music, it's almost eighty years old, but everyone in the class was fascinated by this song."

Within moments, the cab of the truck was echoing with the sounds of Jackie Paper and his friendly dragon. Raven smiled from ear to ear as the song ended. "Again, Mommy." Travis hit replay and the song started from the beginning.

"I think I am going to have to download this song into my daughter's playlist. It seems she's made a connection to the music." Savanna entered the search parameters into the database. She downloaded the music and lyrics so Raven could memorize the words as she listened. Before the second playing of the song ended Raven had pulled up the song on her own data pad. She sang along with the artists as the words scrolled with the music.

"Do you think we'll all know the words before this journey is over?" Travis grinned at Savanna as she studied his face. "So, Dr. Taylor, your father told me you haven't had the opportunity to date much, but he's hoping that will change once you get to Haven."

Savanna could feel the heat blooming on her face. "I think the dating opportunities are going to be severely limited, after all the population of Haven is eighty percent female."

"Yeah, but you don't have to spend all your time at Haven. The basic contract allows you off-campus hours and your research will allow you extra time at other facilities. At least that's what your father said." He flashed her a grin.

Savanna didn't look up. Plucking at the cotton spurs on

her pants, she refused to make eye contact with the man sitting next to her. "I focus on my research when I'm at other facilities. I guess I don't think about dating very much. There are other things that take my focus."

"So, have you ever gone on a date?" His dark brown eyes seemed to be laughing.

Savanna looked back at her daughter and then at Travis. "I started college when I was twelve and my medical residency when I was fifteen. I never spent time with boys my own age. When all my classmates were going to keg parties and hanging out in the quad, I was going to the library and the research center. I wasn't legal, why would anyone want to date me?"

Memories of her experiences at school came flooding back. She was the darling of the Medical Department. Professors loved to call on her during class and point out to her fellow students that a teenager knew more answers than many of the more mature students. This didn't endear her to any of her classmates and caused even further resentment as she entered her residency. It was easier to focus on her research and forget about trying to create relationships with those around her.

Travis smiled. "Well, maybe I'll take you out. You're definitely legal now."

Savanna's jaw dropped. What was she supposed to say to this? She wanted to say yes, but she wouldn't know what to do on a date.

"Mommy, Mommy," Raven called from the backseat. "Mommy, I have to potty."

Travis turned back to the navigation computer. "There's a gas station two miles ahead. We can stop there." He turned back to Savanna. "So, what about it? We can go to dinner in New Las Vegas."

"Umm." Savanna paused for a minute. "I guess."

Travis chuckled.

"What? What's so funny?" Savanna's chest tightened. She knew she did something wrong, but she couldn't figure out the mistake.

"It's just the way you accepted the date. Don't worry, it gets easier. Why don't you pick a restaurant while we're inside? Unless you need to go in." Savanna shook her head and picked up her pad as Travis pulled into the gas station. He parked the truck and hopped out. Grabbing his jug, he headed for the front door. Emily helped Raven out of the truck. She grinned at Savanna as she led Raven into the building.

While Savanna was waiting for the others, she looked for restaurants in the New Las Vegas area. When she first started planning this trip she thought about bypassing Vegas altogether. However, to avoid the city they would have had to travel over a hundred miles out of the way on poorly developed roads. With traditional modes of transportation this wouldn't have been a problem, but with the solar truck it would have added another four hours to the trip and they would be traveling through foreboding high-mountain desert terrain. Since the border delays in Utah were always longer than ones in Nevada, the Vegas route was the most logical one to take.

There were several restaurants meeting Savanna's search criteria in New Las Vegas. She was surprised she was able to find so many that offered a variety of certified organic foods on their menu. She narrowed her search perimeters to include those that scored a hundred percent on their last health inspection and offered hand washing stations at the door for customers. By the time the others returned to the truck she had narrowed her list to five restaurants and had the list loaded into the navi-computer so Travis could see it. Travis opened his door, slid into the driver's seat and placed his jug on the tray beside him. He put his seatbelt on as he looked at the computer.

"Nice choices. Why don't we go to the New Bellagio?" he asked as he scanned through the list. "Emily has agreed to babysit Raven, so it'll just be the two of us."

Savanna felt the heat rush to her cheeks. Looking in the back seat, she watched Emily buckling Raven's seatbelt. Raven had a little plastic cup with a blue lid and a red straw protruding out the top. The girl shook the cup and Savanna could hear the ice rattle and the slosh of liquid swirling inside.

"Look Mommy, I have a jug, just like Uncle Travis." The little girl took a swallow of the liquid. "Aunt Emmy gave me 7UP. It doesn't taste like Uncle Travis's does, but it's still yummy." She took another long sip from the cup.

Emily had the good grace to look slightly guilty over providing the soda for Raven. Or was it because she knew how uncomfortable Savanna would be going out with Travis alone? Savanna shrugged. What could she say? She might as well indulge the child now. There wouldn't be much opportunity to indulge her while they were living at Haven. The cup had distracted her enough for her cheeks to lose some of their heat before she turned back to face Travis. She cleared her throat before she spoke.

"I think that would be fine. We should be able to make it to Vegas by five tonight." Savanna was surprised her voice sounded so clear. She expected it to be shaky. It did sound a little bit louder than normal in her ears.

Travis grinned. "Great, I'll set a reservation for seven o'clock." He tapped a sequence on the key pad and pushed enter. "All set. Is everyone buckled in and ready to go?"

"Yeah," Raven called from the back seat. Savanna nodded and Travis put the truck in gear. As he pulled onto the road Raven scrolled through her music selection. Within moments, 'Puff the Magic Dragon' was playing from the device. Savanna pulled out a set of adapted ear buds from a compartment under the seat and handed them to Emily. Her father thought of everything, even considering his granddaughter's love of music.

"See if you can get her to wear these. I don't think we all need to memorize the lyrics." Emily plugged the ear buds into Raven's pad as Travis pulled back onto the road.

Chapter Fourteen

RAVEN WAS SLEEPING WHEN Travis pulled into the overlook park above Hoover Dam. Savanna reached over and tapped her daughter's knee. The girl stretched herself awake and looked at her mother. Savanna signed for her to turn on the implant.

"Hey, Little One, we're here." Raven gave her a blank look, and then brightened.

"The 'lectric place?" Savanna nodded. Raven stretched and reached to unbuckle her seatbelt. "I have to potty."

"I'll take her." Emily unbuckled her seatbelt and helped Raven out of her seat. Savanna stepped out of the truck and watched as the two walked towards the low brick building containing the bathroom.

"She takes care of her almost as well as you do. It must be nice to have someone around to help you." Travis came around the side of the truck to stand beside her as he spoke. He wasn't watching the two walking towards the bathroom; his eyes were on Savanna.

"Emily loves Raven, but she usually doesn't do this much for her." Savanna said. "I think she knows how stressful this trip is for me and she's trying to help out."

Savanna had the picnic table cleaned and had a snack laid out by the time Raven and Emily returned from the bathroom. Raven sat between Savanna and Travis as they ate. Emily sat opposite, facing them. For a few minutes, everyone ate in silence. Suddenly Emily grinned and a slight chuckle escaped.

"I wonder what people think when they see all of us traveling together," she said.

Savanna was confused by the statement. She looked at Emily, then back at her daughter and Travis. "What are you talking about?"

"Well, Savanna. I'm old enough to be both your's and Travis's mother and Raven's grandmother, yet Raven is the only one who looks anything like me. And with the three of us being of different races, we have to be the most non-traditional family anyone has ever seen."

"But, we're not a family." Emily wasn't making any sense. "Besides, the basic family unit has changed so much over the last fifty years with the changes in marriage laws and adoption. No one should look at us any differently than they do the gypsy and migrant groups traveling as extended families, or the polygamists' communities living on the communes."

"Savanna, you've lived a very sheltered life. You have no idea the prejudices and judgments some people carry around with them. When the outbreaks happened there were entire groups who claimed the world was being punished for any number of sins." Emily took a bite of fruit before continuing. "You have no idea what's been happening in the world because you're so wrapped up in your work you don't have time to pay attention to the news."

Raven's tiny hand was brushing up and down Savanna's arm, causing tiny hairs to stand up. A slight breeze caused goose bumps to sprout on her forearms. "It's not like I don't pay attention, I just don't understand how people can believe such ridiculous rhetoric." Savanna started cleaning the leftover food from the picnic table. She handed a sanitary wipe to her daughter. "There isn't a curse on the land. Terrorist released devastating diseases into the world. People need to take responsibility for their own actions."

Raven started to brush her hand up and down Travis's arm. The man smiled indulgently at the little girl.

"Raven, what are you doing?" The sharpness in Savanna's voice caused her daughter to look at her with a pouty expression.

"I just wanted to see what it felt like. You're so soft. I wanted to see if his arm felt the same."

Savanna started to wonder how soft Travis's skin would feel. The thought made her blush and she turned away from the table. Emily must not have noticed Savanna's reaction. She started to gather food from the table. Savanna helped Emily gather the last of the food. "We need to get going." She said.

Emily carried the food to the truck. Savanna pulled a pair of gloves out of the pocket of her shirt and headed to the bathroom. When she returned Raven, Emily and Travis were standing by the observation deck. Raven had her face pressed to one of the binoculars overlooking the dam.

Savanna observed them for a moment, trying to see the differences Emily had been talking about. Raven's black hair cascaded past her shoulders and down her back. Her narrow, brown arms reached up to curl around the spyglass. Emily was standing in profile to the others. Savanna couldn't help but notice Emily's skin tone and facial features did match Raven's. She looked down at her own arm. The pale skin was turning slightly pink, warmed by the sun. Travis had his shirt tucked into his shorts. His arms were folded behind his back, emphasizing the angle of his broad shoulders, narrowing to his waist and down to his snuggly fitting shorts. His brown skin shone in the sunlight. Savanna couldn't tell if he was suffering any ill effects from the heat.

Emily turned and said something Savanna didn't quite catch, but the others turned and started walking towards her. Raven ran ahead and jumped into her mother's arms. All thoughts of the differences between them flew from her mind as Savanna looked into her daughter's laughing eyes. The girl's hands were flying as she explained to her mother what she saw. Savanna hadn't mastered her daughter's language as well as the child had. She placed the girl on the ground and knelt so she could face the child.

"Slow down, Angel," Savanna signed. "You know I can't speak as fast as you."

Raven paused and then she started to sign again, this time slow enough for her mother to understand. "Water is spraying so big. It's spitting out like a giant fountain. I want to stand under it."

Savanna laughed. "Well, I think the water is a little too powerful for that. We'll have to find another fountain for you to play in."

"Can we go inside and look at the electric stuff?" Savanna knew Raven didn't have the word for turbine yet. She was hoping the child would by the time they reached Haven.

"They don't allow tours inside, Sweetie. Not since the turn of the century. Are we ready to go?" Travis and Emily nodded.

Crossing over the Dam didn't take long. The cab was silent for a while. Savanna pulled the data from the cryotank and started checking the status of the embryos.

"What are you working on?" Savanna looked from her pad to see Travis looking at the data she was studying.

"I'm just checking the status of the embryos in stasis," she said. "A number of them are scheduled to be implanted over the next year."

Travis nodded. "So, your father uses stem cell research to strengthen cellular defects. Do you do the same type of work?"

"In a way." Savanna closed the application on her data pad and placed it on the charger. "My father uses genetic testing and code markers to create embryos with specific traits. Usually parents want a child with certain characteristics and aren't asking for a child with their specific genetic markers. In fact, some parents carry character traits they don't want to pass on to their children, like the cancer gene or a propensity towards obesity or diabetes. My father uses genetic codes from individuals with traits requested by parents, donor DNA. I'm working on ways to give parents the traits they request using the parents' own DNA."

Travis looked out the window and then back at Savanna. "So, essentially you and your father are creating designer babies."

Savanna sensed disapproval in his voice, something she had heard from many others before. She was used to being judged by those who didn't approve of her work. "I don't use my research to decide the gender or appearance of the child. This isn't about blue eyes verses brown, or trying to make bigger, stronger babies. I'm making healthy babies, with lower risk of birth defects and disabilities. Over fifty-percent of the population of the world is either sterile or has fertility problems. My research can help people have children with their own DNA when nature can't."

Travis shrugged. "I still don't understand, I guess. There isn't much difference between making a smart baby and a strong baby. All you have to do is look at the NFL and see this. There isn't one member of a professional team that hasn't been genetically altered to be bigger, stronger and faster. Scouts wouldn't even look at me my first year of college because I didn't have the proper genetic make-up. And when they started to look, I tore my ACL. The injury ended all my hopes of going Pro."

Savanna was used to defending her work. What she heard from Travis didn't surprise her. Most people were familiar with the initial experimentation with genetics from the last seventy years. The term designer babies became popular near the turn of the century, when parents would hand the fertility clinics a list of traits and the clinic would provide them with DNA that fulfilled those requirements.

"I know there are scientists out there willing to create children to specifications given to them by parents, but that isn't what I do," she said. "Most of my research involves working with embryos with some form of genetic defect, or the possibility of defects. I screen DNA and use stem cells to correct defects."

Savanna looked at her daughter and smiled. The girl was caught up in her reading and didn't even look up. "When Raven was an embryo her DNA was so damaged that if she was allowed to develop naturally she wouldn't have been viable. I was able to repair most of the damage with stem cells, but she was still born with a defect. Even though she isn't what the world sees as perfect, I wouldn't change anything about her."

"So, the rumors are true. Raven isn't your natural daughter."

Savanna shook her head. "I gave birth to her, but no, she's not my natural daughter. She does carry some of my

DNA. I used some of my own stem cells to assist her neural development, but her mother was Navajo."

Travis was silent for a few minutes. When he finally spoke Savanna didn't hear the judgment she expected in his voice. "I don't think I'll ever change my stance on genetic design, but I can see where your research may have some validity."

"There's still a lot of controversy surrounding genetic research," she said. "The public thinks we're all just a bunch of mad scientists trying to create a superior race of children destined to take over the world. My father has been called Hitler more than once. It didn't help the cause when I was born."

"What do you mean?" Travis looked at her with a steady gaze, no longer taking in the scenery.

"Blonde hair, blue eyes, genetically altered." Savanna gestured to her hair, today pulled into a pony-tail to flow around her shoulders and cascade down her back. "My father wanted to make sure I took after my mother. He always thought she was the most beautiful thing ever created. He didn't think it would be an issue to make sure his own brown hair, brown-eyed gene sequence was turned off."

"Hmm." Savanna watched Travis's eyes travel down the length of her thin frame and then back up to look in her eyes. "Well, your father did have one thing right. If you do look like your mother, she was the most beautiful thing in creation."

Savanna felt the heat flare up her face. She knew her face was bright red. Ducking her head, she pretended to focus on her data pad, pressing random icons to keep her hands busy. She couldn't think of a response.

The trip into New Las Vegas only took another hour. Savanna had heard the statements released by the Islamic Jihad to the media about the city. The terrorists claimed they didn't need to release any of the diseases into Las Vegas, explaining Americans' greed and desire for sin would bring the great city down. In some respect, the terrorists were right. Within a week of the initial outbreaks all five illnesses were in the city of

Vegas. Travel restrictions kept tourists from spreading the diseases out of the city. They were trapped in the city and had no way of bringing the illnesses home.

As a way to combat the diseases hotels adopted new sterilization procedures, but they were not always effective. Millions were infected by more than one of the illnesses. Daily death tolls numbered in the thousands. Sections of the city were sealed off completely as hotels and casinos were converted to hospitals and sanitariums. Crematories couldn't keep up with the number of bodies and citizens started to take matters in their own hands. They would pile the dead and dying into houses, pour an accelerant on the outside and light it on fire. There were too many fires for the already strained resources of the fire departments. Fires raged out of control in sections of the city where death tolls were at the highest. The city that never sleeps almost died.

Savanna had heard about the heroic efforts to try to save the city. Once the height of the crisis was over Vegas began to rebuild. Casino owners realized visitors wouldn't be interested in staying in a hotel that had doubled as a sanitarium, so they traveled to the outskirts of the city to rebuild. Hotels were contained in glass domes with filtered air systems.

A complicated series of glass enclosed pathways crisscrossed over the city, allowing visitors to travel from casino to casino. All the buildings were created using new, easily sanitized, building material. Hotel and casino employees had to pass a health inspection every month. Old hotels were imploded and new ones built in their place. The glass walkways started to travel over the old city of Vegas, connecting the new buildings. A monorail soon joined the skywalk to take visitors to certified clean casinos. Although the buildings were still, technically, in Las Vegas, the casino owners called the enclosed buildings New Las Vegas as a way to show they were disease free.

In order to enter New Las Vegas visitors had to show a permit from a doctor proving they were healthy and had been cleared for travel. Clinics sprung up on the outskirts of the city offering visitors free health exams with qualifying insurance. Those without health permits could still enter the old city where many hotels and casinos still operated.

Travis drove the truck to the gates of New Las Vegas. The guards scanned the microchips imbedded in the padded palms of the travelers. Once the four had been cleared Travis drove into the city. He found a spot in the massive parking garage. It didn't take long to set the alarm and activate the surveillance system on the van. They walked to the elevator at the end of the row and rode it up to the monorail. Once in the car, Raven sat on Savanna's lap and Travis sat beside them. The little girl rested her feet on Travis's leg. She grinned at him and rested her head on Savanna's shoulder.

"So, should I meet you at your hotel room at six forty-five?" Travis asked.

"What?" Savanna had been focusing on her daughter to avoid looking at Travis.

"For dinner." Travis's eyes seemed to be laughing again. "We have reservations at seven. We want to be on time."

Savanna couldn't seem to escape from his laughing brown eyes. "Um, yeah. That should be fine." She buried her face in her daughter's hair so he wouldn't see her blush.

Once in the hotel room Savanna and Emily made sure to wipe down the surfaces with antiseptic wipes before putting down the bags. The women pulled fresh sheets, still wrapped in the sanitary packaging from the cleaners, out of the closet. They had the two queen-sized beds made within a few minutes.

With over an hour and a half to go until dinner, Savanna started pacing. On her third circuit around the main sitting room Emily stopped her.

"So, what are you going to wear to dinner tonight?" she asked?

Savanna stopped. "What do you mean? I'm going to wear this." She gestured to the cotton drawstring pants and tunic top that was her standard wear. The clothes were comfortable and sturdy with deep pockets for supplies. They served her purpose and she didn't see any reason to wear anything else.

"You can't go to the Bellagio in those," Emily said. "Don't you have anything else to wear?"

Savanna shook her head. "I never needed anything else. Besides, these are made from natural fibers and are guaranteed to be child labor free."

"Savanna, I'm sure we can find something that fits your requirements here in Vegas. I'll call the concierge." Emily pulled out her data pad and started tapping. The concierge answered almost immediately and cheerfully responded to Emily's requests. Less than a half-hour after the call a knock sounded at the door and a smiling woman with a rack of dresses was ushered in to the room.

Chapter Fifteen

EMILY'S PICK OF A red dress fell off Savanna's shoulders and exposed much more of her front than she was used to. Cinching in at her waist and flaring at the hips, it gave the illusion of curves Savanna didn't know she had. Her blond tresses were curled and braided into an intricate weave she knew she didn't have a prayer of duplicating and her blue eyes and bright, red mouth seemed to dominate her features. If the stylists weren't still in the room when Travis showed up, she would have washed the makeup off her face. As it was, Emily was just zipping her into the dress as Travis knocked at the door.

"Wait right here. It's always better to make an entrance." Emily rubbed Savanna's shoulder. "I'll go open the door. You count to twenty, slowly, and then come into the foyer."

Savanna took a deep breath and looked in the mirror. For the first time in her life she felt she looked her age. Maybe now people would believe her the first time she said she was a doctor. She realized she had forgotten to count. Figuring enough time had passed, she walked out of the bedroom and into main room of the suite. Travis smiled as she walked into the room.

"I didn't think you could get any more beautiful," he said. "Wow, excuse me while I pick my jaw up off the floor,"

Savanna felt the heat flare up her neck. She pushed her hands down the front of the dress, trying to stretch the length a little, to see if she could extend it beyond the middle of her thighs. It didn't work.

"Are you ready?" Travis extended his arm to her. She placed her hand in the juncture of his elbow. He placed his other hand over hers and smiled. "You're so beautiful." The warmth of his hand was soothing. More soothing than Savanna could imagine. For the first time she smiled without blushing.

"You look really handsome, too." This much was true.

He was dressed in a black suit with a black shirt and a red tie. The tie matched Savanna's dress perfectly. As they walked out of the room Savanna stumbled a little. She wasn't used to heels, but Emily had insisted on cramming her feet into half-inch, patent-leather pumps. According to Emily they wouldn't be walking much, so she could survive one night in heels.

Travis put his arm around her as they stepped out of the room. "Emily told me you weren't used to walking in heels. Don't worry. I'll catch you if you fall."

It seemed ridiculous, but his comment made her feel better. "Wait. I need to kiss my daughter goodnight. She'll be asleep when we get back." Raven stood by the door, studying her mother. Savanna leaned down and kissed her daughter, leaving a red lipstick mark on her face. "Good night, Little One. Be good for Aunt Emily."

Savanna was surprised at how relaxed she was at dinner. She thought her nerves would get the best of her, but Travis kept the conversation easy and light. The Bellagio offered a wide variety of menu options and Savanna was able to order fresh, local food guaranteed to be preservative and hormone free. She had researched proper dating behavior and was very careful about topics she brought up as they ate.

Travis told her about growing up in California and how he was recruited to play football at Boise State University. He had hoped to go pro when he finished college, but since the pro leagues were allowing genetically altered players onto the teams, his dream was almost impossible.

"Your father's the one who encouraged me to go into law enforcement after I injured my ACL. I went to the police academy right after I graduated. It was the best decision I ever made. I've been working for your father ever since."

The waiter moved to refill their wine glasses. Savanna waved him off and asked for water instead. She didn't drink very often and didn't want to muddle her thoughts with alcohol. One glass was enough. Both of them declined desert and the waiter took their plates in the back to wrap the leftovers.

"So, did you sign a contract with Haven, or do you just work for my father?" Savanna ran her fingers around the edge of her water glass. The crystal sang and she removed her finger, placing her hands in her lap.

"I work at the campus. We don't have many problems since we're so secluded, but an occasional disgruntled spouse or a group of protesters will try to come on the grounds. We tend to discourage that kind of behavior."

"My father told me about it." Savanna couldn't take her eyes of his shoulders. "He said one guy tried to break in to find his spouse. From what I understand, the guards gave him a taste of what he had been doing to his poor husband."

Travis laughed. "It wasn't as bad as all that. We had to tase him a little bit, that's all. He didn't believe we weren't going to let him see his husband, so it took two or three times." Travis' eyes became slightly unfocused as he reminisced. "Once he realized we meant business he went away. He hasn't tried to come back either. His husband is doing great, though. He's become a group leader in the counseling sessions." Travis paused and took a sip of wine. "He came to the shelter with his daughter. I think she's about Raven's age."

Savanna smiled at the thought of Raven having a companion her own age at Haven. One of the drawbacks of working in Phoenix was the hospital child care center was small and only cared for a few children. Many of Raven's playmates had graduated to preschool the year before. She was the only four-year old left in the center. Savanna knew the benefits of socialization for young children. She sorely missed that opportunity while she was growing up.

The waiter brought out their leftovers in small cardboard boxes. "We can have these delivered to your hotel, if you would like to spend more time walking the strip."

Savanna reached for her box. "Thank you, but I don't think my feet will take very much walking in these shoes."

Travis reached for his own box. He stood and offered Savanna his arm. "Well, my lady, since we're headed in the same direction, please allow me to walk you to your door."

Savanna stood and took his arm. He escorted her out of the restaurant and onto the sidewalk.

"The tram'll be here in a few minutes." Travis put his arm around her, gently rubbing his fingers across her shoulder. "There's a bench over there. Would you like to sit down?"

Savanna smiled and nodded gratefully. As they headed towards the bench the maitre de opened the door behind them to allow another couple to enter the restaurant. Savanna's attention was drawn to a commotion down the street. A group of about six or seven people were approaching the restaurant. They were staggering and yelling as if they were intoxicated. One of the members of the group pushed against another, causing the other to stumble. The ensuing shoving match involved much cat calling and teasing. The maitre de took a few steps toward the group. Three of them broke away from the others and blocked him from re-entering the restaurant.

"Are you really going to stop us old man? Move out of the way and you won't get hurt." The man who spoke was obviously the leader of the gang.

The maitre de stood his ground, though Savanna could see the fear in his expression. "Street rats. Leave before I call security. Go back to The Fringe, where you belong."

The leader sneered. "Even rats will attack, if they're hungry enough. If you call back to the kitchen and have them bring out some food we'll leave you in peace. If you don't, well, you'll find out what a rat's teeth feel like."

Savanna's eyes were drawn to a small, dark figure in the rear of the group. She wasn't sure if she was correct, but she thought she recognized her. The figure was wearing a hooded sweatshirt, obscuring part of her face and disguising her stature. Travis handed her his box of leftovers.

"Wait right here. I'm going to help." He moved to stand beside the maitre de. Savanna backed away, never taking her eyes off the small form in the back of the group.

Travis positioned himself beside and slightly in front of the diminutive man standing by the front door. The group spread out, separating Savanna from the others. Suddenly the small, dark figure broke away from the group and darted towards her. Savanna's suspicion was confirmed just as the girl crashed into her, knocking the boxes of leftovers to the ground. While Savanna stumbled and tried to regain her footing, Kai grabbed the food from the ground and started running. Without even thinking, Savanna followed her. The heels tripped her up at first, but once she caught her balance, she was able to find her stride.

"Savanna! Wait!" Travis called.

Savanna ignored Travis' call as she followed Kai around the corner. She barely saw a flash of dark hair as a door to her left swung open. The other side of the door revealed a staircase leading down, disappearing in the darkness. Standing at the top of the stairs, Savanna hesitated for a moment. She could hear the echo of footsteps quickly descending. Obviously, this was a door leading to the depths of the old city. Savanna knew there were a few of these doors around the new city. They were entrances and exits for workers from the old section of the city.

"Kai! Kai!" Savanna hoped to stop the girl before she got too far. "Kai, stop. I can help you." Savanna raced down the steps. She could barely see the dark figure as Kai ran down the street. "Kai! Kai, let me help you." The dark figure didn't pause. Kai darted into an alley. When Savanna arrived at the entrance of the same alley all she saw was yawning darkness.

"Kai? Kai, answer me. I can help you. Please. Kai!"

"Kai, Kai, Kai!" At first, Savanna thought it was her voice she heard echoing back at her. "Kai, Kai, Kai!" The echoes seemed to surround her. Figures separated themselves from the darkness, the alley swarmed to life and Savanna found herself surrounded by people. All of them were dressed in torn and dirty clothing. Their hair straggled down in shaggy, greasy locks, many of them wearing it past their shoulders.

A mass of shadows moved away from the center of the alley, revealing a trash can spewing bright flames into the air. Savanna was able to see more of the shapes and make out facial features of individual gang members.

A sound drew her eyes to a huddled mass in the middle

of the alley. The fire revealed a young boy, no more than two, huddled next to a prone shape on the ground. The child's white-blond hair was matted and gray with dirt. His face contorted in pain as tears streaked his face, leaving clean tracks. The figure on the ground arched as seizures shook her body. Pink foam coated her lips and disarticulated grunting noises escaped her throat. Savanna took a step towards the woman.

One of the men stepped forward, blocking her. He was taller than Savanna and carried himself in such a way as to advertise his wiry strength.

"Kai, Kai," he said. "Who are you calling for, my Little Bird? I can give you what you need. Come here, my Little Bird. Why would you want Kai when you could have me?'

Savanna backed away as he continued to creep towards her. A sudden image of a cat stalking its prey flashed into her mind. Suddenly she came up against a solid mass. Hands closed over her forearms and she realized she had backed into one of the gang members.

"Listen." Her voice was shaky, but she cleared her throat and tried again. "Listen, I'm a doctor. I can help you. I can help her." Savanna nodded towards the woman on the ground. "Just give me a chance. I'll get you what you need. It's not hard for me."

The man continued to stalk towards her, keeping a steady gaze on her face. "What, Little Bird? You're a doctor? Do you have the mark?" He reached out and grabbed Savanna's wrist. She gasped in pain as his grip tightened and her wrist made a cracking sound.

"I… I don't know what you are talking about." Savanna grimaced as the pain radiated from her wrist. Her fingers started to tingle.

"The mark. The mark of the beast, you know. The computer that controls the world." He shook her wrist. "Is the microchip in your hand, or your eyelid? Should we take your hands and your eyes, just to make sure?

Savanna started to shake. Her stomach clenched and her bowels turned to water. The sound of pounding feet caused everyone to turn towards the entrance of the alley. The man restraining Savanna let go of her arms. The other one still had a grip on her wrist. He swung around to confront the intruder. Savanna tried to pull away from him, but he grabbed her upper arm and pulled her to his body.

"Oh, no you don't, Little Bird. You're not going to fly away from me so easily." He pulled her close to his side. Her entire arm started to go numb as he cut off the circulation with his grip.

"Let her go!"

Savanna's knees went weak with relief, easily recognizing the deep timber of Travis's voice. She could feel, rather than see, the gang close ranks around her.

"What are you going to do if I don't?" The gang leader growled.

"Let go of her. You don't want to find out." Savanna could see a spark flashing from something in Travis's hand. It was too dark to make out the shape, but he obviously had something aimed at the gang leader. He began to speak in a very calm voice. "Savanna, I'm going to shoot the leader first. As soon as he goes down you run as fast as you can. Don't look behind you." Travis's voice was very calm, but it didn't do anything to assuage Savanna's fears.

The leader sneered. "Do you really think you're going to get away? I'll kill you first and then I'll kill your little doctor."

Savanna didn't even see Travis move. Suddenly the man holding her twitched and collapsed. He didn't let go of her arm as he went to the ground. She heard a popping sound and pain radiated from her shoulder, across her chest and down her arm. The pain staggered her and she fell to the ground. Struggling to her feet and biting back nausea, she pushed herself towards the brightest area and ran. She could hear screams and running feet and then the screech of metal against metal. A transport truck pulled up beside her and the side door slid open. Hands grabbed her from behind, lifted her from the ground and thrust her inside. She tried to kick out, but her foot didn't connect with anything. She collapsed on the floor. Hands grabbed onto her body and she tried to slap them away. She was lifted off the floor and placed on the seat where she immediately pulled herself against the wall and curled up in a ball. Voices seemed to be coming from all sides, drilling into her. She leaned over and emptied the contents of her stomach onto the floor.

"Ma'am? Ma'am, are you okay?" Savanna looked up but all she could see were a pair of piercing green eyes. The voice Savanna heard was distorted by the filter obscuring the lower half of the face. A riot helmet hid the rest of the soldier's head. A dark shadow filled the door. Savanna looked up just as Travis jumped in the van. A soldier gestured to the driver and slammed the door shut. Travis reached for Savanna and pulled her into his arms, away from where she had just been sick, as the van accelerated away from the alley.

Chapter Sixteen

"MA'AM ARE YOU HURT?" The same voice penetrated through the painful haze surrounding her. Savanna flinched away from the distorted face. Reaching up, the soldier removed the helmet and face mask. Bright red hair fell out. Some of the strands had come loose, framing a pale face and curling to her shoulders. Something about the pale face and earnest expression evoked a feeling of trust. Travis was holding Savanna, his arms wrapped around her shoulders. He must have realized she was hurt because he was barely touching her.

Savanna blinked, trying to clear her thoughts, before she answered. "I think—" She had to swallow before she could continue. "I think he dislocated my shoulder." Just saying the words made the shoulder throb. "He also did something to my wrist. I don't think it's broken.

Savanna cradled her arm against her rib cage. The self-splinting helped.

"What's your name?" the woman asked.

"Savanna. Dr. Savanna Taylor."

"We're on our way to the hospital. Would you like something for the pain until we get there?" Savanna shook her head. The red-head continued, "Why did you go into The Fringe? Don't you realize the risk you placed yourself and your friend in? Did the girl steal something valuable from you?"

Again, Savanna shook her head. "No, I recognized her. I know her family. She ran away, and her family wants her to come home."

"Well, she's in The Fringe now. Even if she does go home, she won't be the same girl who left. The family won't want her back. The Fringe does that to people. I'm Captain Gabrielle Egan, by the way."

Savanna felt the shakiness in her legs. Her body was cold and clammy. Her respirations rapid. She knew the symptoms of shock and realized she was quickly destabilizing. Knowing she needed to stay conscious, Savanna tried to ask more questions.

"What happened to the woman and child?" she asked. "The woman looked like she overdosed."

"The mob scattered when we showed up," Captain Egan responded. "They left the woman there. Medics got her and the child. They're in the ambulance right behind us. We're going to take you to Emmanuel Hospital. It's the closest. Once you're stabilized they'll probably transfer you to Saint Luke's in New Las Vegas."

The van rolled to a stop and the side door flew open. Captain Egan backed out of the way as two medics appeared. Travis slid his arm under Savanna's legs and lifted her off the seat. He carried her out of the van and gently placed her on a gurney.

"We have it from here, sir." A medic said. They started to wheel her towards the hospital doors. Savanna reached out with her uninjured arm and grabbed Travis's hand.

"Don't leave me." The thought of Travis leaving her made her heart race. He intertwined his fingers in hers.

"Don't worry. I'm right here. I promised your father I'd protect you and I haven't broken a promise yet." The warmth of Travis's hand penetrated through her confusion. The radiating warmth spread up her arm and she relaxed back onto the gurney. Bright florescent lights blinded her as she was wheeled into the curtained exam room.

The medics closed the curtain and turned towards Travis. "Are you her husband?" Travis shook his head. "Then you're going to have to wait outside. We can't have you in here while we examine her."

Savanna gripped his hand tighter and then released it. She knew they were going to have to cut her clothes off. She nodded to let him know it was fine to leave.

"I'll be right outside if you need me." He brushed her hair back from her face. The warmth of his hand caressed her check. Without even thinking about it Savanna turned into the caress. He brushed his fingers across her lips. "You'll be fine. If you need me, scream." He left the room.

The medics made quick work of the red dress. Savanna closed her eyes and focused on the sounds around her. She could hear a child crying on the other side of the curtain. The crying turned into a piercing scream, one that Savanna recognized as resulting from a blood draw. Someone called for narcan and a course of other drugs. She recognized as a rapid detoxification process. She realized the woman and child from the alley were right next to her.

She heard the screech of the curtain flying open, and then a voice she recognized. "Savanna! What are you doing here?" She opened her eyes and stared straight into the face of her former assistant.

"Haru, I didn't know you were here. I thought you were going to Japan," her voice sounded thick and heavy, even to her own ears.

He shook his head. "No. Japan has closed its borders to me. Since I've worked in some of the highest contaminated areas they're afraid I will bring the diseases with me. But, you're the patient here today. Tell me what happened."

"I think my right shoulder is dislocated. We're going to need to get a full right-arm series. Order a full spectrum MRI in case there's any muscle or tendon damage." Savanna paused as a grin spread over her former assistant's face. "What's so funny?"

"You always were a better doctor than a patient." The curtain slid open again as a technician wheeled in the portable MRI. "I'll be back in a minute. The nurse will bring in something for the pain." Omoto left and the technician maneuvered the machine into place.

"This'll only take a few minutes, Dr. Taylor." She positioned the machine beside the bed, its arm just over her head. "Okay, the first scan is just going to set the machine to your body position. The second is going to take the X-ray and MRI. Please don't move."

Savanna stayed as still as she possibly could as the bright light from the machine scanned her body from head to foot, traveled back to her head and repeated the process. A nurse walked in just as the light reached her feet the second time. He was carrying a small plastic bin with syringes protruding out of the top.

"Hello, Dr. Taylor," he said. "I'm Jim, the nurse on duty tonight. I'm going to give you a little something for the pain. Dr. Omoto also wanted me to start an IV and get some blood work."

She watched as Jim started an IV in her left arm and filled two vials with blood. He started her on lactated ringers and injected two syringes of medication into the port. "You should feel the effects in just a few minutes. I'm going to attach some monitors to your wrist here." He placed sticky tabs with wires on her wrist. Pulling a blanket from the shelf above the bed, he covered her from her feet to her abdomen. "Let me know if you get cold. Can I get you anything?"

Savanna shook her head. He placed a small device in the palm of her hand. "Here's your call button if you need me." As he opened the curtain to leave Savanna could see Travis standing just beyond the border of the curtain line. As she stared at his back a blue haze surrounded him. Realizing the pain medication was starting to take effect she relaxed into the pillow and closed her eyes.

It seemed to be only a few seconds before she heard the curtain swing open again. She didn't want to open her eyes, even when she heard the voice beside her bed.

"Dr. Taylor? Dr. Taylor? Savanna!" She opened her eyes and looked up at Omoto. "Dr. Taylor?" Savanna knew he was looking for acknowledgement, so she nodded her head. She tried to speak, but her mouth wasn't working. All she could manage was a noncommittal hum.

"I have the results of your tests."

Savanna opened her eyes wider and tried to focus.

"It looks like you do have a slight dislocation of the right shoulder. You're very fortunate. There was minimal tearing and stretching of the muscle. All your tendons appear to be in good condition. You don't have any fractures anywhere, but there will be some bruising on your wrist. Your right knee is also abraded with debris. Do you understand what I am saying to you?"

Savanna nodded.

"You are going to have to relocate the joint." Savanna's mouth was dry and she wished she could take a drink of water. She licked her lips to try to hydrate them.

"I hate having doctors as patients. They always want to treat themselves." Omoto smiled. "You know the procedure. I'm going to give you a muscle relaxer. After about twenty minutes I'll come in and put the shoulder back in place, but you already know all of this. We'll get another MRI when we're done. While we're waiting the nurse will clean your knee. I'll write you a prescription for pain medication and an anti-inflammatory to take home with you. I should be able to release you in a couple of hours. Do you have any questions?"

"Could I get a drink of water?" Since she knew there wouldn't be a need for surgery she felt safe in asking for a drink.

"Yes. Oh, your family is here. Do you want me to allow them to come in?"

"Wait until after the procedure. Raven doesn't need to see me like this." Savanna tried to adjust into a more comfortable position.

"I thought you would say that." Omoto said. "I haven't told them anything. What would you like me to tell them?"

"Let them know about the procedure and how long it'll take." She tried to get comfortable again. "I don't want them to worry."

Omoto nodded. "I'll send the nurse in right away. We want to get this done as soon as possible and get you back to New Las Vegas."

The pain medication made Savanna drowsy. Once the muscle relaxer entered her system she lost all sense of time and place. She was barely aware of Dr. Omoto and his nurse coming in the room. She only realized what was happening when Jim leaned across her chest. A sharp pain in her shoulder joint let her know the procedure was done. She could feel the muscles relaxing into place almost as soon as it was over. Drowsing slightly, she didn't even realize when the others came into the room.

"Savanna." Emily's voice drew her attention and she opened her eyes. She saw the concern in her friend's face when their eyes met. "Oh, Savanna. Thank God you're okay."

Raven crawled into the bed and stretched herself out beside her mother. Savanna wrapped her good arm around the child and pulled her close. Travis stood at the head of the bed.

"What was going through your head? You can't go into Old Vegas. You're could've gotten yourself killed!"

"Emily, it was Kai. Kai was with that group. I just wanted to find her, to tell her she needed to go home." Savanna was almost in tears. Raven perked up at the sound of Kai's name. She had met the woman a few times, when Savanna had taken her to the Reservation.

"Kai was there? Kai hurt Mommy?" Her clear soprano voice echoed in the room.

Savanna kissed the top of her daughter's head. "No, Little One. Kai didn't hurt Mommy."

A shrill scream interrupted Savanna's explanation. It was coming from the next curtain.

"No, you can't have him!" The curtain flew open and a woman carrying a child stumbled through. "You already ruined my high. You're not going to take the boy."

Two police officers followed the woman into the room. She screamed again, a wordless, ear piercing scream.

The boy's cries joined the woman's screams as she backed away from the officers. Struggling, the child kicked at her. She released him, allowing him to fall to the floor. He scrambled to get away, crawling under Savanna's bed, and proceeded to scream on the top of his lungs.

"Get back here!" The woman lunged towards the bed, trying to get to the child.

Travis stepped between her and the bed.

"Back off!" The woman's voice came out a glottal growl. She looked wild and fierce, her hair sticking up all around her head.

Travis crossed his arms across his chest. Savanna could feel Raven trembling against her. She pulled her daughter close and wrapped her good arm around her. "Don't worry Little One. Travis will protect us."

The woman lunged towards the bed, trying to bypass Travis. As she approached, he wrapped his arms around her. They disappeared as he wrestled her to the floor. One of them kicked the bed, moving it about three inches. The jarring motion brought a twinge to Savanna's shoulder. She was grateful for the effects of the pain medication.

The police officers dove to the ground. When they stood they pulled the woman up with them, her arms cuffed behind her back. "Listen lady, you just made a lot of trouble for yourself. CPS is taking your child and you're going to jail."

The woman struggled against her captors. "Don't take me to jail! I need to go home!" She continued to yell and struggle against the officers as they carried her out. Not once did she look back or mention her child. An officer closed the curtain, cutting off the view as they strapped the woman to a gurney. Raven huddled against her mother, tears streaming down her face.

"I hate Kai! She hurt Mommy."

Savanna soothed the child, brushing her fingers through the black hair and humming softly.

It took the nurses ten minutes and a pudding bribe to coax the boy out from under the bed. Dr. Omoto ordered another scan of Savanna's shoulder before splinting it and releasing her.

Chapter Seventeen

THE MEDICATION IN SAVANNA'S system allowed her to sleep deeply, but her dreams wouldn't let her rest. The angelic face of the young boy was imprinted in her brain. As she tried to push his face out of her mind Kai's brown eyes replaced his blue ones. The pain in her eyes seemed to penetrate into Savanna and reverberate in her soul. Pain was replaced by the shine of fever, and Anaba's face appeared. The boy's face reappeared. His features contorted with seizures and then transformed to the woman in the alley, her red, foam flecked mouth contorting with angry screams.

Still groggy when Emily woke her up in the morning, Savanna needed assistance getting dressed even though she was back to wearing the simple pull over tunic and drawstring pants. A knock sounded at the door and Travis entered the room with a wheelchair.

Once they were on the freeway driving out of town Emily called Savanna's father to let him know they were on their way. Savanna was extremely groggy and was only able to answer her father's question in monosyllabic tones. Emily explained what had happened and Dr. Taylor insisted on receiving a copy of Savanna's test results himself. Emily forwarded them, along with a copy of the police report. Savanna dozed off as Travis set the auto-pilot.

Savanna was startled awake by a cloying, slightly skunky, smell. The truck was rolling to a stop as she sat up and looked out the window. Great, billowing clouds of grey-white smoke were rolling across the road. Bright sparks chased the clouds, spinning and swirling as they were caught by the wind. A fire truck, lights flashing, blocked the road, halting traffic. National Guard soldiers directed the traffic to turn back and park in an empty field about two hundred yards back. Travis followed the directions and parked in an empty field.

Emily assisted Savanna out of the truck. Together the two women joined the crowd gathered to watch the fire.

Savanna flinched as pain radiated from her shoulder with each step. Travis guided her to a large rock and helped her sit down. A man standing nearby looked over as she was trying to position herself comfortably.

"Are you in a lot of pain?" Savanna glanced at him, briefly. The man continued as if he hadn't just been dismissed. "All you have to do is take a few deep breaths. You won't be feeling any pain in a few minutes." The man laughed and joined a group who were dancing and singing.

Savanna turned to Travis for an explanation.

"Some protestors torched the cannabis fields. They did it at exactly the right time, too. The drought dried out the fields and it didn't take long for the fire to spread. The fire shouldn't be too hard to contain. Right now they're having more of a problem with crowd control."

Savanna looked around at the people gathered at the edge of the field. There seemed to be a great diversity in the crowd. "Who are all these people?" Savanna wasn't sure if it was the pain medicine that made everything appear crazy, or if it was the overwhelming roar from the crowd.

Travis sat on the ground beside the rock. "Most are just travelers trying to get from one place to the next just like us. Some are here to protest the use of marijuana. Others are advocates for the use of medical marijuana. The group over there," He gestured to the group singing and dancing. "Appear to be recreational users."

National Guard soldiers passed out filter masks to the crowd. Savanna needed Emily's help with hers. "This is medical grade marijuana?"

Travis nodded.

"Why would someone want to torch medical grade Marijuana? It's been legal in all fifty-two states for almost fifteen years."

Travis shrugged and his voice was garbled as he spoke through his mask. "The guardsman said they should have the road open in a couple of hours and we can get on our way then." He relaxed, leaning back against the rock. "You might want to take some more pain meds so they have time to kick in before we get back on the road."

Emily brought Savanna her pills and a glass of water. She had to remove her mask to swallow them. Trying not to breathe too deeply, she took the medication. Raven tried to climb on her lap, but Emily picked her up.

"Mommy, I have to go potty." Savanna looked around. There didn't appear to be any bathrooms in the area. Emily pointed to a rock pile covered with scrub brush. Savanna shook her head. She really didn't want her daughter relieving herself in the open.

"There aren't any other options," Emily said. "It'll be completely private and I'll watch out for her."

Savanna shrugged her good shoulder. She realized if they didn't get on the road soon she would be facing the same dilemma as her daughter. Emily led Raven behind the rock pile. As they disappeared from view Savanna's attention was drawn back to the burning fields. A figure ran out of the smoke, carrying what appeared to be a bundle of plants in his arms. He yelled something as he came closer, Savanna could barely make out his words.

"I saved some! I saved some!"

Two soldiers ran behind him. One of them pulled out a taser. The man collapsed, throwing plants in the air as he went down. He was immediately surrounded by a group of people. At first Savanna thought they were there to help him up but, as the soldiers trained their weapons on the mob and made them back off, she realized the plants around the man had pretty much disappeared. The soldiers forced those who weren't quick enough to hide away their stash to drop it, but Savanna had seen plenty of hands flash into pockets and under clothes. She knew the soldiers didn't get it all.

Savanna heard her daughter crying and immediately turned to see what happened. Emily walked towards her, cradling the child in her arms. She noticed Emily was carrying Raven's pants and shoes.

"It's fine, Savanna." Emily smiled. "She just doesn't

know how to squat. Her pants and shoes got a little wet. She refused to put them back on. I'm going to take her to the truck and help her change." Savanna nodded, relieved it wasn't anything more serious.

It didn't take long for Emily to return from the truck. Although Raven was in a clean pair of pants her aunt was still carrying her. Savanna noticed her daughter's feet were still bare. Emily carefully placed Raven on Savanna's lap.

"I couldn't find her a clean pair shoes. Does she have another pair?" Emily asked.

"Oh." Savanna brushed her child's hair out of her face. The baby face still had tear streaks creating a trail to her chin. She kissed Raven's forehead and brushed away the tears. "She only has the one pair. She outgrew her other ones. I left them for the recyclers."

Emily picked up the shoes and inspected them. Savanna could see dark marks and mud splatters marking the inside curve. "Maybe I can clean these up. She just refuses to wear them."

Raven looked up, her mouth twisted into a pout. "I don't want to wear them. They're dirty." She buried her face in her mother's shoulder and refused to look at Emily.

"We'll get you some new shoes when we get to a town." Savanna tried to pry her daughter off her shoulder, but she couldn't manage to move her with her one good arm. "Raven, you need to put something on your feet. We can't leave the little piggies exposed."

Raven tucked her feet between Savanna's legs so Emily couldn't get them.

"She's as stubborn as you are." Savanna smiled at Emily's comment.

"Call my father and ask him to make sure there are extra shoes for her at Haven. We'll buy something to get her through until we get there." Raven uncurled her feet and wiggled her toes. "I like your little piggies." Savanna wrapped her hand around her child's foot and started to massage it. After a few minutes Raven removed her foot and put the other one in the hand to receive the same treatment.

Emily extended the data pad towards Savanna. A red light flashed in the corner of the screen. "We're out of service area. I can't get a signal. Raven's feet are dirty. I'll get a towel and some water to wash them."

Before Emily moved away another woman approached. Her dark blonde hair curled past her shoulders and her broad mouth curved into a smile, reaching her blue-grey eyes. She carried what looked like a roughly woven pair of sandals. Holding the shoes towards Savanna as if making an offering, the woman spoke in a rich contra-alto voice.

"I see the child doesn't have any shoes," she said. "We make these out of hemp. They'll protect her feet if she needs to get up and walk around." Savanna inspected the sandals. The soles were created by weaving hemp flat and shaping to fit the bottom of a foot. Straps were braided in strategic locations to go over the top of the foot and wrap around the ankle where they would be tied in place.

Thinking they would be better than allowing her child to walk around bare foot, Savanna nodded to the woman. "How much do you want for them?"

The woman's smile broadened as she shook her head. "We don't work for the money of man. Anything we need we trade for. If you have food or clothing we'll gladly take it in exchange, but we don't want any money."

Emily moved to the truck to get some food to exchange for the shoes. She also brought back a white towel and a bottle of water. The woman took the food Emily offered and handed it to a young girl standing nearby. She knelt on the ground in front of Savanna and extended her hand to Emily.

"Allow me to wash the child's feet." Emily handed he woman the towel and water bottle. Raven extended her feet and allowed the woman to gently wash them. After all the dust and grime was washed off the tiny appendages the woman pulled a bottle of lotion out of her pocket and rubbed the white cream into the child's dark skin.

"You're going to be so spoiled after this, child." She

looked up at Savanna. "You're so blessed to be able to serve such a beautiful child. There is no greater bond than the one between mother and daughter." The woman tied the sandals in place. With a soft, graceful movement, she rose to her feet. "I'm Tawnya. May I know your names?"

"Savanna." Savanna pointed to herself and then to her daughter. "This is Raven. My friends, Emily and Travis."

Tawnya nodded to each of them. "Thank you. You have a beautiful family. May the Goddess bless you."

As Tawnya walked away Savanna ducked her head to look at her daughter. The girl's eyes were half closed as she snuggled into her shoulder. Savanna knew Raven wasn't sleeping because every once in a while she would kick a foot up so she could see her new shoes. Soon her eyes closed completely and her foot stopped twitching. Her deep breaths signaled she had fallen asleep.

Raven was still sleeping when the National Guard released the crowd to continue their journey. Emily took Raven and, without waking her, gently transferred her to her car seat. Savanna eased herself into the backseat. It took a couple of tries to get her seatbelt positioned comfortably. By the time Travis pulled back onto the freeway, she was half asleep too.

She didn't wake again until the truck slowed for the border crossing. Travis joined the queue of vehicles approaching the gates marking the border between Nevada and Idaho. Savanna tried to stretch and hissed involuntarily in pain. Emily turned in her seat and rolled her eyes down her frame.

"Are you okay?"

Savanna was still a little groggy so she didn't answer right away.

"It's too soon for another dose of pain meds, but I can give you some Tylenol to take the edge off," Emily said.

"No." Savanna shook her head to clear it. She managed to push herself up into a more comfortable position. "I'll be fine. I'm mostly stiff. In fact, I think I want to try to go without the pain meds right now. We're only a few hours outside of Boise. I want to have a clear head when we get there."

"Let me know if you change your mind," Emily said.

Savanna looked out the window to study the cars slowly creeping towards the guard station. Travis pulled into the far outside lane. There were only three vehicles ahead of them. Guards stood on either side of the vehicles with scanners, preparing to check microchips or verify travel papers. As the lead car pulled up the driver and passenger reached their arms out the window. The soldiers at the gate scanned their microchip and waved them through.

The truck was two cars back from the gate when a sudden commotion caused the gates to crash closed and the guards to draw weapons.

Voices from all sides yelled. "Stay in your vehicles! Stay in your vehicles!" The guards converged on an RV two lanes away and started to pull people out. Savanna watched as they forced the family to the ground and made them put their hands on their heads. She counted nine people, some of them women and children.

The family huddled on the ground while a group of soldiers converged on the RV. One of them yanked the door open, three others rushed inside, guns drawn. A few minutes later all three emerged. One soldier was carrying a young child in his arms.

Travis' window was lowered and Savanna could hear the echoing pleas of one of the women. "My daughter! My daughter! Please, she's healthy. Please, give her back. Please." The woman reached out and fell to the ground.

The soldier behind her barked out an order and two men grabbed her by her arms and pulled her back to her knees. The child was carried to a waiting van, where she disappeared inside. The woman's wails grew louder as the van drove out of sight.

Chapter Eighteen

A SOLDIER WAS STANDING next to Savanna's window. He turned at the whirring sound it made as Savanna lowered it. "Stay in the car, Ma'am. This'll be over soon and we'll open the gates."

"I'm a doctor. If the child is ill I can help." Savanna couldn't help but notice the soldier only looked about seventeen or eighteen.

"These gypsies are just trying to slip a TB carrier through. They hide them in compartments and try to disguise the heat signature. This isn't the first time this family has tried to do this. We're transporting the child to a hospital. Don't worry ma'am, we'll get you on your way soon." He eyed the others in the truck. "Your Native American friends aren't carriers, are they? You're in the fast lane and it'll be a problem if you hold us up here."

"Raven's my daughter. Emily's her aunt and caretaker." Savanna looked into the concerned face of the soldier. "Neither is carrying any diseases."

"You better be telling the truth, woman." The soldier took an offensive stance, his gun across his chest. "We don't need no carriers coming through the borders helping terrorist kill citizens."

Savanna bristled. Despite the pain in her shoulder, she sat up straight and stared him down. "Listen *boy*, I'm Dr. Savanna Taylor. I helped come up with the vaccines to treat half these diseases. You're just a kid with a gun on a power trip."

The soldier reached over and pulled open the door. "Step out of the truck, now!"

Savanna reached for her seatbelt. She didn't notice Travis and Emily doing the same. Another soldier came up behind Savanna's antagonist. He put a restraining hand on the boy's shoulder.

"What's going on here, son?" Savanna recognized the

voice. She looked up into Captain Grey's face, not quite sure if she was relieved to see him.

"Captain, this woman is causing problems and being disruptive," the soldier said.

Grey looked past the boy, into the car. He immediately burst into laughter. "I don't doubt she is, Private. Dr. Taylor, it's good to see you again and this must be Raven. I heard you had a daughter." Raven peeked up at him.

"Captain Grey, are you in charge here?" Savanna realized her voice had dropped into the bass tones she used when she was trying to assert her authority.

He laughed again. "Surprised? It has been a few years since I've seen you. Yeah, I'm in charge of this unit." He turned towards the Private. "Go back to the second gate. We need to get these cars moving again." The boy saluted the captain and double-timed it to his post. Grey put his hand on the door. "I understand you're going to Haven, Dr. Taylor."

"I am." Savanna didn't take her eyes off him. "My father wants to retire and he needs me to take over the facility. He's going to stay on as adjunct at the University, but he says he wants to focus his time and energy on research." Savanna moved to get out of the truck, but Grey held up his hand to stop her.

"It's okay. I worked in a program with Dr. Smith, before he and your father dissolved their partnership. I met your father a few times. He's a real decent guy." He closed the door and Savanna reached for her seatbelt. "The gates are opening now. We'll get you on your way. Enjoy your trip, Dr. Taylor." He waved Travis on. The truck rolled to the gate, where the soldier scanned the four passengers and sent them on their way.

Travis managed to pull out onto the freeway before any of the backed-up traffic was released. Savanna suspected the guards were being extremely thorough in their searches of the other vehicles. She had seen more than one vehicle attempting to make a U-turn and escape the lane of traffic while the guards were busy with the RV. Emily had a frown on her face and was looking straight ahead as Travis merged into traffic and set the auto-pilot.

"We'll ladies, welcome to Idaho." Travis relaxed into the pilot's seat and flashed a grin at Savanna in the rear-view mirror.

"I have to potty," Raven announced.

Travis sighed. "There's a rest stop two miles ahead. Can you wait till then?"

Raven nodded and picked up her data pad. "I'm going to read a story."

Savanna picked up her own data pad. She dialed the connection to her father's office. A beep told her she had connected. He didn't pick up right away, which concerned her. He knew she was expected any time. She checked her missed messages. There was one from him asking for a status update. The time stamp showed he sent it when they had been out of the service area during the fire, but there wasn't anything since then.

Travis pulled into the rest stop and everyone used the bathroom. He refilled his and Raven's jug with soda at the service station and they got back on the road. Savanna dialed up her father's house and his domestic answered. Rosanne was a graduate of Haven Project. She worked as her father's housekeeper for the past seven years. Her blocky, red-cheeked face filled the screen.

"Rose, is my father home?"

"No, Dr. Taylor." She shook her head. "He said he was going to wait until you called the office and then he was heading straight for Haven. He wanted to be there when you arrived."

Savanna's concern grew even stronger. It was after six o'clock and she knew he wouldn't head out to Haven until he had heard from her. Haven shut down their video conference system at eight o'clock and he wouldn't risk missing her call. "He's not answering at his office. I'll try again. Then I'll try Haven." Savanna disconnected the call and dialed his office again. Still no answer.

Savanna desperately typed in the address for Haven. A deep, gnawing feeling grew in her gut. Something had to be wrong. She didn't recognize the woman who answered.

"I'm sorry, Dr. Taylor, but Dr. Taylor isn't here. He said he was going to wait for your call in his office. If you hadn't called by eight o'clock, he was going to leave a message for you to call him at home."

Savanna disconnected and tried the office again.

Travis and Emily had turned to face her as she desperately tried again and again. Emily reached out and took the pad from her.

"He probably just had an emergency at the hospital. Let's leave a message for him to call us when he gets in." She placed the data pad on its charge station. "We're not going to run into any more blind spots between here and Boise. If he still hasn't called by the time we get there we'll stop by his office and the house." Savanna leaned back and put her hand over her eyes. She couldn't shake the feeling that something was wrong.

They pulled over at a rest stop outside of Twin Falls. Emily set out a meal for them. Savanna just picked at her food, not noticing what she was eating. In addition to the worry she felt her shoulder was bothering her again. Emily wrapped up the leftover food and put it back in the fridge. Savanna crawled into the front seat next to Travis while Emily and Raven took the back. They travelled in silence as the sun descended into twilight. The two hours it took to get to Boise seemed to be the longest two hours of Savanna's life. They finally rounded the hilltop, curving into the view of the buildings and trees of the city.

As Travis dropped down the hill and took the Broadway exit Savanna's heart started to race. She leaned forward and grabbed the bar just above the glove compartment. Peering out the windshield, she studied the road ahead. Although it had been almost seven years since she had been on this road, she knew every curve, street light, and building. There on the right, Ono Hawaiian Café, up the street to the left the liquor store, further down the Chevron station. Boise State University sprawled ahead; its campus taking up both the right and the left side of the street. Her father's office was two blocks off Broadway, just up Warm Springs Avenue. Streetlights flashed on as dusk settled over the valley.

Travis turned on to Warm Springs and was immediately stopped by a police officer. The road was filled with flashing lights. The officer approached the truck and Travis rolled down the window.

The officer shone his light into the cab. "This road's closed. You're going to have to find an alternate route."

Savanna leaned over Travis so she could see the officer's face. "My father's office is the next building over. I just got into town and I haven't been able to get ahold of him." She could hear the desperate panic in her voice.

The officer brought his light up to Savanna's face. She flinched as the light blinded her. "What's your name?"

"Dr. Savanna Taylor. My father's Dr. Jackson Taylor."

The officer lowered his flashlight and signaled to another man. "Drive on. Captain Peterson will want to talk with you."

Another officer moved the wooden barrier out of the way as Travis drove the truck through. Savanna's heart raced. She couldn't sit still as they pulled into the parking lot of her father's medical building. She had her seatbelt unfastened and was out of the truck before Travis even put it in park. Another officer met her at the entrance and escorted her to the Captain.

Captain Peterson appeared to be in his early fifties. He was shorter than Savanna, stocky and what hair he had was grey. When Savanna was introduced he turned and gave her his entire focus. Emily and Travis were standing on either side of her, Raven in Emily's arms. Captain Peterson put his hand on Savanna's arm.

"Dr. Taylor, why don't we go into an office where we can talk in private?" Savanna looked at her friends.

"They're my family. Anything you have to say to me you can say in front of them." Savanna suspected what she was about to hear wasn't going to be pleasant and she wanted someone to be with her. The captain let his hand drop. He set himself in a posture Savanna recognized. She used it herself when she needed to deliver bad news.

"Dr. Taylor, I'm afraid there is no good way to say this. When the cleaning crew came in this evening they found your father's body. He had been viciously attacked. When EMS arrived on scene they declared him dead."

Savanna could feel her entire body tingling. A sharp, stabbing pain shot through her shoulder and she realized she was trembling uncontrollably. "My father is dead? My father is dead!" She could taste the salt of her tears as they poured down her checks. "How? What happened? Who did this?"

Travis put his arm around her as her knees gave way. She felt herself being lowered to the floor. Tucking her knees into her chest, she released a wail from deep within her body. She didn't know where the sound came from. It felt like it was being drawn from her toes, through her chest and echoing out of the vaults of the emptiness in her head. Suddenly her daughter was in front of her, trying to work her way inside the ball she had turned into.

"Mommy, Mommy, oh Mommy!" Tears were streaming down the child's face. "Mommy, what happened? Mommy, are you hurt?" Raven tried to pry Savanna's arms away from her chest. Savanna could feel her tiny hand against her cheek as she wiped away the tears.

Savanna pulled the child to her chest, rocking back and forth. Emily reached down and tried to help her off the floor, but Savanna pulled away.

A young officer approached the captain. She was carrying something in a clear, red sealed, evidence bag. "Captain, this appears to be the murder weapon."

Savanna looked up. The heavy glass sculpture was easily recognizable. It was on the shelf behind her father every time she called. She stood up and reached for it. "That's my father's Nobel Peace Prize! How could it be used to kill him?"

The officer pulled the statue out of Savanna's reach.

"This is evidence, Ma'am. The Doctor received several blows to his head, the blood and tissue on this is consistent with it being the murder weapon."

"Officer Carter!" The officer's explanation was stopped by the captain's tone. "We don't need to discuss this here. Take it to the crime lab."

Carter paled then nodded and walked away.

"Dr. Taylor, can I offer you an escort? Where would you like to go?" Savanna was drawn back to the conversation with Captain Peterson. She could see the concern on his face but she couldn't connect with what he was saying.

Her shoulder was throbbing. Raven clung to her leg, tears streaming down her face. Savanna put her hand on her daughter's head and ran fingers through her hair. "I would like to go to my father's house. I want to go home." Emptiness filled her. She couldn't get enough air into her lungs and her stomach clinched in a knot. "Who did this?"

Captain Peterson stepped closer and put his hand back on her arm, Savanna flinched and he drew his hand back. "We aren't sure. We have a short list of suspects, but the investigation just started. We found his body about half an hour ago, but it appears this happened at about five-thirty this afternoon."

They had just entered the service area at about that time. If she would have called her father right away, instead of waiting, maybe she could have interrupted the assailant and her father might still be alive. She couldn't stay in the building any longer. The air was stifling and she felt as if she was going to be sick. Turning to Emily she reached for her friend's hand. "Let's go home," she whispered.

Travis wrapped his arm around her and guided her to the parking lot. Emily helped her into the car and handed her some pills. Savanna swallowed them without thinking about what she was doing. Nothing registered in her mind in the short drive to her family home. She didn't acknowledge Rose when they got to the house. As soon as she crawled into bed she closed her eyes and the world went dark.

Chapter Nineteen

SAVANNA OPENED HER EYES to the vastness of space. A dark blue sky expanded to the horizon, dotted with pinpointed lights denoting constellations. Her left side felt clammy and warm. She closed her eyes and tried to clear her thoughts. When she opened her eyes again she realized she was in her own room. The ceiling above her was a mural of an exact replica of the night sky; a relic from the time she had told her father she wanted to be an astronaut and wanted to find other planets so humans could live in space. Memories flooded her mind and she realized what had happened the night before. She felt a scream building in her throat, but a nudge made her realize the warmth at her side was Raven.

Looking down at the long, midnight hair of the little girl calmed her. The dampness was from her daughter pressing against her body in the night, causing them both to sweat. Raven's dark eyes looked into hers. The little girl stared with such intensity that Savanna had to smile at her. Raven sat up in the bed.

"I'm hungry, Momma. What's for breakfast?"

Savanna forced herself to sit up. She had to see to the needs of her daughter before she took care of anything else. Dressing her daughter helped her focus. Raven refused to wear any of the new shoes Savanna found in the closet for her. Obviously, her father had expected Savanna and Raven to visit frequently from Haven. Savanna helped Raven tie on her sandals from Tawnya. She felt an occasional twinge in her shoulder as she dressed herself, but it wasn't too bad so she left her sling off. Savanna led her daughter down the stairs into the kitchen.

Rose was already at the stove preparing breakfast. Emily sat at the kitchen table looking completely lost, like she didn't know what to do.

"Savanna, where's your sling?" Emily stood to help her to table.

Savanna waved her away. "I don't need it right now. If I start to hurt I'll put it back on." She pulled out a chair as Travis walked in the room. The kitchen was a little crowded when all five of them were seated at the table. She had a hard time forcing food down as she listened to the others talk.

"I don't know what I'm going to do," Rose said. "Dr. Taylor saved my life when I entered rehab at Haven. I don't know if I would have survived if he hadn't given me a place to stay and a job after I finished my program. Not very many people in the world are willing to hire a former drug addict. He even helped me get back custody of my daughter and let me raise her here. This is the only stable home Chelsea has ever known."

Savanna moved the eggs and toast around her plate. "This will always be your home, Rose. This is my family home and I want it to be maintained for my children. I want them to have a place they'll always be able to come to, no matter what happens. If you leave now I'll just have to find another caretaker and I can't even think about doing that right now."

Thinking about the house made Savanna realize she had a lot of matters to take care of now. Her father's death left a gaping hole in her life, but she wasn't going to have time to think about it. Her responsibilities were going to be overwhelming and she needed to find a way to focus. Emily glanced down at Savanna's plate and then looked at her face. Just as she started to speak the doorbell rang. Savanna stood before anyone else could move, forestalling any comments.

"I'll get it. Finish your breakfast." The security screen showed Captain Peterson standing outside the door, his cap in his hands. Savanna placed her hand on the door sensor, opening the door. Escorting him to the kitchen, she offered him a seat at the table. Emily had already started to clear away the breakfast plates.

Rose offered Peterson a cup of coffee, but he politely declined. Savanna could tell he had some information, but was extremely uncomfortable. She waited for him to speak.

"Dr. Taylor," he began. "We have some news for you.

Umm, I'll start by telling you that we know who murdered your father." Savanna waited, expectantly.

"Finger print and DNA analysis point to his former partner, Dr. Devon Smith." Peterson continued. "It appears they had some type of argument. Security video shows him entering your father's office. He was in the room for about fifteen minutes. We can see him on the video running from the room and down the hall. No one else entered the office until the cleaning crew showed up at about eight o'clock."

Savanna stared at Peterson. "Did you catch him?" The expression on his face told her they hadn't. "Where is he? How did he get away?"

Captain Peterson reached across the table to take Savanna's hands. She pulled back before he could touch them. Travis pulled his chair closer to Savanna and put his arm around her, gently caressing her back with the tips of his fingers. She relaxed into his warmth, waiting for the captain's response.

"Dr. Smith has access to resources beyond the average citizen. His financial resources are varied and vast. He also has a pilot's license. He made it to the airport where he flew out on his private plane. He did log a flight plan, but deviated from it as soon as he got in the air. He's jamming radar, so there's no way of tracking him. Our best guess is that he's somewhere in Western China. There are several defunct airstrips in the Xinjiang province. He has connections in the Chinese government, since he did so much work for them during the one child law crisis and later with the North Korea incident. There's so much unrest in the area, we can't risk sending anyone in to extradite him."

Peterson paused and fingered his cap resting on the table. Savanna was slow to process the information. It seemed to be so much to take in all at once.

Savanna turned her face into Travis's chest. She smelled the clean linen scent of his cotton shirt. Tears welled in her eyes. Blinking, she forced them back. "Why? Why would he want to kill my father? He was such a good man. All he ever wanted to do is help people." Although Savanna managed to keep her tears from falling, her throat was tight as she spoke.

Captain Peterson watched Savanna as she struggled to control her emotions. He cleared his throat before he continued. "Dr. Smith has become increasingly unstable in the past few years. He's a brilliant scientist, but some of his experiments crossed the boundaries of ethical standards. Your father refused to work with him on his latest project. You need to know that Dr. Smith had numerous government contracts. The experiments leading from his research were extremely controversial and there may be some fallout."

Savanna sat up straight. This was something she could understand. Something she could relate to. "I know every experiment my father ran. In fact, I worked with him on some of them, from the time I entered medical school until today." Savanna adjusted her aching shoulder. "My father is an honorable man and I'll do everything in my power to protect him, his name and his work. I'm going to Haven to take over there, just as we planned." Savanna paused and looked at the others sitting at the table. "It's the least I can do to honor his accomplishments. I want to know what's being done to bring his murderer to justice."

Captain Peterson picked up his cap and spun it in his hands. "We don't have an extradition treaty with China. He's also headed into an area that still flooded with fallout from Korea."

Although the incident happened over twenty years ago, Savanna was aware of the devastation of the two bombs. The North Korean government claimed the bombing was an accident. According to the information coming out of Pyongyang a computer malfunction sent two nuclear bombs into Southeast China.

The nuclear fallout made it impossible for relief workers to safely enter the affected areas. Aid had to be air-dropped to survivors and even that wasn't sufficient.

In one of the most devastating events in world history, over a billion people lost their lives. Survivors suffering from the side effects of radiation poisoning pleaded for help from anyone who would listen. Savanna's father was deeply involved with developing treatments for those suffering from long term medical problems from the fallout. Much of his work in this area was still ongoing. The resulting war, known as the Korean War II, sent soldiers through the demilitarized zone to ravage North Korea, ending a fifty-year stalemate and uniting North and South Korea, making the entire country a protectorate of the United States.

Peterson put on his cap and adjusted it over his eyes. "You'll want to make plans for your father's body. We've finished the autopsy and will be releasing his body to the mortuary this afternoon."

Savanna stood to escort him to the door. "I'll have him buried in Haven, beside my mother. He built the community. It's where he'll have his final rest." Opening the door, she dismissed the officer.

The next two days were filled by planning the funeral and the transfer to Haven. Her father knew he was approaching what was considered a high-risk age. He was in his mid-fifties when Savanna was born, her mother was forty-five. Savanna was their fourth and only successful attempt at in-vitro fertilization. As he approached eighty her father had prepared himself to face death. Medicine had come a long way, but it hadn't found a way to cure old age. His will outlined his wishes to the letter, although being murdered wasn't in the plans.

After her final trip to the funeral home to arrange to have her father's remains sent to Haven, Savanna returned to the house on Warm Springs. Rose met her at the door. Travis and Emily sat at the kitchen table looking over information on their data pads.

"What are you two working on?" she asked.

Travis handed her his data pad. "We're looking over our contracts. It appears we work for you now. Emily and I both signed contracts to work for your father and we wanted to make sure the contracts were still valid. It seems they just transfer to you. You're my boss now." Travis smiled.

"Isn't there a clause in there that allows you to opt out of the contract if anything happened to my father?" Savanna wasn't quite prepared to talk about Haven, but since the matter came up she felt this was as good as any time to deal with it.

Emily stood up and came around the table. "We're not going anywhere Savanna. *'Intreat me not to leave thee, or to return from following after thee: for whither thou goest, I will go; and where thou lodgest, I will lodge: thy people shall be my people, and thy God my God.'"*

Savanna smiled. "Emily, I didn't know you were such a fan of the Bible."

"I only know a few verses. That's one of my favorites." Emily embraced Savanna, engulfing her in warmth. Savanna felt tears welling in her eyes. This time she let them fall, allowing the grief to overtake her. Travis came up behind her and put his hands around her waist.

"Since you're my boss, does it mean we're not going to be able to date anymore?"

Savanna stepped back and turned to face Travis. "I... I'm not sure. I'll have to review the code of conduct."

Emily burst into laughter. "Savanna, he's joking. It's not against the rules to date at Haven. In fact, building relationships of trust and love is encouraged."

Raven came into the room, her hair flying around her shoulders. She bounced into the center of the group and held up her arms to be picked up by her mother. "I was sleeping in the room with the stars. I like sleeping in there. It's like sleeping outside."

Savanna loved to listen to her daughter. The only thing keeping her centered was caring for the little one. Holding the girl close, she inhaled the clean scent of her hair. Raven started to squirm, causing a twinge in Savanna's shoulder, so she put her down.

"Is everything ready to go?" Savanna wanted to get to Haven as soon as possible. She wasn't doing any good here and her experiments had already been sent ahead to the compound.

Travis nodded. "Everything's packed in the car. We were just waiting for you."

Savanna looked down at her daughter. "Are you ready to go to our new home, Little One?"

Raven looked up, her forehead scrunched up to show her confusion. "We're not going to stay here where the stars are?"

She knelt so she could be face to face with Raven. She spoke in her gentlest voice. "No, Little One. I have a whole new home for you, a happy place, where you'll be taken care of forever."

Travis drove down dark, paved, quiet roads leading to the secluded Haven complex. Savanna watched the scenery slide by as they passed fields ripening in the hot summer sun. The rich soil offered fertile ground for a variety of crops, one of the benefits of building Haven in this area. The lowlands offered wide fields for growing grains or root crops, rolling hills were covered with green trees covered in rich fruit. The trip to Haven took an hour and a half. An electric car had been exchanged for the truck Travis had used to move Savanna from Arizona. All the contents of the truck had been stored away. Her S290 had been sent ahead to the medical center at Haven along with Savanna's embryos and experiments.

The car approached the metal gate denoting the border of Haven property. Before they could proceed onto Haven grounds the guard at the gate had to scan the micro-chips in the palms of their hands. After he confirmed their identity he pushed the button, allowing the metal gate to slid open. Once they passed through the electric gate the paved road ended. The dirt road leading to Haven was so well maintained Savanna didn't even notice when the car made the transition from the paved highway. She sighed, deeply. She was finally home.

Chapter Twenty

THE CAR DIPPED INTO the tunnel leading to the underground garage. Rows of cars, trucks, four-wheeled and two-wheeled motorcycles, all designed to use solar, electric or nitrogen power, filled the spaces. Travis pulled into a spot. Power cords crisscrossed, dangling from the ceiling. The vehicles were plugged in, keeping batteries charged and ready for service. Savanna stepped out of the car, followed by the three people she now considered her family. They walked directly to the dressing cubicles at the back of the bay. Savanna stepped into a cubicle with Raven, closing her and her daughter off from sight of Emily and Travis.

Savanna helped her daughter strip out of her clothes and took off her own. She placed the clothes and all their belongings in a bin on a shelf. The last thing she removed was the butterfly necklace. The only jewelry allowed in Haven was religious symbols and wedding rings. She placed the necklace on the small pile of clothing, sealed the bin and pushed the button beside the shelf. It rose up and she watched as the vacuum drew the bin into the tube. Savanna pricked her finger with a lancet and forced a droplet of blood onto the test strip provided by the computer. Doing the same for her daughter, she sent the strips into the computer.

A warm mist of water sprayed down from the ceiling. Raven shrieked and raised her arms to the cleansing mist. Savanna assisted her daughter with the sanitizing cleansers, allowing the warm mist to wash away any external contaminants. The shower ended and a disembodied female voice directed them to close their eyes and prepare for a body scan. Savanna covered Raven's eyes. The scanner light wasn't very bright, but repeated exposure could cause retina damage

. It didn't take long for the scan to finish. Determining the newest arrivals weren't trying to smuggle in any contraband or bring in infection, the computer opened the cubicle doors leading to Haven.

Savanna stepped into the dressing room through the air dryers. The warm air caressed her, puckering and dimpling her skin as it removed the water from her body. Her hair was still wet when she put on a blue Haven uniform. The color denoted her affiliation with the medical team. The soft linen clung to her skin, stretching to fit her form. The leather soled shoes were a little stiff, but Savanna knew they would conform to her feet with time.

She ran a brush through her tangled hair and pulled it back. Her daughter had on her own green uniform and was looking around the dressing room. There wasn't much there, so after walking around the room once, she stood in the center and turned around in circles.

"What are you looking for?" Savanna asked.

"Where are my shoes?" Raven asked.

Savanna picked up the shoes provided by Haven. The canvas, slipper-like shoes conformed to Haven's policy of only using natural fibers in clothing.

Raven looked at the shoes in her mother's hand. "Those are not my shoes. I want my shoes!" The little girl's face was twisting into a tantrum.

Kneeling she looked her daughter in the eyes. She kept her voice low and calm, hoping it would help. "Raven, we can't wear our old clothes. They may be contaminated by pollution and disease. We need to wear the clothes provided by Haven."

The reasonable tone wasn't working. Raven's chin started to quiver and her lower lip protruded. Savanna could see the shine in her eyes, signaling the beginning of tears. "Mommy, I want my shoes." Raven's posture stiffened, she arched her back and threw back her head. Savanna knew the small dressing room would soon be reverberating with the child's screams.

"Raven, I'll look for your shoes as soon as we get to our apartment. Could you please just wear these shoes until we get there?" Even as she spoke Savanna realized her reasonable tone wasn't affecting the child.

Raven fell to the floor and started to kick the heels of

her feet against the ground. "No. No. No!" Each syllable was punctuated with a kick. "I want my shoes!" Her wailing almost drowned out the knock on the door.

Savanna waved her hand in front of the sensor, allowing the door to unlock and slide open. Emily walked into the dressing room, looked down at Raven and stood over her with her hands on her hips.

"Why is she throwing a fit?" she asked.

"She wants to wear the shoes that woman gave her back in Nevada. She refuses to wear our shoes," Savanna explained.

Emily shook her head, looking at Savanna then at Raven. Savanna looked down at her daughter, knowing she had to get control of the situation. Taking a deep breath, she cleared her throat. "Raven, stop it!" The voice was much more authoritarian than she wanted it to be, but it made her daughter pause. "You are not allowed to throw temper tantrums and you know it." Raven continued to study her mother. Her breath came out in hiccupping sobs. "Now stand up and put on your shoes."

Tears still streaked down the child's face as she slipped on the shoes. Savanna helped her off the floor and straightened her uniform. "Raven, you know better than to act like that. You need to be a big girl. This new home is going to be a good place for us. Now, let's go see where we'll be living."

Raven's breath still shook with ragged sobs, but she took her mother's hand when offered. "I want to wear my shoes." Her hand pulled on Savanna's like a reluctant weight trying to hold her back as they walked to where Travis was waiting.

His black linen uniform fit snugly over his body. Savanna's eyes traced the outline of his muscles, resting briefly on the thickly defined thighs, the narrow waist and the stacked pectoral spread. She blushed slightly when she realized she was staring. Her eyes met his and she realized he had just finished perusing her form as well.

"Well, these outfits don't leave much to the

imagination, do they?" He grinned at her, white teeth flashing against the darkness of his skin.

Savanna could feel the heat increase as her blush deepened. "They're designed for ease of use and functionality. No one was planning on winning any fashion awards with them."

Travis took Savanna's hand in his. "Are you ready to see your new home?"

With the warmth of Raven at her left and Travis on her right and the quiet strength of Emily behind her, Savanna stepped into the courtyard of Haven.

Savanna knew the layout of the facility. She had studied the plans as she was growing up, trying to understand why it was designed in its unique layout. The main campus of Haven nestled in a valley by a stream, supplying the facility with its main source of water. The octagon shaped building encircled a paved courtyard filled with fruit trees. A walkway skirted the edges of the courtyard, abutting with the sheer walls of the buildings. The walkway was exactly a mile in circumference.

In the center of the courtyard was a two-story brick building, known as the Rec Center. This housed the cafeteria and the public school, kindergarten through twelfth grade. Community members gathered here in the evenings to work on projects, watch movies or play games. On Saturdays and Sundays it was used for religious services. Each of the eight substructures of Haven proper, stretching to cover the length of an acre, connected to form an unbroken wall around the compound.

Haven was the brain child of her father, mother and a team of psychologists and scientists. Her mother had wanted to provide a secure facility for women trying to escape abusive spouses, as well as a place for them to heal physically and emotionally.

Savanna had heard the story of the origins of Haven many times growing up. Her mother was grooming her to take over the reins of the facility almost from birth. The original idea was to create a community where women could stay temporarily, receive counseling and get help finding a job. The first Haven shelter was established in downtown Boise in a refurbished gated apartment complex. Problems cropped up immediately.

Although many women entered Haven with the intent of changing their lives, very few accomplished any real change. Many times the husbands would find the women and break into the complex, initiating late night calls to police. Women would bring addictions with them and it was difficult to keep drugs out since the program was voluntary. Some of the women would refuse counseling or would go for a couple of weeks and quit. These women would, inevitably, return to their abusive spouses.

The residents weren't required to work and could come and go as they pleased. As time went on Savanna's mother became extremely frustrated by the revolving door aspect of the program as well as the women's seemingly inability to be active participants in their own healing. She expressed her frustrations to her husband and together they developed a plan to create a new Haven program. The rules and regulations instituted in the program eliminated many of the growing problems at the facility.

One of the most important regulations was a code of conduct for any resident. In order to join Haven women had to sign a contract promising no drug or alcohol use while in the program. They had to either get and maintain a job or be in an educational program while at the facility. The women were required to complete six months of counseling before they were allowed furloughs off campus for anything other than work or school. The rules were strict and women who didn't follow them were expelled, but the waiting list to get in the program kept getting longer.

Within a few years the Haven Project outgrew the tiny apartment complex and Savanna's parents started exploring options to expand. They lucked into a few research and educational grants and started to plan a self-sufficient, self-sustaining program. The Taylors purchased a forty acre farm an hour and a half outside of the city. By the time the land went into escrow they had recruited a number of highly influential government officials into the program. Two years later, they held a ribbon cutting ceremony for their new building on their now two-hundred-acre parcel of land. The end result was a one-thousand bed facility with a two-hundred bed, in-patient, drug treatment facility; a one- hundred bed hospital, a research laboratory, a counseling center, an agriculture department and an education program offering on-line degree programs from numerous universities.

The main campus was an octagonal building with windowless outer walls built of solid concrete blocks. The only way into the facility was through the basement parking garage on the south side and the entrance to and from the fields to the North. Both entrances were difficult to find, hiding the residents in a cloister-like setting. The location of Haven was not secret. In fact, more than one husband had come to the facility to rage against the acre-long, impenetrable walls.

Anyone could apply to join Haven, but the main focus of the program was the treatment and training of women. The rules became even more stringent, but women who completed the program left completely self-sufficient with marketable job skills. The waiting list became even longer.

It was late afternoon when Savanna arrived at Haven. As she stepped into the courtyard a cool breeze tickled her skin, causing goose bumps to bubble up on her forearms. Raven shivered and huddled close to her mother. Savanna put her hand on the girl's back and rubbed it briskly.

"It's cold, Momma," Raven said.

The temperature was around seventy-five, but the wind chill made it feel closer to seventy. Savanna knew most people in the area felt this was the perfect temperature. In fact, before she moved to Phoenix, this was her favorite climate. The extreme, dry heat of the desert had spoiled her. She looked up at the sky and saw the boiling thunderheads, foreshadowing a thunderstorm in the mountains.

"We're going to have a flash-flood warning tonight."

Savanna could never understand why Idaho was considered high-mountain desert. It always seemed to rain more in the summer than just about anywhere else. Living in Phoenix had taught her exactly what hot, dry desert summers could be.

She could feel eyes studying her as she crossed the courtyard. A crowd was gathering outside the Rec Center. Dropping her hand away from Travis' she stepped forward, her daughter close behind. She knew all these people were under contract to her. They were her responsibility now. A man started walking towards her, a young girl trailing behind him. He approached Savanna and, without a word, embraced her.

"You poor thing. We heard about your injury, and now your father oh, you've really been put through the ringer, let me show you to your apartment and then I will bring you back here for dinner we're so glad you decided to come to Haven right away we have been positively lost without your father. I'm Erik Marshall by the way."

Savanna was trying to figure out where he had paused for breath in his welcome speech and, quite frankly, was shell-shocked by his greeting. This had to be the man Travis had told her about. The little girl trailing behind him, shyly clinging to his pant leg, must be his daughter.

Erik stepped aside and pushed the little girl forward. "This is my little girl. I know your daughter and mine will be close friends."

The girl was obviously shyer than her father. She looked at Raven with big green eyes and a slightly stunned expression on her face. She looked at her father and then back at Raven. Taking her thumb out of her mouth, she gave a shy little smile.

"My name is Aida. Like I eata spaghetti."

Chapter Twenty-One

ERIK LED SAVANNA, EMILY and Raven to the eastern end of the complex, the first block of the residential levels. Travis stayed behind, explaining he needed to check in at the security office and report for duty. Savanna and Emily's apartments were on the third level, right beside the door leading to the research lab. Savanna and Raven's room had belonged to her father and was kept vacant for his frequent visits. Savanna knew exactly where the room was located, but she allowed Erik to lead her down the hall, past white walls devoid of decoration. He showed her to the door and, after another hug, led Emily to a room a few doors down. Savanna placed the palm of her hand on the sensor. The door slid open, revealing the austere room beyond. The door was designed to slide open at the touch of the occupant, but could be temporarily opened by others to allow for cleaning, inspection and medical emergency.

Theft was not a problem at Haven, mainly because residents weren't allowed to keep personal belongings in their rooms. All the physiological and safety needs of the residents were provided by the program. Food, water, clothing and shelter covered basic needs. Security forces patrolling the grounds ensured the safety of the residents. This eight foot by ten foot room would be her home for the rest of her life.

Savanna stepped inside the short entry way. To her left was a double-door closet containing changes of clothing, shoes and a drawer for socks and underwear. To the right was what was commonly called the cubbyhole bathroom, just big enough to contain the toilet, sink and shower. A king-sized bed dominated the room. Everything in the room was white: white walls, white bedding, white cabinets. The room was designed to encourage occupants to use it only for sleeping. The idea was to encourage residents to spend waking hours working on projects outside of their personal space.

As Savanna walked into the room she saw the cubby

hiding the extra shelf-like beds. When she was a child she slept on the bottom of the three bunks. Now her daughter would sleep there, at least until she was twelve. At Haven, a child's twelfth birthday occasioned getting their own room. About half the apartments had these built-in bunks. This allowed residents to stay together as a family. The rooms were connected in pods of four rooms per block. When a family would show up with more than three children they would be housed in pods right next to each other, the older children in one room and the adult and younger children in the other.

Savanna slid open the closet. Uniforms were lined up in precise order. Everything was exactly how it should be. She walked into the bathroom. Toothbrush, hairbrush, soap, towels; everything she needed.

Raven flew past her mother and jumped on the bed. She skidded across, displacing the white comforter. Landing face down, she wrapped the blanket around her body until all Savanna could see was a shock of black hair sticking out of the top of the wrap. Flinging her arms wide Raven burst out of the blanket, like a dark bird taking off in flight. Savanna laughed at the little girl's playfulness. Raven showed no interest in her given name. There were times Savanna considered changing the name on her birth certificate from Bly to Raven, but she wanted her daughter to have the opportunity to use her real name if she ever grew tired of the childhood nickname.

Savanna jumped on the bed and wrapped her arms around her daughter. The ensuing tickle fight left them both giggling and breathless. An alarm on her data pad reminded Savanna dinner was in twenty minutes. She made Raven help her straighten the blankets on the bed before they headed to the Rec Center.

Emily was waiting for them. The women walked with Raven dancing between them. She had obviously overcome her disappointment in her shoe options and was back to being her cheerful, bubbly self. Travis waited for them in the courtyard and, together, they joined the lines for dinner.

All meals at Haven were served cafeteria style from four

different kitchens. Residents were assigned to a cafeteria based on their residential block. Savanna, Emily and Raven were assigned cafeteria A; Travis was in cafeteria C.

He escorted the ladies to their line. "I think I'm going to have to request an apartment change so I can eat my meals with you." He walked around the building to join the block C queue.

Savanna looked over at Emily. "I'm glad he wants to eat with us, but do you think his transfer request will be approved? I mean aren't apartments assigned based on your job requirements? Block C is reserved for security personnel."

Emily started laughing uncontrollably. She physically doubled over, her shoulders twitched with the laughter. When she straightened, she wiped the accumulated moisture from her eyes. "First, he doesn't want to eat with us. He wants to eat with *you.*"

The emphasis made Savanna's face warm. She felt the tips of her ears get hot.

"Second, you're now the administrator of Haven. You're the one who approves room transfer requests. If you want him to move to block A, all you have to do is sign the order."

Savanna could feel the heat radiating off her face. She was glad the line to the cafeteria was moving fast so she wasn't required to speak. Every once in a while Emily would glance at her and giggle. Savanna's face would pink up even more.

Moving through the cafeteria line was a quick, efficient process, orchestrated by careful planning and organization. The logistics of feeding over a thousand residents at one time could have been a nightmare but, since her father had built Haven from the ground up, the project planners were able to design a cafeteria system that worked.

Each cafeteria had its own kitchen overseen by a team of nutritionists. Meals were prepared under strict guidelines. Haven residents would enter the cafeteria and run their micro-chipped palm over the scanner or place their thumb on the scanner if they didn't have a chip. A tray would be dispensed on the roller belt and the resident would take it and step up to the counter. Cafeteria workers would hand them their plate already filled with food.

The entire coordinated effort took less than fifteen minutes. When residents finished their meals they would return the tray to the kitchen, where workers would scan the barcode on the tray, record what was eaten and make a note in the records. If the resident hadn't eaten enough of their meal to fulfill dietary requirements a reminder was sent to their data pad and they were required to return to the cafeteria at snack time. There they would receive some form of snack, depending on their food intake, to supplement their diet.

Once Savanna received her tray of food, she turned to find a place to sit with her family. Although the cafeteria's capacity was only two hundred and fifty Savanna felt there were a lot more people here. And it seemed like every one of them were staring directly at her. For a moment she just stood, staring into the sea of faces. She caught movement out of the corner of her eye and noticed Erik waving her over and pointing at an empty bench. Shrugging, she looked at Emily. Emily nodded and walked to the table. Savanna and Raven fell in step behind her.

The food was better than she remembered. One of the many grants used in building Haven involved nutrition and mental health recovery. Savanna's father had recruited several health and nutrition students and specialists from a program at Boise State to help build the nutrition program at Haven. He also tapped into the food service program to build his kitchen staff. A number of those former students now ran the meal program on the Haven campus. This was also the height of the growing season, so the meals included a high percentage of fresh summer fruit and vegetables.

Savanna savored the food on her plate. She knew she would soon be out in the fields with the other members of the community helping plant, harvest and prepare the food. A rule of Haven was if you wanted to eat, you had to work. No one ever went hungry while they were living in Haven, but community members were required to put in at least ten hours of food prep labor per week, no matter what program or job they had at the campus. If a resident ever slacked in their duties, or decided not to participate in the program, and all counseling failed, a council was called. If it was determined the individual was noncompliant with Haven policy they would be expelled from the program.

Savanna had nearly cleared her plate of all her food, but Emily was pushing her steamed green beans around her plate. She sighed and put down her fork. "I could really go for some chocolate cake right now."

Raven's eyes lit up and she looked at her aunt. "Can I have cake, too?"

Savanna put her arm around her child and pulled her close to her side. "Aunt Emily was just teasing, Little One. We don't have any cake here." She moved the bowl of fresh cut peaches closer to her daughter. "Eat your peaches. That'll satisfy your sweet tooth."

Raven looked at her peaches and sighed. "I miss cake." She picked up her spoon and started in on the fruit.

Erik chuckled. "Our daughters are so much alike. I couldn't keep Aida out of the cookie jar from the time we brought her home. I never knew anyone who had a sweeter tooth than she did."

Aida picked up green beans with her fingers and put them in her mouth. She grinned when she heard her father talking about her. Erik gently placed a fork in the little girl's hand. "Use your fork, Honey."

He returned to the conversation. "It didn't take long for her to get used to the food here. In fact, she's lost quite a bit of weight since we came to Haven." He pinched the little girl's cheek and kissed the top of her head. "She was a pudgy little thing."

Savanna studied the child sitting across from daughter. She couldn't help comparing the two girls. Aida was slightly shorter than Raven and lacked some of the physical coordination seemingly ingrained in her daughter. Raven held her spoon with more skill and determination than Aida, whose fork tended to waiver and spin in her pudgy fingers. Aida's golden-brown hair was trimmed to shoulder length and had a slight wave. Raven's long black hair fell straight to the small of her back. Both girls were concentrating on their food. The intensity on their faces echoed each other. Their brows furrowed into a knot, mouths held tight in a slight pout and eyes, Raven's brown and Aida's green, focused on every scoop going from the plate to their mouths.

Savanna turned her focus back to Erik. He had finished his dinner and was removing the sterilizer pad from its package and cleaned his hands. "How long have you been at Haven?" she asked.

Erik looked at the ceiling, "Well, it's been about a year now." He continued talking without being prompted. "Ronnie and I had been married for about a year when I asked if we could adopt a child. He never really wanted to have children. I think Ronnie had kind of a rough childhood. His family was very poor and, he never explicitly said anything, but I suspect there was a fair amount of abuse involved in his childhood. He was afraid we wouldn't have the resources to care for a child. Ronnie wanted to make me happy though, so we started adoption procedures."

Erik paused and looked at Savanna. "Everything was fine for awhile. Aida was such a good baby. She was a little over a year old when she came to us. I decided I wanted to be a stay at home dad, so I resigned from my nursing position at the hospital. Ronnie was working as an IT specialist at a startup software company. The company was downsized and when he lost his job it seemed like he lost himself. I went back to work and he stayed home with Aida."

Savanna had heard so many of these stories over the years she could almost predict exactly what Erik was going to say next. "Ronnie was rarely physically violent, but he just couldn't seem to work himself out of the depression he spiraled into since he lost his job. We started fighting like we never had before. He became physically abusive and the way he used to rage at me was terrifying. At first I thought he would find a job and it would all stop, but then one day I came home and he was just tearing into Aida. I couldn't let him do that, not to my little girl. I packed my bags and went to a community shelter."

The tables surrounding the group were all starting to empty. Erik looked around and started to pick up his tray. Savanna reached out and stopped him. "No, I want to hear more."

Erik put his tray down and continued his story. "There's not much more to tell. Most shelters are designed for single men or women with children. The community house I entered is one of the few designed for families. The shelter was over-crowded, so one of the counselors recommended I apply for Haven. Your father interviewed me personally. He got me in here and offered both me and Ronnie counseling. I started my Master's in social work about a month after I entered Haven. I'll graduate in a year."

"Did Ronnie take up Dr. Taylor's offer?" Emily asked. It appeared she was as caught up in Erik's story as well.

"Yes, he started counseling sessions two months ago. I've been joining him for couple's therapy on my furloughs. When I finish my program, we're going to try to get back together." This time as he started to gather his tray Savanna didn't stop him. She wiped her hands with the sanitizing cloth and helped Raven with hers. They were the last group to leave the cafeteria, but Savanna felt the time she spent listening to Erik was valuable. His story emphasized why she came to Haven.

Chapter Twenty-Two

THE FUNERAL FOR SAVANNA'S father was the next morning. A small plot of grass in the shadow of the research center was excavated. The residents of Haven all gathered, vying for the best position to watch. Savanna wanted to keep things as simple as possible. She placed the urn containing her father's ashes in the vault lining the bottom of the hole. Next to it she placed her mother's urn. She had taken it from the mantle of her family home and had it sent to Haven. Travis helped her seal the tiny crypt and cover it with a layer of sandy soil. A small group of people helped plant a flowering almond over the gravesite.

Savanna approached the lectern. Microphones and cameras winked in the sunlight. The world wanted to see Dr. Jackson Taylor laid to rest. Savanna knew her image was being sent all over the world. She was glad Raven was tucked away in the mass of people watching the service. Savanna made it a goal to keep Raven as far away from the public eye as possible. Closing her eyes, she tried to still the echoing beat of her heart and stop the quivering of her knees. Her mind went blank as her heart raced and blood roared in her ears. The sea of faces blurred together and tears gathered in her eyes. Her throat tightened and she had to work to get the words out. Raven stood at her side as she prepared to say the final words to honor her father.

Savanna couldn't speak. Sorrow and fear choked her and she was unable to force the words past the knot in her throat. Movement in the front of the crowd drew her eye. Travis had taken a step out of the crowd towards the lectern. The movement brought Savanna's thoughts into focus and she started the speech she had prepared to honor her father.

"My father was the greatest man I ever knew." She realized her voice was too quiet. She tried to adjust the volume.

"My father dedicated his life to helping others. He studied genetics as a way to help those who couldn't conceive.

He built Haven to protect victims of domestic violence and provide them a place to heal and grow. My childhood home was a happy place, full of joy and love. He provided me with a safe place to grow and instilled a love for learning that I know I'll pass on to my daughter and any other children I may have."

Savanna paused to look down at her daughter. She placed her hand on the black hair and brushed it back. "My father may have passed from this life, but his work and his dream didn't." She gestured at the building behind her. "I will continue his work and grow his dreams here at Haven. Even though he is gone, his spirit will never leave this place."

Savanna left the platform and walked towards Travis. Before she could reach him, the crowd moved forward, surrounding her. She was engulfed in a sea of faces, all of them with tears flowing down their cheeks. Voices clamored for her attention begging for words to relieve their own pain. Raven moved to stand by her legs and Savanna reached down and picked her up, trying to protect her from the massive crowd. A twinge of pain shot through her shoulder, but she held Raven close to her chest. She heard Emily call her voice and automatically turned to her friend. Emily wrapped an arm around her and used her other arm to maneuver through the crowd.

"Please, give her room." Emily's voice seemed to soothe the crowd and they started to move out of the way. Savanna felt a presence at her other side and she looked up to see Erik standing beside her.

"Everything'll be okay." His voice soothed her and quieted the crowd. "Allow Dr. Taylor to go to her office. We all have work to do. Please, the best way to honor Dr. Taylor is to continue his work at Haven."

The crowd started to disperse and Travis was able to make his way to her. Emily took Raven from Savanna's arms, moving out of the way. Travis traded places with Emily, putting his arm around Savanna. She felt protected by his warmth. Erik led them all through the entrance of the research center. The closed doors blocked the crowd outside.

A girl sat at the front desk. As the group moved closer she stood up. Savanna judged her to be about seventeen or eighteen years old. The girl's long blond hair was pulled back into a loose ponytail, curling in ringlets until it brushed her shoulders. Like Savanna, Emily and Erik, the girl was wearing a blue uniform. A pink smock over the top classified her as an intern in the nursing program.

Erik moved around to the other side of the desk and pulled a data pad out of a pouch on his belt. "Molly, go do your rounds. The other staff members will be here in a few minutes to help." Molly left the desk and headed down the hall to attend to her duties. Erik looked at Savanna and motioned her over.

"I know you're familiar with the operating system here at Haven, but this kiosk was put in just six months ago." Savanna approached the desk. A number of touch screens were imbedded in the panel. Erik placed his palm over the red scan light and all of the screens lit up. Savanna quickly scanned the readouts. The center screen was the most prominent. It displayed vitals for patients in the hospital. Erik used a stylus to tap a few times on his data pad and the patient list changed.

"This is my job," Erik said. "I manage the hospital and rehab center nursing staff and monitor patient progress from this desk. I know exactly what's happening with every patient in every room." He pointed to several monitors, each showing patients rooms and the activity inside. "These are patient rooms in the rehab center and in the high-risk unit."

Savanna watched the screens for a moment. Most of the residents were sleeping. A few were involved in activities in their room; reading, walking around, using the bathroom.

"Most of the people in these rooms are new arrivals. They're still in the early stages of their recovery, that's why they stayed in their rooms during the funeral."

Erik aimed the camera down the hall to follow Molly as she made rounds. "Molly came to us two years ago. Her story is indicative of the residents of this unit. She started using drugs when she was ten and developed a drug addiction. By the time she was fifteen she'd been arrested four times and was a habitual run away. Her parents didn't know what to do with her, so they sent her here. Haven has helped her find purpose and she's become one of the best nursing interns we've ever had."

Savanna watched Molly as she walked from room to room bringing changes of bedding and clothing. Screens flashed showing patients in rooms and displaying vitals to correspond with the person. It was a lot of information to take in at once. Erik tapped his stylus against the pad again. "This system can also alert me if there's anything that needs attention. The work station in your office runs on a similar setup. Your father was planning on training you on how to use it before, well…" Erik let his voice trail off.

"I've been studying the computer system over the past couple of months." Savanna ran her hand over the scanner and uplinked her data pad to the work center. "I know the operating systems, but it's different being able to see it in action." She studied the information as it was loaded onto her pad. "There are a hundred and seven patients in the rehab center right now?"

Erik nodded. "Some are ready to be assimilated into Haven. It'll be your job to assign them quarters and sign them up for work duty."

Savanna knew she had a big job ahead of her. It wasn't going to be easy taking over as the administrator of Haven. When her father originally offered her the job they planned on slowly phasing her in over the course of five years. She wasn't expecting to be thrust into management right away.

Savanna's life become a whirlwind of logistics and management. Over the next few months she dedicated herself to learning the logistics of running the Haven program. Knowing the theory of Haven and running the facility were completely different things. Savanna didn't have any spare time to work on her experiments as she was learning the ins and outs of managing the facility.

Savanna had read the case histories of all the residents,

but she wanted to meet with each one of them and listen to their stories. Many of them were echoes of Erik's or Molly's. Almost all of them involved a history of abuse either in childhood or in relationships, sometimes both. Drugs and alcohol abuse were prevalent in almost all the histories. Learning the stories was not difficult, Haven residents were encouraged to talk about their life as part of the healing process. They were required to attend at least one group counseling meeting a week, as well as specific individually assigned counseling. Savanna and Emily joined a weekly group session, but Savanna would occasionally attend other sessions as an observer.

All the residents were required to submit a weekly work schedule to the main database. Their weekly work schedule, counseling, exercise, education plan, rest and relaxation and ten hours of labor in food production a week kept residents focused. Savanna joined the work crews headed to the fields or gardens at least once a week. Emily and Travis joined her as often as they could and Raven was always at her side.

She was glad she wasn't required to work with animals as part of her responsibilities. All the meat and dairy products were provided by off-site sister farms. The knowledge base and time commitment for this type of work didn't fit into Haven's program.

The farms were managed by experts trained in Animal Husbandry. Farm hands were culled from residents of the project. In some cases, they were individuals who needed a little more time in a structured program and the farm became a type of half-way house for them. In others, the residents wanted to earn a degree in Animal Husbandry or veterinarian medicine and the farms became their training grounds.

There were other, similar, programs scattered throughout many states: clothing factories, food manufacturers, technology programs, research and medical programs, all outcrops of the Haven project. Graduates of Haven were practically guaranteed a job in any field they were interested in, or had the skill set to perform. This program had helped thousands of people, most of them women, when society or life circumstances failed them.

One week after she took control of the facility Travis' room transfer request appeared on Savanna's data pad. She had to wait until an opening came up on block A before she could approve the request. In the meantime, they scheduled their exercise and work duties to coincide. Travis continued his flirtation with her and, after a few weeks, she barely blushed when he would make a comment about her beauty. She started to develop a sense of comfort she had never felt with a man before.

Emily took over many of Savanna's responsibilities in the lab. Savanna had cultivated several fetuses and they were ready for transplant. The parents anxiously awaited the opportunity to attempt implantation. Once a week Emily would leave Haven to bring the prepared fetuses to the medical center in Boise and assist with the transplants. She would return to Haven and describe what was happening outside the shelter walls.

A new outbreak of tuberculosis, a strain mutated from the terrorist strand, developed in upper New York State. The announcement caused wide-spread panic throughout many of the previously affected countries. Border control became even tighter. Cities and towns began developing their own militias. These militias were illegal, of course, but it didn't stop them from forming.

Perhaps the hardest news for Savanna to hear was stemming from the extreme sects, both religious and political. During the interviews with the women in the compound Savanna heard a variety of opinions about the current government managed health care.

The people of Haven came from a variety of backgrounds. Domestic abuse was a problem without class, age, race or gender discrimination. The women and men of Haven brought their personal beliefs with them, and they were encouraged to continue to develop those beliefs as part of their therapy. Some of the extreme opinions Savanna heard included the idea that the five plagues were designed by the current United States government as an attempt to gain more control of the health care system.

Theories about the plagues weren't discussed openly in the counseling sessions, but many of the residents shared their thoughts in community or religious meetings. Travis attended one of the Sunday services every week and invited Savanna to join him. She declined, wanting to spend the time in her lab, but when Raven expressed an interest Savanna allowed Emily to take her. Savanna used the opportunity to spend a few quiet hours in her lab, something she wasn't usually able to do for long blocks of time.

Raven, like any young child introduced to a new situation, adapted to living at Haven as if she was born there. Savanna rarely saw her daughter without the company of Aida. The two girls spent most of their time together, heads bent close, whispering and giggling to each other.

Raven entered school in the same pod as Aida, their birthdays falling only two months apart. Intellectually they almost matched although developmentally, Aida seemed to lag slightly behind her friend.

Savanna spent some time studying Aida's medical records. The child had spent the first six months of her life in an orphanage in New Orleans. Both of her parents had died from an E. coli outbreak. Her mother was pregnant when she became infected and delivered Aida a month early. Due to the health and development concerns of premature infants, it was difficult to find an adoptive home for her. The orphanage wasn't the best place for an infant with special needs and by the time Erik adopted her she had some severe delays. Erik's love and work with the child helped overcome some of those delays, but she still had a ways to go.

Savanna's free time was dedicated to her daughter. Emily worked the evening shift at the hospital, taking a shift that allowed her to care for Raven during the day while Savanna worked. Between the two of them and Erik they were able to care for and supervise both girls. Aida and Raven would take turns sleeping in the bunks in either Erik's or Savanna's room. Erik sometimes took Raven when Savanna needed to spend extra time in the lab, allowing her to do experiments she otherwise would not be able to perform with limited lab time. The familial atmosphere gave Savanna the opportunity to heal from the loss of her father and continue to develop her experiments and projects.

About six weeks after Savanna arrived at Haven a room in A Block opened up and she completed Travis' transfer. Much to everyone's delight he joined the family in the cafeteria for meals.

Summer slowly faded into fall and the rate of harvest increased. Savanna spent some time working in the food processing factory to learn how food was prepared for storage. Her goal was to spend time working every job at Haven, as long as she had the skills to do it, so she had an idea of the inner workings of the facility.

Fresh, raw food always had the best nutritional value, but during winter accessibility to fresh fruits and vegetables was limited to what grew in the green houses and what could be shipped from sister farms in warmer climates. To maximize the nutritional value of food coming through the process centers the food was either flash frozen or freeze dried.

One of the most remarkable aspects of Haven was the policy of living life with zero waste. The majority of energy used by the facility was provided by alternative fuel sources. Massive solar panels installed on the roof of all the buildings, windmills and water turbines all contributed to providing energy. The farm equipment ran on solar energy. Food was stored in paper or cloth bags or reusable glass containers. This type of storage wasn't optimal, but it helped reduce the carbon footprint.

Savanna enjoyed the hard work and Raven thrived in the nurturing climate of Haven. Much of the exhaustion Savanna felt from the past six years seemed to fade as Haven took her attention. She felt safe and secure, locked away from the dangers in the outside world. Her focus turned to developing stem cell research attempting to increase the disease resistance of embryos. Life was good and the new lives she was creating were even better.

Chapter Twenty-Three

THE BEGINNING OF WINTER brought changes to Haven. Harvest season was over and the focus turned to land preparation. Savanna grew to trust her support staff and gave them more management responsibilities. The temperature started to drop and outdoor activity slowed. Savanna turned her focus to genetics.

The fetuses she had brought with her to Haven had all been implanted, but other couples sent their genetic material or requests for fetal adoption. Savanna reveled in her research. This is what she had dreamed of doing since she had moved to Phoenix. Here she could focus on her work in the safety and security of her lab.

Savanna was in her office in the late afternoon reviewing work orders when the chime at the door drew her attention. Molly's pretty, moon-shaped face appeared on the screen beside the door. Savanna put aside her work and opened the door. Gesturing to the girl, she invited her in to sit down. Molly sat on the edge of the chair twisting her hands in her smock, wrinkling the fabric. Savanna gave her a glass of water to calm her nerves.

"How are you doing Molly?" While Molly took a sip of water Savanna pulled up the girl's records. The original intake photo of the girl was completely unrecognizable from the girl sitting in front of her. Savanna noticed the intake date at the lower right-hand corner. Molly had been at Haven for two and a half years, exactly two years longer than Savanna.

Molly placed her glass on the corner of Savanna's desk and wiped her hands on the legs of her uniform. "Dr. Taylor, I wanted to talk to you. I mean we wanted to talk to you."

The girl became more nervous, so Savanna stood up from her desk and moved to a chair beside her. She took Molly's hands in her own. This seemed to calm her down and she began again.

"Dr. Taylor, when I came here I was a mess. You've

seen my records. You know I've not always made the right choices in my life. I broke my parents' hearts more than once. I also drained their bank accounts. My college fund is gone." Molly paused and took a breath. She stood up and paced for a moment, Savanna could tell she was fighting back tears. "Haven saved me. I found my sense of purpose here."

Savanna smiled, she could tell Molly was well on her way to being one of Haven's success stories. Just her mention of wanting to go to college showed the progress she was making. The faded scars on the girl's arms gave testament to her shaky past and the desolation the girl had felt in her hopes for the future. Molly leaned forward, her nerves still apparent, but she had a sense of intensity in her eyes.

"It sounds like Haven was here for you when no one else was." Savanna felt a sense of peace as she realized her father's legacy had every chance of continuing.

Molly nodded. "I'm going to graduate from high school next month. When I came here, I had three credits and I was sixteen years old. I'll turn nineteen in three months. Some of the classes I took gave me college credit, enough so that when I applied to a nursing program, I was accepted."

"That's wonderful Molly. I'm glad you have found success here." Savanna said.

Molly stood and paced again, this time she didn't return to her chair. "I can't afford tuition." She blurted the words out, as if she was afraid of their affect. "I applied for financial aid and I've been offered some loans, but there're no grants available. I don't want to start my new life in debt."

Savanna nodded, beginning to understand where Molly was headed. "There are a number of grants and scholarships available. We have a few specialists here who can help you find them. Would you like me to set an appointment for you?" She reached for her data pad.

"That's just it." Molly sat down in the chair and leaned towards Savanna. "We found one. It's called Scholarships for Surrogates."

Savanna had never heard of this program before.

"Molly, I don't like the sound of this program. There are strict laws surrounding the use of surrogates. Surrogate mothers aren't allowed to profit from carrying a child."

"We know. We've researched this." The determination in Molly's eyes didn't fade, if anything, it became more intense.

Savanna stood up. "Who's the 'we' you keep mentioning?"

Molly swallowed, her nervousness becoming more apparent. "There're twenty of us interested in the program. We researched it and it's completely legal. Prospective parents pay into a scholarship fund to reimburse the surrogate. All medical expenses are covered as well as tuition for any state college." She paused. "The surrogate promises to carry two children for parents who invest in the program. The first pregnancy needs to be confirmed before scholarship funds are released. We've all signed up for it."

Savanna knew there was more information coming. She waited for Molly to continue, completely at a loss for words.

"There's a campus for the girls in every state in the union, except for Idaho, Utah and Cuba."

"Are you girls going to need travel papers to another state? It's going to take a while to get Visa's and health checks together." Savanna was disappointed the girls wanted to leave Haven. She wasn't sure if all of them would be ready to graduate the Haven program.

"That's just it," Molly continued. "It's easier for fetuses to travel across state lines than people."

Savanna started to get what Molly was hinting at. "Emily has applied for a grant to open a facility in Idaho. She's been working with us since the beginning."

This piece of information surprised Savanna. Emily was usually pretty open with any of the programs with which she was involved.

"So, the thing is, we obtained a grant, but it's not enough. But, well…" Molly took a deep breath and suddenly started talking very fast. "We have everything we need to open a facility here at Haven. The grant will pay for the medical supplies. We'll all continue to follow Haven's policies. Emily has it all worked out on paper. Your father's dream was to help families who couldn't conceive. We believe this is our way to help him accomplish this goal."

Molly handed Savanna a data disk, a little square inch black cube. "All of the information is there, including Emily's proposal. She was planning on presenting it to you, but I felt it would be better if one of us approached you with it." Molly smiled, the nervousness was still in her face, but it carried with it a sense of relief. "Please, consider it. For some of us it's the only way we'll be able to fund our education."

After Molly left, Savanna reviewed the information Emily had sent. The surrogate program appeared to have some validity to it. The girls had to sign contracts acknowledging they had no claim on the children and would willingly surrender all infants at birth. There was a list of rules and covenants each surrogate needed to follow and commit to before she could be considered for candidacy. Her pad alarm went off, signaling the dinner hour. Savanna didn't feel she had enough information to make a decision, so she carried her pad with her to the cafeteria.

Her family was already seated at their table. Raven and Aida were whispering to each other. Aida had one arm around Raven's shoulders. Savanna sat beside Travis and placed her data pad on the table so she could focus on her food. Erik glanced at the pad in front of Savanna.

"What's this, Doctor? You usually don't bring your work to dinner with you. Surrogacy? Is this going to be an extension of your genetic research?" he asked.

Savanna picked up the pad and started to scroll through the document. "It's a program that was brought to my attention today. I want to look into it before I okay it."

"What's it all about?" Travis smiled at her. Her heart sped up and her ears tingle.

Savanna looked back at the pad and scrolled through the information. "It's a surrogacy program, called Surrogacy for Scholarships. It looks like it's legitimate, but I don't want to make a snap judgment on this. It could have some pretty severe consequences for the young women involved. Going through a pregnancy with all the hormonal and emotional baggage and then giving up the baby can take a severe emotional toll on someone, even if the baby isn't genetically theirs."

Erik took the pad back and started scrolling through the information. He spent a few minutes studying the screen. Emily placed her tray on the table. She dropped into the seat beside Erik.

"Sorry I'm late. I had to replace an IV at the rehab center. The woman pulled it before the anti-narcos could get in her system. I have a feeling she's going to have a tough time in the program. It's an involuntary placement. So, anything exciting happening?"

"Molly came to see me today."

Emily froze. "What do you think of her idea?"

Savanna chose her words very carefully. "I haven't made any final decisions yet." Savanna studied her friend for a few minutes. Emily had changed over the past six months. The diet and exercise program helped her drop forty pounds and her face reflected her growing health. Savanna returned her focus to her meal. "I need to spend some more time studying the details. On paper everything looks good, but I want to make sure to protect the girls."

"Savanna, you need to understand a few things. This world is going to pot." Savanna tried to interrupt her friend, but Emily held her hand up to forestall any comments. "No, you have to listen to this. You've lived a sheltered life. Your father protected you from the realities of the world. Infertility isn't the only problem we're facing. Crime, drugs, divorce, it's all on the rise. There isn't a lot of hope in the world right now."

"I'm not clueless, Emily!" She hated it when Emily treated her like a child.

"Just listen." Emily's tone was one Savanna had never heard her use before. "The world has been in a negative population decline for the past fifteen years. The population spiked at nine billion in 2022. Now it's back down to just fewer than six billion and it's steadily decreasing. There aren't enough healthy babies being born. At this rate, humans are going to be an endangered species." Emily completely ignored her food. "This is our chance to affect real change in the world. Babies are being sold on the black market. Women are selling their bodies to become surrogate mothers. They're clinging to men who have proven fertility, begging them to get them pregnant. There's even a sect whose entire premise is based on a fertilization program. Girls are not considered women until they have given birth to their first child and have no rights until they do. It's degrading, but they're so brainwashed there's no way to help them. This program gives those girls a future. It helps parents who want children and have the resources to care for them. We can make a difference in this world."

"Will twenty babies really make a difference? I mean were talking about millions of children here." Savanna pushed the dregs of her soup away. Her stomach was tied in knots and there was no way she could eat any more.

Emily moved the data pad in front of Savanna and showed her a screen. "Twenty babies is just the start. We have thousands of women moving through Haven. We can provide strong, healthy babies for countless women. And what's the trade-off? Eighteen months of pregnancy? The girls will each have a college degree when they finish the program."

Savanna took the data pad and looked at Emily's numbers. "Emily, not every member of Haven is going to want to participate in this program. Even if every woman is willing to participate, less than half of them would be eligible to be surrogates according to the guidelines."

"I know, Savanna." Emily sounded tired, but she persisted. "I don't expect to change the world. I just want to make a tiny difference." She stood up and picked up her tray. "I need to get back to work. Think about it, please, Savanna. You know I've been spending some of my furlough volunteering at a free clinic in town. You should come with me some time. Leave your nice sterile lab and see the world the way it really is." Emily turned and took her tray to the depository.

Savanna looked down at her daughter. The girl was looking at her with bright brown eyes. "Mommy, were you and Aunt Emmy fighting?"

"We weren't really fighting. We just have different opinions about a few things. We'll work things out." She brushed the hair out of her daughter's eyes

Raven turned back to her tray. "Look Mommy, I finished all my food. Can Aida and me go for our walk now? Uncle Erik will take us." Savanna nodded and watched as her daughter left with her friend, following Erik to the track.

Travis was still sitting at the table studying the data pad.

"It doesn't seem right for girls to have to pay for their education this way." Savanna said.

"But if they're helping women who can't have children it's their choice." He put the pad down and took her hand. "What would you do if you discovered you couldn't carry another child? Wouldn't you be willing to do anything you could to have a baby?"

Savanna's finger tips tingled from the warmth of Travis' hand. She swallowed down her nervousness before she answered. "I wouldn't mind having another child, sooner rather than later. I have several zygotes stored away just for that possibility. Since I've finally settled in here I've been thinking about attempting another in vitro procedure, probably in the spring. I don't want to be pregnant during the heat of summer, like I was with Raven."

Travis brought her hand up to his mouth and gently kissed her palm. "Have you ever thought about having a child the natural way?"

Savanna felt her face heat up and she knew it was a bright cherry red. Looking around the room she noticed it had cleared out, only a few workers were left, but they were busy cleaning the tables. She stammered for a few seconds. "I— I… umm, well I trust the tests I have run on these zygotes and I know they're genetically stable. If I do have a child with someone, I would want to make sure they're genetically stable as well, for the sake of the child. I would also want to make sure I had a commitment contract with the father."

"Hmm." Travis leaned in, close to her face. "You've really thought about this, haven't you? So, do you ever stop thinking and just feel?"

He was so close to her she could feel his hot breath on her face. Her pulse started to race and her breath quickened. She held herself completely still as he closed in on her. His lips gently brushed against hers. Savanna opened her mouth slightly as he pulled her closer. She loved these little tender moments when they could be together. Travis released her, whispering against her lips. "Why don't you go into town with Emily? Don't worry. I'll go with you. I'll protect you." Savanna relaxed in his arms.

Chapter Twenty-Four

THE NEXT AFTERNOON, FOR the first time in six months, Savanna prepared to leave Haven. Raven looked forward to spending the night at Aida's apartment. Erik was thrilled with the prospect of watching her overnight. Emily had been staying at Savanna's family home the twenty-four hours she was off-site. Savanna dialed up Rose to let her know to expect two other visitors in addition to Emily. She put in a request to have clothes ready to change into as she left the facility.

The group left in the early evening. Emily had talked Savanna into wearing a pair of jeans and a T-shirt, an outfit more appropriate for fitting in with residents of the city. Travis drove Haven's unmarked hydrogen powered van. Savanna climbed in the passenger seat and buckled her seatbelt. Emily was rearranging some supplies in the back of the van before she took her place.

"Why aren't we taking a solar powered vehicle?" Savanna asked. "They're more eco-friendly."

Emily fastened her own seatbelt before answering. "We're going to be heading into some pretty tough neighborhoods. The solar powered vehicles don't have enough power to get away if we run into any trouble. Plus, all the other vehicles are marked with the Haven symbol. It's pretty recognizable."

Travis turned the key in the ignition and backed out of the parking space as Emily continued talking. "Everyone knows Haven has a medical center and the vehicles sometimes transport medical supplies, food—"

"And other things," Travis interrupted.

Savanna noticed Emily's lips thinned and disappeared in a straight line, a sure sign she was upset. "Drivers have been attacked a couple of times by gang members trying to steal their load. It can get pretty rough out there."

Emily looked out the window as they drove out of the

garage. She pointed to the clouds visible through the sunroof. "Besides, it's cloudy today. The solar vehicles could have problems getting enough energy to maintain their charges."

Savanna looked at the grey clouds weighing heavily in the sky. The van's tires crunched on the grey snow. It seemed the whole world was grey. Even the wool coat Savanna was wearing was grey. Back in Phoenix the temperature was 54 degrees, she looked it up this morning before breakfast, balmy compared to the 29 degrees now registering on the van's external temperature reading.

The guard looked miserable as he huddled in his gate house, bundled in a coat and gloves. His hands were wrapped around a mug emitting steam. He put the mug down and, leaving the warmth of the gate house and scanned the palms of the passengers in the van.

"Dr. Taylor, I almost didn't believe it when I saw your name on the furlough list. I've heard a lot about you, but I haven't had the chance to meet you yet."

Emily reached her hand out of the car, interrupting the young man's greeting. "We need to get on the road. Could you scan us so we can get through?"

The young man looked stricken, but did as he was told. After scanning the passengers, he typed in the code to open the gate and waved the group through.

"You were pretty short with the guard at the gate, Emily." Savanna flipped her mirror on the visor down so she could see Emily without twisting in her seat.

"I guess I'm just a little anxious about this trip. I'll apologize tomorrow when we get back." Emily turned and looked out the window.

Emily didn't speak for the rest of the trip. Savanna and Travis chatted about the plans to rotate crops in the spring and discussed what jobs they would sign up for once planting season began. Savanna was surprised by how much knowledge she had gained in the farming arts since she started working the harvest.

"I think I'm going to start working in the green houses

this winter." Savanna watched the sun peek in and out of the clouds as she spoke. "There's a whole aspect of natural medicine I haven't even explored in the herb gardens. Sometimes science is so caught up in chemical composition we tend to forget the natural remedies available. We sometimes run short on medical supplies and I'd like to find some alternative medicines to supplement our pharmacy."

Travis pulled on the freeway and programmed the auto-pilot to cruise at ninety-five. The freeway was clear of snow and ice and there was very little traffic to impede their progress. Rays of sunlight strained through the clouds, turning the edges of the clouds a silvery white, and streamed down beams from above. Savanna stared quietly out the window, watching the play of the sun reflecting off the snow on the mountain. A bright shaft of light burst through the clouds and played across the top of a snow-capped mountain peak, dancing its last homage to the setting sun.

The rest of the trip passed in silence, the occupants of the van lost in their own reflections. Travis exited at Broadway and started the decent into downtown. Savanna remembered the last trip down this road and its tragic end. A knot formed in her throat as she thought about her father and she swallowed back tears.

Travis pulled into the driveway of Savanna's family home. The white-sided building stood out from the grey background, like a beacon in the fading light. Savanna stood on the front porch for a moment, staring at the broad oak doors. This was the house she grew up in, but she couldn't really call it home any more. How could she? Everything she loved was at Haven. A wave of homesickness overwhelmed her and for a moment she couldn't move. Then Travis looked back and his dark brown eyes drew her into him. She took the last steps toward the door and, together, they entered the house.

In the kitchen, the table was set with her mother's white china and a roasted chicken smell welcomed them. Rose stood in the kitchen putting the final touches on a salad. As soon as the group walked in the door, Rose brought the salad to the table.

"Good, I'm glad you made it on time. I was afraid dinner would get cold. Emily, the movie starts in forty minutes, if we want to get there on time we better leave now." She took off her apron as she spoke and picked up her purse. Savanna looked between her friend and her father's housekeeper.

"Rose and I go to a movie every time I come to town." Emily had two dark spots on her cheeks, as if she was embarrassed about something. "The movie has an early start, so we'll eat dinner when we get back." The two women walked out before Savanna could say anything.

Turning to Travis, Savanna saw a huge smile on his face. "That was strange," she said. "What's Emily hiding? I've never seen her act like that before."

Travis took Savanna by the elbow and led her to the table. "It's nothing. We just never get the chance to be alone. I asked Emily if she and Rose could find a way to get out of the house for a while."

"Oh." The tips of Savanna's ears were burning. She couldn't focus on dinner and, for once, she was glad there was no one around to record her food intake.

Travis kept the conversation light as they ate, putting her at ease. The conversations steered itself around to life before Haven. Travis was telling Savanna about his college years and the goals he had before he met her father. "Do you know I received my teaching credentials after I graduated?" he asked.

Savanna shook her head. This new information surprised her.

"I thought if things didn't work out for me at Haven I could always coach and teach high school. I was about to start applying for jobs in some of the school districts, but then your father sent me to fetch you."

Savanna ducked her head, feeling the blush rise on her cheeks. "You shouldn't give up on your dreams, just because you met someone. If you really want to coach you should go for it." Savanna's heart raced at the thought of Travis being anywhere but with her at this moment. He reached across the table and took his hand in his.

"As soon as I saw you, Savanna, I knew I needed to stay at Haven. You looked like an angel standing in the hallway. I think you were even glowing."

She felt like her face was on fire. "Pheromones."

"Huh?"

"When two people are physically attracted to each other, they release pheromones to signify their interest. It's a carryover from days when humans mated based on estrus cycle. Women would enter estrus and release pheromones to let the male know they were ready to conceive. We still have the pheromones, even though…" Savanna trailed off, realizing Travis had a strange look on his face.

"There you go, analyzing everything." He shook his head, but smiled as he spoke. "Let's clear the table and go in the living room. I've been talking about me this entire time. I want to give you a chance. For one thing I want to know what it was like living in this spectacular house."

They cleared the table and put the food away. She helped Travis load the dish sanitizer before they retired to the living room. He programmed the TV to display a roaring fire and the two sat on the couch, not quite touching.

Travis pulled Savanna's braid over her shoulder and started to play with the end of it, rolling it through his fingers. "Tell me about your childhood. All I ever see of you is Dr. Savanna Taylor; Savior of the World, Curer of Disease and Protector of Women. It makes me think I need to buy you a cape. I want to know about you as a little girl. I want to figure out your epic flaw."

Pulling her knees close to her chest, Savanna wrapped her arms around her legs. She hadn't talked about her childhood much these past months. The pain was too fresh. It made her feel like she failed her father when he needed her most. Something in Travis' eyes invited her in and the warm memories of her childhood came flooding back. The corner of her eyes tingled, but she knew she wouldn't cry.

"My parents loved me to distraction." Savanna rested her chin on her knees. "My Dad was always distracted by his work, but he really tried to make it up to me by being there when I really needed it. Every time I came to him and told him what I wanted to be when I grew up he provided me with everything I needed to learn about the subject." Savanna grinned at the memories pouring into her head. "I remember the day I told him I wanted to be an astronaut. He hired a slew of designers to paint my ceiling to reflect the night sky, bought me a telescope and had a star named after me. I still have the certificate hanging in my room."

"What about your mom? You don't talk about her very much."

"If my Dad and I didn't have each other to hold on to after her death, I don't think we would have survived." Savanna stretched and Travis pulled her feet into his lap. He removed her shoes and socks. His warm hands kneaded the tension out of her instep. "That feels so good. I haven't had my feet rubbed since I was a child."

"Emily believes you've lived a sheltered life." His fingers didn't stop their gentle circular motion. "She says you don't understand a lot of the world around you. We've butted heads more than once over our relationship. The woman is extremely over protective of you, almost like she's your mother."

Savanna was sure she heard a little bit of bitterness in his voice as he spoke. She wondered if this was why Emily was so quiet today. "Emily thinks I'm completely naive. I've dedicated my life to research and gaining knowledge. She thinks just because I'm young I haven't experienced life enough to know how to take care of myself." Usually Emily treatment of her didn't bother Savanna. She just passed it off as part of her quirky behaviors. Now, for some reason, the thought of Emily and Travis discussing her behind her back frustrated her.

"I didn't mean to upset you." Travis stopped rubbing her feet and leaned closer to pull her into his arms. "I was just trying to explain why I haven't been pushing things with you.

Emily said I needed to give you a chance to get used to the idea of dating and falling in love, because you haven't experienced it before."

So many emotions were coursing through Savanna she didn't know what to think. She didn't understand when he said she didn't know what it was to be in love. Savanna knew exactly what love was. She loved her daughter more than anything. She loved Emily as if she were a sister and Aida and Erik as if he was a brother and she her niece. The emotions she felt about Travis were a little more complex. She knew she loved him as she did the others, but her physical response was caught up in it too. The emotions she felt for him couldn't be categorized into neat little packages of familial ties.

"I think I would know if I were falling in love," Savanna scoffed. "It's not like I'm blind to love. I mean, love isn't just a physical response. You have to build trust and caring in a relationship. It takes work and the ability to care for and sacrifice for one another. People don't fall in love, they choose to love. And they choose to fall out of love. I know all the rhetoric about love."

Travis reached up and stroked Savanna's cheek. His warm fingers caused her face to tingle and shivers to climb up her spine.

"You're so analytical. Don't you ever stop analyzing things and let yourself feel?" Travis' hands were constantly in motion. He had slipped the band off the end of Savanna's braid and unwove the honey-blonde hair. "I fell in love with you from the moment I saw you. Are you telling me you didn't feel the same?"

Savanna swallowed, trying to hide her nervousness. "I can't deny I was, I still am, very attracted to you. I do love you. You're one of my best friends and I know I would never be the same if you left. I don't believe in love at first sight, I think what you had was a—" His lips connected with hers, interrupting her.

He pulled back slightly, his lips still touching hers. "This isn't a choice Savanna, I love you. I want to be with you.

Any moment I'm not with you, I feel like a part of me is missing. You can't tell me you don't feel the same way. I see the way your eyes follow me when you think I'm not looking." He pulled her closer to him, brushing her fingers through her hair and whispering in her ear. "Your heart is racing. I can feel it against my chest." Savanna realized he was right, her heart seemed to be pounding in her ears. "Are you telling me that you need to make the choice to love me?"

Savanna shook her head and then realized he couldn't see her. She cleared her throat. "No. I've already made the choice. You make me feel safe. I know I love you. I'm just saying—" The words were lost in another kiss.

When they separated, he spoke again. "I don't want to break any of Haven's rules, but I want us to live together. I think we should sign a commitment contract and start thinking about becoming a family."

Savanna couldn't think straight. His kisses where making her head spin. "Isn't it a little fast?"

"Think about it." He separated himself from Savanna and stood up. "Emily's going to be back soon. I convinced her to give me a couple hours alone with you, but I don't think she is going to let us be alone for long. I'm going to bed." He leaned down and kissed her on the forehead.

Chapter Twenty-Five

SAVANNA STARED AT THE stars on her ceiling, trying to get to sleep. She had traced the pattern of the Big Dipper and found Orion's Belt when she heard a soft knock on her door. Travis poked his head inside.

"Can I come in?" he asked. "I feel like I'm not finished talking."

Savanna moved over so he could sit beside her on the bed. She propped a pillow behind her back. Travis moved into the room, actually tiptoeing.

"Emily and Rose got home about an hour ago. They both just went to bed." Travis lay down on his side, his head propped on his hand. "You left your hair down, I never see it down around your face. You look younger."

Savanna swept her head from side to side so she could see her hair as it fell around her. "That's why I wear it pulled back. I know I look young, so anything I can do to make myself look older and more experienced helps give me the aura of authority." She gathered her hair and dropped it over her shoulder. The gentle kink marks from the braid gave it a soft wave. Travis ran his fingers through the shiny lengths.

"You are so beautiful," he whispered.

Savanna tipped her head back and Travis lowered his face to hers. He paused right before his lips touched hers. "You know you can kiss me back, don't you?"

"What do you mean?" Savanna's words came out as a soft whisper.

"Haven't you ever kissed anyone before?"

"Sure," she said.

"I mean someone other than a family member." Travis' tone revealed he already knew the answer so Savanna didn't respond.

Lowering his mouth to her, Travis gently brushed his lips against hers. "Tense up your lips a little bit. When you feel pressure move them slightly." He tried again. "There you go."

He kissed her a few more times. "I'm glad you're a fast learner."

"I know how to kiss."

Travis chuckled.

"Knowing about something and knowing something are two different things." Savanna felt the blush creeping up her face. Travis rolled on his back and stared up at the ceiling. "Wow, you weren't lying about the sky painted on your ceiling. It's just like camping out under the night sky."

"I've always been fascinated with space. I wanted to be an astronaut from the time I was eight until I was about eleven." Savanna studied Travis' form lying beside her. His long, lean body was stretched out, showing the muscle definition. It was difficult to make out his specific features in the darkness, but his eyes shone brightly.

"What happened?" His eyes never left the ceiling.

"My mom was diagnosed with ovarian cancer. I saw the pain and suffering she went through and I couldn't do anything to help." Savanna swallowed past the tightness in her throat. "When I found out she was born with the cancer gene I couldn't believe there was nothing anyone could do to help her. I decided to become a doctor and study genetics."

"How old were you when you decided that?"

"I think I just turned eleven."

Travis rolled onto his side and gathered Savanna into his arms. "So much weight for such a little girl. Did you even have a childhood? Or were you born all grown up?"

Savanna closed her eyes and allowed herself to relax in his arms. Travis stroked her hair, curling his body around hers and engulfing it in his own. "Go to sleep, Savanna. Everything will be okay."

Travis wasn't in the room when the alarm woke her. Savanna reached over and turned it off. She sat on the edge of the bed, thinking about everything they had talked about. There was no way she could deny she had strong feelings for him, but this was the first time she had ever been close to a serious relationship with anyone. She had no basis for comparison and had no idea if what she was feeling merited a commitment contract.

Breakfast was on the table by the time she was dressed and left the bedroom. Travis stood when Savanna entered and held her chair for her. Emily's lips tightened and a wrinkle appeared in the middle of her forehead. Savanna could tell she was upset about something. Travis's secretive little smile gave her a hint about what her closest friend was feeling. Emily had always been overprotective of Savanna. Although the woman liked Travis, Savanna suspected that Emily's protective instincts were roaring forward in full force today.

"Are you ready for some excitement today, Savanna?" Travis took his seat and started scooping eggs on to his plate.

"How exciting is it going to be? Aren't we just going to be seeing a few patients?" Savanna looked from Travis to Emily.

The furrow on Emily's brow grew deeper. "I know you are used to running things at Haven, but I need to ask a favor." The seriousness of Emily's tone drew Savanna's focus. "Today, when you're at the clinic, I need you to follow the directions I give you. This isn't like any medical facility you've ever seen and some of the things that happen there might surprise you. You can't identify yourself as a doctor until after the patient is brought to the room. In fact, we all use a pseudonym while we're working. I'm Juanita. Travis is called Nick. And you're going to be called Sarah. Don't forget." Emily paused and waited until Savanna nodded at her. "You'll be assigned a nurse. Don't allow yourself to be separated from whoever it is. If things get crazy, listen for my voice. I'll be watching and will let you know what to do. Do you understand?"

Savanna nodded; Emily sounded so serious it almost frightened her. She could feel her pulse speed up as they all took their places in the van. The clinic was only a few miles away from the outskirts of Boise. Travis drove the van through a neighborhood full of rundown homes. Broken windows repaired with plastic and duct tape, chipped and faded paint and missing roof shingles testified to the abject poverty of the residents. A number of houses gaped with open doors and sagging front porches, suggesting they were devoid of occupants. As they passed one such dilapidated house Savanna thought she saw a flash of white. When she looked back, she saw a child's pale face peering out of the calcium-stained window.

Pulling into the parking lot of an unobtrusive brick building, Travis dropped the women off at the front door and pulled away. The van disappeared around the back of the building. Emily led Savanna through the double doors into the lobby. A row of uncomfortable orange chairs lined the walls. At the front desk, a receptionist flipped through a pile of papers. She looked up, a tired expression on her face. For a moment Savanna flashed on brown eyes peering from above a white surgical mask, the memory passed and she looked at the grey haired, matronly woman in front of her.

"Oh, Juanita, I'm glad you're here. This must be Sarah." The woman reached under the desk and Savanna heard a buzz. "Everything's arranged for your one o'clock appointment."

Emily nodded. Savanna had a feeling there was more being said between the two women and wondered what was going on. She followed Emily through the heavy wooden door and into the back of the building. The clinic was set up much like many of the small-town clinics Savanna travelled to while studying disease outbreak patterns. The nurse she was assigned was called Becky, but she doubted that was her real name, especially since the woman tended to react slowly when Savanna called her by that name. Becky was a slim red-head and appeared to be very competent in her job.

Becky gave her a quick tour of the building; showing her where everything was kept in the rooms. Some of the equipment was out of date and would slow down the diagnostic and treatment process. She decided the next time she came, she would bring Sam with her. The S290 had several applications she could use to analyze test samples and Savanna felt having him could help facilitate some diagnosis and treatments.

The nurse closed the door and turned to Savanna.

"Doctor, do you know what we do here?"

"This is a medical clinic. I assume you see patients on a walk-in basis."

"Sit down, Doctor. I want to explain a few things here." Savanna sat on the low rolling chair beside the exam table. "The people who come here don't have medical insurance for a large variety of reasons. We do our best to help them with the limited resources we have. Our job is made even more difficult because sometimes the patients aren't always honest with us." Becky's green eyes flashed with emotion. "Most of our supplies come through donations or from Canadian and Mexican pharmacies. Although, technically, these clinics aren't against the law, we have no governmental support. In fact, a number of our clients don't trust the government and would have nothing to do with us if we did."

"How do you make sure your supplies are safe?" All sorts of red flags popped up in Savanna's head.

"We have enough resources to ensure the safety of our patients and an ambulance for emergencies. It's still illegal to deny medical attention to individuals, even if they don't have insurance. Most of our clients pay cash, if they have it. All the money we bring in goes for supplies and to pay the few staff members we can afford." Becky opened the door. "We better go get our first patient." She handed Savanna a surgical cap, lab coat and mask. "It's better if you go out as covered as possible to protect your identity."

Savanna covered her hair and face and put on the coat to disguise her willowy frame. The receptionist led a girl to the room and handed Savanna a clipboard with a piece of white paper attached. Savanna had never seen a medical chart on anything except a computer screen before and it took her a moment to decipher the text. Becky took the chart from her and had the girl sit on the edge of the exam table.

"Hi Michelle. Tell me why you're here." Becky glanced down the chart with an ease that showed she was familiar with the paper work.

Michelle had dark, curly hair falling past her shoulders,

an olive complexion and light brown eyes. She kept her eyes down-cast, refusing to make eye contact as she spoke.

"I've been married for six months, now."

Savanna studied the girl. She looked to be about seventeen, very young to be married.

Michelle's face was bright red with embarrassment, but she continued. "My husband and I haven't been able to conceive and we wanted to see if it's because I'm having problems or if it's because of him."

Becky asked a list of questions regarding Michelle's sexual history, menstrual cycle and frequency of intercourse. Each question made the girl blush even brighter, but she answered each question as it was posed to her. "We have to follow the rules set by the Elders. We don't have sex before marriage. I was pure before I married Benjamin and he has only been married to his first wife for two years. She hasn't been able to conceive either, but she doesn't cycle regularly, as I do. The Council of Mothers thinks it's just her and that I could conceive if we tried hard enough."

Savanna held her tongue as long as she could, but she needed to know some key information if she was going to help this child. "Michelle, you need to be completely honest with us if you want us to help you. According to this chart you were born in 2023 and you're currently nineteen. Is this correct?"

"Yes ma'am." Michelle nodded as she spoke. "We're not like sects that marry their girls off too young. We're required to wait, at least until our eighteenth birthday, before we're allowed to marry. Girls are not physically ready to bear children until they're sixteen, though we can get pregnant earlier. The Lord has shown us that babies who are born to women when they're older are healthier and the mothers have fewer complications."

"You are your husband's second wife? What happened to his first wife?"

"Oh, we're all still married. If I conceive, my first born will belong to her, unless she conceives as well." Michelle didn't seem to be distressed by this statement. In fact, she seemed elated at the idea.

"What will happen if you don't conceive?"

"Well, like every woman I'll have a choice." She spoke in a resigned manner. "My sister wife and I can put aside our husband and remarry, or we can attempt to become pregnant by the second husband."

Savanna was about to ask what she meant by the second husband, but Becky waved her hand to stop her.

"Michelle, I'm going to run a few tests. First, I need to draw your blood." Becky said. "I'm going to send you home with some ovulation tests and some specific instructions on how to use them." She handed a slip of paper to the girl. "Can you read that to me?"

Michelle read the instructions off the paper and handed them back to Becky. "Good. I want both you and your sister wife to test for ovulation for three months and both return here and report your results. Can you do that?"

Michelle nodded. "I know I can return. I'll see if she can come as well. Neither of us wants to put aside Benjamin. He's a good provider. I don't know who the sect would pick to be the genetic father for our children if the problem is his."

Becky drew blood and performed a pelvic exam before she and Savanna left the room to allow her to dress. The woman pulled Savanna off to the side, where no one could see them, and spoke in a quiet voice.

"She's a member of a polygamist sect. This group is very careful to stay on the correct side of the law, but the right to be in a polygamist marriage is still very new and not many people accept it. If we ask too many personal questions the women will stop coming here and we won't be able to help them." The intensity in Becky's eyes showed how much she cared about her patients. "Treat the patients who come to see you. Offer them what help you can, but don't step on any toes."

Savanna was shocked. When it came to medical care, she was usually the one on the offensive, but this Becky woman had her beat hands down. The nurse left her standing in the hall as she went to talk to the receptionist. After a moment she came back, Savanna gathered her wits about her and followed her back to the room. Michelle sat on the edge of the exam table, her simple cotton dress back in place and her hair tied back, covered by a head scarf.

"Michelle, do you think you could convince your husband to come in some time? If we can get a sample from him we may be able to determine if he's the problem and get him what he needs." Becky's voice was soothing and calm, not anything like a few minutes before when she was reprimanding Savanna.

The girl took the paper bag of supplies Becky handed her and stood up. "I can try. The men sometimes prefer not to know and it's hard to get them to come in and see anyone."

"Well, talk to him and see what he says." Becky opened the door and led Michelle out without even glancing at Savanna. Not knowing what else to do, Savanna followed.

The rest of the morning Savanna worked with Becky seeing several patients. It felt good to get back into the mix of seeing patients. She didn't realize how much she missed it. At lunch she spoke to the clinic manager to sign up for additional shifts. She coordinated her schedule to coincide with some of Emily's shifts, volunteering to come in once a month.

Chapter Twenty-Six

SAVANNA HAD AN APPLE for lunch and went back to work side by side with Becky. Obviously, the woman had overcome her initial ire. She explained the case history of the patients she was going to see in the afternoon. Becky explained the next patient was an elderly dementia patient. Her husband mistrusted government health run nursing facilities and was trying to care for her at home. It wasn't going well and Becky was trying to facilitate other options for them. As Becky was explaining the situation Emily came up behind Savanna.

"Mrs. Tulu is here for her appointment." Her tone indicated there was much more to the statement than the words she was saying. Becky nodded and turned to the other staff members.

"Okay, this is what we've been waiting for. Let's get all other patients in rooms and lock the front doors. Sarah..." It took a moment for Savanna to realize she was talking to her. "Stick close to Juanita. You two will be leaving quickly. I'll see you next month. Someone tell Travis to get the van ready."

Savanna was caught in the epicenter of activity within seconds. She had a clear view of the waiting area as it was cleared of all patients. The only people left in the room were a couple, the man in a suit, the woman in a traditional Ethiopian garb, and a woman sitting with them. From their behavior the woman appeared to be a translator. The man was filling out a form with the help of the translator. The woman in the Ethiopian garb shifted in her seat and Savanna noticed she was holding an infant in her arms. She reached down to the floor and into her diaper bag. Almost immediately, a familiar odor permeated the room. The mother lifted the baby close to her face and sniffed, her nose wrinkled. Turning to the translator, she asked a question. The translator looked around until she spotted the receptionist.

"Excuse me?"

The receptionist looked up from her charts.

"Is there a place to change diaper?" the translator asked.

The receptionist stood up. "I'll show her."

The man started to stand, but the translator said something and he sat back down. She turned to the next page of documents and started reading to him. Opening the door to the back, the receptionist led the woman into the restroom. Emily positioned herself near the door to the lady's room and guided Savanna there as well.

"Watch for a distraction," she whispered. "We're going to slip into the bathroom."

Seconds later a young woman came charging out of the exam room. She screamed at the top of her lungs. "No!" She pushed the receptionist down and charts flew everywhere. "I won't let you touch me! My parents can't make this choice for me!" A crowd of people rushed her, blocking the view of the front reception area from the back of the clinic.

Savanna took a step towards the girl, but Emily took her by the arm and pulled her towards the bathroom. They slipped inside while a group gathered around the girl, blocking the door from view. The tall, graceful Ethiopian woman stood in the middle of the bathroom, clutching her infant, a look of absolute terror on her face.

"You help?" The question had the full force of a pleading prayer behind it.

"Come." Emily led them both to a door at the back of the bathroom. They entered a storage room with a sliding loading door. She had to strain a little bit to get the door open. The Haven van sat in the loading bay, its rear door standing open. He van was completely unrecognizable. It had a red stripe down the side and lettering identifying it as an ambulance. Emily helped the woman inside. She waved Savanna to the passenger side where Travis was waiting with the door open. Emily climbed in the back and closed the door.

Savanna turned around and looked at Emily, sitting with the woman in the back. The intensity of the situation was weighing on her so she kept her voice low. "What's going on here?" The words hissed through her teeth.

Emily put her finger to her lips.

The scream of sirens echoed down the streets. Travis flipped a switch, lights flashed and the sound of a siren joined the others. He pulled out of the back of the clinic and turned onto the main road. He floored the pedal and seemed to fly out of the subdivision.

Travis steered the vehicle behind a row of trees, hiding them from prying eyes. He flicked off the lights and sirens as he slowed to a stop. The woman beside Emily stripped out of her traditional garb. Underneath she wore a tee shirt and jeans. Emily held the infant. Travis climbed into the back and pulled a coat out of a box on the van floor. He handed it to the woman, helping her put it on.

"You're safe now." Emily's voice was soothing, even though it appeared the woman couldn't understand the words. Placing the infant in the woman's arms, Emily took the bundle of clothing and placed it in a bin. They stayed hidden behind the trees for about fifteen minutes before Travis took his place back in the driver's seat, dialed up the local news broadcast and pulled back onto the main road.

Savanna couldn't keep quiet any longer, too much was happening and her mind was reeling. "Emily! What's going on here?" Her voice came out harsher then she intended and the Ethiopian woman flinched, pulling her baby closer to her chest.

"We had to move quickly if we wanted to save this woman and her child." Emily gestured to the woman huddled in her seat. "She's a political refugee from Africa. The tribe this woman and her husband come from still practice female circumcision, even though it's been banned by the World Medical Association. When Aamina was born her mother had some serious complications. She also had a son two years ago and the complications were just as bad. Her husband was also preparing to have his daughter circumcised."

"The infant?" Savanna looked at the child in the woman's arms. She couldn't have been more than six months old.

Emily nodded. "The surgery wouldn't be performed until the child turned eight, but the father is concerned there's no one in the United States willing to do it. He's making some serious inquiries. Nulie is afraid her daughter will have to go through what she and her sister suffered when they were children. Her sister died from complications and Nulie's afraid her daughter will suffer the same fate. I've been working with the clinic the past few months, trying to find ways to protect women. This is the best way we could find to help Nulie and her child."

"Shh." Travis turned up the volume on the news broadcast.

A reporter stood on the sidewalk near the clinic. She was wearing a bulky coat and a blue stocking cap with dark brown hair flowing from underneath. Her microphone picked up wind interference, but her words were perfectly clear.

"Yes, Jim," she said. "I'm standing outside a Garden City neighborhood where a woman and her infant daughter went missing approximately thirty minutes ago. The woman was in a clinic for a check-up when she went into the restroom to care for her daughter. A severe disturbance broke out and in the confusion the woman disappeared. After the police were called and order was restored, the woman's husband realized she hadn't returned from the restroom. At first, he assumed she was hiding out of fear and she would be found quickly. This doesn't appear to be the case. The man and woman are refugees from Africa and neither of them speak English. The man has been speaking to the police through a translator, but it appears there's still a communication barrier. The husband believes the woman is hiding somewhere in the neighborhood and the police are preparing a search grid to cover the area she could have gotten to on foot."

The image changed to a split screen to show a black suited man sitting at a news desk. "Trina, do the police have any other information?"

"At this point this is all the information we have. Of course, we all know there has been a sharp increase in kidnappings over the years and immigrants fall into a high-risk group as victims." The reporter paused as a police car rolled behind her with its siren blaring. "These individuals are less trusting of authority and are less likely to be registered with the domestic registration services. Unless a child has been marked with a microchip, they're almost impossible to recover."

Travis turned down the news broadcast. Emily grinned as she looked at Savanna. "It looks like we're going to make it."

"Don't get too complacent," Travis said. "We haven't gotten away yet."

"How did you make the van look like an ambulance? When we left Haven yesterday it was white." Savanna said.

Travis tapped a display screen beside his right hand. "Holographic projection. Right now, we're driving down the road in a dark blue van. There's enough energy in the battery to maintain the image for a little over an hour. That should get us to the back road leading to Haven, I hope. Once we're inside the gates we'll be able to file papers to protect the woman and child."

Savanna didn't breathe easy until they entered the gates of Haven. The van lost power as they rolled into the garage, not even making it into the marked stall. Travis parked it where it died. Emily led Nulie to the locker room and the sanitizing showers while Travis and Savanna cleared out the van.

A black garbed man approached Travis and handed him a data pad. "Sir, here's the information you requested." The man nodded to Savanna before he turned and walked away.

Travis slid the pad into the pocket on his sleeve. "Just the paper work we need."

It didn't take long for Savanna to process through and dress in her Haven uniform. A red light was flashing on the screen outside the sanitizing shower when she exited. Savanna pulled the information feed up on her pad, reading the message. She pushed a button, opening a link to the other dressing room.

"Emily, we need to bring Nulie to the isolation section of the hospital," she said. "She has a mild bacterial infection.

We need to treat it before we allow her access to main campus."

Medics brought a gurney to the dressing rooms. Savanna helped direct Nulie into the service tunnel leading from the garage to the hospital wing. Once the woman was settled in as exam room, Savanna started an IV and placed the vitals monitor just above her heart on the upper left pectoral. Nulie appeared to be in stable condition, so Savanna turned her attention to the infant.

Savanna checked the baby from toe to head. She appeared to be perfectly healthy, but Savanna ordered a full spectrum of tests just to make sure. Aamina's large brown eyes stared silently into Savanna's the entire time. When she finished, Savanna swaddled the infant in a blanket, sat in a chair next to the bed and slowly rocked the baby to sleep. Travis found her like that a few minutes later.

"You're a natural. I bet you could have a dozen more just like her and be perfectly happy." He kneeled beside her and studied the baby.

Savanna looked down at the infant and then at Travis. "I don't want a dozen, but I wouldn't mind having one more. That conversation we were having earlier, what type of commitment contract were you thinking about?"

Travis' entire face lit up when he smiled. "I have one right here." He handed her the data pad he received from the guard in the garage. "Look it over, tell me what you think. It's not as binding as a marriage contract, but it does protect our assets and family, just as a marriage contract would."

The expression on his face was hopeful and full of love. Savanna was drawn into his eyes and was lost for a moment. The infant fussed and stretched and the moment was lost. She looked at the tiny bundle of perfection in her arms then looked back at Travis.

"I don't know how you're going to react to this question, so I'm just going to ask. Would you be willing to go through genetic testing to ensure any child we have won't have any genetic defects?" Savanna watched the minute changes in

Travis' face as he processed the question.

His eyes dropped to the infant and then back up to hers. "I want my children to be mine, genetically. I'm willing to go through the tests, but I don't want any of my children to be genetically altered."

Savanna glanced at the pad in her hand. "You do realize any child we have will have my genetic markers, too. I'm genetically altered."

He reached down and brushed his fingers through her hair. "But, they'll be half mine, without any other genetic alterations. I think I can live with that."

Savanna nodded her understanding and glanced at the pad in her hand. "Let me read this. I'll let you know, but I'll probably say yes."

Travis kissed her briefly on the lips, stood up and left the room. His feet didn't even seem to be touching the ground.

Savanna placed the infant in the basinet next to the bed. Nulie woke and reached out for her baby. Savanna helped her settle the child in her arms and showed her how to operate the nurse's call button. Although there was a language barrier, Savanna was able use some iconic sign language to express to the woman she was not to nurse her baby and to use the call button if she needed anything. She expressed concern the antibiotics she was using to treat the infection would affect the infant, gesturing to the IV in her arm. The woman appeared to understand.

It was still early evening, so Savanna went to her office to look over the commitment contract. It was standard contract, renewable every five years. It protected assets obtained by each partner prior to the joining, as well as equal division of any property obtained through the course of the partnership. Any children born as a result of the relationship would be the responsibility of both parents and if the relationship was dissolved the children would live with the parent who could provide the best environment for the children's development.

By the time the alarm signaled the dinner hour she had

made her decision. Savanna put in the requisition for a privacy screen dividing the children's bunks from the rest of the room, allowing privacy when the contract was finalized.

Travis was in line with Raven and Emily when she crossed the courtyard to join them for dinner. He watched as she approached, his eyes studying her face. She smiled at his anxious expression, his returning smile lit up his eyes and as soon as she was within reach he pulled her close and kissed her. Raven patted Savanna on the leg drawing her attention.

"Mommy, why you kissing Uncle Travis?" Raven's face was perplexed as she looked up at her mother.

Savanna reached down and picked up her daughter and hugged her close. "Well, Little One, what would you say if I told you I decided I wanted to live with Uncle Travis?"

Raven's forehead wrinkled as she thought for a moment. "Where would he sleep? Will he fit on the top bunk?"

Emily threw back her head and laughed uncontrollably.

Savanna grinned at the image of Travis trying to cram his long, lean body into the five-foot bunk. "We'll find room for him, don't worry."

Travis pulled them both into his arms and kissed Savanna on the forehead. "You're so beautiful. I know we're going to be happy together."

Savanna smiled and kissed him. All around them, the crowd broke into applause and cheers. Savanna buried her face in Travis' chest to hide the growing blush on her checks.

Erik walked up behind the group and Raven squirmed to get down so she could stand with her friend. Aida wrapped her arm around Raven's shoulders. "Guess what, Aida? Uncle Travis is going to come live with us. Maybe you and Uncle Erik can come live with us too."

Erik grabbed Savanna, pulling her out of Travis' arms. "You're making a commitment? I should've known. You two can't keep your eyes off each other. It was only a matter of time. Where are you going to hold your commitment ceremony?"

"We're just going to have a simple commitment

contract, we don't need a ceremony." Savanna knew she had to rein Erik in before he got his teeth into this thing. She loved him, but she didn't need to put her life on public display. Erik held her at arm's length and smiled.

"We'll see," he said.

Chapter Twenty-Seven

IN THE END, ERIK got his wish. About a week after Savanna accepted Travis' proposal the two held a commitment ceremony in front of her father's memorial tree. Savanna did manage to convince Erik to keep the ceremony simple, but the majority of residence of Haven still attended and offered their approval.

Travis' move into the apartment was smooth. A privacy barrier was installed, enclosing Raven's bed, but she spent most of the next week at Erik or Emily's apartment so Savanna and Travis had privacy as they explored their new relationship. Savanna was nervous at first, not quite sure how to adapt to living with a man. Travis was patient and gentle, calmly taking everything in stride. By the time Raven returned to the apartment the two had developed a closeness Savanna had never felt with anyone before. He fostered such a feeling of safety and security Savanna couldn't help but trust him implicitly.

Savanna was surprised at Raven's ability to adapt to the new situation. Just like any five year old, she was jealous of the attention her mother gave Travis, but soon she learned two adults meant she got twice as much love. Savanna tried to encourage her to sleep in her own bunk, but most nights she climbed between her and Travis. Once she fell asleep, Travis would put in her own bed. It was a quiet and peaceful time.

Raven had a major meltdown when Caleb was born a year later. She had been sleeping in her own bed since early summer, but regressed back to snuggling between Travis and Savanna. When Caleb cried for his three a.m. feeding, Savanna would nurse him in bed. Raven tried pushing and pinching the baby until he fussed and wouldn't nurse.

Savanna brought up the issue in the weekly therapy sessions. Many of the women were supportive and gave her the tools to help her deal with the sibling rivalry. Savanna made sure her daughter realized she was just as important to her as

Caleb was, but it wasn't an easy transition.

Savanna was deeply entrenched in her work on analyzing a new strain of the Smallpox virus when she received a call from the school. Savanna couldn't stop what she was doing, so Travis agreed to pick Raven up and bring her back to the office.

This new strand of Smallpox had developed in south Florida. Despite attempts to create global vaccination programs, several impoverished nations still didn't have the resources to protect all their population. Even though efforts were made to close borders there was no way to build a wall around an ocean and refugees still managed to make it into Florida and other coastal states.

While Savanna helped prepare the slides of the newest outbreak other research assistants were manually extracting the viral DNA from the new samples. She put aside her work when Travis brought Raven to her office and left the lab to meet them there. Raven was huddled in a ball on one side of the couch, her entire body shaking with sobs. Savanna sat down and pulled the child into her lap. At first the little girl resisted, but Savanna held on, rocking and soothing her until her sobs quieted.

Travis moved from where he stood by the window and joined them on the couch. He put his arm around Savanna and used his free hand to brush the hair out of Raven's eyes. Savanna studied her daughter's face, looking for an indication to why she was so upset.

"The teacher said Raven had been acting out and had gotten into an argument with another child." Travis explained. "He had been teasing her about not looking anything like her mother and brother. Raven slapped him and burst out crying. The teacher said she couldn't get her to calm down."

"Raven, what's going on? Why are you acting this way?" Raven turned her face into her mother's shoulder and mumbled a few words. Savanna gently turned her so her face wasn't buried and prompted her to repeat what she said.

"He said since I didn't look like you, you were going to

return me to the orphanage and get a new baby like you got Caleb. I told him you didn't get me from an orphanage, but he just laughed and pushed me. So, I hit him." Tears streamed down her cheeks and the sobs made her words hard to understand.

"Hitting is never the answer to anything," Savanna gently reprimanded. "I love you more than the whole world, Little One. We need to do something about this problem."

"Don't send me to an orphanage, please?" Raven's fear was apparent, so Savanna didn't laugh. She did suppress a small smile.

"Raven, you're my daughter, true and firm." Savanna kissed her forehead and continued to rock her. "You were born of my body. I'll never let you go. Your Uncle Travis is right here, too. We're a family. We belong together." Savanna held her daughter close and rocked her until her sobbing stopped.

Once Raven calmed down, Travis took her from her mother's lap and stood up. "I think I'm going to take her back to school. She has a couple of apologies to make."

"Talk to the teacher and set up an appointment with the boy and his mother while you're there," Savanna said. "We need to address this bullying issue. Hitting doesn't solve anything, but bullying isn't acceptable either."

Travis nodded and turned to leave, but before he made it to the door, Emily entered. The expression on her face made everyone stop and stare. Emily drew up short when she saw the family standing in the office.

"I... I didn't realize everyone would be here."

"What's wrong? You look as if you've seen a ghost." Savanna stood. Emily was pale and shaking.

"It's Kai. They found her." Emily was so pale Savanna thought the next words out of her mouth would be the girl was dead.

"What happened?" Savanna asked.

"She's in jail. This is her third arrest and the judge wants to send her to prison." Emily's voice echoed with intensity as she spoke. "The public defender heard about

Haven and knows we have a drug treatment program here. He pulled a few strings and the judge agreed to let her try rehab if she entered this program. Savanna, I've spoken to her. She's in pretty bad shape."

"Well, what's the issue? We have room in the rehab center. Bring her here." Savanna knew this was the least she could do for her adopted family.

"But this jumps her up the list above others who are trying to get in. We don't have enough room for everybody who needs our help." Emily's voice quivered with emotion. "We need more room."

Savanna picked up her data pad. "I know we don't have enough room for the programs we have. I've been speaking to some engineers about expanding. It wouldn't take much to add more wings to the facility. All we would have to do is build more octagons attached to the outer walls of this one."

Savanna handed the pad with the schematics to Emily. "We're also adding more family units. It's going to look like a beehive when it's all said and done, but when it's created we'll be able to add three thousand more beds to the living quarters." Emily studied the schematics as Savanna took her daughter from Travis. "The campus for the surrogate program will be opening next month. That'll open up two hundred more beds here and provide room for another three hundred since the program is growing faster than anticipated."

"This isn't going to help everyone who needs it now, though. These won't be finished for another five years." The tension was still apparent in Emily's voice.

"Yes, that's true, but we can help Kai. Bring her here. Judge's orders have a way of opening doors."

Emily's face still showed her concern as she left the office, but at least Savanna knew Kai would be in a safe place. Travis left with Raven to bring her back to class and Savanna took a few moments put things in motion to bring Kai across the border before she went back to her lab.

Over the next few weeks Savanna made sure to spend extra time with her daughter. She volunteered time at her school to help monitor the on-line classes and scheduled her lunch and exercise time with her. The extra time helped alleviate some of the child's stress and Raven began to adjust to the new family dynamics.

When Kai made it to Haven she was high on Meth. Savanna checked her into the rehab center. The rapid detox was painful to watch, but Savanna attended to her, wanting to make sure the girl had everything she needed. The rehab center wasn't usually part of Savanna's job responsibilities, but she made it a practice of visiting Kai at least once a day. It took three days to flush her system of narcotics. During that time, she didn't make any sign that she recognize either Savanna or Emily.

Once the ravages of detox waned, Savanna was able to see the girl she knew beneath the ravages of scars and time. She was shocked by what she saw. Kai was only twenty-two years old, but she looked closer to forty. Most of her back teeth were broken off or missing. In addition to the wounds left by smallpox her face was covered with scars and pockmarks where she had picked the skin away. A collection of wrinkles around her eyes and mouth and the graying hair that hung in clumps from her scalp aged her formally beautiful face. Looking beneath her scars, Savanna could see the beautiful girl she had helped nurse through the trauma of smallpox and rape. Savanna could see Raven in her face, especially when she looked into the young woman's eyes, but there was a pain there, a suffering she never wanted to see in her daughter's face.

Kai was lethargic when she came out of detox. She refused to eat or talk and barely took care of her physiological needs. The only thing she asked for was something to take the edge off her pain. She would beg for cigarettes or methadone or any other number of drugs. Claiming back pain from an injury, she begged for morphine. Each request was denied and she became more and more desperate.

The clinic staff had seen all of this behavior before and they treated Kai with professional detachment. Emily came to treat her in much the same way.

Emily explained she wasn't acting distant because she didn't love her niece, in fact, it was quite the opposite. She loved the girl to distraction and if she didn't keep her distance her sympathy could become detrimental to the girl's treatment. After a week of Kai not responding to her, Savanna decided to stop visiting. She monitored her progress and received regular reports, but she wanted the girl to have a chance to heal on her own.

It was early spring when Kai's review board came up. She had spent the entire three months of her treatment cycle in the clinic, not being able to enter the general population due to her outbursts and violent behavior. The board felt it was time to transfer her so she could start working as part of her program. Savanna and Emily were both on the review board this month and so they joined the other ten members in the counsel room as Kai entered and sat.

Savanna surveyed the woman, mentally comparing her to the image she had of her when she first entered rehab. Kai's gaunt cheeks had filled out, the grey tinge in her skin was gone, her teeth had been repaired and her hair had filled out, growing long, sleek and black. Kai's eyes met Savanna's and a look of shock crossed her face. Savanna realized Kai didn't remember her visits. The council took their seats and the proceedings started.

Savanna and Emily sat at the end of the council table. They had both determined they wouldn't say anything about Kai's past before she entered rehab, so prior bad acts wouldn't be considered. The head council member rapped a gavel on the table to get everyone's attention.

"This council is brought to order," the woman began. "We're here to assess the fitness of Kai Silva to determine her fitness in mind and body. This hearing will determine Kai's progress and placement in the Haven community. Nothing said in this meeting is to leave this room as to protect the privacy and rights of Kai. Is that understood?" The woman looked at each member of the council, waiting for an 'aye' and a nod from each before continuing. "We'll first hear medical testimony."

At a gesture from head council the head of the rehab unit stood and began speaking. "Kai is twenty-one years old. She was brought into the rehabilitation facility as a result of an arrest on possession of a controlled substance. Upon initial intake tests revealed she had methamphetamines, tobacco and alcohol in her system. Levels indicated she had ingested the toxins within forty-eight hours prior to her arrival. Also, further tests revealed physical damage indicating long term use of these substances. Medical tests also reveal the patient has had smallpox and has been exposed to several other diseases. The smallpox infection had been resolved eight years ago, all other disease has been resolved. Detox treatment is complete; however, her behavior indicates if she would go back to using if she was released. Medical recommendation is for her to stay at Haven for at least another six months as we help her resolve some of the underlying psychological problems."

Kai sat quietly during the reading, her eyes downcast. She glanced up when the woman read the recommendations as if she wanted to say something, but immediately ducked her head again.

Savanna studied her. She had never seen anyone exude such a level of self-defeat. Tears pricked the corner of her eyes, but she blinked them back. This was Savanna's greatest weakness. No matter how hard she tried, she couldn't distance herself from some of her patients.

"Kai, the council is going to recommend further treatment. You have a choice in where you want to go. The judge wants you to complete six months of in-patient rehab and then three years in prison for your crimes. If you sign an agreement to spend two years at Haven and agree to follow the rules, he is willing to release you and expunge your record. We've explained to you the expectations of residents of Haven. What are your thoughts?"

Looking up, Kai's eyes met Savanna's and then Emily's. Savanna could see her throat move as she swallowed. As she spoke the words came out too quiet at first, but then she cleared her throat and started again.

"I...I don't know. I was fine until I saw—" She gestured towards the end of the table where Savanna and Emily sat. "Will I have to spend time with Dr. Taylor's daughter? I don't think I could handle that."

Savanna couldn't let this girl get away if there was a chance she could save her. She had to speak up. "Kai, I could arrange your housing and your work schedule so you would never be around Raven. In three months the first of the new wings will be open and I'll transfer you there. We'll make this work, if this is what you want."

Kai's expression showed her doubt, but when they offered her the contract she signed it. The committee disbanded and Emily volunteered to show Kai her room and orientate her to the facility. Kai didn't speak to Savanna or even look her in her eyes as she left the room. She looked so broken as she walked to the door. Savanna wanted to do more for her, but her strength was in healing the physical body not in the psychological. If you could point to it and touch it and say it was broken she could easily fix it. The mind continued to be a mystery to her.

Chapter Twenty-Eight

EVEN THOUGH SHE HAD promised Kai she wouldn't force her to spend time with Raven, Savanna made sure she tracked the young woman's progress through her program. As the new units were constructed the builders created a walkway across the top of the buildings, accessible only through Savanna's office. This design was created partly because the original design of the facility made it too difficult to interconnect the wings and partly because Savanna wanted to find a way to offer better quarantine options as disease continued to appear and spread rapidly through the world.

The walkway was encased in glass and gave Savanna a view of the valley she wouldn't have gotten anywhere else. She started to use the walkway for exercise. Strapping Caleb on her hip with a sling and joined by Travis and Raven, her family would walk the circuit of the buildings for an hour. The sun would set over the clouds, bathing the valley in reds and golden orange and finally fading into violet twilight. It was her favorite time of day. All the worries of the world faded away. There were no more diseases, no more reports of militant groups attacking National Guardsmen as they enforced Martial Law, no more pain, abuse and suffering.

As Caleb grew he rebelled against riding in the sling. He took his first steps on his first birthday and soon he was toddling after them as the family took their evening walks. His first word was Wavie, and he mimicked everything his sister did, much to the older girl's frustration.

Travis hinted around that it was time to think about adding to the family, but Savanna wasn't sure she was ready yet. Caleb had been unexpected, but not unwelcome. She hadn't finished testing Travis' DNA when she discovered she was pregnant and had decided to stop testing because if she didn't want to find anything. She was glad when Caleb had been born healthy, but she wanted to observe his development a little more before she decided to have another child.

From all outward appearance Kai adapted well to life in Haven. She participated in work crews and therapy sessions. Savanna was observing her therapy group when one of the women brought up a child she had lost to the state. She was expressing her desire to try to regain custody of the boy when Kai spoke.

"Why? Why would you want him back? Kids are nothing but trouble. I'm glad I'm not going to have any more." Her voice dripped with bitterness.

The therapist grabbed onto the comment. "How many children do you have, Kai? Where are they now?"

Kai looked directly at Savanna. "Dr. Taylor has the only surviving one. More power to her if she can fix what's wrong with her. The other two were born early and addicted. They died. After the second, the judge ordered me to get an IUD. I'm fine with that. I don't need no kids messing up my life."

Savanna sat quietly. This was information she didn't know. How much damage had been done to this girl? If only she could have done something to help her heal her mind like she could her body.

Savanna covertly studied Kai as the therapist pried for more information. Kai had been seeing the dentist in the clinic and most of her teeth had been repaired. Her face was starting to heal, but there were still several pock marks disfiguring her features. There were also several deeply scarred burn marks on her left hand and forearm. In reviewing Kai's medical chart upon intake Savanna had learned they had come from an attempt to make a small batch of quick meth. Kai had put the ingredients for the drug in a two-litter pop bottle and shook it to mix them together. The resulting explosion had caused second and third degree burns on her hand and forearm and led to her first arrest for drug possession.

At dinner that evening Savanna was deep in thought, trying to think of ways to help Kai. She pushed her peas around with her spoon, mustering up the energy to eat when a giggle got her attention. She looked across the table and noticed her children mimicking her movements. Raven was separating each pea and had arranged them on her plate in a star pattern. Caleb, at nearly two, was using a spoon to push the peas to the far edge of the plate and attempted to keep them there. When they would roll to the center of the plate, or off the edge, he would attempt to pick them up with his pudgy little fingers. Usually all he succeeded in doing was smashing the tiny green balls. Savanna laughed at their antics and finished her peas to set an example.

Travis picked up his family's trays to take to the counter. The family group seemed smaller since Erik left them. He was now living at the surrogate dormitory as the in-house therapist. Savanna had the facility built in Boise, closer to University Row, to give the girls in the program more educational opportunities. Ronnie had moved in with him and together they administrated the program.

Raven missed her best friend, but Savanna took the children with her when she made her twice monthly furloughs to the clinic. Aida, Raven and Caleb would stay with Erik while Savanna worked.

Savanna had access to greater resources than the clinic staff. She was able to use the obscene amount of money left to her upon the death of her father to fund needed medical supplies. She extended Haven's grant program to encompass the clinic and, as a result, the clinic was able to service a larger number of patients.

Work at the clinic had been quiet, despite the initial excitement of her first shift. Women rarely needed to make as dramatic of an escape as Nulie did when she first came to Haven.

A few days after Nulie's escape she released a statement explaining why she ran away. Her husband filed many appeals to her, but she refused each one. Her fear for her daughter greatly outweighed her love for her husband. She mourned the loss of her son and expressed hope her husband was raising him well.

Nulie spent the last three years at Haven, learning English and working on her education. She earned her high school diploma and was looking into various nursing programs. Savanna convinced her she could help her with her scarring and pain. After more than a dozen surgeries, Nulie's mutilation had been repaired on the aesthetic level. She would never fully recover, but if she ever chose to remarry, she at least had the opportunity to have a normal relationship with her spouse. Even though Nulie could safely move from Haven now, Savanna had offered to let her stay and finish her nursing program. She had offered her the position of Dorm Manager of East Wing, the third addition at Haven.

Haven quickly became more than a facility to assist women. As states tightened border security and towns started to develop their own militias more and more appeals for shelter were crossing Savanna's desk.

Entire families camped outside the gates leading to Haven, begging for refuge. Travis would take a troop of men to the tent cities to try to disband them, but he would be confronted by a solid wall of resistance. Men pleaded with the security forces to at least take their wives and children. They could fend for themselves, but the women and children were at risk from disease or starvation. The militias soon became gangs, hoarding food, exacting taxes, creating mobs and subjugating entire communities to acts of all-out terror. The National Guard could do little to control the situation. They were spread too thin to help.

Despites Savanna's attempt to help the families outside the gates, the situation grew worse. New families arrived at the gates, bringing disease with them. More than once Savanna was called to the shanty town to deal with outbreaks of typhus or scarlet fever or any number of diseases. When Haven was built her father had purchased all the acreage surrounding the community, thinking he could sell it off for lots to help fund the project. Haven had become a self-sufficient community before he ever needed to do this, so Savanna was left with acres of land with which to work. She built several dormitories on the land. Long one-story buildings, to house these families.

These buildings were not as protected as Haven and

were susceptible to raids from marauding bands of thieves and renegades, but at least they offered some protection from the elements. The families taking residence in these shelters had to follow the same work program as the members of Haven to live in the dorms, but there was no way she could offer them the same training and medical care she did for the women inside her walls.

The dormitories became a haven for undocumented workers, those who refused to be marked with the government microchip. Savanna built a health clinic and staffed it with graduates of Haven's medical program. With this and the medications she was able to acquire through the government subsidies provided for Haven, she was at least able to keep disease and starvation at bay in what was becoming known as Little Haven.

It was Caleb's third birthday and Travis and Savanna were bringing him with them on furlough, leaving the others. Emily had opted to stay at Haven, needing to get some things done at Little Haven Clinic. Raven had a project she needed to get done for school so she begged her parents to allow her to stay. Savanna felt this was also a good time to get Kai out of Haven and start her on furloughs.

Although she hadn't shown much interest in the programs at Haven, Kai had completed a certified nurses' aide program and Savanna was encouraging her to look for a job outside of the community. Kai sat in the back seat of the car beside Caleb. She made a point of staring out the window and refusing to look at the boy, even though he kept tapping her on the hip and saying 'Wavie, Wavie, Wavie'. He would brush his hand through her midnight black hair, so much like Raven's.

Savanna studied the girl in her visor mirror. Many of the scars and marks on her face had faded with laser treatments and multiple surgeries had repaired most of the damage on her arm and hand. She still carried scars from the severe burns, but now she could at least use the hand with almost a complete range of motion.

Rose had dinner waiting for them when they arrived at

the Warm Springs house. She convinced Kai to go with her to a movie after dinner, knowing Savanna wanted some quiet time with her husband. Savanna and Travis both played with Caleb until they wore him out, showing him the stars in the big room and running around with him in the big back yard with Rose's cocker spaniel. When he was sufficiently exhausted they laid him in the big boy bed they had used to replace the crib in his room. He was asleep as soon as his head hit the pillow.

Savanna brushed her hand through his springy curls. "He had so much fun with the dog, today," she whispered to Travis. "It makes it wish animals were allowed at Haven."

"Little boys and puppies do seem to belong together." Travis kept his voice low. They tiptoed from the room silently, making their way down the hall to their bedroom.

Placing the video monitor beside the bed, Savanna took a moment to study the image of her sleeping son. He was curled in a ball with his thumb plugging his mouth, a habit he had only when he was completely exhausted. Smiling, Savanna lay down on the bed next to Travis. She studied the star pattern on the ceiling, tracing each constellation in her mind. Travis brushed his fingers against her cheek, leaving a warm trail on her skin.

"We need to go camping sometime so we can look at the stars as they really are." Savanna turned her head and met his soft, full lips with hers. They parted and Savanna caressed her lips with her tongue, feeling the honeyed taste left behind.

"Did you know they've been able to reestablish the space program? Private companies are sending scientists to the space station and the moon colony. One of the further reaching probes may even have found indication of life on another planet."

Travis grinned and leaned in to kiss her again. "I think I'm satisfied with the life on this planet. We still have a lot of work to do to rescue this planet before we send probes into space to wreck the universe."

Savanna was still lost in the moment of the kiss, so it took her a second to respond. When she opened her eyes, it was to find Travis' staring back at her. "Well, some of the research is helping us here on earth. We're using the same technology they use on the moon colony to grow crops in the green houses at Haven."

Travis reached down and kissed her again. "I don't want to talk about Haven right now." He kissed her again. "I just want to enjoy being with you. Haven takes so much away from you. I want to be selfish and have you to myself tonight." He gently nuzzled her neck, right at the pulse point.

Savanna reached up to gently push him away until he was looking in her eyes again. His expression was puzzled, but her warm smile smoothed the wrinkle from his brow. "Speaking of life here on this planet—" The wrinkle was back and Savanna broadened her grin. She reached up with her finger and smoothed the furrow. "I'm at about three weeks." It took a moment for comprehension to flood into his features, but once it did, his reaction was priceless.

Travis whooped and leaped to his feet, flying in the air and bounding on the bed. At the moment, Savanna was grateful for the motion resistant mattress because she was sure she would have been bounced off the bed without it. A fussing sound from the monitor caused her to glance at the screen. Caleb stirred and rolled on his back, his thumb popping out of his mouth. Savanna hushed Travis and watched until she was assured her son went back to sleep. Travis settled back down and pulled her into his arms. He gently kissed her and caressed her hair. Savanna reveled in his warmth as his kisses became more ardent. Her love for this man grew even stronger at the thought of all the love and protection he provided for her.

She started her shift at the clinic early the next morning. After Travis brought Savanna, Kai and Sam, the S290, to the clinic he drove away with Caleb. He planned to take Caleb to the YMCA water park as a treat. The boy loved to play in the water and, since there wasn't a pool at Haven, the furloughs were the only time he could swim.

Savanna had developed the habit of bringing the S290 to the clinic with her as a precaution. Ever since Nulie had escaped using the clinic as a refuge the tiny building had become a target for protesters. The S290 had a built-in unit they could use to store harvested embryos from women who were putting them up for adoption. The clinic still performed abortions, much to Savanna's disappointment. She couldn't convince the staff fetal adoption was a preferred method of dealing with unwanted pregnancies. No one outside the clinic staff knew the robot had the storage center, so protesters didn't harass them on the way out.

Today, a group of protesters stood outside the gates harassing patients as they attempted to enter for their appointments. They had to stay at least fifty yards away from the doors of the clinic, but their voices could be heard as Savanna and Kai approached the front door.

A young, obviously pregnant, girl stood at the front door. As Savanna approached she could see the girl was pale and shaky. A flash of pain registered in her eyes and Savanna realized she was in labor. She couldn't understand why the girl didn't enter the clinic, but instead stood staring at the protesters. Savanna listened to the voices yelling across the way and slowly made out the words they were chanting.

"They're going to steal your baby!"

"Baby stealers!"

"Don't go in. We'll save you. Come with us!"

The crowd was working themselves into a frenzy and Savanna realized the girl was not responding well to the heckling. She wrapped her arm around the girl's shoulder and pulled her close.

"Don't listen to them. I'll protect you." Savanna gently led the girl into the clinic and shut out the noise behind her.

Chapter Twenty-Nine

THE WAITING ROOM WAS quiet and tense. There were hardly any patients sitting in chairs and the clinic staff looked nervous and edgy. Savanna sat the girl down in a chair, far away from anyone else, and motioned one of the clinic staff over. The staff member brought a chart, but when she moved to take over the patient, Savanna waved her away.

"It's okay. I'll help her." Savanna sat down next to the girl. The plain, long dress and triangle shaped head scarf proclaimed her to be part of the same polygamist sect as Michelle. Savanna pulled a chair close to her and sat down.

At first the girl was either nonresponsive or spoke so quietly Savanna couldn't understand her during the questioning. Savanna leaned in close and put her hand on the girl's arm, in what she hoped was a reassuring gesture.

"What's your name?"

"Katy." The whisper was barely audible.

"Katy?"

The girl nodded and Savanna continued. "It's okay. No one is going to take your baby. We're here to help you. How long have you been in labor?"

The girl started to speak but another contraction stopped her. When the spasm passed she looked up. Savanna realized the girl was trying to assess if she could trust her. Katy must have decided Savanna was trustworthy because she started to speak. "I've had back pain since last night. My family brought me here, but I had to wait until the clinic opened before I could come in. The others left when they saw the mob. Many people don't accept us." Another contraction caused the girl to curl in pain. "Is this your first?" Savanna asked. A quick nod through the pain offered confirmation.

"Not mine," Katy said through clinched teeth. "Belongs to first wife." Savanna realized the girl was a member of the polygamist sect Emily worked with occasionally.

Savanna didn't approve of the lifestyle this community

led, but everything happening there was well within the bonds of the law, so she could do nothing about it. She ordered a wheelchair to take Katy to a labor and delivery room. Savanna paused outside the door to scrub her hands and dress. It only took a few moments to put on her gown, cover her hair with a cap and put her mask in place. When she was dressed she entered the room.

A quick ultrasound revealed Katy carried twins. She smiled when Savanna told her. "I'm going to get to keep the second born," she said, before another contraction hit.

Hooking Katy to the fetal heart monitor frustrated Savanna. The machine was so archaic compared to the technology she had at Haven or even at Surrogate house. She felt fortunate there didn't appear to be anything wrong with the babies. The fetal heartbeats were strong.

The labor progressed normally, Savanna asked Katy if she wanted an epidural, but the girl declined. Katy was fully dilated and on her first push, a foot presented, an indication of a possible breach birth. Savanna called in a team in to help.

"Stop pushing Katy," Savanna instructed. "Breathe through the next few contractions. One of the infants' leg is out. I need to put it back in and turn the infant."

Katy, drenched in sweat and straining from the pain, looked at Savanna with clear eyes. "Tie a ribbon around the foot." Savanna was puzzled by the girl's request, but when Katy handed her a yellow ribbon from her hair, she tied it around the tiny ankle and continued with the procedure.

Using gentle pressure to push the foot back in and turn the baby only took a few minutes. Katie gasped in pain and her face turned red. Savanna wished the girl would have allowed her to give her an epidural, but it was too late now.

After completing the procedure, the baby crowned. Two more big pushes and the shoulders were out. As soon as the shoulders were out, the rest of the body emerged without any difficulties. Savanna wrapped the infant in a blanket and placed her on her mother's stomach as she clipped the cord. Katy automatically reached down and held her in place.

"Well, your first born is a little girl." Savanna prepared for the delivery of the second baby as Katy looked over the one on her stomach.

"She doesn't have a ribbon."

Savanna looked up as the next baby's head crowned. "What?"

Katy held the blanket away from the tiny, wrinkled feet. "There isn't a ribbon tied to her foot."

Just then a contraction shook Katy's body. A nurse took the baby girl and Savanna's attention was drawn back as the head of the second baby emerged. She gently twisted to alleviate the pressure as the shoulders and the body soon followed. Noting the child was a boy, she immediately looked down and noticed a bedraggled ribbon tied to his ankle.

"Well, it looks like I was wrong. Your first born is a boy. He was the first to emerge. It looks like his foot went back in and he was turned when his sister was born. You gave birth to two healthy babies." Savanna finished cleaning off the boy and cut his cord.

Savanna could tell Katy was tired, but the after-birth euphoria of the hormone flood would kick in soon. Savanna removed her gloves and washed her hands as the nurses brought the babies to Katy and placed them on either side of her. Katy looked at each infant, gently rubbing the toes and caressing the ears. She paid special attention to the little girl.

"Anna is going to be so happy to have a little boy. And I'm so excited I have a little girl. I just wish..."

"What do you wish?" Savanna prompted.

Katy looked down at the infants in her arms. "I wish I wouldn't have to go through the ceremonial second husband. I wish my husband could have proven his worthiness."

Savanna looked at each of the children. She realized they were probably the result of a ritual marriage performed amongst the polygamist group. Savanna had studied the family dynamics of the polygamists group as she encountered them over the years. Many of the members were anti-government groups who banded together after citizens were required to be implanted with a microchip. They formed roving bands, many times consisting of extended family groups.

The work policies they adopted were echoed by Savanna's father at Haven. The workfare program guaranteed no one would go hungry, if they worked for their food. Since the members of the group refused the microchip, many mainstream jobs were unattainable for them and they were forced to create a barter system to live.

Polygamy was incorporated into the group due to the lack of options for health care. One of the basic rights of citizenship was health insurance. Since the group didn't have the microchip, they couldn't be classified as citizens. When infertility became a growing issue, the female members of the group started asking men of proven fertility to father their children. The group leaders realized there was no way to control this behavior, so they established strict guidelines to monitor conception and protect the genetic line from incest and the women from being exploited.

Savanna didn't condone the methods they used, but since she couldn't change the behavior, she did her best to care for those who came to the clinic.

Emily had been invited into the encampments of the group to care for members of the community who could not make it to the clinic. She'd been present during one of the ceremonies and was horrified by what she witnessed. At least the parts she saw and was told about. When she returned to Haven, she described the procedure to Savanna.

The young woman participating in the second marriage was completely covered from head to toe in a ceremonial robe. She was led to a tent, where twelve elderly women from the community watched over her. The man who had been chosen as her second husband would be led into the tent. Usually it was a man who had proven his fertility with multiple wives. Both parties would be completely covered, no hint of identity showing. The act was consummated in just a few minutes. After it was over parties would be led from the tent. The hope was the brief encounter would result in pregnancy.

Savanna studied the two infants that were the result of one of these ceremonies. Katy rested quietly. Savanna encouraged her to go to the hospital to recover, but the girl refused. Her family had given her a disposable cell phone and she called them to arrange a ride. She gave her a bottle of pain medication, knowing she had no way to fill a prescription at a pharmacy, as well as some information on after-birth care, breast feeding and infant care.

She had the nursing staff round up a wheelchair and was helping Katy move from the bed to the chair, still trying to convince her she would be better off in a hospital. Katy refused, explaining the only reason she came to the clinic was because she was a first-time mother and the community thought she was getting too big to have a normal delivery. Since this birth was so easy, she insisted that from now on she was only going to use midwives and avoid any medical facilities.

As the nurse wheeled the girl out the door a sudden crash came from the front of the building. Almost immediately the back of the clinic filled with an acrid, burning odor. A woman's scream echoed through the hallways and a flash of orange lit up like a wall. Savanna ran from the delivery room and saw the entire lobby engulfed in flames and dark, black smoke rolling across the ceiling. The mask covering her face protected her from most of the smoke, but she knew it wasn't going to be much protection for long.

Savanna grabbed a sheet from a cart and threw it over Katy and the infants, tucking in the ends so they wouldn't drag on the floor. They were right outside the bathroom leading to the loading dock in the back alley, she opened the door, waving the nurse through.

"Take her and wait in the alley. Only come out if you recognize clinic staff." The nurse nodded and pushed the chair through the door.

Savanna closed the door and turned back to the exam rooms. She had no idea how many people were trapped by the raging fire. A form emerged from a cloud of gray smoke. Savanna grabbed the incoherent woman and recognized Becky.

She pushed her towards the bathroom door.

Acrid smoke rolled across the ceiling, causing Savanna's nose and eyes to burn. Tears soaked the surgical mask covering the lower half of her face and a coughing spasm racked her body. Blinded, Savanna could only make out shadowy forms fading past her. She reached out and grabbed one as it moved by. "How many?" She was confronted by a blank stare. "How many people are in the building?"

The woman shook her head. "I don't know. We only had seven patients. I think they all got out." Savanna pointed the woman to the bathroom.

"Go through there!" The woman disappeared through the door. Savanna dropped to her knees and crawled through the heat. Her hands touched the broad wheel base of her S209. "Sam!" The unit beeped in response. "Sam, find people. If they can walk, guide them to the bathroom and out the cargo bay. If they can't walk, carry them!"

She wasn't sure how much of her vocal commands the robot could hear, but he rolled off towards the back of the building. She probed around until her hand touched the wall. Creeping through the smoke, she brushed her fingertips against its surface until she came to the void of a doorway.

"Is anyone in here?" Calling into the emptiness didn't elicit a response. She knew she didn't have time to go in and investigate. She was already starting to feel dizzy. Crawling to the next doorway, she called again. The third exam room door was closed. She reached for the handle and turned it. As soon as the door opened, a hand reached out and grabbed her arm. Savanna grasped onto the attached arm and pulled the person from the room. She couldn't tell who it was, but whoever she was, she grabbed onto Savanna as if she were a lifeline. Savanna pulled the person to the floor and pushed her against the wall.

"Crawl against the wall. Two empty rooms. The third door leads to a bathroom." The woman didn't move at first. Savanna prodded her ribs. "Move!" This propelled the woman forward and Savanna watched her disappear into the smoke.

The heat pressed down on her body, seemingly entering

every pore and pulled the oxygen from her lungs. She was starting to feel the sweat soaking the cap covering her hair. Turning around, she started back towards the bathroom, feeling along the wall. When she reached a void, she thought was near the bathroom she turned inside. Her hand touched the burning hot metal of a rolling chair. She didn't know where she was. Her head spun.

Heat pushed her to the floor and she couldn't draw air into her lungs. Flames crept around the doorframe as she dragged herself forward. Unable to see anything she felt around for the wall.

She couldn't breathe. Her heart rate accelerated to a marathon pace. Pain flashed through her hand. Sparks flew as she disturbed a pile of burning coals. She couldn't breathe. Her head throbbed with pain. She buried her face in her arms to filtered air through her clothes. She couldn't breathe.

Suddenly, a metal vise gripped her arm. Pain flashed through her wrist as hot metal burned into her skin. "Dr. Taylor, this way." The metallic sound of her S290's voice filtered through her consciousness.

She was lifted from the floor. Searing pain flashed through her body. Everything clouded over and she couldn't breathe. She saw stars popping before her eyes and felt the searing pain in her lungs.

Then nothing.

Screaming sirens brought her to consciousness. Her lungs burned as oxygen was forced into them. Voices buzzed in her head. Buzzing but no distinguishing words. Pain radiated from every cell in her body. Cold penetrated her to the core.

"She's waking up. Morphine. Now."

Savanna grabbed the arm of the medic. "No."

The medic stopped the needle posed above the IV port.

"No morphine. Pregnant."

"Doctor, we need to give you something for the pain. You have second and third degree burns all over your body." The needle continued its journey toward the port.

"No!" The word came out with as much force as she

could muster. "I can wait. In hospital—take fetus. Put in cryo. Then give drugs."

The medic shook his head, but put away the syringe.

"How many trapped?"

"We don't know," the medic responded. "The fire department is still fighting the blaze when the robot burst out. We don't know how he made it through. His circuits were pretty fried when we plucked you off him. I'm afraid we left a little bit of your skin behind on his metal frame. He got pretty hot in there."

Savanna barely heard the final words through the haze in her mind. She stared at the ceiling of the ambulance, focusing on breathing through pain and staying strong for her child.

She welcomed the blackness.

Chapter Thirty

EVERYTHING WAS HAZY AND confusing. She remembered waking up and seeing Travis beside her bed and closing her eyes and then opening them to see Emily and Raven. When she tried to talk she realized she was intubated. She lost all sense of time and reality as she drifted in a state somewhere between awareness and dreams. At one point, she woke up and realized she no longer had a tube down her throat. When she asked what happened everyone hushed her and told her to get rest. Asking questions became burdensome. She knew the words she wanted to ask, but they weren't coming out of her head.

The nurses gave her a button and told her to push it when she felt pain, but she couldn't feel anything and then the pain would come and she would push the button and then it seemed to take forever for the pain to go away. It was all too complicated and not worth it and she would forget the button was there and soon she just gave up. The nurses would remind her of the button and she would forget again. At one point, they just replaced the button with a morphine drip.

She remembered asking about Kai, but no one answered. The only response she received when she asked again was from Raven. "Kai was there? Why does Kai want to hurt Mommy?"

And the nightmares. Incoherent images floated through her mind. She saw Kai, the woman, suffering through withdrawals, fading into Kai, the girl, covered with weeping blisters, fading into Yanaba, the child, arching with seizures. She was lost in a world of shadows and flames and no one was there to save her. She called over and over for Travis and he wasn't there.

Sleep was the enemy, but she couldn't wake up. Waking up was extremely painful. Every time she woke, she asked what day it was. Someone would tell her, but she would forget and ask again the next time.

Eventually the pain started to fade and become bearable and the doctors slowly reduced the morphine levels.

Finally, things started to make sense to her. The first thing she saw when she awoke was Travis' concerned face staring down at her. She attempted to smile at him, but felt a sharp twinge in her lips. She reached up and felt the dry chapped skin attesting to her dehydration.

"Water?" Relief flooded Travis' eyes as she spoke the word.

"The doctor says I can give you ice chips. I don't think you're getting enough fluids though." Travis spooned a few chips in her mouth. Savanna relished the cooling effect. It soothed her pain ridden throat.

"How long have I been out?" The words came easier even though her throat still hurt.

"The doctors kept you in a drug induced coma for about a week. They wanted to give your burns a chance to heal and the tissue grafts to take." Travis placed his hand on her shoulder and brushed his fingers against her cheek. "I was so scared, Savanna. The thought of losing you, I couldn't take it."

Travis buried his face next to her shoulder. Savanna could feel the whiskery growth of his unshaved cheeks tickling her neck. She tried to reach over and brush her fingers through his hair but flinched back from the pain. Travis sat up and scanned her body, looking for the source of pain.

"How bad?"

Travis's eyes met hers. She knew it was worse than she thought. The morphine was probably taking the edge off. "You have second and third degree burns over much of your body. Most of them came from the hot metal of the S290. You also suffered some smoke inhalation. But you're alive and you're coming home to me." Travis ran his hand up and down her forearm.

Savanna watched his hand gently caress her milky-white skin. She always liked to look at the contrast his dark skin had against hers, it soothed her in a way nothing else could. "What about the others? Was anyone else hurt in the fire?" Savanna could feel the throbbing pain on her face and shoulder and her stomach started to lurch. She willed the sensation away.

Travis' forehead wrinkled. Savanna recognized the expression as the one he would use when he wasn't quite sure how much information he wanted to give her. "Three people were trapped in a rear exam room. They were in the middle of an embryo retraction when the firebomb exploded. There was no way they could stop where they were. They managed to keep the door closed and finish the procedure. It took them a few minutes to get the patient ready for transport and by the time they did, the fire had spread to the hallway. The patient and the doctor were able to escape, barely. They only had mild smoke inhalation. The nurse never made it out, but the embryo was safe in its storage container."

Travis stopped and took a breath. "Everyone else made it out. The clinic is a complete loss. It's going to need to be rebuilt and no one knows where the funding is going to come from. It's a shame. A lot of people counted on it. Oh, and Kai disappeared. We think she took the opportunity to cut and run."

"What?" Savanna almost sat up in bed, but the pain stopped her. "She only had three months left on her probation and she would have been free."

Travis didn't speak. Savanna leaned back into her pillows. She was almost afraid to ask her next question. "What about our baby? I asked them to harvest before they gave me drugs. What happened?"

Travis' smile didn't quite reach his eyes, but Savanna could see the relief in his expression. "Safe. Emily brought him back to Haven. The doctors feel as soon as you're strong enough it can be re-implanted. They're confident there shouldn't be any complications, if the implantation works."

Savanna tried to smile, but the pain shooting across the side of her face prevented any movement. "Where are all my burns? I think I hurt everywhere."

The smile didn't come this time.

"Just tell me," she said. "It's like ripping off a Band-

Aid. Do it fast, so it doesn't hurt as long."

Travis sighed and took her hand in his. "The right side of your face, your right shoulder down onto your chest, your right hand, your left hip, right across the joint and your entire right calf, in some places nearly to the bone."

As he listed off the injuries, Savanna attempted to assess and localize the pain in each area. It was impossible. As soon as he named one the pain would flare and radiate. She tried to take deep breaths, but it wasn't helping. A low groan escaped.

"You're in pain. Let me call the nurse."

Unable to use her voice, Savanna nodded. It didn't take long. Savanna kept her eyes closed against the nausea. She felt the burn of the morphine as it traveled through her veins. Soon she was floating in welcome oblivion.

She woke to fiery pain on her chest. A nurse was standing over her, gently removing the bandage covering the burn. Savanna sucked in her breath as the gauze came up and exposed the burn to the air. The pain was unbearable and she couldn't suppress her gasp.

"I'm so sorry, Dr. Taylor." The nurse paused in removing the layers of gauze. "I know this is extremely painful. We don't want to rush this, though. We want to try to minimize scarring so this is going to take some time. Let me know if this is getting to be too much and I'll give you more morphine. Do you think a virtual reality device would help?"

"I'm willing to try anything." Savanna spoke through clinched teeth. The nurse helped her place the VR glasses over her eyes and plugged ear buds into her ears. The images and sounds transported her to a cold mountain top as gentle snowflakes fell around, coating the landscape with a soft blanket of white.

The images helped her deal with the pain, but it wasn't enough to shut everything out. She didn't know how long she was lost in the cloud of white, but when the nurse removed the VR device she was enshrouded in fresh gauze. Savanna realized she recognized the nurse.

"You were at Haven, weren't you?"she asked.

The nurse was adjusting the IV drip, but stopped and turned to Savanna. "I was in a six-month rehab program. I don't know if you remember me very well, my name is Karen Pierce. Haven saved my life and my marriage. Some days I wish I was back there."

Savanna studied the worn face of the woman by her bedside for a moment. "Are you in danger of relapse?"

Shaking her head, the nurse turned back to the machine pumping fluids into Savanna's arm. "No, it's just that life is so much harder here on the outside. Sometimes it's hard to find enough food and supplies. We were so cared for in Haven, the world is just so hard right now."

Savanna couldn't keep her eyes open. Exhaustion overtook her before she could process what the nurse said. Her dreams led her to dark places in her mind. The pain overshadowed everything. Feeling so cold and alone, tears escaped the corner of her eyes and soaked her hair. Pain thrashed her body as if fists were pounding her from all directions. Trying to pull into a ball to protect her body, the pain shot through her. She couldn't move. She couldn't stay still. She woke up screaming.

Travis was by her side almost immediately. His voice soothed her and the warmth of his touch helped ease some of the pain. She realized her thrashing had loosened some of the bandaging materials and she could see yellow-stained, raw skin beneath. A nurse entered the room, a young girl Savanna didn't recognize. She checked the vitals on the machine, made a note on the computer and left the room. All without making eye contact, or talking, to Savanna. A few minutes later, she came back with a doctor.

"Dr. Taylor, it's good to see you awake. My name is Dr. Carlsen." Savanna vaguely recalled him working on her in the emergency room. "It looks like you're running a low-grade fever. You might be developing infection in some of the wounds. I'm going to have to remove the bandages and get some cultures. Are you going to be okay with me doing that?"

Savanna hissed through her teeth at the thought of the pain this was going to cause, but she nodded her head. "It has to be done." Travis wrapped his hand against hers and she lost herself in his eyes.

"I'm going to give you some morphine," Dr. Carlsen said. "It'll take the edge off the pain. I'll also get you set up with the VR device. Nurse Pierce said it helped when she changed the bandages last time."

Soon Savanna was lost in the cold winter scene. The coolness of the mountain seemed to stab into her at times. A deep, sharp pain shot through her hip, despite the virtual landscape. She screamed and tried to arch away from the pain. She heard Dr. Carlsen's apology, but the pain shot through her again, making her scream and thrash. Reaching up she pushed the glasses off and pulled the buds out of her ears.

"Dr. Taylor, it looks like there's some infection developing in the wound on your hip. I'm increasing your dosage of antibiotics." Dr. Carlsen continued to probe her hip as he spoke. Travis had to hold her arms to keep her from lashing out at the doctor. "We're probably going to want to do surgery to get the pocket of infection out before it gets to the joint. The last thing we need is infection in the bone. If that happens, we'll have to take the leg. Don't worry, I'm going to do everything I can to prevent that."

Between the antibiotics and the increase in morphine, Savanna was overwhelmed with nausea. She couldn't keep any food down and she knew she was losing weight. The bland, preservative-filled hospital food brought on severe, blinding headaches.

Travis convinced the doctors to allow food to be brought in from Haven, hoping the lack of chemical preservatives and unprocessed foods would help. When Emily arrived with the food she also brought jars full of a thick, sticky salve.

Karen came into the room to change Savanna's bandages. She wouldn't allow anyone else to do it, even coming in when she was off-shift to do the scheduled changes.

Technically this was against policy, but since she took over the infection decreased and the incision Dr. Carlsen made on her hip to drain the infection healed better than he anticipated the hospital overlooked the breach in procedure. Emily pulled Karen aside and handed her one of the jars. The two women held a whispered conversation in the corner of the room. Savanna could tell there was an undercurrent of argument in their mannerisms.

Emily obviously won the argument because when Karen approached the bed she was carrying the jar. She held it up so Savanna could see the golden salve. "Emily says she wants us to start using this on the burns instead of the ointment we've been using. I'm hesitant because if I use this I'll be going against doctor's orders, but she insisted that I ask you about it."

Savanna took the jar and studied the contents. Removing the lid revealed a sweet, pungent scent. She thought she could smell a hint of honey. "What's in here?" She wasn't questioning her friend's intent, she was just curious as to what was in the medicine.

"It's a natural antibiotic blend I created." Emily described the medicine to her just as she would if she was talking to her about a patient they were treating at Haven. "I used a blend of raw honey, fresh aloe vera, golden seal and garlic as well as a few other herbs. Everything is food grade material, so you don't have to worry about contamination. We even tested the honey for botulism. I promise it's safe, Savanna. The bacteria you've picked up in the wound has probably become resistant to the antibiotics they're using now."

Savanna handed the jar back to Karen. "Let's try this for a couple of days. I'll be covered in bandages so the doctor won't even notice." Her eyes met Emily's and she saw a flash of triumph there. "I trust Emily."

Emily grinned, the smile finally reaching her eyes. "You should take some internally as well. It isn't the greatest tasting, but it'll help you fight the infection." She picked up a plastic spoon and scooped out a glob. Savanna opened her mouth.

There was a bitter after-taste and the garlic overpowered the sweetness of the honey, but overall, it wasn't too bad.

Savanna's obvious trust in Emily won Karen over and the two women began to remove the gauze covering her wounds. The pain wasn't as intense this time, until they started removing the bandages over her hip. Savanna studied the gapping, oozing wound over her hip bone and had to swallow back a wave of nausea.

She was surprised by her reaction. After all her years in the medical field, she should have gotten used to the sight of pus, but it was the one thing she still had trouble handling. Closing her eyes, she felt the sting of the ointment as it made contact with the wound, but it wasn't as bad as she thought it would be. Even though she didn't have the VR device she closed her eyes and imagined away as much of the pain as possible. Her mind drifted to cool mountain tops and she let the sensation carry her away.

Chapter Thirty-One

SAVANNA'S RECOVERY TOOK A turn for the better once they started using Emily's ointment on her burns. The infection cleared up and her temperature went back to normal within the week. Dr. Carlsen was impressed by her progress and attributed it to Karen's expert care. He never did discover Emily's ointment and when he released her he didn't know Savanna had shanghaied Karen to work at Haven.

The return trip to Haven was blissful. Savanna finally met Karen's husband, David. He was a quiet, unassuming man of average build and intelligence who had managed to obtain a degree in computer engineering. He found it difficult to find a position in a field already burgeoning with applicants. Although there wasn't an overwhelming need for technicians at Haven, Savanna figured they could always use more help. If nothing else, she could use his help in repairing Sam and perhaps help build a technology program for incoming residents.

Savanna needed help in the sanitizing shower before entering Haven. Emily and Karen helped her remove her clothing and the bandages from the burns. Although the skin grafts had been incorporated into most of the burned areas on her body, the new growth was not as flexible as her natural skin. She found it almost impossible to move her right hand and her left leg wouldn't support her weight.

Emily helped support her as they moved into the shower. The range of motion in her right arm was severely limited so Emily helped her apply the antibiotic wash to her hair and the areas of her back she couldn't reach. Karen waited, already dressed, as Savanna stepped out of the shower. While Emily took her own cleansing shower, Karen covered Savanna's wounds with ointment and gauze. The two of them helped Savanna dress in her Haven uniform once again.

The warm cotton fibers caressed her skin, filling her with a sense of peace and harmony she hadn't felt in a long time. The uniform meant home, comfort, and gave her a sense of purpose. Travis ordered a wheelchair from the medical ward and wouldn't let Savanna argue her way out of using it. David waited with his and Karen's twelve-year old son, David Junior, for the others to emerge out of the changing room. Once they had all gathered they moved into the courtyard of the main compound.

It seemed the entire population of Haven was present to welcome her home as Travis wheeled her through the doors into the open air of the courtyard. The roar of voices echoed off the walls as the residents gave a welcoming cheer. It was after the dinner hour, a time when most residents would either schedule exercise time or work on individual or family projects. Savanna realized there were more people in the crowd then just those from the main wing and figured the residents from the other buildings must have come in through the field gates. There was no way this many people could have entered through the roof access.

Travis wheeled her through the crowd as they parted before her, allowing an alley way to form through the of crush bodies. Hands reached out to touch, reaching for her hands, brushing her hair. Then, into her frame of vision, a form blotted out the sun. Coalescing in the afternoon sun, seemingly emerging from out of nowhere, Etu appeared. His grey hair glowing as a shaft of sunlight caressed it. Savanna pushed herself out of the chair and fell into his embrace. She didn't realize she was crying until she felt the moisture against the front of his shirt.

"Father, why are you here?" The joy she was feeling could not be expressed in words.

"I came to see my children and grandchildren. I have missed them over the years. I did not know you had been injured until I arrived." Etu's deep voice reverberated from his chest rumbling against Savanna's cheek. She allowed him to help her into the wheelchair and the family continued into the community center, the only building large enough to house them all.

"It's amazing how you showed up just when I needed

you." Savanna couldn't keep the joy out of her voice. She noticed Raven leaning on him, never more than a hand span away.

"I've enjoyed spending the time with my grandchildren. Raven has grown so much since the last time I saw her." He reached down and picked up Caleb, settling him in his lap. "It's hard to believe you have another one nearly the same size Raven was when you left home. Haven is nothing like I imagined it to be. You have a fortress out here, Anaba."

Savanna smiled at the name she hadn't heard in a long time. She felt she had fought a battle and now had the scars to prove it. "When did you get here?" She still didn't understand why he was here, there had to be more than just wanting to see his grandchildren.

"I arrived about two weeks ago." Caleb squirmed on his lap, so he put him down. "I just had a feeling I needed to be here. There is no explanation for it. It is a good thing I arrived when I did. Travis was at his wits end trying to be here for the children and there for you. Emily was busy with things here, so I just took over the care of the children. I haven't had this much fun in years."

Emily came up behind her father and sat at a table. A number of dried herbs had been laid out to be sorted in containers. Groups of women were involved in the task, moving from the welcome committee to the task at hand. Emily took up the work at the table in front of her, the others gathered around to help as they could.

"Were the children any trouble today?" she asked.

"Not really, Enola." Etu answered.

Emily's face twisted. "Dad, I go by Emily, you know that."

Etu sighed before answering. "I know. I just like your real name."

"Emily is my real name."

The name battle had been going on for as long as Savanna had known the two. Etu must have realized it wasn't a battle he wanted to fight now because he turned back to

Savanna. "I think next time I visit I am going to fly. It's getting harder to cross state borders. The Guard does not like it when your reason for entering a state is just to visit." He stood up and stretched his back. "I was going to talk to you about allowing Emily to bring Raven to Arizona to visit since she's older now, but I think that is going to be a conversation we will have after you've had time to recover."

Savanna looked at her tall, dark daughter standing beside her grandfather. She could see the adoration in the eyes of the young girl as she studied him. Etu's hands flashed as he unconsciously signed as he spoke. She realized it was a habit they both shared. Raven complained of headaches from her colloquial implant so often Savanna allowed her to turn it off and used sign language at home.

"She's going to be nine this year. Time really goes by fast. Let me see how my recovery goes and I'll think about it." Raven kept her eyes on her mother's hands as she spoke. Most of the words had to be signed with Savanna's left hand, the right being almost completely useless. "Does anyone know what happened to Kai?"

Raven came and leaned against her mother's leg. Travis reached to stop her, but Savanna held up her hand. "It's okay, just be careful, Mommy's broken." Raven leaned against her hip, barely touching her.

"Why does Kai always hurt Mommy?" Savanna realized the times she had been hurt Kai had been on the periphery of the situations. She could see how a child could take the events out of context. She reached across with her good hand and caressed her daughter's hair.

"Kai didn't hurt Mommy. It was an accident." Savanna could tell that Raven was not mollified.

"How did this happen in the first place." Etu sat down across from Emily and was helping her sort herbs. "Wasn't the building up to code? Why did the sprinklers not kick in and put out the fire?"

"The assailants knew what they were doing." Savanna leaned forward as Travis began his explanation. She hadn't heard any of this before. "There was a water main outside of the building that supplied the fire sprinklers. Someone managed to turn it off during the night. The man's fingerprints and DNA were on the faucet. They used an accelerant with a high flashpoint to start the fire. The flames caught quickly and spread before anyone could do anything." Travis reached over and brushed the hair out of Savanna's face. "If it wasn't for Savanna and Sam a lot more people would have been lost."

"How many people did Sam get out?" Savanna asked.

"You know, they say it was the most amazing thing. He led at least five people to the bathroom before he rescued you." Savanna leaned her head on Travis's shoulder as he spoke. "The heat destroyed his circuitry, though. It's doubtful he can even be repaired. It's a shame. He's quite the little hero."

Savanna was saddened by the thought of losing the robot. At times he had been the only friend she had. Working on his programming brought a sense of escape from the human cost of the terrorist attacks and allowed her to clear her mind and refocus. She was going to have to see what she could do to repair him.

"How long is physical therapy going to take?" Etu's question drew Savanna back to the conversation.

Savanna extended her right arm so Etu could see the white gauze covering the palm. She couldn't open her fingers all the way as the scar tissue was tightening and pulling against the muscle. "The doctors can't say how much use I'll get out of the affected joints and muscles to any certainty."

She tried to extend her fingers a little more, but they didn't budge. "I'm still feeling an extreme amount of pain in my shoulder, hip and calf when I try to move. The consensus is I may never have full function in my left leg because too much of the calf muscle was destroyed. Fortunately, most of the joint function has been maintained, so I should be able to walk and use my arm again. I just have to work on stretching the skin to allow further mobility."

Etu took his hand in hers, gently running his fingers over the gauze covering her wounds. "I will do the best I can to help you heal, my Anaba. You have done much for the hope and the healing of The People. It is time we paid our debt."

Savanna tried curling her fingers around his hand. Her grip was weak, but the connection was there. "The People owe me no debt. You have done more for me than anyone else ever has. My heart belongs to The People, it has since the first moment I met Yanaba."

Etu placed his hand on the side of Savanna's face. She leaned forward and he pulled her into his chest. Closing her eyes, she drew in the aroma of sage on his shirt. The pain seemed to fade as she lost herself in the scent of the desert. A low rumble echoed in his chest and Savanna realized he was chanting. She knew there was no empirical evidence to show spiritualism could influence healing, but nonetheless, the chanting soothed her. Without realizing it, she fell to sleep in his arms.

She woke as she felt herself being placed in a bed. Opening her eyes, she found Travis staring down at her. The familiar room came into focus, austere white walls devoid of decoration. Travis smiled as she took in her surroundings.

"Welcome home, my love." He gently kissed her on the forehead as he positioned her on the bed.

"How on earth did I fall asleep in that position?" Savanna was wide awake now, horrified at the thought of falling to sleep on Etu's shoulder.

Travis chuckled. "I don't know, but you slept better than I've seen you sleep for a long time."

"Why didn't anyone wake me?"

"I was going to, but Etu wouldn't release you." Savanna heard a hint of possessive jealousy in his voice. "He said you needed the healing."

"How long was I out?" Savanna felt a little disoriented.

"About half an hour. You didn't even stir when Emily removed your shoes." Travis reached for the zipper of her uniform. "I was beginning to think I was going to need her help getting you dressed for bed."

He helped her remove her uniform and put on her

night gown. It took him about ten minutes to place the pillows around her and under her arms and legs to position her. She knew he would be up every two hours to reposition her to keep the blood flowing and relieve pressure points throughout the night. The most frustrating aspect of her injuries was the inability she had to comfortably move herself as she slept. Hopefully, the physical therapy would relieve some of those issues. Travis crawled in beside her staying near the edge of the bed. He rolled to his side and placed his hand on her stomach, one of the few places he could touch without causing her pain.

Savanna could feel his eyes on her as she dozed off and on. Sleep seemed to elude her. In the outside world, the division between the social classes was becoming more pronounced and clashes were becoming more frequent. The appeals to join Haven were coming at a more intense rate and Savanna knew she wasn't going to be able to help everyone who needed it. She didn't even know if she could help herself.

She went to a dark place in her dreams again. Travis woke her. Whispering soothing words in her ear, he slowly brought her back. Her nightgown was drenched in sweat and pain throbbed in her hip and shoulder in rhythm with her racing heart. She couldn't bring her breathing back to normal. Her head throbbed and she couldn't get herself calm enough to go back to sleep. Travis called Emily and she sent a medic over to help transport her to the hospital wing. Etu came over to stay with the children.

Savanna suspected her problem stemmed from withdrawal from the morphine. Emily offered to give her some to take the edge off, but Savanna refused. She didn't want to become dependent on it. Instead, she asked for some chamomile tea, hoping the soothing affects would help. A headache throbbed in her temples and the bright hospital lights seemed to pierce her eyes. She asked Travis to turn off the lights and bring her a blanket from the warmer. It seemed to help and she dozed off again.

She wasn't sure what time she woke the next day, but she was still in the hospital. Travis was gone and Etu was in his place beside her bed. Her head still throbbed, but the pain was more manageable. Etu must have heard her stir because he stood and approached the bed.

As Savanna studied his face, she realized he didn't seem to be as old as she remembered him to be. Thinking back, she realized he had only been in his early fifties when the Smallpox outbreak first occurred, meaning he was in his early sixties now. He just seemed so much older to her because of his strength and his wisdom.

Chapter Thirty-Two

SOMEONE WAS CONSTANTLY BY Savanna's side as she struggled through nightmares and headaches. Travis' duties pulled him away from her bedside often, as he dealt with rising security concerns cropping up on the edges of Haven property. Emily made several soothing tea blends to alleviate her pain. Physical therapy had to be delayed because Savanna tired so easily. She had no reserve from which to pull any strength.

Emily brought in a cream blend she created to soften some of the scar tissue and bring some of the elasticity back to the atrophied tissue. It became Etu's responsibility to massage the cream into the scars and stretch the muscles to increase Savanna's range of motion. At first Savanna was uncomfortable with the intimacy of the therapy, but soon Chief Etu's gentle hands and soothing voice allowed her to ignore the placement of his hands as he massaged the scars. He would chant as he manipulated the tissue's angry red and purple ridges.

Savanna could feel the joints relaxing and stretching under his competent hands. He helped her stretch the joints, flexing them and forcing them to move. They would be painful and throbbing afterwards, but after a while the pain would fade and she would relax and be prepared to start all over again.

Days passed before she could be moved from the hospital bed back to her home. Still, she couldn't put any weight on her left leg. She had to rely on those around her for help. Strength slowly returned to her arm and she had full range of motion in her left leg, despite the injury to her hip. Every waking hour was dedicated to recovery. Meanwhile concerns mounted over the security of Haven.

Travis would come home every evening, weary from patrols along the border of the property. Haven's property consisted of about four hundred acres and abutted several Federal Reserve lands.

The beginning of spring was the busiest time for security and this year was no exception. Several traveling refugees had set up camps on the border of the Federal land, hiding from rangers in gullies and wooded catches. The spring floods forced them to high ground and groups of them had crossed over the boundary lines onto Haven property. Usually this wasn't a problem, the groups would move on as soon as they realized they were on private property, but this year they harassed the workers as they prepared the fields for planting.

The early spring work involved clearing fields, plowing and spreading fertilizer. Most of this work involved the use of tractors and heavy trailers and only a select group of residents were trained in the use of the farm equipment. The rest of the residents worked on collecting water samples to ensure the purity of water or in the greenhouses preparing small plants for transplant. There were several other jobs requiring only small groups of laborers in the field, and it was these groups who were being harassed.

Gangs armed with clubs and firearms would come out of hiding and surround the small work crews. Asking for food or supplies, they would threaten to hold them hostage if they didn't capitulate. The female residents would balk at going out alone and there weren't enough security personnel to protect the individual groups.

Savanna looked into hiring more security, but she ran into the issue of housing any possible guards. All of the beds were taken in the wings of Haven facility and Savanna had no idea where she could add more. There was the option of using the barracks she had built for construction workers when she was adding the wings to Haven, but even that idea ran into problems. The waste treatment plant was already running at maximum capacity, she would need to build another one before she could add more residents.

The harassment of the work crews increased. Savanna needed to do something to protect the members of her community. It would take three months to get the waste treatment plant built and running, but it was a necessary step, so she ordered the equipment and put in the work order. In the meantime, she made sure work crews didn't leave the facility in groups smaller than twenty and the children were not to leave the compound to work the fields until the problem was solved.

The number of attacks lessened but didn't stop entirely. Savanna wanted to join the work crews to find out what was happening, but she didn't have the physical strength. Travis brought her regular reports, but it wasn't the same as being there. She missed her walks along the rooftops with her family. The children became bored with exercising in the gym while she did her physical therapy and would act up, distracting her from her exercises.

She pushed herself in her recovery but didn't seem to be making much progress. The wheelchair was more of a hindrance than a help. As long as she was inside Haven she could cruise the hallways and push herself among the groomed paths, but once she was outside the gate the uneven ground prevented her from moving forward. She needed to strengthen her leg so she could put weight on it to walk.

Standing on the atrophied muscles was torture. Savanna struggled to take steps, but she never made it more than five yards before her strength gave out and she would collapse back into the chair. There was no relief from the pain. It was constant, throbbing, as she tried to walk or stretch. She was slowly regaining strength in the rest of her body, but her leg refused to cooperate.

The days started to get warmer and Savanna bristled at the thought of staying inside. Travis started taking her to the glass enclosed walkway spanning the rooftop of the Haven hive.

Savanna realized she could see much of the work being done in the fields from the rooftop and started spending most of the day wheeling herself around the walkway. On warm, clear days she would open the doors and wheel around the security balcony encircling the stone structure.

Emily and Etu joined her one morning to watch the sun rise. Bright, white rays dashed across the sky and reflected off the tops of the mountains. Work crews left through the gates of each wing of the facility, heading into the fields.

Savanna watched as a large group headed to the barn where the farm equipment was stored. The crews started to split off, some of them headed towards the orchards and berry fields. It was time to trim the dead branches and brambles from the fruit bearing plants. Tractors pulled out of the shed, having spent the night charging engines in the solar battery bay.

Tools were distributed and groups were formed. Everyone dispersed to various tasks. The tractors headed for the fields to plow deep into the rich soil. This was the final plowing before planting and hundreds of Haven residents gathered near the storage sheds to prepare seeds, grains and sprouts. The tractors shrank into the distance as they entered the farm fields. Tiny dots represented groups of workers, mostly women, fading into the trees and bushes. One group drew Savanna's eye. They just didn't look right. As they emerged from the brambles, she noticed the group wasn't wearing Haven uniforms. She drew Emily's attention and pointed out the group as they slowly walked across the field and approached one of the tractors.

"Call security. We have a situation." Emily turned to follow her directions, leaving Savanna and Etu to watch from the walkway.

The tractors had pulled too far away from the groups working in other areas. Savanna couldn't see what was happening. She had to get a better vantage point.

Reaching forward she grasped the metal railing and, using every ounce of strength in her body, pulled herself out of the chair. The muscles in her leg screamed in pain, but she had to see. Gripping tightly, she used the strength in her arms to hold herself steady.

The scene played out like a poorly scripted movie. As work crews realized what was happening they dropped equipment and raced for the safety of the rock walls of Haven. The mob approaching the tractor was larger than ones Savanna had received reports about. It was difficult to get an accurate count, but Savanna figured there was close to a dozen people emerging from hiding. Their target was apparent, congregating on the one tractor in the furthest field.

All the tractors had separated and pulled away from the work crews as they plowed the fields. The mob approached as the drivers turned around and tried to make it back to the security of Haven. The invaders chose their target well, however. Electric tractors had the benefit of being powerful, but they weren't built for speed. There was no way the driver was going to make it back in time.

Haven security rushed to the scene. Savanna could see the two and four wheeled vehicles leaving the gate. They were too far away. The invaders surrounded the tractor, forcing it to a stop. Two of them leapt on the ladder leading to the cab, pried the door open, dragged the driver out and threw her to the ground. The others fell on her, kicking and punching until she stopped struggling against them.

It was hard to see exactly what each individual was doing, but Savanna could make out items being thrown to the ground. The mob stripped the tractor. Small solar panels and batteries were the first to go. Savanna kept her eyes on the woman lying so still in the field. A sharp, piercing whistle shattered the silence carried on the wind to where the assailants where stripping the tractor. A gesture from the lookout informed them Haven security had made it through the mass of workers running for the walls.

The invaders grabbed what booty they could and headed for the safety of the brambles. Savanna could tell most of them were going to make it. She saw a flash of light in the brambles and realized it was the reflection off a mirror. The mob had at least one vehicle waiting for them, hidden in the brush. A cloud of dust trailed behind the security force as they approached the scene.

Savanna's grip tightened on the railing as vehicles surrounded the woman on the ground. She didn't take a breath until she saw they had her c-spined and lashed to the back of one of the four-wheelers. A medic straddled the woman as the vehicle turned and headed back to the facility. The rest of the force took off after the fleeing assailants. Savanna turned to settle back in her chair, not bothering to watch the rest of the pursuit.

"Take me to the hospital wing, please. I want to be there when they bring her in." Savanna's focus was now on the injured woman, all other concerns became peripheral.

Etu grasped her chair. "It looks like they caught at least two of them. The others made it to the brambles." He pushed her into the glass enclosed walkway and down the ramp into her office.

They made it to the hospital just as the medics brought the injured woman in, but they were too late. The injuries to the woman's head were extensive. The assailants had used rocks to hit her over a dozen times. She was dead before the rescuers even got to her. Savanna had Etu wheel her out of the room and back to her office. He offered to stay with her, but she sent him away. Locking the door, she pulled up the security footage of the event.

Her stomach clinched as she replayed the attack, noticing tiny details she should have seen before. She reviewed previous attacks and border footage. Every where she looked she saw increasing elements of desperation.

Half-starved attackers surrounding work crews, forcing them to give up whatever supplies they had. Her entire property was surrounded by tent cities, hidden by a variety of camouflage techniques. Savanna realized the attacks weren't malicious, just desperate attempts to find food and supplies.

Savanna knew the attacks wouldn't end as long as food shortages continued to grow. She'd seen enough evidence of the disparity between the classes while working at the clinic. The government insisted any citizen living in the United States needed to be marked with a microchip containing their identification, immunization status and residency in order to obtain government benefits. Entire subgroups refused the chip and decided to live a life flying under the government radar. Martial law couldn't enforce the chip policy. The attacks came from groups who refused to have any connection with the American government. These groups gained momentum as the government continued to take control of many aspects of the country's private sector.

Savanna rubbed the palm of her hand, trying to feel the tiny bump of her own microchip. Social security, bank records, medical history, marital status, education and career was all programmed into the almost microscopic device planted under her skin. The financial investments her father and grandfather made through their lifetimes, and she had inherited, along with all the grants she used to build this oasis were filed away on this chip.

Microchip marking wasn't a requirement to enter Haven, but so many things necessary to live a comfortable life required the chip. The least of these was a work pass and health insurance. Many of the women of Haven requested a chip before leaving to pursue their lives outside the facility. Savanna had a microchip device brought to the facility and had a government permit to program chips and mark residents.

Savanna had to find a way to defend her community against marauders. In addition to the raids on Haven, there were also attacks on trucks bringing supplies from sister farms, although the drivers hadn't lost a cargo, yet. The rising desperation of the attackers made it clear this would no longer be the case. Something needed to change.

Pounding on her office door drew her away from the security footage. She pulled up the camera feed and saw Travis shaking the handle, trying to gain entrance. Savanna tapped the lock icon and the door flew open.

"Savanna, why did you lock everyone out?" Travis pulled himself up to his full height. He rubbed the handle of his taser, an unconscious gesture he made only when he was angry.

Savanna pushed herself away from the desk and wheeled over to him. "I'm sorry." She kept her voice low, trying to assuage his anger. "I just needed to collect my thoughts in private. This woman was my reasonability and I let her down."

Travis lifted her out of her wheelchair and carried her to the couch against the far wall. He sat and held her close as she shed tears of grief. "You're so young to have all this responsibility on your shoulders," he whispered. "You're not even thirty and it's like you're a mother to all the people here. You need to learn to delegate responsibility. Your recovery will be much faster if you did."

He took the pins out of her hair and ran his fingers through the honey waves. She felt the tingle of his fingers against the scars on her temple. Most of her head had been protected by the cap and mask during the fire, only the exposed part of her face that was resting against the S290 had been burned. The hair above her temple was growing back a light, silvery grey. Savanna pulled her head from Travis' shoulder and studied his eyes. They were so full of love and concern. She buried her head in his shoulder and allowed her body to relax into his warmth.

"I don't want any more crews going out without security with them. Start hiring. I want the force up to five hundred by planting time."

Travis fingers stopped massaging her scalp and he shifted so he could take out his data pad.

"We have six weeks before work crews go out in force." Savanna continued. "Invest in tasers. I want every single resident trained and armed before they go out again. Contact the Bureau of Land Management. They're in charge of the border land. Give them all the reports and video from the security cameras. We're not going to lose any more people." Savanna paused and took a ragged breath. "We've created a safe haven here, but we're not going to be able to maintain it if we are can't get our crops planted."

Travis cupped her face in his hands. "Will you promise to get more help if I do?"

Savanna took his hand in hers. "I promise."

Chapter Thirty-Three

A UNIFORMED OFFICER STOOD when Savanna entered her office. For a second Savanna bristled, this was the first time any one was allowed on Haven property in civilian clothes. Savanna walked to her desk and picked up the data pad waiting for her. She wasn't quite comfortable with the braces the tech crew developed. She kept trying to fight against the mechanized joints as she moved.

Savanna braced herself against the edge of the desk to hide the struggle she was having with the device. The federal ranger stayed quiet as Savanna found a favorable position. He seemed to know she needed a moment to center herself. Pretending to read the information on the data pad, Savanna surreptitiously studied the man standing in front of her. He was lean and wiry, just barely over five-eight, and was exuding a sense of quiet strength. He tilted his head in her direction.

"Ma'am." He had a slight twang to his voice; a dialect Savanna couldn't quite identify. "Thank you for allowing me to meet with you here. I know you can't get around too good since your accident."

Waving his statement away, Savanna pulling up information on her data pad then handed it to him. "Jacob, I asked you to come here to see if we can solve some of the problems we both seem to be having."

Jacob Schneider and Savanna had been talking for the past two weeks, trying to find a way to manage the rogue attacks. He was young to be in charge of the BLM land office, but many of the healthy young people in the nation had been drafted into the military to either fight overseas or to serve domestically with enforcing martial law. The president mandated a two years service requirement for every male citizen and a voluntary one-year service for women to shore up the flagging military membership. This law created even more dissension among the citizenship.

Savanna's main concern was the residents of Haven.

There were over four thousand souls she was directly responsible for in Haven and Little Haven. Most of those residents were women and children. Haven was becoming a refuge from the violence and hatred in the world, but it still wasn't enough. Hopefully the steps she was taking in this office today would help.

Jacob handed the pad back. As he moved, Savanna noticed the unnatural angle of his left arm and realized he had a prosthetic. "We're short-handed, just like everyone else, Dr. Taylor." The frustration was apparent in his voice. "We'll attempt to patrol the border more frequently, but you're surrounded by miles of federal land. We don't have the manpower necessary to round up all the squatters."

"I intend to build stations on the border of my property," Savanna said. "I'll man them with my own security force. It's just going to take a little bit of time to get the security force in place. I want the people I have now to join you and your men in patrolling the borders and cleaning out these scavengers..."

"Ma'am," Jacob interrupted. "We don't need interference from private forces. We have enough problems with militias and private armies."

"My forces are well trained and I intend to have them patrolling the borders of my property." Savanna stood as tall as she could, relying on her braces to support her body. "I just need your men to patrol the other side of the border more frequently."

Jacob replaced his hat on his head, pulling it low over his eyes. "We'll see what we can do. Most of our men are injured soldiers returning from the wars. We just don't have the manpower to patrol a border of this size."

Savanna realized she wasn't going to get cooperation from this boy. She looked at the floor studying the pattern in the rug, trying to get her temper under control, before she spoke again. Looking into the face of the young man, locking eyes with him, she measured her words for greatest effect. "A woman was murdered here."

The young man's cheeks reddened, either from anger or embarrassment, Savanna wasn't sure which. "And those perpetrators where caught, weren't they? They're sitting in jail, right now."

Her heart thumped against her rib cage and her fingers curled into a fist. Savanna knew there was not going to be any help coming from his direction. She was on her own when it came to protecting the residents of Haven. Travis wasn't going to be happy to hear this.

Savanna dismissed Jacob, having security escort him off the campus. Travis joined her in the office. He sat on the couch and opened his arms to her. As she relaxed into his embrace, she could feel the tension leave her shoulders. He was her safe place, her love. She kissed the warm pulse on his neck.

"We're on our own, Babe," she said.

His arms tightened around her shoulders as he drew her closer. "I'll start looking into some private security forces. Maybe we can use some of your connections in the National Guard." His fingers gently massaged the tip of her shoulder blade. "The waste treatment plant will be running at half capacity next week, so we can start bringing in the first wave of personnel. It'll be fully operational in four months, although I don't know why you had such a large plant built. The new treatment plant can service a town of ten thousand."

"I want to be prepared." Savanna was subdued. She was passionate about wanting to protect her people and she could feel tension all through her body. Having Travis hold and caress her soothed away some of the tension she was feeling. "I'm having a number of outbuildings constructed and am extending the fields. We always produce more food than we can eat here, so I'm increasing the size of the facility."

Travis sat up, pushing Savanna into a sitting position, and looked at her.

She brought her hand up and brushed his cheek. "Don't worry, love. I'm delegating more of the responsibility. There're a number of people here ready and willing to take on more challenging roles. We're also not going to have as much turnover." She smoothed the wrinkles out of his forehead, gently caressing it with her hand.

"What do you mean?"

"I'm going to offer more of the residents here permanent placement." Haven policy allowed the women to stay until they completed their educational program and assisted them in finding permanent homes and job placement. It was becoming more difficult to find jobs and safe placement outside of Haven walls.

"Where are you going to find room for all of them?"

"Little Haven has proven to be very successful." Savanna had to talk fast to assuage Travis' concerns. "I'm going to build some more family residences on the border of the land. I'm hoping that spreading out the population and bringing in security forces will eliminate some of these problems. I've already sent in the work orders and asked for bids from construction companies."

Travis stood up and ran his hands over his closely shaved scalp. "Savanna, you're already pushing yourself to the limit. You need to give yourself time to heal. I feel like I'm losing you to Haven."

Savanna reached up, taking his hand. Pulling him back down beside her would have been much more difficult if he hadn't let her. "No, no Travis." She spoke in soft tones, brushing her hands against his shoulders and chest, attempting to soothe him. "Emily has taken over the genetics lab. You're going to be in charge of security. Dr. Omoto is coming in to run the hospital and rehab center, I've already talked to him. I have other people lined up to take charge of other areas."

Travis sat back on the couch, but Savanna could tell he wasn't relaxed. "I'm letting go of the reins, my love. I promise, I'm giving up control."

He embraced her, allowing her to relax into his warmth. "I'm sorry. It's strange to be jealous of your job. I just went through so much when you were hurt and I can't stand the thought of losing you. Do you realize the renewal of our contract is coming up?"

Savanna nodded against his chest. "I know. I want to renew. What about you?"

"Of course." Travis brushed his fingers through her hair. "You and I belong together."

Warmth flooded her. Savanna closed her eyes and drew in his scent; the clean, cotton smell she so loved. He held her against his body for a long time as she slowly relaxed into him. His breathing was much slower than hers and she tried to match his slow even breath. She was just starting to doze off when the rumble of his voice jerked her awake. Shaking her head, she attempted to clear her thoughts. Travis repeated his question.

"So, where is this security force I'm supposed to be in charge of coming from?"

Savanna took his face between her hands and kissed his soft, full lips. "I don't know. I'm delegating that responsibility to you."

Travis stood, dislodging Savanna from her very comfortable position. "Well, I'd better start the recruiting process. I need to post job openings and run background checks on any applicants. I'm going start bringing in staff by the end of the week. I hope the barracks are ready by then."

Building the security force took more time then Savanna anticipated. The biggest issue seemed to be finding applicants who were physically capable of performing the work. Most skilled, able-bodied, members of society were in the military or already had jobs with the police force or private security agents.

Travis was able to recruit several former soldiers who, for various reasons, were no longer considered fit for duty. In most cases, they had received severe injuries in battle, but with prosthetics and specialized equipment they could perform their job duties at Haven.

Arming the workers with tasers was the biggest deterrent from daytime raids, but the number of night raids and thefts from the outbuildings increased. Travis couldn't hire enough security to protect the grounds from the night raids. As the summer growing season continued the number of raiders entering the fields and stealing crops increased. One of the sister farms reported the theft of a hundred heads of cattle, most of them heifers pregnant with their first calves.

Savanna's growing concern and stress from the situation was starting to take its toll. She tried to hide it from Travis, but there was no way to prevent him from seeing the dark circles under her eyes and the physical pain her injuries were causing. Night was the worse time. The nightmares were unrelenting, causing her to wake drenched in cold sweat; her heart racing and throbbing in her ears. Travis did everything he could to alleviate her fears, but another harvest season waxed and waned and still the raids continued.

More seasons waxed and waned and reports crossing Savanna's desk became more desperate. Harvest was coming and Savanna was terrified. She needed to send work crews out on tractors to reap the grains and unearth the fields of root vegetables. Horrifying nightmares, reliving the attack in the previous spring, haunted her, stealing her sleep.

Another nightmare woke Savanna and she sat up in bed, her heart racing and nightgown drenched in sweat. She buried her aching head in her hands, trying to shake off the pain. Travis sat up beside her and wrapped his arms around her shoulders.

"What is it, Love? Another bad dream?" His arms soothed her tremors. After a moment, he got up and got her a glass of water.

Savanna drank, quenching her thirst. Once the dryness of her throat was relieved she handed him the glass, moving to the edge of the bed. "I just can't shake them."

"Raven?" Travis didn't even have to say anything else to evoke memories from Savanna's latest nightmares. Raven was nearly fourteen and had been going out with the work crews as part of her duties. Savanna worried every time she saw the girl join her classmates to go work in the fields. She only had twelve more credits to go before she completed her secondary education and had already started on some medical courses. Savanna was really hoping she would spend more time in the hospital and less time working outside, but the child seemed to revel in the hard work and physical toil as much as she did working on her studies.

"Etu would love to have Raven spend some time with him. Why don't we send her to Arizona for two weeks?" Raven loved visiting Arizona. She had flown to see her grandfather three times over the past two years and had always returned full of energy and with stories of life on the Reservation. Travis rubbed Savanna's shoulders, kneading the tension away.

Savanna thought about the option for a minute, but then dismissed it. "I can't be seen as showing favoritism to a member of the community." The thought of sending her daughter away so soon after she moved into her own room distressed Savanna. She still wanted to keep her close.

Travis' hands stopped rubbing her shoulders and cupped her face in his hands. She turned her face to receive his kiss and saw the concern in his eyes. "Raven is not just a member of the community, she's your daughter. It's within your rights to protect her."

"There haven't been any attacks on the work crews recently. She's perfectly safe. I'm the one having issues with this." Savanna stood and stretched her tense muscles in her back. "We'll keep the younger members of the community near the facilities and double up the guards."

Travis took hold of her hand and pulled her back on the bed. "You know I love Raven as much as I do Caleb. She's my daughter in spirit, if not in body. I want to keep her safe too."

Relaxing into his body, Savanna allowed his gentle hands to soothe her. "I'm strong enough to join the work crews. I'll be going out with everyone else. It's going to be difficult for raiders to attack work crews if we go out in force."

Travis took her hands and gently rubbed circles into her palms. "I'm going to train her to use the taser, just as I trained you. She's already as comfortable on the motorbikes as you are."

Travis had taught Savanna how to ride the cycles used to patrol the perimeter of the facility since she had difficulty walking across the uneven ground. At first, she was intimidated by the machines, but now she could ride them with ease. She still struggled with using the taser, though. The thought of holding a taser and using it to harm someone made Savanna's chest tighten. She had to take a moment to catch her breath. Every time she hefted the cool, plastic weapon in her hand, she felt as if it was preparing to strike out at her. Travis' eyes were on her, watching as she slowed her breathing. His dark brown eyes held such strength and warmth, she couldn't help but trust him.

"You know, I've been talking to Dr. Omoto and he thinks I'm strong enough to carry a child," she said. "I think we should consider implanting the embryo that was taken after I was burned."

Travis' face lit up. "Are you sure? I mean, I wouldn't want to push you too hard." The excitement reverberated in his voice and Savanna couldn't help but caught up in the moment.

Savanna reached under her pajama top and rubbed her hand over the scar on her hip. The skin felt smooth and slick, almost like plastic. "I can walk without the brace now and he thinks the skin on my stomach and hip will be flexible enough to stretch through the pregnancy."

Travis reached down and felt the scar, taking her hand in the process. "I can start the hormone regiment and have Emily prepare the fetus for transplant. Of course, we'll have to be careful. One of the side effects of hormone therapy is the over-production of ova. We can't get pregnant while I'm preparing for implantation."

Travis grinned even wider. "It'll be nice to have a baby in the house again." Leaning across he kissed her gently on the lips.

Savanna looked around the cubicle room and at the screen, hiding the children's sleeping section from the rest of the room. Caleb's gentle snores were echoing from behind the screen. This wasn't much of a house, but it was home. Travis pulled her close and they both relaxed back onto the bed. His hands caressed her, bringing a flush to her skin and a warmth to her cheeks. She drew him closer and relaxed into his embrace as he started to remove her clothing. After they made love, Savanna fell asleep wrapped in Travis's warmth.

Chapter Thirty-Four

THE NEXT MORNING SAVANNA sent a message to Emily, asking her to report to the office after her shift in the lab. She just pulled up the records of some of the women she was considering promoting to house leaders in the outbuildings when she received a call from the security guard on the front gate.

"Dr. Taylor." The guard's voice cracked and Savanna realized just how young he was. The young man cleared his throat and started again. "Dr. Taylor, a convoy of transport trucks and buses just pulled up to the security gate leading into the main drive. There's a General here who says he knows you and needs to talk to you."

The guard was obviously flustered and at a loss for words. Savanna could hear an authoritarian voice in the background. "Go fetch that mouthy little doctor of yours. I need to talk to her."

Savanna smiled when she realized she recognized the voice. "Yes, I know him. I'll be there shortly." She used a four-wheeler to drive to the gate and meet with Commander Grey. Travis met her there with three other guards. She waved the men back as she approached. General Grey stood on the other side of the black and red striped arm bar as Savanna approached. She could see the residents of Little Haven coming out to observe the situation, curious as to why a military brigade was pulling up to their front gates.

"Hello, General." Savanna acknowledged his new rank. "I haven't seen you in a few years. How have you been?"

The smile on Grey's face made it obvious he didn't miss the sarcasm in her voice. "Dr. Taylor, a pleasure as always." His own voice carried a heavy dose of sarcasm. "Doctor, I'm not going to pull any punches here. You need help and we're here to give it to you. We both have situations here and my solution can benefit us both."

Savanna's curiosity was piqued. She gestured to the

guard to raise the gate so she could talk to the General without having a shouting match. Savanna caught Travis moving up behind her out of the corner of her eye, motioning his men to stay back.

Grey motioned her to follow him and they walked to the line of buses with darkened windows and trucks with camouflage canvas coverings. He stopped at one of the vehicles. Savanna counted thirteen buses and five trucks, along with several jeeps and all-terrain vehicles. The General stepped to the back of the truck and waited until Savanna joined him.

"Doctor, we've taken over the duty of guarding your borders from the BLM." Grey untied the cords holding the flap down on the back of the truck. "Our troops will build barracks on the edges of your property and perform guard duty while you and members of your community are working in the fields. We're also going to provide guard duty for your transport trucks from other facilities."

Savanna looked down the row of vehicles. "There are a lot of people here just to guard one community. Why would the guard send so many soldiers?"

"Well, Doc, that's the thing. We're not just here as guards. We need something from you, too," he said.

Savanna's confusion must have shown because Grey motioned one of his men over to help him remove the covering from the back of the truck. "Your father and Dr. Smith started this program before they ran into creative differences. In fact, many people suspect this is what they fought over the most. Your father felt Dr. Smith was pushing the limits of genetic manipulation. Dr. Smith felt your father was doing everything he could to build an Über child. Neither of them could agree on what that child should look like."

The soldier helped him flip the covering off the back of the truck. At first Savanna couldn't see into the darkness, but slowly she started to make out white-rimmed eyes peering out at her. She blinked and peered deep in the truck. Children crowded in the bed, looking up at her with emotionless faces. Looking from the back of the truck down the row, she mentally recounted the vehicles.

"Exactly how many children are we talking about here?" Savanna calculated the food production and care facilities she had in place.

"Children? We have about two-thousand, so far." Savanna looked at the sea of faces in front of her. The realization of what he just said hit her.

"So far?"

Grey had the good sense not to make eye contact with her. He walked to one of the buses, motioning her to follow. The door opened at his gesture and he led Savanna inside. Every seat on the bus was taken up by a woman, each in various stages of pregnancy. Not one woman was smiling in the expectant-mother glow. Then one of the women shifted in her seat. Savanna heard the rattle of shackles and caught a glimpse of metal at her wrist. She took a step forward, attempting to get a better look, but Grey grabbed her arm and led her off the bus before she could say anything.

They got two steps away before Savanna pulled up short and turned on him. "What in the world is that?"

"It's not what it looks like, Doc." General Grey placed his hand on her shoulder in a failed attempt to calm her. "Every one of those women volunteered to be part of this program. We were having problems finding surrogates in the general population. When the program first started, we would cull volunteers from the enlisted, but since the unrest in the Middle East flared up again and we're still dealing with the Korea and China fallout, we needed all the able-bodied soldiers we could get."

Savanna could feel her pulse pounding in her temple and the tension in her neck muscles. "Where, exactly, did you find these women?" The words came out from between clenched teeth.

Grey removed his hand, a smart move considering Savanna was tempted to separate him from the much-needed appendage. "The court system granted them leniency or commuted their sentences if they agreed to be surrogates.

These women have come in from all parts of the country to be part of this program. Some of the woman are in restraints because they have a tendency to harm themselves or others and the only way we could transport them safely was to hobble them."

"How many?" Savanna could hear the low growl in her throat. The past eight years of her life had been spent preventing the exploitation of women and here they were dropping off busloads of victimized women on her doorstep.

Grey stepped back. Savanna could tell he was getting nervous. "Five hundred and sixteen."

Savanna didn't speak for a long time. When she did her voice came out in a low hiss. "All pregnant?"

"Well, some of the most recent in vitros may not have taken." He looked back at the bus. "The facilities we were using were threatened and we had to transport as many embryos as we could by transplantation. We still have over a thousand embryos in stasis and will need to get them in your storage as soon as possible."

Savanna didn't see the point of arguing. She remembered the heat she felt when she stepped on the bus and knew the pregnant women were suffering, so she allowed the trucks to enter the gate and set up camp in one of the fallow fields. She wasn't going to have the women sitting in the buses waiting for answers in their condition.

Telling Grey she would talk to him in her office, she left him at the gates and returned to Haven. Showered and changed, she spent the next hour fuming in her office waiting for him to appear. Travis showed him to the sanitizing shower and had him change into one of Haven's uniforms.

She fingered her father's Noble Peace prize, trying to think what he would do in this situation. Her pad beeped, letting her know General Grey was in the hallway. The man looked extremely uncomfortable in the black uniform, especially because Savanna had ordered it one size too small.

Travis opened the door and motioned Grey into the office. Savanna kept her back turned until Travis made sure the man was seated in one of the gray covered chairs. Crossing her arms across her chest and pulling her face into the tightest scowl she could, she turned to face him. She knew the tightened skin from the burn on her face pulled the corner of her mouth down, making the expression seem even more fierce. Not that she minded at this point, she wanted him to realize exactly how angry she was.

"I don't have the capacity for the numbers you're bringing me." She decided she would get right to the point. "You expect me to incorporate, what, twenty-five hundred more into Haven society overnight and add five hundred more over the next nine months." She kept her voice low, but intense.

"Well." Grey's tone sounded ominous. "There might be a few more than five-hundred. The most the law allows us to implant is five embryos, but most of the surrogates didn't retain more than two fetuses. Altogether we're expecting about eight-hundred and ninety live births."

Savanna had to take long, deep breaths. "How do you expect me to care for that many individuals? This facility wasn't built to be a child producing factory."

"Dr. Taylor, we've been operating the surrogate program for thirty-five years. You don't have to take care of any of these people." Grey handed her a data pad. "All the pertinent information is here. We have the resources to provide for the subjects. The issue is their safety. Our original site was compromised and we need to set up a new base. Barracks will be built on Federal Reserve land and we'll have our forces patrolling the dividing line."

Savanna glanced at the data pad. There were several documents on the file, it would take time to go through them all.

"What's all missing from this mess?" she asked.

Grey looked at the pad she was holding in her hand. His expression showed concern, like he was waiting for her to throw it at him. "You have the highest security clearance there is. All the information you need to know is there." He paused and looked across the desk to her. "Dr. Taylor, the decision has been made. We're not setting up camp on your property, so you have no say in it."

Savanna bristled, feeling the tension in her jaw and neck. The worst part was he was right; there was nothing she could do about it.

"What kind of medical care have these women received?" If she couldn't do anything about the program she could at least help the women.

"We have a number of OB/GYN medical personnel who have been checking the women regularly," Grey explained. "They stayed behind to help with the final load and evacuation."

"What's forcing you to move from your facility?" Savanna pulled up information on the data pad. She couldn't find anything about the previous location of the program.

"We were located on a military base in an undisclosed location." Grey attempted to adjust his uniform. "Although the base is still operating, it's being manned by a skeleton crew. There have been several raids on the base from pirate groups and the program director feared for the safety of the subjects. There have also been several dissenters who have been protesting this program. Threats have been made against the facility and we felt it was better to move the subjects rather than risk their safety."

"How do you propose to protect the safety of this facility and your own program here if you couldn't even protect them on a military base?" Savanna's voice was steady despite the turmoil in her mind. There was no way she could guarantee the safety of her people with this imminent threat looming in their back yard.

General Grey held up his hands to forestall any argument. "Doctor Taylor." His voice was calm. "We have the Corps of Engineers building barracks and medical facilities. The outer walls and fences have already been built. You haven't seen them because they're too far out. No one is going to get across those lines. The guard towers and medical facilities will be up in the next two weeks."

Savanna could feel her jaw tighten even more. They were surrounding her facility, her home. Attempting to stare down Grey, she moved across the room to stand directly in front of him.

"I have built a safe haven for these people. I am not going to allow you to destroy it." Grey wasn't backing down, but Savanna needed to get her point across. "If I discover these women are being exploited I will bring them into Haven and lock us down. You won't be able to come near them, or their children."

Grey took the data pad and pulled up a document. Handing it back he pointed at a passage. "The women aren't important, but the children are the property of the United States government." As he spoke Savanna read the passage he pointed out. "If you do anything to interfere with us, you will be declared an enemy of the state and all funding for Haven will be cut off. If I'm not mistaken, you rely heavily on funding from the government to run many of these rehabilitation and education programs."

His last statement was not a question and Savanna bristled at the implied threat. She turned her back on him and paced across the room. Many of Haven's grants and funding came directly from the United States government. The federal insurance payments alone funded the entire medical and rehabilitation centers. The government paid a significant chunk of the research program as well.

"I don't see why you have such a problem with what we're doing here anyway. You came from this program." Grey's words stopped her in her tracks. She turned to face him and his accusation.

"What do you mean?" Savanna didn't like the implication in his voice.

"Where do you think you came from?" Grey pinned her down with his eyes. "Your father developed you at the same time he developed this program. He used the genetic research to create a smarter, stronger, more disease resistant human and then used that knowledge to build you. You're one of these Über children."

Savanna narrowed her eyes. "I'm genetically altered, I know that. I read all of my father's research. It's not like you're telling me anything I didn't already know."

Grey took the data pad away from her again. This time he didn't return it right away. "I don't think you have seen all of your father's research. I think you'll be surprised by what you find out when you delve into it."

He tossed the data pad down on the edge of the desk. "Your genetic code is so scrambled and spliced, I'm surprised you had any of your parents' genetic markers. Why do you think you can do the things you can do? I have doubts that you are even fully human."

Savanna felt her jaw tic as the muscle twitched.

"You should analyze your own genetic code before you pass judgment on us." He gestured to the pad. "Now, if you'll excuse me Doc, I need to get out of this straight jacket and back into my uniform."

As Travis escorted the man from her office, Emily walked in the door. There was a moment when the three did a little jig, trying to move around each other. Emily stood aside and allowed the men to pass before she entered the room.

Savanna picked up the data pad, moving around the desk to sit in her chair. She skimmed through the information as she waited for Emily to have a seat. It only took a few seconds to find her file and bookmark it for future reading. She knew what General Grey was implying. Her father had spent countless hours researching genetic code and developing stem cell research to create a healthy child. He had told her many times how he had slaved for hours developing the perfect combination of genes to create a healthy, intelligent, beautiful child. Savanna knew her genetic code, having studied it carefully over the years. She did want to see what General Grey saw in his perusal of her medical records. She didn't like the idea of him knowing something she didn't and using it as a weapon against her.

Chapter Thirty-Five

EMILY CHOSE A SEAT across the room, sitting on the edge and folding her hands in her lap. She rubbed her finger tips, picking at her nails. Emily always seemed nervous lately.

"Emily," Savanna started, tying to help her feel at ease. "We're going to need to store some embryos in the nitro tanks. What kind of room do we have in there?" Savanna hadn't spent very much time in the genetics lab recently. In fact, now that she thought back on it, she realized she hadn't done any significant genetic research for about three years.

Emily looked up from her hands, a puzzled expression on her face. "Is that why you called me in here? We need to make room in the lab?"

"Well, no," Savanna explained. "This just came up. General Grey brought in about a thousand embryos and we're going to need to store them."

Emily stood up. "Well, it shouldn't be a problem. We just expanded the embryonic storage lab. The surrogate program is continuing to grow and Erik and I decided it would be safer to store the embryos here."

"Why would they not be safe at the transplant facility?"

"It's just the unrest in the area. Not everyone believes the surrogacy program is as innocent as it appears." Emily returned to her seat and continued picking at her nails.

"Are any of the women in danger?" Savanna calculated the space she had at Haven and realized there was no way she could accommodate five hundred more women in the space she had.

"No," Emily reassured her. "We've just had a couple of break-ins at the clinic. Surrogate House is well protected. In fact, the walls hide it completely from view. Very few people know exactly what the campus is all about."

Savanna was confident Emily could easily manage the incoming embryos. She decided to get right to the point. "Travis and I have decided to try implanting the fetus I was pregnant with before the fire. We need to get started on the hormone therapy and prepare to harvest the excess ova. I'm pretty sure this will be our last child, but if this one doesn't take we may decide to try in vitro."

Savanna missed the startled look on Emily's face. When she looked up from the pad, the woman was staring at her with a lost expression on her face. "What's wrong?"

Emily gave a start and shook her head. "Nothing. I'm just trying to remember in what section I stored the fetus." Emily wiped her hands on the pant legs of her uniform. "If this implant doesn't work, you might have some problems convincing Travis to contribute his DNA. We've been trying to convince him to donate for the surrogate program for years. He keeps putting us off, saying he doesn't like the idea of his children being sold to the highest bidder and would rather have children with someone with whom he is in a committed relationship."

"Well, we're in a committed relationship." Savanna waved off her concern. "We'll work things out. Let's start the hormone therapy tomorrow. By the time we're ready to implant, things will be settled here."

"Well, I better get to the lab if I'm going to make room for the new embryos." As she spoke, Emily stood. "Do we have any idea how long we're going to store them?"

"No. Right now we just have to take care of them." Savanna clenched her fist under the table. "We're going to have to take things one step at a time."

"Well, I better get back to the lab." Emily walked to the door.

"I'll be in tomorrow to start treatment." Emily nodded, but didn't turn around to face Savanna, who was already engrossed in the data pad.

Nothing on the pad surprised her. Grey must not have realized how much she knew about her father. Savanna had been studying his work since she was twelve years old. She had found her medical files when she was fourteen. Her father had used stem cells from fourteen different individuals when he was developing her. His biggest concern was the fact that both he and his wife had the genetic marker for cancer and he was afraid his children might be born predisposed to the disease. He also eliminated the genetic marker for obesity, diabetes and near-sightedness. Turning genes off and on was an easy process, once the human genome was mapped. Savanna's father knew what he wanted in a child, and he made sure he had it.

Her mother insisted genetics was only half the battle. You could manipulate genes to make a smart, healthy child, but it took love and strength to teach a child to walk the right path. She used to tell Savanna her father made the shell and it was her job to fill the vessel. Hearing people talk about the evils of genetic engineering frustrated her. Her existence couldn't be wrong. If it wasn't for her father's research she would never have been born. Her work was dedicated to the creation of life. Nature could only do so much; her research fixed the chinks in the building blocks of DNA.

Savanna left her office and entered the glass enclosed walkway. The only ones in the passageway were sentries watching the fields as Haven residents worked. They were all at their posts on the outside of the glass walls, walking their sections. She acknowledged their nods as she passed, but didn't stop to talk. She needed to clear her head and think.

She found her favorite outpost, a tiny overhang overlooking the south fields and orchards. Since the two sentries on either side were able to observe this area, no one was posted on this balcony.

Savanna had installed a patio swing and she would go up there to think whenever she was feeling overwhelmed. In the evenings Travis, and sometimes Raven and Caleb, would join her. Today Savanna needed time to think about what she was going to do with Grey and the problem he brought with them.

The medical charts of the women revealed at least fifty of them would be ready to deliver within two weeks, before the medical team was scheduled to arrive. She did a quick lookup of the staff she had trained in obstetrics and sent a message for them to meet her in the office in the morning.

Savanna stood up and stretched the kinks out of her back. She was glad she was going to attempt this pregnancy now. She wanted to be finished with her family by the time she was thirty-seven. Walking to the railing she scanned the fields of grain ripening in the hot summer sun. Cherry harvest would start soon, other fruits would follow suit. This year was going to be another bountiful harvest, as long as they didn't lose too much to raiders. The genetically altered plants produced high yield fruits and vegetables in shorter growing seasons. Many of the residents of Haven became fascinated with food cultivation and, when the south wing was built, she had incorporated an agricultural research lab into the structure.

Movement in the orchard startled Savanna and she leaned forward to get a better look. It was too early for harvest and all of mowing and weeding had been done on the south fields for the week. No one should be out there. She pulled up the camera views on her pad. Focusing the telescopic lens on the area she saw movement. There was someone out there. It looked like there was only one person so she knew it wasn't any of her residents, no one was allowed out of the facility alone.

Savanna called security on her data pad and headed for her office. She didn't receive a response right away so she grabbed her taser from her desk and headed for the elevator bay. As she entered the elevator, Travis finally called her back. Pulling his image up on her pad, she quickly explained the situation.

"Our forces are completely committed right now, Savanna. We weren't expecting any one on the south side of the complex because nothing over there is ready for harvest." Savanna could see Travis' data as he was scrolling through status updates trying to find the crew closest to the south fields. "I'll pull a crew and have someone there in fifteen minutes."

Savanna knew she was the closest to the field and was going to make it out there before the security crew. She felt drawn to the orchard, as if she needed to be there. Something was happening out there, a situation she needed to control. Overriding the security lockout on the elevator, Savanna took it down to the basement. When the doors slid open she pulled up the codes to the motorcycles and pushed the remote start key on the pad. One of the bikes roared to life. Savanna threw her leg over the seat, kicked the stand and rolled out of the parking spot. She wasn't quite at full speed when she left the parking structure, but she was close.

As she entered the access road, she saw clouds of dust approaching from the east. Her backup was on its way, but they wouldn't make it to the invader before her. Savanna pushed the bike faster, wheels spinning in the dust as she sped towards the orchard. The trails between the fields were well maintained and she didn't have any problems keeping the bike under control. It didn't take long to leave the flat grain fields behind and approach the gentle slopes of the orchards. She aimed for the area where she had seen movement and pushed faster. Catching a flash of color behind a tree, she brought the bike to a halt.

The cold, hard plastic of the taser felt uncomfortably in her grip. She slowly worked her way from tree to tree, trying to keep a barrier between herself and whoever was in the orchard. As she approached one of the dark, twisted boles of a tree, she saw a flash of blue.

It took a moment to recognize the form of a woman huddled on the ground. Savanna kept her taser aimed low as she approached, knowing invaders used a variety of subterfuge techniques to lure in victims. Savanna knelt beside the woman, rolling her to her side. She could feel the heat of a fever radiating off the woman's body as soon as she touched her. As Savanna rolled the woman over she realized she recognized her. This was Michelle, the girl she had met at the clinic the first time she volunteered there.

Placing the taser by her knee, Savanna assessed the woman. Michelle's face was flushed, her lips dry and cracked. Bloody sputum coated her lips and chin. Her breathing was shallow and labored. Savanna knew she was going into respiratory arrest. A sudden sharp wail drew Savanna's attention. It took a moment to locate the direction of the sound and decide if she could leave Michelle to investigate. She heard tires crunching on gravel and looked over her shoulder. The security team had arrived. Crossing her arms to warn them back, she gave the signal for them to gown and glove. One member of the team pulled out the med kit and started distributing the barrier devices.

Savanna rolled Michelle into the recovery position, picked up her taser and walked deeper into the grove. It took her a moment to locate the source of the wailing. A tiny child, perhaps about two years old, sat under a tree, tears making a course down his dusty cheeks. Savanna immediately scooped him up and headed back down the slope. The security force had bundled Michelle onto a board and had her strapped to the back of a four-wheeler. Savanna handed the child to one of the guards.

"Both of them need to be taken to quarantine," she ordered. "You are all to go through the sanitizing process before you enter the facility. None of you are to leave quarantine until you've been medically cleared."

The team members nodded their acknowledgement as they prepared to return to the facility. Savanna followed them in on the cycle. She entered instructions on her pad for all the rescue equipment to be sanitized before being placed back on their chargers. Travis was waiting for her when she left the sanitizing showers.

"She was taken directly to quarantine." He handed her a data pad. "The TB test came back positive. The child tested negative. We placed him in a quarantine room for now, but Omoto thinks he'll be able to be transferred to the nursery soon. We want to keep him isolated from his mother until she's no longer contagious." This news confirmed Savanna's suspicions. She went to the quarantine area of the clinic to check on Michelle, but the woman was unconscious. Dr. Omoto had everything under control, so Savanna returned to her office and to her work.

Savanna kept an eye on Michelle's medical progress, but was too busy to visit her for the first few days the woman was in quarantine. In the meantime, she started her hormone therapy and treatment. On the fourth day of Michelle's quarantine she received a message from Omoto, prompting her to visit. The hollow echo of her footsteps on the tiles followed her down the halls of the quarantine center as she approached the nurse's station. Nulie looked up from the chart she was holding and smiled.

"I was told she's awake and can talk." Savanna spoke in a hushed voice, not wanting to break the silence of the unit.

"She is getting much better." Nulie still had a deep accent, but her English had improved in the years she had lived in Haven. "The antibiotics are working. She is still contagious, so she is still quarantined."

Before she entered the room, Savanna put on a gown, gloves and mask. Michelle was sitting up in the bed, combing the tangles out of her hair. An oxygen mask covered her mouth and nose. Savanna pulled a stool to the edge of the bed.

"Michelle." The girl put down the comb and turned to Savanna. "I'm Dr. Savanna Taylor. You're a very lucky girl. If I hadn't found you when I did, you would probably have died."

Michelle shook her head and lay back in the bed. "You don't know how lucky I am. I ran away from the family." Michelle closed her eyes. "I didn't have any choice, though." Tears crept out of the corner of her eyes. "The first wife was angry when I became pregnant and she couldn't. My first born was supposed to be hers, but she said she didn't want him. A little boy has no value to her. She wanted me to go to the second marriage to try to get with child again so she can have a daughter, but then I got sick. She told me to take my son and leave. Our husband was going to challenge her and he ordered me to stay. I refused and took my son with me. When I left I wasn't feeling as weak, but when I entered the trees I knew I was dying. I laid my son under a tree so I could walk away from him to die. Thank you for finding me and saving our lives."

Savanna was thankful for the mask to hide her

emotions. This girl wouldn't have survived if she had stayed with her people. "Michelle, you're very ill." She paused, searching for the words to say. "You have tuberculosis and it's very contagious. Everyone you've come in contact with is at risk. We need to inform the CDC and provide treatment for your family."

Michelle opened her eyes and studied Savanna. "Don't you know about the plagues? The coughing sickness is taking too many people to count. No matter what doctors try, there's no controlling it. My family would rather take the risk of the disease rather than go under the control of the government."

Savanna knew the plagues were still having devastating effects on the world population, but seeing their effect first hand was extremely distressing. "Have you been able to see your son?"

Michelle smiled through her mask. "They bring him to the window to see me every day." There was obvious joy and pride in her voice as she talked about her son. "He's such a good baby, worth everything I went through to get him."

Savanna offered Michelle a few words of encouragement before she left. She took a moment to look in on the little boy before returning to her office. She needed to spend some time organizing the hospital and preparing beds of the women who were ready to deliver in the next few days. This news of the diseases pushed at the edges of her mind and a real fear of the world these newborns were coming into crushed her heart.

Chapter Thirty-Six

DESPITE SAVANNA'S PREPARATIONS, IT was still another eight months before she began her hormone treatments. There was just too much work to put in order with the addition of the surrogate units to prepare for the implantation of her fetus. Fall harvest passed, then winter and finally spring planting, before she could start her therapy. The hormone therapy was as brutal as Savanna remembered from her first treatment. Her pregnancies were a walk in the park compared to the emotional and physical turmoil she felt as she prepared her body to accept the embryo. Travis was understanding and gentle as she suffered through mood swings and hot flashes. The worst of it was the sudden dizziness and lightheadedness striking at the most inopportune times. She focused on the end result, figuring she could lived through three months of twice daily injections if the end result was going to be another child.

Michelle was recovering and, since she was no longer contagious, was able to join the general population. She joined the women in the harvest and was thriving in the supportive Haven environment. The heat of summer was approaching and the entire community was involved in strawberry harvest, one of everyone's favorite times.

Savanna crawled on her knees between the rows, picking the plump, red fruits hidden beneath green leaves. She passed Michelle's little boy. He had a berry in each hand and his face was covered in red juice. His golden hair glistened in the sun, bright blue eyes shining out of his pale face. His mother was two rows over, dark curls tickling her shoulders, falling from beneath her scarf. The little boy looked nothing like his mother, making Savanna wonder what his father looked like.

Savanna looked around the field for her own family. Raven and Emily were a few paces ahead of her, their matching straight, dark hair braided in a rope down their back. Travis was further up the field, swiftly picking the bright red fruits. Caleb was nowhere in sight.

Standing up, Savanna stretched the kinks out of her back and scanned the rows for him. It took a few moments to find his small frame since he wasn't in the field where he was supposed to be. She finally located him on the edge of the fields. He was staring at the young soldier walking the perimeter. Caleb followed the man as he paced from one corner of the field to the other. His eyes lit up when the soldier stopped in front of him. Caleb reached up to touch the butt of the soldier's gun. The young man pulled it out of his reach and spoke a few quiet words to him.

Savanna left her bucket of strawberries in the row and walked to where Caleb was talking with the soldier. The soldier smiled as she approached, causing Caleb to turn to see who was walking up behind him. He gave a start and ran to pick up his bucket.

"I'm working, Momma." He ran down the row and set his bucket down beside his father. Travis reached over and rubbed his son's short curls. They continued down the row, picking as they went.

The soldier grinned at Savanna, eyes roamed up and down her frame. Savanna knew what he was thinking, what all the soldiers were thinking and saying about her. "I hope he wasn't disturbing you too much, Private," She said. "Ever since your unit showed up we can't seem to get him to focus on anything but being a soldier."

The soldier looked down the row to where Caleb was working. "We can always use good soldiers. He's more than welcome to join the others in their training."

"It's okay." Savanna looked at her husband and son and then to her daughter. "I want to keep my little boy a while longer. Nine years old is a little young to be trained as a soldier."

"I started when I was four." The pride in the young man's voice was unmistakable.

"When he turns seventeen and is legally eligible to join will be soon enough." Savanna turned and walked back to the field.

"Yes, ma'am, hot Mamma."

The comment was said in a tone so low Savanna wasn't supposed to hear, but it wasn't low enough. Savanna could feel the tips of her ears burning as she walked past her family. Raven smiled at her as she passed. She must have read the soldier's lips as he spoke. Emily must have heard as well because she refused to look up and meet Savanna's eyes.

It was hard for Savanna to focus on the berry picking today. In two days, Emily was going to implant the embryo. All Savanna could focus on was the thought that in a few days she could be pregnant again. Travis had been subdued over the past few weeks, and Savanna hoped the pregnancy would bring him out of his funk. Their marriage contract was up for renewal and she loved the idea of starting out the new contract carrying new life. Travis had seemed at a loss since the Guard had come in and taken over security and she wanted to help him find another role in Haven.

Emily left with a batch of embryos to deliver to the surrogate clinic the next morning. Savanna intended to go with her, but Emily convinced her to stay, telling her to get her food service hours in before the transplant since she was going to be on light-duty for two weeks. Raven left with Emily to be dropped off at the airport. She was flying to Phoenix to spend two weeks with her grandfather.

After putting in five hours at the processing plant, Savanna and Travis spent the afternoon walking the rooftops and discussing the day-to-day operations of the massive facility. They stopped at the balcony, relaxing and talking about inconsequential matters.

They had left their data pads in her office, leaving messages that they didn't want to be disturbed today. When they returned to the office both of their pads were indicating they had missed messages. Savanna pulled up her messages. Raven had sent her a text saying she had made it to Phoenix and would call in the morning. There were seven from Erik. Emily hadn't shown up at the clinic with the embryos and she hadn't called. He was afraid she had been attacked or waylaid. There was a message from Caleb's instructors, explaining he hadn't returned to the classroom following lunch.

Savanna looked up from her pad to see Travis' concerned expression. "It's the hospital. Caleb's been admitted. He has a broken arm." He handed her his data pad with the message.

She sent a message to Erik as they were on their way to the hospital wing, telling him to contact the police and have them begin a search for Emily. Pulling up the leave request Emily had filed, she forwarded the license number of the car she had taken, as well as the data from her friend's data chip. By the time she hit send they were at the hospital being escorted to their son's room. Caleb was resting quietly on the bed. He looked so tiny; his dark skin glowing in stark contrast off the white pillows and sheets. The physician's assistant on duty explained what happened.

"Mr. Baker, Dr. Taylor. It appears Caleb slipped out of the facility with one of the afternoon work crews. He made his way over to the obstacle course in the Guards training field." The physician led them to display screen on the wall of the room and pulled up an x-ray of an arm. Savanna immediately spotted the spiral fracture on the ulna. The white line wasn't serious, but she knew it would cause pain and stiffness for a time.

"He slipped and fell on one of the hills and rolled onto his arm. It won't take long to heal. We put it in a cast. He'll need to take it easy for about six weeks, but he'll be fine, if we can keep him away from the obstacle course."

Caleb refused to look up and meet Savanna's eyes as she approached the bed. She adjusted his pillow and brushed her hand across his cheek. He turned and looked at her and she saw tears glistening in his eyes.

"Caleb, my Little One." Savanna scanned him from head to toe, looking for further injury. "Where are you hurting?"

"I'm not hurting, Momma." A tear escaped his eye and

rolled down his cheek. "I just don't want to get in trouble."

Savanna sat on the edge of the bed and pulled him onto her lap. Travis stood beside them, rubbing his back. "You're not in trouble, son," she said. "I'm not mad at you, just a little worried. Why did you leave school?"

"I hate school, Momma." Savanna could hear the quivering in his voice. "I want to be a soldier."

Savanna wiped the tears away from his cheeks and stood from the bed, holding her son in her arms. "You're much too young to be a soldier."

"I hate it here, Momma." Travis buried his face in Savanna's shoulder as tears fell. "It's no fun here."

Savanna looked over her son's head at Travis. His eyes seemed to sympathize with the child.

He turned away from Savanna and addressed the physician's assistant. "Can we take him home?"

She nodded. "Just let him rest for awhile. He'll be up and about by tomorrow." She turned off the x-ray screen and flipped a switch on the wall. "We'll get this roomed sanitized right away."

Caleb was heavy, but Savanna refused to put him down or turn him over to Travis. The little boy clung to her as they walked the halls back to their apartment.

Savanna tucked him into his bed, changed into her night clothes and joined Travis on the bed. He pulled her into his arms and caressed her arms and shoulders.

"I'm worried about Emily," she whispered. In all the fuss over Caleb Savanna had almost forgotten her friend. Travis pulled away slightly, not breaking physical contact.

"What do you want to do?" Travis' tone implied he would do whatever she asked.

"Can we go into town and try to find her?" Savanna's question was more of a gentle prod.

Travis smiled and pulled her close. "I put in a request for leave as you were putting Caleb to bed. I think it would be good to get off-campus. All of us. We'll take Caleb with us."

The sun wasn't even up when they left the grounds the

next morning. Travis had downloaded as much data as he could from Emily's navi-computer onto his data pad. The computer was turned off, but Travis was able to pull off enough information from it to see she had made it to the airport and to the house in Boise. After that the trail ended. Savanna called Erik and he informed her that Emily hadn't shown up at all. When he had called the police he had been informed the police were overwhelmed, but he was welcome to file a missing person's report. They also said he would probably have more success if he went to a private security agency to find her.

Savanna and Travis dropped Caleb at the house. Rose agreed to watch him as they retraced Emily's steps. Savanna left Rose with very specific instructions regarding school work and meal time, providing enough food to feed Caleb through into evening. She also gave her his prescription pain medication.

Leaving the property meant passing through the security gate, a new addition in recent years. It only took about twenty minutes to travel to the airport. They had to explained to security exactly what they were doing and show them the police reports Erik had filed.

Travis had to show the men his Haven security clearance before they were allowed into the parking garage. In the end Savanna and Travis were joined by two members of the airport security team as they searched the parking lot for the Haven vehicle. The search proved to be fruitless.

Travis followed the path given by the car's computer down Vista Avenue and into the heart of the city. As they drove past chain link fences and cement walls enclosing the population in the safety of their dwellings Savanna noticed harsh, black spray paint marking the walls and fences. She knew the markings denoted gang territories, each area controlled by overwhelming violence.

It was almost as if eyes followed them as they drove the streets. She had heard of the rash attacks of unregistered residents as gangs sought food and supplies. Rough estimates placed about a third of the population refusing to receive a microchip required as a United States citizen. These individuals didn't have work visas, travel passes, rights to bank accounts and other access to basic survival needs. Alternative, often violent, means of survival was a necessity for this burgeoning population and Savanna saw the evidence of the violence everywhere as they travelled.

The path ended not long after they entered downtown. Travis circled the Capital, skirting the five-foot white stone fence surrounding the building. Savanna didn't recognize the graffiti covering the walls and she wondered who would have the courage to tag the walls with the overwhelming security presence on the Capital grounds.

They had just started a survey of the one-way street grid when Savanna received a call on her data pad. She tapped the answer icon as Travis pulled up to a meter. "Erik, have you heard anything?"

Erik looked overwhelmed. His face was pale and the dark circles under his eyes testified to his lack of sleep. He ran his fingers through his hair as he spoke, turning the golden-brown locks into a mass of disarray.

"Savanna, they found the car. It's at the Greyhound station." Erik rubbed his face. "It's been stripped and torched. The embryos are missing and there is no sign of Emily. The police said they'll have an investigator meet you at the station."

In an echo of events eleven years earlier, Chief Peterson met Savanna at the scene of a crime. The car was surrounded by yellow crime tape, warning onlookers away. Travis pulled into a spot a short distance away. Peterson waited as they approached the burnt husk of a car. Nothing was recognizable in the blackened chunk of twisted metal, parked at a slant across two spots. Savanna's chest started to ache as she thought of the number of embryos lost in the fire.

"Where's Emily?" Her main concern was for her friend. Chief Peterson's expression wasn't hopeful.

"The security footage showed Emily pulling into the parking lot," Peterson began. "It appears she took a suitcase and some sort of metal container out of the trunk of the car. She bought a ticket to Phoenix and boarded a bus yesterday morning. Last night a gang stripped the car and fire bombed it. We're going to attempt to track down the gang and arrest them for damage to property, but it appears Emily boarded the bus on her own."

He showed Savanna the security footage. She recognized the small metal container holding nearly a hundred embryos designed for temporary storage. Savanna knew the embryos needed to be implanted within the next forty-eight hours in order to be viable. Her throat tightened and she felt a pain clutching at her chest.

"What about the embryos? Those embryos are Haven property." The words were forced out through her tightening throat.

"Do you have a list of embryos taken?" Peterson voice was condescending.

Savanna knew she didn't have a way of knowing which embryos were in the storage container until she returned to Haven and reviewed the manifest. Even then, she wasn't sure if she would know which ones were missing since Emily had been in charge of the lab for so long. There was no hope of getting the embryos back. She needed to return to Haven and see what damage had been done. Travis was standing a few feet away.

"Let's get back to the house. There's nothing left for us here," Travis said. He helped her into the passenger seat and turned towards the house. The car echoed with silence as they drove.

Savanna sent a message asking Erik to meet them at the house. She also sent a message to Haven, explaining she wanted all the records of the Surrogate program as well as any genetic research information sent to her right away. She wanted a record of every embryo kept in stasis and where every embryo ended up over the past five years. Her anxiety increased. She couldn't help thinking about her embryo. She feared it was one of the embryos Emily took with her. Emily was in charge of keeping all the facility records. She was the only one who knew exactly where everything was kept and how everything worked.

Savanna had been so caught up in the day to day maintenance of Haven, she had let the substructures of the campus run themselves. Now she realized it was a mistake.

Travis reached over and took hold of her hand. His warmth made her fingers tingle. She had to rely on his strength right now, otherwise she would fly apart.

Chapter Thirty-Seven

CALEB WAS AT THE table eating his lunch when Savanna and Travis walked into the house. Travis immediately went to the fridge and pulled out a carton of juice. He poured a glass for himself and Savanna and they sat down to wait. Erik was at the door, breathless and anxious, within fifteen minutes. He joined the others at the table. Savanna sent Caleb to the back yard to play so they could talk.

"Erik, what's been happening at the clinic? What made Emily think she could just steal embryos and leave?" Savanna could hear the hysteria in her voice and she tried to temper her tone.

Erik ran his fingers through his hair. "I don't know. I know she was frustrated with the idea that those who had, as she put it, could just buy an embryo while those who had not went through so many degrading actions to have a child."

"Is she talking about that cult?" Savanna struggled to understand her friend's thought process.

"There are a lot of things going on in the dirty underside of this world, Savanna." Erik's tone was reproachful, as if he were scolding a child. "You don't KNOW because you've locked yourself in Haven and closed your eyes to the suffering."

"Erik," Savanna interrupted. "I'm doing my best to eliminate suffering. Many of the experiments we do at Haven have broad reaching implications. I'm not ignoring the suffering in this world."

"No." Erik stopped pacing and sat down across the table from Savanna. "Your work affects about a third of the population of the world. Hundreds of thousands of people are dying every year from disease or war or violence. Haven has saved a few thousand compared to the billion people alone have died in the past two years. We see it every day, living out here. What you're doing isn't good enough. What we're doing isn't good enough."

"What does all this have to do with Emily? The embryos she stole belong to the families who want to adopt them." Savanna stared at Erik, challenging him to answer.

"Actually, the embryos belong to the program. It's one of the stipulations of joining. Once you have your two children any leftover embryos are property of the surrogate program and can be used for couples who can't produce their own. We make sure every embryo is documented and encode the child's DNA information in their microchip so there is no potential for cross mating." Erik seemed to deflate as he spoke. "I'm not saying what Emily did was right, but she is still, technically, the head of the surrogate program, so she's in charge of those embryos. She's not done anything illegal."

Savanna swallowed, tamping down her fear and anger, hoping it wouldn't boil over. Her data pad flashed to let her know she was receiving an incoming call. Seeing it was from Phoenix, she quickly pushed the answer icon. She was slightly disappointed to see it was Raven calling, wishing it would have been Emily with an explanation. The disappointment passed as soon as her daughter's face appeared on the screen.

"Raven, I'm glad you called." Savanna smiled. "I miss you already."

"I just got here yesterday, Mom." She rolled her eyes, so typical of the teenage behavior she had been exhibiting lately. "Aunt Emily showed up this morning, but she left an hour later. I have no idea why she took the bus, but she left me a message to give to you. She said to tell you she sent a message to your data pad. It's under the file labeled Kai, in the surrogate files."

Savanna scrolled through her files and found the one Raven mentioned. She didn't open it right away, wanting to finish her conversation first. They chatted about her flight and how the family was doing. As always, Raven was in awe of the spectacular scenery and colors of the dessert and was adamantly clear in the fact that she was not homesick. Savanna tried to keep the conversation upbeat, although she really wanted to pull up the message from Emily.

As soon as Raven ended the call with a cheery, 'I'll see you in two weeks' Savanna pulled up the file Emily left to listen to the message. Emily's face appeared on the screen. Her eyes were hooded and she refused to look directly into the recording device. As Savanna listened to her message, her heart sank to her toes.

"Savanna, I couldn't tell you any of this in person and I know I'll never be able to face you again after this, so I left Haven and I'm not coming back." Savanna felt her chest collapse into itself. She gasped for air and she pushed her hand into her chest, hoping it would help open her lungs.

"I can't stand seeing the wealthy pay for designer babies while women subject themselves to degrading acts just to get pregnant. I've been using embryos from the surrogate program to implant in women who come to the clinic for treatment. Since I have discretion over what happens to the embryos in the program I haven't done anything illegal. Although it may have been immoral, since there's no way to track the embryos once they leave the program. I did try to keep sibling embryos in family groups. I don't feel guilty about what I did except for one thing." Emily paused. Savanna could feel a slight twinge grow in her chest. "It didn't seem as if you were interested in the embryo you had removed when you were in your accident. I couldn't stand the thought of one of your children not having a chance at life. Everything you do is for the good of others. I implanted your embryo into another couple at the clinic three years ago. I even see him every once in a while." Emily gave a small smile before she started again. "I also used the other embryos you had stored from when you got pregnant with Raven. Six of the implantations took. I'm sorry I took them without your permission and I know you are never going to be able to forgive me."

Savanna's anger was boiling over. Emily had stolen her children.

"I can't return them. Some of them you won't even be able to trace. I'm sorry, Savanna. I know your children are going to change this world. I'm just giving them a chance to be born. All of them. I took the ova you had stored and used genetic contributions from the surrogate program to fertilize them," Emily paused for a breath. "You and Travis can always have more children together. Don't try to find me. I've deleted the information on my microchip. I have friends helping me hide out and by the time you receive this message all the embryos I have here will be implanted and it will be too late. I love you Savanna, I always have. This is my way of making sure your legacy never dies." The screen went black.

Savanna threw the pad against the wall, shattering it into shards of black glass and plastic. Hardware flew around the room as she screamed.

Rose ran in from the kitchen as Travis grabbed Savanna's shoulders and spun her around. "Savanna, Savanna." His words did not pierce her hysteria and she continued to scream. "Savanna, stop it. You're scaring me."

Her body went limp and Savanna collapsed into Travis' solid frame. Her mind raced as she thought of her friend's betrayal. She had to find out where her children were. She had to get them back. Travis gently rubbed her back as she sobbed against his shoulder.

It took a few minutes to collect herself. Once her tears stopped, she pulled away from Travis and looked towards the wall where pieces of her data pad had landed. "Well, that was extremely childish of me." Savanna felt ashamed of her outburst and wanted to put the incident behind her as quickly as she could.

"Travis, call the police. We need to report this. We have some rights as genetic parents. I never gave up custody of these children." Savanna walked away with as much dignity as she could muster.

The police were at a loss. There was no precedent for this type of case. Captain Peterson listened as the two explained what happened. When Savanna tried to pull up the file on Travis' pad she discovered Emily had only sent the message to her, taking advantage of the privacy stream Savanna had built into the Haven medical records. There was no way to pull it up.

The police gathered up the parts of Savanna's data pad from where they had landed and promised to have their detectives try to pull out the message. Savanna stopped them, realizing she had several sensitive documents in regards to Haven's operations. She told them she would have her own team look at it and get the message to them instead.

Travis convinced Savanna to spend the night in town. They had dinner together as a family. After dinner, Savanna and Travis put Caleb to bed and retired to their bedroom. Savanna laid on her side, glad for the darkness as silent tears slid down her cheeks to moisten the pillow.

She must not have been quiet enough. Travis reached over and gently rolled her onto her back. He kissed her cheek where tears had moistened it.

"Travis, what are we going to do?"

Travis rubbed her back and shoulders. "I'm as angry about this as you are, Savanna. Emily didn't have any right to take our children. But, we have to think of the children we have now."

"The only fetus that's genetically yours is the one I was pregnant with when I was in the fire. The rest of the ova were fertilized with other genetic material," Savanna explained.

"I know I didn't contribute to the embryos, genetically, but they're as much mine as they are yours. I'll help you search for them." He paused. "Savanna, we need to talk." He hushed her when she tried to speak. "I can't go back to Haven."

Savanna was shocked enough to stop crying. She looked into his chocolate brown eyes, silently begging for an explanation.

"I don't fit there anymore. I don't have a job, not since the Guard took over security. I feel completely useless." He brushed tear moistened hair off her face. "Caleb isn't happy there. He needs to be somewhere where he can be involved in normal boyhood activities. He needs to play sports and go to a regular school. We belong out here Savanna, not locked up in the gilded cage you've created."

"Are you leaving me, Travis?" Savanna's voice sounded

so muted to her ears.

"No." He embraced her, but she stayed limp in his arms. "I want you to stay with us. Leave Haven. The facility can run itself. You're not needed there. We need you out here."

Savanna pushed herself out of Travis' arms and sat up in the bed. "You can't ask me to do that. Haven is my home. I'm safe there."

Travis sat up next to her and tried to pull her close again, despite her resistance. "I'll keep you safe here. I've been offered jobs with the police department and with a private security agency. The school where Caleb will be attending is one of the safest in Boise." He gave up on trying to pull her into his arms and sat with his hands resting at his side. "This area of town is safe. This house is safe. We can live here. When Raven comes back we can enroll her in the high school. Please Savanna, I'm suffocating at Haven. I can't go back." He reached over and touched the glass shade of the lamp, bringing a hint of light to the room.

Savanna stood and put on her robe. Pulling the belt tight around her waist, she turned to face the bed. "I don't know. I can't just abandon Haven."

Travis buried his face in his hands and rubbed them over his scalp. "Caleb can't go back there, you know that."

As much as it broke her heart, Savanna realized her tiny son was not thriving at Haven. There was nothing there for her husband to do, but if she abandoned the facility it wouldn't survive.

Travis reached out his hand. When she took it, he pulled her back onto the bed with him. "Will you at least think about it?"

She allowed him to kiss her before she responded. "I'll think about it." Travis kissed her again. "Your right about Caleb, he can't go back to Haven. This house is safe though. Our commitment contract stipulates any decision we make needs to be for the benefit of our children, right?" Travis nodded his agreement. "Would you be okay with living here until Caleb finishes school and decides what he wants to do with his life?"

He wrapped his arms around her and pulled her close. "If that's what it takes. I still want you to live here with us, but I'd be happy to raise Caleb in this house. I know you can run Haven from here. Please, consider it."

Savanna didn't sleep at all that night. So much turmoil was rolling through her mind. She just couldn't get her brain to shut down. She started to doze off around three in the morning but a car alarm started her awake. Her heart was racing as it received a jolt of adrenaline. The alarm was followed by yelling and gun shots. This continued all through the night. Just as she dozed off some noise outside the fence would startle her awake.

In the early morning she gave up on sleep and went to the kitchen to make tea. The noises didn't let up when the sun came up. Instead, the sounds were joined by screaming sirens.

Her first impulse was to pack up her son and immediately return to Haven. There was no way she could resolve herself to allow him to live in this wild world. Then she thought of his broken arm and his undying admiration of the Guard. There was no way she could manage Haven and keep track of him at the same time. Despite her fears, she knew he was much better off out here than at Haven. She pulled the box of parts from her data pad close and started inspecting the pieces, attempting to see what she could salvage.

Travis joined her just as she was finishing her second cup of tea. He brushed her hair away from her face and kissed her forehead.

"Didn't you sleep at all?" The question was asked after he had studied her face for a moment. Savanna didn't need to look in a mirror to know she looked like death warmed over. Her face had to be puffy and pale from crying, not to mention the dark circles under her eyes from lack of sleep. Ducking her head, she trusted her silence to be her answer.

"I think I can salvage most of the information from the data pad." She showed him the jig-sawed pieces she had managed to work into a semblance of the original shape of her device. "I'm going to need to get some new components, but most of the hardware looks intact."

Travis took her to a computer recycling store where she was able to find the parts she needed. It didn't take much effort to place the mother board and data chips in the new device. Much of the data was corrupted, but she was able to salvage Emily's message. She forwarded it to the police.

There wasn't much hope for finding Emily. Savanna didn't realize there were so many subgroups hiding under the radar. The District Attorney filed custodial interference charges against Emily and swore out a fugitive warrant, but they let Savanna know they had some serious doubts about ever finding her.

Registering Caleb for school was a simple process. The small private school, two blocks away from the house, was more than happy to accept him as a student, especially since Savanna was willing to pay three years tuition up front. His test scores made it possible for him to enter as an eighth grader, but Travis wanted him to have the opportunity to join sports team, so they decided to register him as a sixth grader to give his body more time to develop.

After a week in the new school it was obvious they had made the right decision for their son. Caleb thrived in the highly social atmosphere of his new environment. Teachers sent glowing reports home of his academic and social progress. Savanna still hadn't had a good night's sleep.

In addition to the noise pollution outside the house keeping her awake, she suffered from extreme stomach aches and heartburn. At first, she thought she could be pregnant, but the tests all came back negative. When she could get to sleep noises in the middle of the night would shock her awake, causing her to bolt up in bed, heart racing, gasping for air. The worst part of it all was the extreme headaches. Sharp, blinding pain that would start behind her eyes and radiate around her entire head. With throbbing temples, all she could do was sit in a cool, dark room trying to force the pain away. She desperately missed Emily and her herbal teas, but just thinking about her friend brought back thoughts of betrayal.

Savanna made every effort to adjust to the world outside of Haven for the sake of her husband and son. Raven was due home in four days. Savanna hadn't done anything to prepare her room in the house for her homecoming. The school Caleb's attended was K-12, but Savanna was concerned her daughter wouldn't fit into the traditional school. Although Raven's hearing was fully functional with the implant, she hated the sound it made in her head when it was on and would leave it off most of the time, relying on lip reading to understand what was being said around her. She was significantly ahead of other students her age, needing only seven more credits to receive her high school diploma. Savanna was concerned the school would consider holding her back, just so she could graduate with her peers.

Her biggest concern, though, lay in the conversations she had with her daughter. Raven couldn't wait to return home, and the home she kept mentioning was Haven. She had plans for what she wanted to study and the internships she could start in two years.

When Savanna mentioned she was considering moving out of Haven, Raven said it didn't matter she had her own apartment and could easily live at Haven by herself.

Ultimately, Savanna knew there was only one decision to make. Her health and her daughter's future demanded it. She needed to be at Haven. Telling Travis was the most difficult thing she ever did in her entire life. He accepted she just wasn't adapting to the world outside, her deteriorating health gave testament to that. Savanna wanted to beg him to return to Haven, to stay with her, because even though Haven didn't need him, she did. The words just wouldn't come, though. His new job at a private security office was giving him a sense of purpose, something he hadn't had for nearly two years. She couldn't take that away from him.

Chapter Thirty-Eight

TRAVIS DROVE HER TO Haven the next morning. She had explained to Caleb she was returning to Haven, but would call him every day and come see him as often as she could. He had let her hold him a little tighter and longer than usual in the morning before he hopped out of the car and ran to the school building. Savanna had managed to hold her tears back up until that point, but then they started in a steady stream. It wasn't helping her headache.

The drive through the back roads was quiet. Travis had just turned off the main road leading to the gates of Haven when she started to experience clenching stomach pains. She begged him to pull over. Throwing open the door, she struggled to a ditch at the side of the road. Heaving, she emptied the contents of her stomach. Travis tried to come up behind her and pull her hair back, but she waved him off. She didn't want him to see her like this. Her body shook with tremors and tears poured down her face as she knelt in the hot soil. Sandy grit rolled under her hands as she steadied her body. A goat head sticker pierced the palm of her hand, drawing blood.

She was shaking when she stood, but her headache was starting to fade. Travis stood by her door holding a bottle of water. Swishing the taste out of her mouth helped a little and she wasn't feeling quite so weak as she sat down. Nothing was said as they drove down the road, leading to the gate.

Turning the car around, Travis backed up to the gate while they waited for the guard shift commander to arrive to pick up Savanna. He reached across the seat and pulled Savanna into his arms.

"I'll wait for you at the house. Come to us as often as you can. I'm still committed to you, even without a contract. I'll always be there if you need me." He gently caressed her hair and kissed her forehead.

It didn't take long for the jeep to show up at the gate.

Savanna felt Travis' arms tighten around her, as if he couldn't let her go. His arms suddenly released, taking her by surprise. She sat back to study him. The muscle in his jaw was working up and down as if he was trying to hold back some strong emotions. Leaning forward he kissed her on the mouth, the jaw, down the side of her neck.

"Don't leave me, Savanna." His whispered plea stabbed into her heart.

"Travis." Her own voice held a plea, a desire to be released from the pain. He let go and repositioned himself behind the steering wheel. Savanna opened the door and stepped out of the car.

Savanna had a few minutes to compose herself as the gate opened. Refusing to look back, telling herself it was better this way, she walked to the waiting jeep. It took her a moment to arrange the safety harness, once it was in place the young soldier put the vehicle in gear and raced down the road to Haven. Savanna could tell from the grin on the soldier's face that she didn't drive very often and this was a thrill for her. A dust trail kicked up behind the jeep, obscuring Savanna's vision in the rear-view mirror. Through the dust, she could see the white car still sitting at the gate, facing the road. The jeep dipped into a gentle valley, hiding the car from view. When they crested the next hill, the car was still sitting there. It wasn't until they dipped and crested for the third time that Savanna could see Travis finally pull away and turn onto the main road.

She managed to keep her emotions in check as the jeep approached the entrance of the facility. The soldier slammed to a stop, forcing Savanna forward into the harness. They were parked in front of the main entrance to the garage. One of the rules Savanna made when the Guard first showed up on her doorstep was the facility was hers. They could have everything from the front door to the border but, unless it was an emergency, no soldier was to enter the main campus of Haven.

Savanna walked into the decontamination area by herself. Stripping out of her civilian clothing, she threw them in the waste recycler bin. She had no desire to see those clothes ever again. The cool shower of water and antibacterial spray felt like icy spikes hitting her skin. Her stomach roiled again and she crouched on the floor over the drain. There wasn't anything left to expel, though. Shuddering and heaving, nothing came up except burning bile. Wrapping her arms around her body Savanna huddled in the floor not knowing if the water on her face was from the shower or from tears.

The water stopped and a beeping invaded her thoughts. She knew the computer was asking for a sample of her blood to screen for infection. Savanna just couldn't pull herself off the floor to place her hand under the screener. Shaking with cold and pain, she curled into a ball. Huddled on the floor, she tried to shut out the noise. An alarm claxon echoed, startling her, but she still didn't move. It wasn't until the doors slid open and she felt her body being enshrouded by a sheet that she started to respond. Hands lifting her off the floor and she reached out to steady herself. Gentle whispers soothed her as she was placed on a gurney and wheeled out of the room.

"Don't worry Doctor, we have you." Nula's thick accent pierced through the darkness. "You are home now. You are safe."

Savanna allowed the darkness to take her. She woke in a sterile hospital room dressed in a gown, an IV in her arm. The fluid dripped from the bag, clear of any other medication. Nulie walked into the room, a smile lighting up her face.

"Doctor, you are awake." There was obvious relief in her tone. "This is good. You scared us all. Your body does not tolerate the chemical additives in processed food and you have a bad reaction."

Although Nulie's sentence structure was a little twisted, her meaning was clear.

Dr. Omoto brought in her test results and allowed her to look over the details. Savanna didn't even realize how serious her reaction to all the chemical additives in processed food could become. Apparently, she had been slowly poisoning her. Omoto explaining Savanna's system would take a few days to clean out the toxins, but now that she was back on a natural diet she should be fine. She was suffering from dehydration and was close to going into systemic shock. He insisted she stay in the hospital one more day for observation, but he did remove the IV from her arm so she could move around the room.

She steeled herself to return to the apartment the next day. The tiny room seemed so much bigger without her husband's and son's belongings. For a moment she regretted asking housekeeping to remove the items and redistributing them to members of the community, but she realized holding on to them served no purpose. The bed was huge and empty as, for the first time in ten years, Savanna spent the night in it alone. She pulled a pillow close to her chest, curling her body around the soft form.

Raven returned home the next day. Travis picked her up at the airport and dropped her off at the gate. Savanna was waiting for her daughter when she left the dressing room, sanitized and in her Haven uniform. Leaping out of the room, Raven flew into her mother's arms. Embracing her made Savanna realize just how big her daughter was getting. A healthy diet and daily exercise helped Raven develop lean, wiry muscles, emphasized by her tall frame. She would never reach the same height as her mother, but she far surpassed her in physical strength.

Savanna brushed the hair out of her daughter's eyes and smiled. "How was your trip, Honey?"

"Good." Savanna could still feel the moisture in Raven's hair and fluffed it out to help it dry. "Grandpa misses us. He wants you to come with me next time. So, what's going on with Travis and Emily? Don't they want to be with us anymore?"

Savanna had hoped these questions wouldn't come up until later, but it was just like her daughter to rush head long into things. Raven always demanded answers, and she wouldn't be satisfied until she received them.

"Travis and I agreed it would be better for Caleb to live outside of Haven for a while. They're going to live in the house and we're going to live here." Savanna tried to keep her voice neutral, but a slight crack betrayed her.

"Are you getting a divorce?"

Savanna never thought about it in those terms before. "No, we're just not renewing our contract. If things change we want to try to get back together."

Raven furrowed her brow. "It seems so cold and calculated."

Savanna stopped walking and turned to face her daughter. "There's nothing cold and calculated about this. We made this decision because this is what was best for everyone. Travis needed to work. Caleb needed a safe place to grow up."

"Safe!" Raven's eyes flashed. "How is living out there safe? I swear Haven is the only safe place in the world!"

Savanna wondered if her daughter's vehemence was from normal teenage exuberance or if she truly believed what she was saying. "Why do you enjoy your visits to your grandfather so much, then?" The question wasn't meant to be challenging, Savanna was just curious.

"Oh, Grandpa keeps us safe enough. No one usually bothers us on the Rez." Raven's expression had smoothed out somewhat. "I just hate going to the city and no one goes out after dark."

Dinner was being served, so Savanna and Raven joined the queue to receive their trays. The cafeteria was full of pregnant women. Savanna moved most of the surrogates into the facility during the last phases of their pregnancies, where she could monitor their progress. They had just sat down to eat when Savanna received a call from maternity.

"Dr. Taylor, we're having a problem with one of the surrogates." The nurse's eyes were slightly wild, obviously unable to deal with whatever was happening. "Usually Emily is here to deal with this, but..." The woman's voice trailed off.

Savanna pushed her tray away from the table and stood up. "I'm on my way."

Raven stood up with her. "Mom, I just got home. Are you just going to leave me here?"

"Do you want to come with me? You'll have to wait by

the nurse's station, but this should only take a few minutes."
Savanna held out her hand for her daughter. They went to the
hospital wing side by side.

Savanna could hear screaming as soon as she entered
the wing. It didn't sound right. The voice sounded angrier than
pain ridden. Turning to her daughter, she saw a glimpse of fear
in her eyes.

"It's fine Raven. It's all part of being a woman and
giving birth. It's not a pretty process."

Guiding Raven to the chairs set up in the lobby, she
turned to go into the patient's room. The door flew open as she
approached and she was almost knocked to the ground by the
person forcing her way out of the room. Managing to catch
herself, she grabbed hold of the arm of the woman and
restrained her.

"Let go of me!"

Savanna could only see the profile of the woman, but
she immediately recognized her. "Kai!"

The one syllable brought everyone up short. Kai turned
to face Savanna, revealing horribly twisted and grotesque
features. One side of her face was burned and twisted in an
almost macabre mask-like distortion of a real face. Pock marks,
scars, wrinkles and weeping sores disfigured the rest of her
face. The painful expression in her eyes made Savanna's throat
tighten and her eyes burn.

Raven approached the two women. There was a look of
pity and shock on her face, one with which Savanna could
empathize.

Kai drew away as the girl approached, struggling away
from Savanna's grasp. A growing sneer twisted her features.
"So, this is her, huh? Does she know she shouldn't even have
been born? Is she a good little girl, or does she take after her
mother?"

Savanna couldn't help comparing her daughter to the
woman in front of her. Although Raven had been subjected to
numerous genetic alterations before she was born, her core
genetic makeup still came from the woman standing in the

stark hallway wearing a simple hospital gown. Beneath the scarred and aged face Savanna could still see the face of the beautiful young girl she met almost seventeen years ago. A face that was a perfect echo of the child she gave birth to two years later.

Ignoring the questions, knowing Kai was just trying to get a rise from her, Savanna turned to the nurse who had accompanied the woman out of the room.

"What's the problem?"

The nurse looked frazzled and her voice was stressed when she answered. "The patient is in the early stages of labor. She's insisting on a c-section, even though it isn't protocol." She consulted her chart. "She's carrying twins and has a prior history of three natural births. There's no reason to believe she can't deliver these children through natural delivery."

"Except that I don't want to!"

"Kai, how long have you been part of this program?"

"They brought me in a year ago." Kai's anger was obviously building and it was reflecting in her voice. "It was either that or prison. As soon as these things are out of me, I'm gone. They can't force me to stay here. I'd rather be in prison."

"You do realize the risks of surgery? Any surgery?" Savanna knew she was losing the battle. There was so much bitterness and anger in Kai's voice, she had the overwhelming sense the woman was lost.

"Just get them out." As she spoke, Kai curled her body, obviously fighting off a contraction.

Savanna turned to the nurse. "Get her prepped. If we don't do it this way she will fight us at every turn. Our main concern right now is for the infants."

Kai sneered. "If you really cared about babies, you'd try to find the boy they took away from me two years ago." The nurse escorted Kai back into the room as Savanna turned back towards her daughter. Raven's face was distorted by anger.

"I hate her!" She spat out. "Every time she shows up you get hurt."

Pulling her daughter into her arms, Savanna attempted

to soothe her. "Raven, honey, she's lived through more things than you could ever imagine. Why don't you go eat your dinner? I'll stay here until we get her ready for surgery. I'll join you for a walk on the roof."

Raven relaxed into the embrace, as much as any teenager would allow a parent to embrace them. Savanna watched her walk out of the lobby before she turned back to Kai's room.

Savanna didn't stay with Kai very long, just long enough to make sure she was comfortably sedated and the staff on duty had the situation under control. After sending a message to General Grey to let him know she wanted to meet with him the next afternoon, she returned to the cafeteria to eat her interrupted meal.

It took weeks of reviewing all the records Emily had kept over the past five years to make sense of what the woman had been doing. Although many of the things she had done over the years may have not been morally or ethically correct, technically, the only illegal behavior was taking Savanna's embryos. Every other embryo had been turned over to her willingly to be used at her discretion in the surrogate program.

Kai recuperated in the hospital wing after the delivery of two healthy boys. Savanna had asked Grey how he had kept her secret from her for the year she was in the program. He explained Kai insisted she would only be a part of the program if she was kept away from Haven as possible. She was kept in the outer barracks until the last days of her pregnancy.

Grey and Savanna both agreed Kai was not fit for the surrogate program and, when she had recovered enough, she was transferred to the women's prison in Boise to serve out the rest of her sentence. Savanna tried to question her about her son, but she remained tight lipped about him, telling her he was better off where he was and to mind her own business.

Chapter Thirty-Nine

WHEN SAVANNA TOLD RAVEN Kai had been transferred she noticed a great weight seemed to be lifted from her daughter's shoulders. Raven's energy and appetite improved, and she smiled more as she went about her work. That week they both went to the south potato fields to do row work. Bending over the rows, violently hacking weeds to allow water flow, causing sore shoulder and back muscles was strangely therapeutic. Savanna had just finished her row and was stretching the kinks out of her back when she saw a man approaching the edge of the field. He was wearing a BLM uniform, so she assumed he was coming in to look for General Grey.

The man was a few steps away and he still hadn't said a word. There was something about him that made Savanna uncomfortable. His uniform looked wrinkled and dirty, as if he had been rolling around on the ground.

"Are you looking for General Grey?" Savanna asked. "I can have someone take you to him."

The man looked at Savanna with a calculating expression on his face. "Are you Dr. Taylor?"

Something about the man-made Savanna uncomfortable. She looked around the field for the closest guard. None were close enough.

"Are you Dr. Taylor?" The man's voice was a desperate growl. He didn't wait for an answer. "Where's my wife and son?"

Savanna's eyes widened as she started to realize exactly who this man was. Michelle wasn't out with the work crews today and Savanna was grateful. She looked at the man, directly in his eyes. "I don't know what you're talking about. You're trespassing on private property. I suggest you leave before I have you arrested." Her voice sounded stronger than she felt. She could feel her heart racing, the blood echoing in her ears.

The man growled a bestial, animalistic sound she had

never heard before. "I killed the man wearing this uniform. I'll kill you too."

Before Savanna could pull her taser from her belt he was on her. She fell to the ground and his fingers were closing around her throat, squeezing. Kicking and thrashing, she tried to dislodge him, but darkness started to shadow her eyes and bright lights popped and dimmed as she gasped for air. She felt his hands spasm before they suddenly released her. Gasping for air she sat up and looked around. The man was on the ground, twitching in full body spasms, a number of white electrodes protruding from various parts of his body. Looking beyond him, Savanna saw a crowd of women, her daughter in the front, all holding tasers and pointing them at the man.

"Well, I think he got the point that he wasn't welcome here." Savanna stood up and studied the man. She thought she spotted drops of blood on the uniform. "He said he killed the man wearing that uniform. We need to find him and see if he's still alive."

The women all scattered, some of them running to guards, others back to the facility. Raven ran directly for one of the Haven cycles sitting on the edge of the field.

"Raven, what are you doing?" Savanna knew her impulsive daughter and feared she was going to do something foolish.

"Mom, I know this area better than anyone here." She threw back over her shoulder. "These hills are my back yard, remember. I saw the direction he came from. I think I know where to look."

Some of the guards must have heard her statement because, as she put on her helmet and took off, they followed. Savanna watched her daughter speed towards the edge of the orchard, knowing there was nothing she could say to stop her. She returned to Haven, showered at the entrance and made sure she was prepared to meet whoever came in at the hospital wing. Dr. Omoto insisted on examining her. She patiently allowed him to assess her injuries. Other than a few superficial scratches and some red marks that were already starting to turn into deep purple bruises, he gave her a clean bill of health.

A half an hour later Savanna received a message from the search team. They found a badly injured ranger in a valley by a stream. He was still alive, and they were transporting him to Haven. The EMS crew met the four-wheeler carrying the patient by the entrance and transported him to the trauma unit. The young man was bleeding from several deep lacerations on his head, his long, wavy, black hair had turned crimson from blood and was matted with dirt. His shoulder looked dislocated and his right leg lay on the gurney at an unnatural angle. Savanna did a complete work up on him and ordered a full body scan.

To clean his head wounds Savanna ordered the man's hair cut and his head shaved. He had a skull fracture in addition to his dislocated shoulder and broken leg. Putting the shoulder back in place was a fairly simple procedure, one he didn't even wake up for. Savanna helped clean the injuries on his head and stitch the lacerations. It took thirty-seven stitches all together. They had to wait until the swelling went down in his leg to perform surgery, inserting pins into his leg to bind the bone.

Savanna kept him in the drug induced coma, allowing his body's natural resources to heal his injuries. His microchip scan revealed his name was William Sapa and he was registered member of the Lakota tribe centered in South Dakota. He was currently listed as an employee of the Montana, Idaho and Oregon BLM program. Perhaps the most surprising revelation was he was only seventeen years old.

Raven seemed vindicated in her assessment of Kai's visit when she saw the bruises on her mother's neck. Savanna reassured her multiple times she was fine and her injuries weren't serious. She encouraged Raven to help her with the patient since she was showing interest in entering a nursing program. Another six months of school and Raven could start a nursing internship.

Savanna was by the young man's bed when he started to wake up. She slowly decreased the medication level in his system, testing his brain function as she went. He moved from the ventilator, to oxygen, to room air, fairly quickly. Savanna was very pleased with his progress.

The boy slept heavily, but it was a healthy sleep. One brought on by the natural healing of his body, not a drug induced state. Savanna was exhausted, and her head ached from where her hair had been pinned up in its French twist all day. She loosened the tight roll and allowed her hair to fall to her knees. She was running her fingers through the tangles, shaking it out, when her daughter walked into the room. The girl's black hair swirled loosely around her shoulders, falling down her back and past her knees, just like her mother's. Raven grinned, reached up and pulled a strand of her mother's hair through her fingers. A noise from the bed forced them both to start and turn towards the patient.

"I must have died and gone to the spirit world." William stared at both of them, his eyes studying their frames. "How in the world did I luck into finding such beautiful spirits to accompany me?"

Savanna saw her daughter's cheeks darken with his words. Her lips compressed at the flirtation. The boy's eyes were glassy from the narcotics used to alleviate his pain.

"It's good to see you awake, Mr. Sapa," Savanna began. "I'm Dr. Taylor, this is my daughter Raven."

"Call me Billy." His eyes ranged from Savanna to Raven, moving as if he was watching a fast-paced tennis match. "You're mother and daughter?"

Savanna smiled at the question, not an unusual one. "What's the most surprising, my youth or her obvious beauty?"

Raven's skin darkened even more and a giggle escaped. "Well, Billy," Savanna continued. "It looks like you dodged a bullet. You're a lucky boy. Can you explain what happened?"

The boy shook his head and then winced, obviously regretting the action. "I was doing water surveys. I remember leaning over to get a sample when a felt a sharp pain in my head and I fell. The next thing I know someone was stripping my uniform off and mumbling something about being disease infested anyway so it didn't matter if he died." Billy's lips suddenly narrowed in anger as he thought about what he just said. "I have all my immunization and have been cleared for service in the military when I turn eighteen next year. It's things like this that makes me think my parents are right for declining citizenship and refusing to be micro chipped. The only reason I did it was because I'm tired of being poor and hungry."

He tried to move but flinched and rested back on the bed. Reaching up he touched his head. Feeling the shaved scalp his eyes rounded and he tried moving his other hand up to feel the effects.

"What happened to my hair?"

Savanna put his hand on his shoulder, attempting to calm him. "We had to shave your head to stitch your wounds. You were attacked by someone who was looking for his run-away wife. We brought you to Haven and treated your injuries. You're lucky to be alive."

"I've heard of this place." Billy's hand dropped and he suddenly grinned. "Isn't this supposed to be a coven of thousands of women who don't have any man around?"

"Don't get so excited, young man." Savanna laughed silently at the young man's eagerness. "You're way too sick to see any women right now, besides most of the women here are old enough to be your mother."

He looked directly at Raven. "Not all of them." Then he grinned. Raven's skin darkened even more.

Billy didn't have any problems recovering from his injuries. It helped that he had a very dedicated nurse in Raven. Savanna checked on him on a regular basis, but she didn't need to since she received regular reports over dinner every night. Raven couldn't stop talking about him, outlining his recovery and rehashing every conversation she had with the young man.

"And he was just working for the BLM between his junior and senior year." Raven was in full bore. "When he graduates he's going directly into the Marines. Do you know that ninety percent of the registered male population in the U.S. between seventeen and thirty-five is either full-time or reserve military? There are soldiers in almost every nation in the world.

They still haven't found all the labs producing the genetically altered diseases."

Savanna knew Raven wasn't interested in her response. She just smiled and nodded as the girl rambled on about what was quickly becoming her first crush. Many of Raven's reactions were similar to Savanna's in the early stages of her relationship with Travis. Watching her daughter's budding romance took the focus away from her heartbreak of being separated from her love.

Security had been tightened around Haven following the attack on Savanna. She had hoped she would have the opportunity to visit her son, but the shutdown of the facility prevented her from leaving. Her daily calls to her son ensured he was adjusting well. Caleb couldn't have been happier. Travis had signed him up for a little league football team and he thrived in his new environment. There was a longing in Travis' voice as they spoke. Savanna wanted so much to join him, but she knew she wouldn't survive in the outside world.

Savanna had just ended a conversation with Travis when she heard the chime on her office door. She pulled up the image from the door cam and found General Grey peering into the lens.

Tapping the icon on her pad allowed the door to slide open and he stepped inside. Whatever he had to say it had to have been important. He rarely subjected himself to the sanitizing showers and strict dress code required to enter Haven. Savanna had gotten over her initial anger over the situation and decided her passive aggressive behavior wasn't helping anyone, so she made sure the uniforms provided for him fit.

He took a seat opposite her desk and sat without speaking. Something was off with his posture and she knew whatever the news was, it wasn't going to be good, and she probably didn't want to hear it. The General waited for her to place her data pad on the desk before he placed the data pad in his hand in front of her.

"There have been fifteen attacks on United States

military bases in the past week." Savanna picked up the data pad and scrolled through the information. Grey continued his report. "Three insurgent groups have banded together and formed a massive militia. They have declared war on the United States government."

Savanna knew the situation outside Haven was tenuous at best, but she didn't see how any of this related to her. Other than one isolate incident, there hadn't been any attacks on the facility for three years. She placed the data pad on the desk and looked up at Grey.

"Why do I need to know this?" she asked.

He picked up the data pad and tapped it a few times before he handed it back to her. "We've received credible threats on the facility here. The insurgents claim this is a secret military base and we're raising a special genetically engineered army designed to take over the world."

Savanna looked down at the information Grey had pulled up on the data pad. "They also claim we're hording enough food to feed a million people for seven years. They've made plans to attack this outpost and raid the food stores. We've put the base in total lock down until the threat is under control. This means absolutely no one besides military in or out. No one."

Savanna didn't mistake the look she was receiving from the General. "How long?" She thought of the number of people she had on the waiting list to enter the facility.

"Until this insurgency is shut down." He paused, but Savanna knew there was more. After a moment he took a deep breath and spoke. "We hope to get the leaders in the first push, so we could be looking at a couple of weeks, or…" He paused again, not quite as long. "It could be up to five years."

Savanna dropped the pad and stood up. Grey took two steps back. "Five years?" She knew she was yelling. "I can't keep everyone locked in here for the next five years. My husband and son are out there. I need to bring them here. I need them to be safe."

Grey held up his hands, trying to forestall her tirade.

"Dr. Taylor. Savanna. We're aware of your situation, but we must take desperate steps, not just to protect the children of this unit, but to protect the members of this community. The insurgents are a very large, desperate group. They're hungry and they're scared. Everyone knows you have food and shelter here. Everyone knows you've created one of the very few safe places in the world right now. They want what you have."

"Then go bring my husband and son back here."

General Grey's expression answered before his words. "We can't. Your husband and son are in a protected zone, but we would put too many of our own men at risk to get to them. Right now, it's all we can do to keep the riots down. We can't go on personal rescue missions."

Savanna clutched the pad in her hands holding it as if it was a shield. "Are we at war, General?"

The echoing silence was the only answer Savanna received.

As soon as Grey left the office, Savanna called her husband. "I need you to come home." She pleaded through tears. "I need you and Caleb here, where we can be together and safe."

"We won't be able to get through the barricades." Travis explained. "It's chaos out on the streets. No one is safe outside of the guarded neighborhoods."

There was longing and sorrow in Travis' voice, but there was also a deep sense of resolve. "Caleb and I are safe here. We have enough food stored to last three years and we have access to more. I know it was a mistake to leave Haven, but there's no going back now. We'll come back as soon as the lock down is lifted."

Knowing there was nothing she could do to help her husband and son, Savanna turned her focus to Haven. There needed to be a place for her family to return to when it was all over.

Billy had no choice but to stay at Haven. He called his parents to assure them he was safe. He explained he wanted to help and pay the community back for saving his life anyway, so it wasn't a big deal. Savanna suspected the real reason he wanted to stay was to be near Raven. As soon as he was physically cleared, he joined the Guard unit in their training. He graduated from school and was sent to Basic Training. General Grey pulled a few strings to have him return to the surrogate unit as his home base.

On her seventeenth birthday, the legal age to sign the contract to join the military, Raven joined the Guard. They sent her to North Carolina for three months for her basic training. Since she wasn't eligible for active duty until she was eighteen, she was sent back to Haven, where she did her weekend rotations and training with the Surrogate Unit.

Billy was sent on a six-month tour in Afghanistan while she was away. Savanna was concerned about how her daughter would react to find her boyfriend gone when she returned, but Raven seemed to take it all in stride. Raven finished her degree in nursing and trained as a medic while she was waiting for Billy to return. Savanna watched her daughter take all her life changes in stride. As her daughter's eighteenth birthday approached Savanna reflected on the events in her life and how things would have turned out so different for her if she hadn't been working in Arizona twenty years before. Raven was making her own way in the world, just like Savanna had found her own Haven.

Epilogue

THE FIRST ATTACK ON the insurgents went horribly wrong. The rebel forces were deeply embedded in communities or they were adept at living off the land. The news showed a number of wanted individuals on a daily basis. The most disturbing bit of information was the leaders of the insurgency were steeped in knowledge. Most of them were former Special Forces and had military training and background.

Savanna focused her energy on ensuring Haven was as well-protected and prepared as possible. Most of the residents resigned themselves to living long term at the facility. Some of the women had family members on the outside and they feared for their safety. Communication outside of Haven was spotty and frustration and fear seemed to rule the community. Savanna tried to be the voice of reason, reassuring the women the military was doing everything it could to protect them so they could return to their families.

She pulled all the surrogates into the main facility. The children born as a result of the program were assigned to dorms created from the construction worker barracks. Patrols around the facility tightened and no unauthorized personal were allowed on the grounds. Haven was no longer the shelter Savanna's parents originally created.

She gave Raven her full support when she married Billy. The two signed a lifetime contract, but Raven kept the last name of Taylor explaining she didn't want to lose that part of who she was. She worked as a nurse in the surrogate unit, helping with implantation, prenatal care and labor and delivery. Two months after the wedding Grey sent her to officer candidate's school so he could give her more authority in the unit.

When Raven came to Savanna just after her nineteenth birthday and told her she was pregnant Savanna congratulated her, even though she thought she was much too young to become a grandmother. She realized she had done everything she could to ensure a safe, healthy existence for her daughter. Now it was Raven's turn to protect the next generation. Billy had just been deployed in North Korea and was on communication lockdown, so there was no way to let him know he was going to be a father.

Raven was seven months along when she received notice that her husband had been killed in action. The news sent her into a deep, spiraling depression and no matter how hard Savanna tried; she couldn't get her daughter out of her funk. Raven went into labor three weeks early and delivered a healthy boy.

Savanna was there for the delivery. Unlike many of the births she attended, even the birth of her own son, Raven didn't scream or yell. She treated it all very business-like and professional. After her son was born, she barely looked at him and the nurses had to work hard to convince her to hold and nurse him. Raven wanted him to be placed in the newborn nursery where the surrogate nursing staff would take care of him, but Savanna insisted Raven take him home with her.

For the first six weeks of her grandson's life Savanna tried to help Raven with the child. Her daughter struggled with post-partum depression and Savanna tried her best to treat her medically. Raven just couldn't seem to pull herself out of it. She couldn't even think of a name for her son, barely even acknowledging him except to feed and change him. Savanna overcompensated for her lack of affection by taking the child as often as she could. She suggested naming him William after his father and Raven shrugged saying it was good enough.

Raven filled out the birth certificate naming him William Lakota Travis Etu Taylor. She said she wanted to give him a name that would make him remember where he came from and would give him the strength to do what he needed to do when the time came. Savanna thought it was a strange thing to say, but at least Raven was finally taking an interest in the child.

It was early morning and a storm was raging in the

mountains as Savanna walked the rooftops of Haven. Approaching her favorite balcony, she saw a form standing in front of the shadowed glass. At first, she couldn't figure out who was standing in front of the glass doors, then the shadow moved and she realized it was her daughter. Raven stared out of the window holding her son in her arms. She didn't turn as Savanna approached. The two stood side by side in silence for a few minutes. Finally, Raven spoke.

"I need to leave."

Savanna didn't respond, allowing her daughter to explain.

"I volunteered for active duty. I'm leaving Lakota with you." Raven's voice was a cold monotone.

Savanna turned to face her daughter. "No, Raven your needed here." The thought of her daughter fighting for her life in some far-flung battle tore at her heart.

"Mom, I'm leaving. You have a calling here. You help people here. I need to help people out there." Raven placed her son in Savanna's arms. "I call him Lakota, so he will never forget where he comes from." Raven brushed her hand over the baby's forehead. "Goodbye, my son." She turned and walked down the corridor.

Savanna wanted to chase her daughter down the hall and yell at her to come back. She wanted to rage against the storm, but she had an infant in her arms. Instead, she held the boy in her arms, watching the lightening flash against the sky and feeling the thunder to boom in her soul.

As the sun rose, the storm cleared. Savanna opened the door and walked onto the rain-soaked balcony. The red and orange tinted clouds brightened the sky as she carried the boy into the light.

Facing the East, she held the boy up to the rising sun. "Fill your body with the wind from the East. Allow your mind to open and think about what's ahead. Turn your thoughts from the past." The words echoed in her head as she thought of what she could offer the boy.

She turned, feeling the wind from the South. "South

winds help me plan. Let me know what is next. Help me fight this battle." Savanna drew in a deep breath of cool morning air.

Turning, she could feel the struggle of the wind as it pushed against the edge of the building. "West winds carry me. Give me your strength, West wind."

She faced north. "North winds follow my daughter. Protect her."

Savanna pulled the child close to her chest, feeling his warmth against her body. The winds buffeted against her, chilling her. She turned back to Haven. Her Haven.

Back to safety.

I hope you enjoyed this book. Please take a few minutes to post an honest review. Thank you.

About the Author

Lucinda Moebius has been a writer since she was a child and was first published in 2010. Since then she has worked hard to create unique visions and stories. Her work includes novels in multiple genres including: Science Fiction, Fantasy, Paranormal, Children's Books, Screenplays and Non-fiction. Lucinda has a Doctorate in Education and loves teaching, but her greatest desire is to help others understand how literature and writing can bring enlightenment and understanding to everyone. She offers book coaching and advice to everyone, whether they want it or not.

Other Books by this Author

Echoes of Savanna: Book One: The Parent Generation
http://www.amazon.com/gp/product/B006RM66QM

Raven's Song: Book One: T1 Generation
http://www.amazon.com/gp/product/B006YJ92GO

Write Well Publish Right
http://www.amazon.com/gp/product

Publish Promote Repeat
https://www.amazon.com/dp/B071KQDRMS

Feeder: Chronicles of the Soul Eaters Book 1
http://www.amazon.com/gp/product/0615968325

30 Days Stream of Consciousness V. 1
http://www.amazon.com/30-Days-Streams-Consciousness-1-ebook/dp/B01BW8JXBU

Haunting
http://www.amazon.com/30-Days-Stream-Consciousness-Haunting-ebook/dp/B01D7T9CFY

Abduction
https://www.amazon.com/dp/B01F1DMOBI

Fire and Ice a Love Story
https://www.amazon.com/dp/B01GGL8QUM

-- in Between
https://www.amazon.com/dp/B075KYN184

Raising Grandpa
https://www.amazon.com/dp/B00OPP1FCI

I Know I am Awesome
https://www.amazon.com/dp/B00QYAQBZI

Oh Brother!
https://www.amazon.com/dp/B01A1PC5YM

Firefighter Jeff
https://www.amazon.com/dp/B06ZZ41W6N

More about this Author

Blog: Moebius Musings
http://lucindamoebius.blogspot.com/
Website:
www.lucindamoebius.com